Harvestman
by Chang Terhune
Copyright 2013 Chang Terhune
Discover other titles by Chang Terhune
on the web at http://www.changterhune.com
ISBN: 9781301153787

Table of Contents

CHAPTER ONE — 3

CHAPTER TWO — 11

CHAPTER THREE — 28

CHAPTER FOUR — 34

CHAPTER FIVE — 49

CHAPTER SIX — 56

CHAPTER SEVEN — 59

CHAPTER EIGHT — 67

CHAPTER NINE — 73

CHAPTER TEN — 75

CHAPTER ELEVEN — 82

CHAPTER TWELVE — 96

CHAPTER THIRTEEN — 103

CHAPTER FOURTEEN — 118

CHAPTER FIFTEEN — 121

CHAPTER SIXTEEN — 127

CHAPTER SEVENTEEN — 140

CHAPTER EIGHTEEN — 143

CHAPTER NINETEEN — 150

CHAPTER TWENTY   **155**

CHAPTER TWENTY-ONE   **162**

CHAPTER TWENTY-TWO   **167**

CHAPTER TWENTY-THREE   **182**

CHAPTER TWENTY-FOUR   **191**

CHAPTER TWENTY-FIVE   **194**

CHAPTER TWENTY-SIX   **198**

CHAPTER TWENTY-SEVEN   **205**

CHAPTER TWENTY-EIGHT   **213**

ACKNOWLEDGMENTS   **216**

CHAPTER ONE
2191 AD, Ocean of Storms Lunar Base

As the pilot walked into the conference room a table grew from the floor, accompanied by a chair. She noted the quiet electric crackle as the furniture fully coalesced then she sat down, awaiting her interrogator. The room was dark, painted a uniform gray, lit only by the ceiling's rectangle of thin light strip. She knew the walls were permeated with unseen surveillance devices.

They kept her waiting for an hour to feed the sensors of the debriefing team. No doubt even the chair was taking in data, monitoring her condition. She obliged the data-hungry chair theory and farted.

The door slid open. An officer walked in; tall, thin, female, with blonde hair pulled back in a utilitarian bun and not a strand out of place. She carried a large pedia under one arm. She made no effort at eye contact, as if the room were empty.

At the table, she put the pedia down, waiting as another chair formed.

Finally she sat and opened the pedia. She looked up at the pilot, giving the pilot an efficient, bureaucratic smile while opaque windows opened around. They regarded each other without expression until the officer produced a small white package from inside her coat and slid it across the table to the pilot. The pilot reached out, drew the package toward herself and smiled at the officer. She opened the top, withdrew a cigarette and lit it by snapping it against the end of the package. She inhaled deeply then blew smoke at the officer. Midway across the table, the smoke was sucked back down into the pack. The officer smiled again at the pilot, who barely cracked one in return.

"Thanks," said the pilot, leaning forward to read the officer's name tag. "*Gorman.*"

"You're welcome. Now then," said the officer. She glanced at her pedia, eyes darting around on the screen. "Please explain what occurred when you engaged the Choudhury drives."

"Again? Okay, I might as well get the weird stuff out of the way," said the pilot with a grin. "I engaged the Choudhurys and the thrusters went off. I saw a Doppler shift through the portholes. But it turned into a swirl followed by a blinding whiteness. I believe I lost consciousness at this point."

The officer glanced at her pedia.

"Agreed. Medical monitors in the flight recorders indicate that Pilot 23 did lose consciousness at this time," said the pedia.

"Thanks," Pilot 23 said with a nod to the pedia. The officer smiled stiffly and made a gesture, muting the pedia's persona. "So, I came to, but ... out of my body, as if separated from it. Similar to when you're drifting off to sleep and can't feel your body; you're unaware of your surroundings yet fully conscious. Like I'd left my body somewhere else."

"What did you see?" asked Gorman, shifting in her seat. "Where were you?"

"I was no longer in my ship. I couldn't see anything, not visually at first. I slowly grew aware of being in a liminal, waiting place. Between states or dimensions, maybe? I couldn't tell how long I was there but I wasn't impatient to be anyplace else. As if time not only didn't exist—I didn't care if it did. Yet, I was fully aware that the last thing I'd seen was my ship accelerating past a point that had killed twenty-two test pilots." She drew on her cigarette and blew smoke out. The package was unable to collect much and Gorman made a face at the cloud.

"What happened then?" Gorman asked.

"An awareness of transiting to a newer place. Like I had shifted to a different ... dimension. There were others there."

"Could you see them?" asked Gorman. "Hear them?"

"No, not really. I felt them—It's ... difficult to describe what happened in terms of senses because I didn't use any of the five we have. All I can say is it was an ... awareness, without sensory input. As if I had suddenly entered a place filled with billions of minds all shouting to be heard and answered. Imagine the thoughts of every other being in the universe. I'd say it was deafening but there was no sound, understand? It was just too much for my mind to handle. And I couldn't shut it out. I thought if only I could somehow block it but I couldn't. Then soon I ... sensed another being there. Coming close to me. It had a familiar human resonance. Female."

"What happened with this female?" Gorman asked. She looked at her pedia and tapped out a short chord on its surface.

"She said, 'Hello.'" The pilot laughed. "Like I said, it was a female presence I could hear through my own senses though it really occurred in my mind. She said, 'You're new to this place, I think. Try not to talk with your body. Let your mind speak. It might take a while.' It did. Again, there was no sense of time; rather, I was without a sense of urgency. I felt her waiting patiently as I struggled to ... speak in this new way, like a baby, forming words without speech. 'Where?' was all I could manage at first. 'Good,' she said. 'You'll get the hang of it. You're in the *Narthex*. It's a kind of waiting place where we queue up before we pick our destination.'

"I managed to get out a question about her destination. Then I was wondering where exactly we were and slowly getting back my wits.

"So she said, 'Where am I going? Oh, I understand the question. Well, from here we call it the *Mapparium*. It's a kind of chart room. You were just in the *Narthex*, right? Jeez, it must be busy in your neck of the woods. I felt you forever out there. But then, you're new.'

"Suddenly I remembered my ship and its status. I began to get somewhat ... concerned.

"'Oh, now I understand,' she said to me. 'Well, I wouldn't worry about that. You could be up here for what seems like hours and you get back and barely a millisecond has gone by. We girls make the jump pretty fast. It's how we broke light speed.'"

Gorman grunted quietly and noted this on her pedia. "Go on," she said.

"So anyway she goes 'Girl, you seem mighty familiar. I want to know your name when you can get the hang of it.' Now I tried to tell her, but all that came out was a flood of images and memories. Like how you say your own name in your head doesn't come straight across as it does in speech. You see what I mean?"

"'See' is an interesting way to phrase it," said Gorman, with a half smile. "Is it telepathy of some sort?"

"No, nothing like that. This was like I was using some kind of long-dormant part of my brain. A weak part."

"Flight data indicated elevated brain activity in the frontal cortex," said Gorman with a glance at her pedia. "Then what happened?"

"So she says, 'Never mind. I just wanted to know your name, I didn't want to meet your family! Take it easy. Concentrate. It's like this: Your brain is feeling about a billion different minds right now, trying to communicate with each of them. Some of these might not even be human—don't even bother with those. Just focus on mine. Filter out all the other stuff that's going on. S'okay, I was a little wet behind the ears once. I felt like I was going to go crazy until I mastered it.' She was so familiar in her speech. And she was right. It was like being constantly shouted at from all directions. I couldn't filter at first. She—I could hear her as if she were speaking close to my ear. It took what seemed like hours but I eventually managed to tune out all the others. Finally hers was clearest while the dull roar slowly subsided.

"When I achieved this she says, 'Okay, I think you got me in focus. Now, here's the fun part. You can kinda see out here. But it's nothing like your real eyes. Again, it's filtering all these other competing frequencies out for just the ones you want. Right now, your brain is experiencing this dimension as a whole. Our brains are not quite ready for that. I'm surprised you're even out here. Your focusing implants aren't working right, I bet. Those make it so much easier.'"

"What did she mean by that? Focusing implants?" Gorman's eyes darted to her pedia and back to the pilot a few times, her interest piqued. "There's no such thing."

"I'm not sure," the pilot said, looking at the end of her cigarette. "Some kind of technology they had wherever she came from. I assume it was something to help them tune out the 'noise.' Then she says, 'Either you're some kind of hotshot or you fooled your way in. Don't worry, though. I'm too far away to rat you out to the Academy. We all know what happens in the *Mapparium* stays in the *Mapparium*, right? Though ... I may never get back.' Right there, I detected a note of sadness in her voice. I got this brief flood of emotion from her. She was holding back, putting up a major front. I must have been very eager to see as she did, trying to put it in words. But words are useless when

7

describing this!" The pilot put her head in her hands and shook her short, spiky hair out. She sat up again and dragged on the cigarette.

"Okay, so then she said, 'All right, sister. Take it slowly. If you open up now, you'll flood your brain and most likely die. They'll either end up scraping you off the butt of a deep space freighter or you'll be a shooting star over a colony somewhere.'"

"A colony?" asked Gorman. She tapped on the pedia again and then looked at the pilot, leaning closer with head in hands, elbows on the table. "Did she specify a colony name?"

"No. Only colonies are on the Moon and Mars, right? Doubt we'll even have Mars for long the way things are going with those separatist assholes. Anyway, I made some sort of understanding impulse. She said, 'Good. Your brain is fighting to keep you from losing it. You're like the little pig and the big bad wolf is blowing down the door. What I want you to do is this.' She described how to keep the mind shielded yet slowly open up—for lack of a better word—a third eye. I couldn't feel my body yet I could feel this point. Like a door holding firm in a tornado. After absorbing what she said I focused and slowly opened ... my mind's eye, I guess." The pilot dragged on the last of the cigarette and looked for an ashtray. When none was found, she dropped her cigarette and watched as the floor ate it up.

"It was somewhat like primitive sonar imaging or radar. There was light and shadow but indefinite shapes or forms. Even so, at first everything was too much. I felt my mind shut down over and over again until I could channel it all through my new eye. Then slowly the space cohered. The idea of shape and form seemed useless. I—I was in a vast place stretching out endlessly in all directions. No ground below, nor was I floating. This place lacked directions, gravity or any of the physics we understand. Up was down was sideways was backwards was inside out. It was as if the impressions I felt in the *Narthex* had become almost visual. Everything hovered at a point between uber- or hypervisual and a mental sensory form. As I said, like radar. But not."

She shook her head, took another cigarette and lit it.

"Things slowly coalesced into a definite point. A sphere—it could have been the size of a handball or a planet since shape or size didn't seem to exist out here—appeared in the midst of this void. Near it was the female presence.

"'Come close,' she called to me. 'Come and see what you've found.' I—*moved* might be the word?—okay, I moved forward to join the female presence at the sphere. Close up, I became aware again of the extra presence watching us from somewhere else. It was not a malevolent presence, just ... something observing.

"Who's watching us? Who are they?' I asked.

"She said, 'The Transparent Ones. We think so, anyway. You've taken the oath so ... The Transparent Ones were gone long before we were around. They're the ones—we think—who created this. They're watching us. Like air traffic control or—'"

"Transparent Ones?" asked the officer.

Pilot 23 just shrugged. "That's what she said."

Gorman typed frantically for a moment before turning back to her.

"I asked how they built it. Something like laughter emerged from her. Like a wave of light in the darkness. She said 'Hey, if I knew that? Well, I wouldn't be here. I'd be up there with them. All we know is the first pilot stumbled on it and we have her to thank for everything. The good and the bad.' Again there was the flash of sadness. Again she said 'Look.'

"I turned my attention to the sphere before us. At first it was a swirling mass of indiscriminate energies. But as I focused more and more, it took shape. Forms split into various areas and different quadrants within." The pilot took a long drag from the cigarette.

"I realized I was looking at a map of many stars, maybe the whole universe; a three-dimensional—at least the three dimensions we can perceive—map. It pulsed and lived in front of us in this globe just as it did around our real bodies. She said to me, 'From here, we can choose wherever we want to go in the galaxy. Known or otherwise. We control it.'

"This time sadness welled out, breaking free from her. I felt it. So deeply. I tried to console her as she made a last attempt to hold it in before a rush of emotion burst from her. I felt her experiences rush by in a barely coherent mass; her life story in a nanosecond. I saw a tall man in a strange pressure suit, snow and a fiery, bright sun. A battle.

"She said. 'He saved me and died. I gave up on him and he did the last thing I ever would have thought of him.' A silence fell over us. You ever been out in snow, Gorman? Like a real snowstorm where it swallows sound? It was like that. I felt her pain, her distinct lack of will to live. I couldn't put into words what I felt, so I simply propelled my feelings to her in a blind rush.

"'I have no idea,' she said to me after a time. 'Maybe when you get back you can tell them where to look for me. This is how you tell where to go. It's kind of easy but be careful. If you get caught in my field, you'll end up either right alongside me out in our space or worse, you will materialize into my ship. That sucks, mostly because you don't usually die instantly.' I followed her presence as it projected a limb of sorts—some kind of focus point—into the sphere. I saw a binary star system and some other stars that seemed dimly familiar. But I had no idea if it was in the Milky Way or far across the other side of the universe. The arrangement was just totally unfamiliar and I'm a pilot for God's sake!"

Gorman nodded.

"She noticed my confusion and said, 'Oh, you poor kid. How the hell did you get out here? You can't even astrogate, can you? No offense, but they're churning out some weak ones these days. Ok, seriously, I'll explain where this is. Listen closely.' She explained what we were viewing. The stars were unfamiliar to me. I struggled to follow her but she nearly overwhelmed me. When she finished there was another silence of indeterminate length. Again, more felt than perceived as passage of time.

"'Now then,' she said after showing me her place in this world, 'where are you from? I bet I can guess, but I want you to show me. Do it like I told you.' I concentrated and projected into the sphere. It was almost like I traveled right to the point and there I was, viewing Sol from just outside the solar system.

"She said, 'Hey, that's right! Good work. You're from Sol. Just like me. I mean, we all are, right? That's weird, though. I don't see the solar orbiting stations. Or the jump beacons. It's almost like before ...'"

"'Before' what?" asked Gorman.

"Exactly. Her thoughts suddenly shut down and scrambled, forming calculations and ignoring me. I felt her doing the math and it was like being bound in heavy steel. I could barely keep up with her as she went into some sort of trance. Then a sudden mixture of panic and awe emanated from her.

"She said, 'It's you. You're here. I don't believe it. Pilot 23.'"

The pilot looked at Gorman, who cocked an eyebrow and glanced at her pedia. The pilot continued.

"Her disbelief became panic. She knew my classified flight number, Gorman. When I took off there were five people alone who knew that number. So she said, 'I have to get you out of here. This could be disastrous.'"

"Why?" asked Gorman.

"I don't know. I asked her what was wrong and how she knew who I was. She wouldn't answer. I could feel her rushing me out from the *Mapparium*. The last place I wanted to be. I protested in vain.

"She said two words to me: 'parens tanta.' Then she backed off for a time. When she returned she said, 'Sorry, whoever you are, I have to get you back to your ship. Right now.' I wanted to help her; find out what she was talking about with me. I felt like she'd been so open then all of a sudden stopped.

"She said, 'Don't worry about me. I'm just a footnote. You're the history. Way more important. Now listen. It's kind of like when you have to pee, right? Only instead of releasing muscles, you're releasing your mind. It's like letting yourself fall. It's freaky, but a relief.' I begged her to stay. She wouldn't. 'No way. You have to go. If I'm right, you're in a tight spot when you get back. At least I had PM backups. Now, close your eye.' Reluctantly, I did. The *Mapparium* subsided and I was left with a sense of all those voices encroaching again. Then the doors rattled in my mental tornado.

"She said one last thing: 'Thank you for your kindness. I wish I could have met you outside.' Her words trailed off as the surrounding noise increased. Soon I was flooded on all sides again. Too much noise, too much light, too much thought. No filters. Then I was back in my body."

The pilot drew on the cigarette then dropped it to the floor.

"Where were you?" asked Gorman.

"Somewhere near Barnard's Star. My ship had stopped itself. It took a while to figure out what had happened. All but the emergency systems were offline. I managed to power everything back up after a few hours."

"You attempted to return home?"

"Yes. I pointed the ship in the right direction. After thrusters came on, I turned on the Choudhurys."

"And then?" asked Gorman, her hands knotted as if to keep from grabbing Pilot 23 by the shoulders.

"Same as before. I reached maximum speed. Doppler shifted to white and I was back in the *Narthex*. But she—whoever—wasn't there. I found my way back to the *Mapparium* and found the sphere. I pointed to Sol and then let myself fall back, so to speak."

"And then?"

"I regained consciousness outside of Jupiter. I signaled the team at Ocean of Storms and they notified the recovery teams at Van Allen SFB to come get me."

"Thank you, Pilot 23. That will be all for today." The officer closed the pedia. She began to rise from the table. Pilot 23 reached over, slamming a hand on the pedia.

"Gorman, who was she? What the hell happened to me out there? I tried to find the coordinates she showed me but there's nothing out there. Just a dim star."

"We're trying to figure that out. We may need to talk a few more times." The officer drew the pedia out from under Pilot 23's hand. She turned for the door.

"She was just so sad and damaged," said Pilot 23. "I wouldn't leave another pilot out there." The officer lingered for a moment at the door, her hand over the control plate.

"Thank you, pilot. An orderly will be around in a moment to take you back to your room. Good day."

Pilot 23 stood alone in the room, a cold, gray silence closing in around her.

CHAPTER TWO
Crash

2468 AD

Mother was shaking Leonardo roughly, jostling his little body as he watched an episode of "Mejia's Marauders on Mars" on his pedia. He tried to squirm away from her but his legs wouldn't work right. First it felt like something wrapped around them as if the bedding got tangled up. Maybe something crawled inside the mosquito and faraday netting to attach itself to him? But when he lowered his pedia he saw Mother as she tore through the gauzy protective barrier on his bunk. Their eyes met. Her hair messily fell about her face and he could tell by the look in her eyes she'd been at the Jimmy-Stim again. He listened for his little sister crying like she always did but couldn't hear her. Mother reached out and shook him, muttering in a weird language as she tied his arms and legs up in the thin, dirty sheets. He wondered what he'd done this time. It didn't feel like he'd wet the bed. Maybe he hadn't tied the house barge to the mooring correctly? Had they drifted out of the canal and into the ocean overnight? The last time that happened they'd almost struck a mine. He looked up at Mother as his pedia fell off the bed and hit the floor, the 3D characters shimmering then blinking out as it crashed. Her face grew darker and light swirled around her hair. He knew he was in real trouble then. She'd be sure to make him stay up all night on watch or worse—

Capt. Leonardo Reyes De la Valencia of the *UFWSS Resurgam* awoke with an astounding hangover and an immediate sense something was very wrong. Dwi8, one of the biped walky-talkies, was stuffing him into an emergency pressure suit. He attempted to speak a restraint code but couldn't work more than a choked rasp from his throat. He tried to push the walky-talky away but his body was totally unresponsive.

The air was cool and cloying on his skin, the gel from the berth quickly turning from gooey clumps into frozen chunks by the second. His vision was blurry, reduced to impressions of darkness around him with swaths of light blazing back and forth. Searing blasts of color stabbed his skull. Was it fire? He took a breath and felt like he was burning inside but from cold. He tried to move but still found himself trapped. His neck was stiff, his tongue thick and sluggish in his mouth. It dawned on him he'd been dreaming of his childhood. The present sharp-edged sensations told him that *this* was the reality.

Most shocking of all was the utter silence; no alarms, no voices coming over the comms, no AIs giving warnings and status. Apart from the sound of Dwi8 closing up his suit he heard nothing. Once the walky-talky had him suited up, it spoke as lights from its wrists, headpiece and chest panel shone on him.

"Captain," it said in its calm, synthesized voice, "*Resurgam* has crashed. The survey team is dead as well as seven of the crew."

Leonardo managed to raise a hand then drop it weakly at his side. With an effort in clearing his throat he attempted to speak a word.

"Ship?"

The biped took this as a cue to continue.

"*Resurgam* is entirely without power. Even redundant base-level systems are nonfunctional. The Wal8 unit is damaged beyond repair." Dwi8 stood like the patient servant it was, voice staccato and uneven, laced with jagged fragments of syllables, a sign of damage.

He felt the suit begin restoration of bodily functions; blood returning to dried, empty veins. Medicines administered by brief, sharp jabs of microscopic needles. He began to feel some small relief. He wondered if he would have been better off dead.

"Alive?" he asked. "Who is still ... alive?"

"Yourself, Lt. Al-Mushtarii and Astrogator Valencia. All others are dead."

Leonardo found this difficult to conceive. Old training kicked in hard, providing some reason to what was already an unreasonable situation. Clearly, he was suffering the effects of early resuscitation from hi-space deepsleep: mental faculties impaired, struggling to maintain consciousness while being buried under layers of chemicals administered into his body to slow its functions and sustain it during the long journey home. His body would be slow to come around under normal circumstances, resuscitation being a week-long process. That he had to take in the idea of a crash compounded his rapidly growing problems.

At least his limbs began to feel slightly less leaden. A flailing attempt at sitting up exhausted him and he dropped back into the sleep berth.

"How?" he panted.

"Unclear, sir. I was activated when *Resurgam* was struck by debris as it left hi-space. Wal8 was on watch during the flight, sir. I was offline during the journey. Without access to ship's systems and AIs, I cannot access astrogation logs or charts. I was only able to access a few seconds of what occurred before my own activation. Even those records are severely corrupted. Something made us exit hi-space early. Flight AI Marconi registered a red-level distress signal and dropped the ship down from hi-space to answer at the originating coordinates. Astrogation AI Magellan predicted open space. Upon re-entry, we were immediately struck by debris. Astrogation AIs Magellan and Vespucci engaged in an emergency search for a suitable planet for landing. Due to further miscalculations, they chose not an E-class planet, but a dwarf planetoid of as yet indeterminate composition. We made a statistically improbable landing on the surface."

"Drina ... help ..."

"Sir? Shall I go see to Asgr. Valencia and Lt. Al-Mushtarii?"

"Yes, " Leonard hissed with exhaustion and a growing exasperation.

The walky-talky departed to the adjoining quarters of Leonardo's wife, the Astrogator. Without its lights darkness swept down upon him. *Not even emergency lighting's working,* he thought. He lay back and let the suit revive him. During the conversation with Dwi8, the suit had fully assessed his physical needs and began to pump in the necessary medication to aid the recovery process. He'd be able to stand in a few minutes. Even with the suit's assistance it would be difficult recovering from a forced revivification. There was no sense in tiring himself out trying to get up before the body was ready.

Something deep in its bowels rocked the ship, reverberating through the hull and shaking him in the suit. He braced himself as well as he could without muscular control but nothing followed the explosion. It was most likely the ship settling in on whatever it had landed on. He sighed and lay still, thinking back to events just before being put into deepsleep.

They'd left Baaklum Cha'am with the survey team after receiving an urgent message from UFW Outpost Keenan. A vessel left Mars, breaking the UFW blockade and jumping to hi-space outside the solar system. Aboard *Resurgam*, preparations for the return journey went smoothly. Their cargo was secured and the survey team was placed in their sleep berths in their modular unit in the bay. Once under way, the crew finished their assigned tasks then they were put in deepsleep with the help of Wal8 and Dwi8.

Finally Leonardo did last checks, gave Drina the OK and went under himself. That was the last thing he remembered, along with thoughts about their return to Earth: his impending retirement, Drina's disengagement ceremonies, and their divorce.

Leonardo saw a light come down the hall towards his quarters. Dwi8 returned and stepped up to the sleep berth. "Sir, Lt. Al-Mushtarii is conscious and recovering from enforced awakening. I have told him of your condition."

"Drina?"

"Sir, Asgr. Valencia's condition is *delicate*."

Leonardo knew he was feeling better; the walky-talky's attempt at tact was annoying *and* alarming. "What's wrong?" he asked.

"Sir, she is unconscious but stable. Her berth's redundant systems are keeping her safe. Without functioning medibots or Dr. Afrika, I am unable to make a diagnosis. My own abilities are limited to—" Leonardo gestured at it, a flick of bent fingers, using a mudra to silence Dwi8. He was about to ask for the doctor when he remembered Ramon Afrika was among the dead.

"Tell Baz ..." Leonardo had to pause several times to let his weak body get the energy to speak the few words he could manage. "Wait until his suit systems tell him he can get up ... *Resurgam* ... Seems stable ... We can wait ... Then go ... check the ship ... Need to make sure we catalogue all ... damages. How much of the ship is ... intact?"

"Unknown, sir. From our angle, we came to rest listing slightly to starboard. I would estimate thrusters and sensor equipment on the starboard side are damaged. Without a full visual examination—"

"Get a full list of damages: systems down, hull integrity, breeches, and anything else ASAP. Go."

"Yes, sir." Dwi8 left.

After twenty minutes lying quietly and breathing slowly, Leonardo heard his suit chime.

"You are now ready to sit upright. Please note that the effects of enforced awakening from deepsleep can last for several hours or even days. Also note that elevated alcohol content detected in your blood may exaggerate side effects."

He responded to the gentle ping of the suit with an emphatic "Go to Hell!"

Leonardo swung his legs up out of the berth and nearly crashed into the opposite wall. Ship's gravity was inoperative. The planet's gravity was significantly less than what he was used to. The world swooned for a moment and he took a deep breath to stabilize himself. Leonardo slapped the front of his suit to activate the chest panel lights and helmet lights.

Illuminated, his surroundings took on a familiar shape. His quarters looked almost exactly as they had when they left Baaklum Cha'am, though any belongings not secured were flung towards the bow and right side of the room. He regarded the small pile and for a moment tried to make out what was broken beyond keeping. He knew it was a pointless effort with the ship in such a state, then sighed and stood carefully. When he felt like he could slowly move without fainting or falling over, he left the cabin.

Adjoining his quarters were those of his wife, Asgr. Drina Valencia. He stepped into her room and listened; silent like the rest of the ship. Without functioning environment systems they were in effective vacuum. God only knew what was in the atmosphere outside. He raised an arm to shine wrist lights over the prone body of his wife. She lay still, breath barely noticeable under the heavy layers of her suit. Her helmet's faceplate fogged slightly where her breath hit it.

Leonardo said, "Capt. Valencia. Disarm," as a chime sounded and his display read "PROXIMITY SECURITY OFFLINE." He sighed at the malfunction. Systems were down, as it should have said, "DISARMED" back at him.

He felt his hopes drop down a crevasse in his mind. An Astrogator was the nerve center of a UFW ship, even a low-level freighter like this. Her survival was the imperative of the entire crew, especially the captain. While there were tight security precautions at all times, when an Astrogator was injured her security precautions became lethal to nearly everyone on board. As a young pilot he'd served on board the *UFWSS Pellomere,* where a curious sailor somehow entered the Astrogator's cabin. Three steps in he was quickly and viciously neutralized by the room's security. Their captain left the boy's bloodstains on the walls outside as a reminder of the rules: the only people who ever saw the Astrogator on a ship and lived were the captain, the XO and the medics.

Now those security precautions were offline and almost nothing could protect her except for Leonardo.

He stepped closer. Safe under the diamond cover of her berth, nothing visible harmed her. No signs of wire overload or nano damage. He looked around the cabin and saw no other apparent damage from the crash. Not that he expected to for two reasons. One was that Drina kept her quarters in a low level of disarray on the best of days. He'd long ago given up fining her for the mess in her quarters.

The other was that though the ship was not designed for planetfall, it was built to withstand almost any spaceborne incident imaginable. Despite the bizarre miscalculations of the rest of the journey, the astrogating AIs Magellan and Vespucci (or "the gemelli" as Drina called them) had masterfully landed *Resurgam* in such a way that even three of the crew had survived. The officers' quarters and those of the Astrogator were shielded and suspended within the ship by a complex system of antigrav and barrier elements. If not utterly destroyed, UFW ships retrieved from battles with the FMR or crashes often had their Astrogator's quarters fully intact with their occupant shaken but very much alive.

He looked closer at his wife. Even with their long and bitter estrangement, he still found her beautiful. Dark brown hair spilled around her face inside her helmet, with thick cables connecting her to the ship snaking into sockets placed around her skull. Drina's slender nose and high cheekbones were accentuated by the slight toll hi-space travel took on an Astrogator's complexion (Drina called it her "throne tan"). Despite her pallor—and everything they'd been through—he'd never tire of looking at her. His heart panged a bit, seeing his wife in her weakened state. Leonardo noted the small mole on her right cheek just under her eye. She hated it and often spoke of having it removed. Leonardo always talked her out of it. He was sure she complained just to hear him tell her how beautiful it made her. But the last time they'd talked like that was years ago.

Drina was alive; this was the most important thing. If the ship was not too terribly damaged and the Choudhury drives were functional, they had some chance of escaping the planet: they could get outside the gravity well of its star and Drina could get them back home. He tucked the idea of how they were going to get a ship that wasn't supposed to land on a planet offplanet into the growing backlog of details about the crash. No sense thinking weeks ahead when he wasn't sure they'd survive the next twenty-four hours.

He watched a tube snake from the side panel of Drina's crèche into a socket on her chest panel. A light blinked red then green as medication was pumped into her suit. He'd let the doctor figure out what the medibots were up to.

"He's dead, asshole," Leonardo muttered to himself. "They're all dead." He let a sigh escape as he thought of corpses in their berths.

Leonardo turned away from Drina's unconscious form and activated his suit systems menu. A bright orange graphic appeared before his eyes with a list of suit functions: Weapons, Life Support, Network Access, Communications, Medical Assistance. He chose Communications and activated the suit's recorder. A small playback transport appeared in the left side of his heads-up display. He squinted his left eye at the red "Record" button and the counter began rolling.

"Capt. Leonardo Reyes De la Valencia, *UFWSS Resurgam*. Suit log engaged. Subvocal recorder working. We have crash-landed. I am now assessing the damage. It seems—"

He stopped short, aware of something just outside his vision. He whirled around to see a pressure-suited figure step into the doorway. Before he was even aware of it his suit noted his reaction and armed itself. A look into the faceplate and he saw it was only Baz, the lieutenant. Leonardo looked at the "Disarm" icon in the upper right corner of his HUD and the suit calmed. Baz held up a hand and Leonardo continued.

"All ship's systems are down. We must rely on suit systems for now. The reasons for this crash are unclear. Something forced us from hi-space, possibly a distress signal. We emerged from intracosmic deep sleep into a debris field, almost like that of a ringed planet. Without data from ship's AI Jason nor the twin Astrogation AIs Magellan and Vespucci, I cannot say how that occurred. Dwi8, the surviving walky-talky, tells me from its internal records that the Twins interpreted open space where the debris field was. Flight AI had registered the red-level distress signal and dropped the ship down from hi-space to answer the call. Upon re-entry to normal space we encountered the debris. Astrogation AIs engaged in an emergency search for a suitable planet for landing. Due to another malfunction they chose not an E-class planet but what appears to be an icy chunk of rock in the depths of uncharted space: an asteroid with a stolen atmosphere." He looked at the stop button, then looked at Baz.

"Sir," Baz said, saluting Leonardo. Leonardo waved him down.

"Don't bother, Baz. We got bigger problems than protocol."

Baz smirked from behind his faceplate. "You're telling me. Leo, what the hell happened? How'd we survive?"

Leonardo frowned as Baz's voice came through his helmet speakers with uncharacteristic static and shook his head. "No idea," Leonardo said, slipping past his XO. "The more I see, the less sense it makes. Let's get some visuals. Find out what state we're in and work from there. I sent Dwi8 out to survey the ship. Let's see what he's up to. No. Actually—" Leonardo turned about-face in midsentence. "Let's head to the bridge and see what we can get up and running."

"Coffee'd be good. The suit's coffee sucks."

"Maybe later, Baz." Leonardo frowned and turned to face the XO. "Look, is your comm setup okay? I'm getting bad static."

Baz looked askance, checking his HUD. "Normal strength. You're coming in a little fuzzy, too. I'll boost signal."

"Copy that."

"Better. Christ, we're gonna need all the help we can get. On to the bridge."

Leonardo was glad his XO felt light. Baz had a talent for easing tense situations as well as taking decisive action in critical moments. It's what kept him on Leonardo's ships for almost three decades.

Leonardo briefed his XO as they walked forward towards the bridge doors from the officers' quarters. During normal hi-space flight the duty AI sealed all doors and hatches. In a crash situation they automatically locked shut to prevent fire or atmosphere loss. Which somehow hadn't worked here. Leonardo banged at the door with his gloved hands then turned to Baz.

"Gotta force it."

"Jesus Sublime. Leo, what the hell did this? We should at least have base power."

"No idea."

Leonardo looked to the left of the portal. A red square was painted midway into the wall. His HUD flashed "Emergency Door Release." He pushed his gloved hand into the square and felt for the handle inside, then pulled. Leonardo cranked it back and forth until the door eased open.

When Leonardo opened the door wide enough they slipped inside. The bridge was a wide semicircle with ceilings sloping towards the bow and the displays. It was painted in varying shades of military gray like the rest of the ship; it remained stubbornly dark except where their lights shone. In the center of the room was a large, waist-high horseshoe-shaped console open at the back. The outer walls of the bridge were featureless wherever the suit lights shone. Baz walked outside the ring and Leonardo walked inside, stepping onto the raised dais. Below the outer panels were five seats spread out evenly before angled white desktops. These were similar to desktops the captain saw inside the ring. Two seats set at each console along the interior of the ring.

One chair was set slightly elevated behind these: Leonardo's chair.

"Looks okay to me," said Baz. "Except—"

"Except nothing," said Leonardo. "No power at all. Baz, I don't think I've ever seen a completely blank bridge before. Maybe during construction, but ..."

Whenever he looked at the desktops, Leonardo's HUD displayed "OFFLINE." He turned around, half-expecting to see the display showing him Drina on her throne. But it was blank. He knew she was far behind them, unconscious and unaware of their plight.

"All right, Baz. There's nothing else we can do right now. When we get power back ..."

"We'll know how fucked we are?"

"Well put. Let's go outside."

Leonardo didn't expect to see much damage on the bridge. It was only slightly less protected than their quarters. They were still deep inside the ship, about thirty meters from the hull behind shielding and sensors and various equipment. Leonardo had to calm himself and not worry about unknown damage. With the total loss of power they might not even have sent out distress beacons before the crash. He quelled his mind's worrying and they exited the bridge by cranking open the port doors.

They walked down the corridor towards the stern. After about a hundred meters of silent walking they came to an open set of doors labeled "Midships Airlock One." The emergency door release was already broken open.

"That's not good," said Baz.

"Maybe, maybe not. Hang on," said Leonardo. "Dwi8, where are you?"

A hiss and crackle with a hint of the walky-talky's voice came through.

"Dwi8. Boost signal and repeat!"

A second later Dwi8's voice came through clearer.

"Sir, I am in the Survey Team Quarters working my way down through the ship to assess damages. I will move on to Engineering presently."

"Good."

"Sir, I believe you should come here and investigate. There appears to be—"
Leonardo shook his head.

"Just secure it for now. Have you been through the port airlock?"

"Yes, sir. Is there a problem?"

"No." He cut off Dwi8 and turned to Baz. "That interference is weird. Signal should be clear up to a thousand klicks."

"Comsats probably didn't get deployed."

"Still. It ought to be clearer this close." Leonardo shook his head again and waved Baz on.

Baz shrugged and looked at the airlock's manual controls. He opened the panel to the left of the airlock. Inside was a large red handle. Warning notes were plastered around the box.

"These airlocks are much harder to pry open. *Exosuit on*," Baz spoke and a slight rippling rolled through the suit's frame, filling it out. He turned the handle counterclockwise as both the inner and outer doors slowly opened in front of him. Leonardo felt the groan of the doors sliding back through stiff tracks. Weak blue light spilled into the dark space and their faceplates adjusted. Baz finished cranking and they looked out the airlock doors.

"Snow?"

A cold blue world stretched out before them, covered in bluish snow with drifting and winding streaks of yellow through it. Far in the distance, yellowish mountains rose up from the horizon. A weak white sun shone down on the landscape.

"The mountains—" said Leonardo.

"—look like scrambled eggs," said Baz. "Hungry."

"Can it. Wonder what *Resurgam*'ll look like from outside," said Leonardo.

Their HUDs told them what naked eyes couldn't. Yellow meant sulfur; the hills were approximately ten klicks away from them. After a few seconds the chromatograph gave a detailed report. The ice was made up largely of ammonia with some other trace substances. A light wind blew some drifting snow into the airlock.

"Gonna be interesting getting down." Baz pointed and Leonardo's gaze followed his hand. Twelve meters below them the surface was snow, rock and ice broken apart by *Resurgam's* landing trough. Under normal circumstances—in a vacuum crash—a ladder or gangway would extend from the ship. But there was nothing here, only a long drop down.

"In this gravity we're pretty light. Should be able to jump," said Leonardo.

"And back up?" asked Baz. Leonardo nodded. The surface could be unstable. Or there could be something underneath. The phrase "known unknowns" popped up from his training.

"Fair enough. Let's tie something here to help us down." Leonardo opened a utility locker. Finding a length of cable inside, he tied it to one of the rails along the wall. He attached the cable to one end, double tying it and tugging on it.

"That'll do for now. Worst case Dwi8 can get us up."

Baz nodded in his helmet then walked and stood at the lip of the airlock with Leonardo. "Who goes first?"

"Me."

Leonardo leapt out the airlock and slowly fell towards the surface. He landed softly in the scramble of rock, dirt and snow. He looked up as Baz raised his hands in resignation and jumped down. He came to land as smoothly as his captain. They stepped back a few paces and surveyed the *Resurgam's* exterior.

Leonardo sighed heavily.

He never liked looking at this ship from the moment he first laid eyes on it.

It was nothing like his previous command, the *UFWSS Wellstone*, a Zeus-class battlecruiser, four kilometers long with its hungry Choudhury drives. As sleek and stark as polished bone with its forward gun ports like empty eye sockets, *Wellstone* was all business. Often, the mere appearance of a Zeus-class ship at a conflict led to swift resolution before shots were even fired. If a situation required weaponized diplomacy, a Zeus-class ship could leave a planet-sized cinder smoking in space. *Wellstone* had a fearsome rendering of Huitzilopochtli, the Aztec god of war painted over her weapons-bristling bow as an extra intimidation tactic.

Resurgam, on the other hand, had a hairy, muscular spider with eight small limbs each holding a tool of some kind painted on the hull.

Resurgam was a Racine-class vehicle, an unarmed freighter. Leonardo could hardly stand to look at it under normal circumstances. Now, seeing it bent and broken, he hated it more. In working order *Resurgam* looked like a large, swollen caterpillar with a fat midsection where the cargo was held. The bridge and bow stuck off the end like a miniature head. Directional thrusters protruded from the front like stubby limbs. The smooth hull was unbroken by portholes, but studded with instrument domes and sensor arrays. Its light gray exterior was blackened near the nose and underside by the crash. The atmospheric burn on entry tore away a good portion of her shielding.

Almost a kilometer in length, *Resurgam* was powered by tiny Choudhury engines compared to the monstrous ones that drove the *Wellstone* and all Zeus-class ships. The fore seemed more or less intact, with a slight list to starboard. Midships the damage became evident with odd holes punched in the hull. *Resurgam's* stern lay crumpled, hull shielding bent at odd angles. But massive openings torn into the hull by the stern meant engine damage. Both could see the trail the ship gouged into the surface stretching behind.

"Christ," said Baz. "We're lucky she didn't strike those peaks. She'd have split in half or worse." He pointed behind the ship where the jagged yellow mountains could have torn *Resurgam* apart like a knife through cloth.

"We're lucky to be standing here," Leonardo said. "Bow's in good shape."

"Yeah, that's ... positive."

"Remember the crash of the *Koln*?" asked Leonardo. "I sat in on the review tribunal for that. *Koln* was Racine class like *Resurgam*. Came down nose first onto Orhun's surface after she took a hit from FMR raiders hiding in the rings there. Her crew was preparing for the hi-space jump then got hit by a direct MHT blast while they were securing cargo. Everything from the cargo bays up rammed into the bow. The bridge crew were just smears on the displays when the rescue team got in there. The Astrogator was crippled."

"Jesus, that's awful. But, look," Baz pointed out the path the ship took in, going from the right down over the mountains to where *Resurgam* lay. "It's like she just glided in," Baz said.

Leonardo nodded. "I'm dying to see the flight data. Figure out how to get such a smooth landing with this and patent it. Get a ... medal for it ... maybe." He knew Baz discerned the tone in his voice. His words hung in the thin air between their helmets like ghosts.

"Whoa. Look there," Baz said, pointing at *Resurgam*'s stern. Leonardo saw two holes blasted into the port side, three-quarters down its length. The first was small, three or four meters across. The second was bigger, further towards the stern and perhaps six to ten meters around. Shards of the hull lay perhaps a hundred meters away from the hole. Strips of shielding, pipes and hull sprayed out from the ship's side in a ghastly metallic wound. Cargo had burst through the hull, debris clinging to the sides or fluttering in the light wind. Open gouges broke up the black scar of atmospheric burn

Like holes punched in burnt flesh.

"That's near the main cargo bay. Let's go check it out." They trudged back to the ship. With the light gravity of the planet and their strength, they should have made the distance in short time. Were they not sleep drunk, Baz would be taunting him to race. But by the time they got to the ship, they were both short of breath.

Dwi8 emerged from the smaller hole in the hull, waving once. "Captain, I believe you must see this." Leonardo vaguely remembered the walky-talky requesting his presence earlier and waved up at the black form looming over him.

"Right, right. Help us up." Dwi8 threw down a cable for them. Leonardo jumped and was grateful when he felt the line pulling him up. He lifted his gaze to see Dwi8 reeling him in with limbs reconfigured for the task into motors and pulleys. Once up and inside he stepped away and waited for Baz to join him. When Baz made it up, the three of them stepped into the remains of the survey team's quarters.

The UFW Scientific Academy Xenoarcheological Survey Team was quartered in a modular multipurpose container attached to the cargo bay floor. This was placed against the port wall near the largest of the two airlocks for easy access. The main bay was enormous, big enough to hold everything for a dozen of these journeys. The team's belongings as well as the container of artifacts from Baaklum Cha'am's surface resided here. *Resurgam*'s bay was fitted with several such modular units, each twenty-five feet long, nine wide and nine tall. These could be preprogrammed for any storage needs: food, live cargo, hazardous waste, even habitation. The survey team's custom-made container came with them from Earth.

Stepping into the dark, Leonardo, Baz and Dwi8 faced a grim scene. A tremendous explosion blew a hole in the container's interior wall and through the hull, venting the module's atmosphere. The hull's layers were blown outward as were the inner walls of the module. The interior walls were blackened with scorch marks from one end to the other.

Anything near the damaged wall was shredded apart, the remains thrown about the cabin. Everything inside the module was scorched; burnt books, smashed pedias, clothes and other items were strewn around the cabin floor and out the door into the cargo bay.

"Jesus Christ," said Leonardo.

Baz stepped around him and began pointing things out. "The explosion blew the control systems for the berths. They probably failed along with everything else in the ship. This module was hooked into *Resurgam's* power grid. Nothing was spared."

Leonardo grunted in assent. There were seven people on the survey team. Six berths were stacked three to a wall on either side with a table for meals or conferences in between. One berth had been where the explosion had occurred, vaporizing the sleeping occupant. Each of the other six berths appeared to have malfunctioned in exactly the same way, killing the occupants.

"These berths have redundant power supplies. They should be able to run on their own for at least ten years," said Leonardo. The window of each was blackened from the explosion, obscuring the faces underneath. From what little they could see peering in, the dead all looked the same: mouths parted slightly as if in mild protest or just breathing slack jawed in their sleep.

"Dead," said Baz. "All of them. Dead."

"Damn it," said Leonardo, his stomach in knots despite his efforts to remain calm. It brought up memories he preferred suppressed. He turned away.

"Dwi8, any ideas?"

The walky-talky stepped forward and looked about the room.

"I believe the damage is related to the explosion as Lt. Al-Mushtarii stated. I do not have an exact sequence of events to explain it. I can say with a high degree of certainty that the ship crashed and these explosions occurred shortly sometime *afterward*."

Leonardo remembered the rocking of the ship shortly after his revival.

"All right." Leonardo peered into one of the berths again, doing his best to hide a deep repulsion. He saw frost on the interior of the glass. "The sleep process should have left no moisture inside the berths. But there's condensation there. What's that from?"

"My guess is somehow the seal in each of the berths was broken. Likely a malfunction of the emergency release mechanism. There was a short period of time where there was atmosphere inside this unit. The berths *may* have broken down before this explosion occurred." Dwi8 pointed to the gaping hole in the hull. "The units all warmed up for a moment, then when the atmosphere was breached—"

"Right. The breach." Leonardo repeated and turned towards Dwi8. The walky-talky's blank eyes regarded the captain. "What about that?"

"When I arrived here the door was open. Perhaps Wal8 opened the compartment to check on the survey team?"

"Doubt it," said Leonardo. "With an atmospheric breach, Wal8 would know not to open any compartment door."

Dwi8 pointed to the cargo bay. "The ship lost pressure due to the larger hole torn into the hull just aft of here. This led to the atmosphere of the planet rushing in."

"Despite the surfeit of doors and airlocks between here and there?" said Baz.

"Due to the journey ahead of us I told Wal8 to do an atmospheric drain. Save us some oxygen." Baz nodded. Leonardo surveyed the berths turned coffins around him. Things weren't making sense even without his head still foggy from deepsleep. "But this explosion here in the compartment? It blew *outwards*. Perhaps the larger explosion triggered the smaller one? Or vice versa?"

"No clue," Baz said. "Y'know, these bodies are fine for now. But when we get power back on with these units all damaged? They're going to begin to decompose pretty quick."

"You're right." Leonardo turned away from Dwi8 and Baz, walking through the rows and looking at each berth in turn.

"Dwi8, continue checking the ship. I want a full damage report ASAP. And when the time comes we'll remove these bodies. Maybe cover them in the snow. Leave a marker so we can find them later."

"Yes, sir." The walky-talky left the compartment.

"Let's get out of here," Leonardo said to Baz. "I've seen enough."

"Agreed." They stepped out of the module. "Hang on a second, Baz."

Leonardo looked for Dwi8 and saw it walking towards the rear of the cargo bay.

"Dwi8, where is Wal8?" The walky-talky turned and raised an arm, one digit extended.

"Near the utility lockers, sir." Dwi8 pointed behind them.

They left the module and entered Cargo Bay 1. The enormous cargo hold, usually kept pristine by *Resurgam*'s crew, autonomous stevedrones and walky-talkies, was torn apart during the crash. A storage container filled with the survey team's artifacts from Baaklum Cha'am was torn loose and smashed into the forward wall. Deep gouges in the floor showed its path. It apparently exploded in the abrupt atmospheric pressure change, contents spilled onto the floor of the bay.

There they found the remains of Wal8 pinned between the wall and the container. From its appearance, Leonardo surmised that the walky-talky must have been moving when the crash occurred. During travel walky-talkies stayed in their charging berths. But Wal8 was wedged in tight, its waist crushed, legs splayed at odd angles even for a walky-talky not constricted to human anatomy. The head was smashed in and the thoracic trunk blown out. The arms appeared to have been torn from the body.

"Damn. What happened?" Leonardo asked Baz.

"I don't know," answered Baz, looking about the cavernous bay. "Wrong place, wrong time." He knelt closer, delicately poking at the innards. "God, Wal8's blasted to hell. How'd he get so knocked around? See any Wal8-sized dents around the bay?"

"No, but see if you can cannibalize anything from it. I'm sure it has some data from the crash. Let me know what you turn up."

"Got it." Baz pulled tools from his belt. "Where you going?"

"To check the crew." There was a moment of eye contact and both knew what the other was remembering: UFW soldiers, mutilated corpses. Miners and their families thinking they were going home only to die in the cold of space.

Baz broke the tension by nodding curtly. "Okay. Let me know if you need anything."

"Will do." Leonardo left as Baz began dissecting the walky-talky.

Leonardo walked towards *Resurgam's* bow.

Over half the ship was built for carrying cargo. Engines took up less than a quarter of its length and the rest was living areas for crew and a small number of passengers. The bay's reconfigurable design made it suitable for almost any mission. Since taking command, Leonardo oversaw a variety of missions from diplomatic support, humanitarian aid, and emergency supply runs and even other archaeological missions. Most had been simple support runs to larger ships and nonessential missions. He'd been in command of the ship only a few years. He commanded the *Wellstone* for almost twenty years until the incident at Newhope15.

He thought that perhaps his short time as captain of *Resurgam* might have made the scene in the crew bunks somewhat easier to bear despite the incident. Leonardo had not known this new crew very well. Baz gave up a chance to command his own vessel to serve under Leonardo as he had on the *Wellstone*. This crew was wary of Leonardo from the beginning and he knew it. No doubt they heard and perpetuated the rumors about the old man. There was little love lost between the captain and almost all of his crew. They kept to themselves, followed orders and were civil towards Baz, Drina and himself.

But finding his crew dead in their berths filled Leonardo with neither joy nor relief nor sadness. It was just as it had been at Newhope 15. He would see they received the proper burial. He would speak of their bravery and dedication.

And they can no longer whisper about you on deck or behind closed doors, he thought.

Nor could they help him now when he needed them most, as they lay dead like the survey team members.

Leonardo stepped closer to the nearest berth and peered in at the face of Chief Engineer Guacharo Himanako. Himanako had been one of the more likable ones, as eager to show off his capoeira skills as to keep the ship running. Leonardo would miss his intimate knowledge of Choudhury drives and loving care of *Resurgam's* engines. He might have known how to right the ship and get them back to space. Now they'd be lucky if they got the AI to show them how to repair the engines.

Leonardo looked closer at Himanako's head. Through the clear panel he could see the temples were distended, his skull bloated and misshapen. Frozen blood ran from his ears, nose, mouth and eyes. His limbs were flung out and the body contorted as if he had died in pain, not resting for a long journey home; completely unlike the restful forms of the dead back in the modular container.

The captain looked at each of the berths in turn, finding every single occupant in the same condition: heads distorted and swollen, faces and bodies contorted painfully with blood coming from all orifices. He hoped they hadn't suffered too long and wondered what could have caused such horrific deaths.

Leonardo lingered over the berth closest to the door, that of Lt. Regina Badawi. Her black hair was flung across the pillow as if in tormented sleep. One hand was pressed against the glass of the berth, palm flattened, the print of her skin frozen into the glass. Leonardo put his gloved hand over hers, not daring to look too closely at the rest of her.

"I'm sorry," he whispered. He drowned out the words of their last conversation and memories of their final coupling in his mind before they could take.

"Baz?" Leonardo called out, the comm channel opening with a short clashing hiss of static. After a second there was a beep in his left ear.

"Yeah, Leo?"

"I'm in the crew quarters. Something's weird. Something happened to the crew."

"How do you mean? Besides being dead, sir." Leonardo noted Baz's delicacy. He knew Leonardo would be thinking of Regina.

"They died in the berths, but ... I don't think it was from the crash. Something else happened." Leonardo left Regina's berth and walked back into the hall.

"I'll be there in a minute. For what it's worth, Wal8 looks odd, too."

"How so?"

"I'd swear this damage isn't from getting crushed by the container. It's as if it got beaten up."

"Really?" Leonardo paused. "Okay, keep these things in mind. First order of business is to join up with Dwi8 and find out the status of the ship. And I think we need to go do a full planetary survey at some point."

"Agreed. Looks like Dwi8's in ..." Baz trailed off as they simultaneously checked their HUDs.

"Rear Bay 7," Leonardo continued. "See you there."

"Copy that."

Leonardo left the crew quarters without looking again. Already he tired of running back and forth, missing the ease of the lifts that would have carried him through the ship much faster than walking. There was a temptation to let his thoughts fester and darken as concerns mounted, recounting the myriad ways they could have prevented the crash. *Stuck here in this ship turned tomb, with a wife in a marriage just as lifeless*, he thought.

There was only futility in following those thoughts.

Leonardo swung out at the nearest wall strut. The exosuit immediately activated, increasing the density tenfold while protecting him with impact pooling. *Feels good to flex a little,* he thought. He straightened up as he made his way down the corridor and through the cargo bay. He passed through the aft doors of the cargo bay to enter Rear Bay 7.

Rear Bay 7 held an array of small craft for various uses. A half-dozen spherical repair vehicles waited in their bays, perfect for zero G and completely useless on a planet with even this little gravity. Extra EVA suits hung in stalls, the names of their owners stenciled on each yellow helmet and over each door. Various pieces of EVA gear were stored in their containers as well.

He found Baz in consultation with Dwi8, standing near *Resurgam's* short-range vehicle, *Sparky*; a hundred feet long, twenty high and twenty wide. *Sparky* was a light shuttle capable of planetary landing and take-off, as well as short interplanetary runs. The door to the cockpit was open to darkness inside. Baz had taken off the rear panel of

Sparky's starboard engine housing and was poking inside it. Dwi8 turned to look at the captain.

"Any luck with that?" asked Leonardo.

"No. Bay doors are locked tight for hi-space flight, for one thing. Nothing'll get it started. *Sparky* just doesn't work like every other goddamn thing on this ship. I'd kick Dwi8 if I thought it'd do any good."

"Sir?" asked the walky-talky.

"Never mind," said Leonardo. "Let's keep moving."

They moved further aft through ship's stores. Darkness loomed in on them wherever they went. Nothing escaped the deactivation of the ship's electrical systems. Each room was empty and devoid of the normal hum of activity of a ship like *Resurgam*.

They stopped when they came to the corridor leading to Engineering. The ceiling was torn open, revealing weak gray daylight above and crumpled, torn-up hull to the sides. They could see the planet's surface. The dim light shone into the jagged space illuminating the other side of the corridor. The floor fell away in a ragged tear of metal, broken conduits and sheared wires. Pipes burst, their contents instantly frozen or shorn off.

"Oh," said Leonardo, his voice like a child's. "I guess ... The engines have broken off."

"We'll never get off this planet," answered Baz in a hoarse croak.

CHAPTER THREE
Everything's Gone Green

"Damn," muttered Baz, headlamp and wrist beams following his gaze up to the torn wall and ceilings around him. "It's a simple break ... but we're still fucked."

"Nope." Leonardo shook his head. "This is a bad break, not simple. Clean, but bad."

"At least the struts appear stable," Baz said, pointing towards supports connecting Engineering Section to the ship. Twenty-five struts, each seven feet in diameter, made of solid ferroceramic reinforced carbon fiber, ran from the rear of the ship to Engineering. These were capable of explosive disconnection in the case of catastrophic engine failure, such as negamatter leakages or sabotage. "I'm surprised they didn't blow."

"The core must've jettisoned before we hit the atmosphere. It's most likely why we're still alive," Leonardo said.

"Sir," Dwi8 piped in. "I estimate a reasonable chance of repairs once the ship's power is restored."

Leonardo turned towards the walky-talky and frowned.

"Yes, Dwi8, but I don't see exactly when that could happen."

"Yes, sir."

"Well, maybe it's not too bad," said Baz, stepping closer to the ragged edge. He waved at the right side of the missing corridor. "We've got no walls here, but some still intact over there. Chances are we could reroute everything to the left."

"True," Leonardo said. "Then the nannies could rebuild the wall here."

"Think there's anything in the soil they could use?" asked Baz.

"Dwi8?" Leonardo said. The walky-talky focused its gaze on the snow below.

"The surface is ammonia ice. Soil is rocky, composed of unknown metals. The ship's nanomech could find a reasonable amount of resources."

"Good." Leonardo gingerly crossed the wide strip of remaining floor and shined his light on the warped doors.

"Dwi8, open these."

The walky-talky edged over, followed by Baz. It stepped in front of the doors, holding out a hand. It reconfigured from five fingers into large gripping metallic claws. Dwi8 slipped these into the gap in the door and spread them apart. Leonardo detected the faint sound of metal screeching in the thin atmosphere as the vibration wound through his suit. After a few seconds of steady wrenching, the walky-talky made enough space for them to pass through.

They entered the darkness of the engine rooms, the power center of the ship. Engineering was nearly a third the size of the main bay. Directly in front of them were the main generators. Far to the back of the space was the beginning of the Drive Works.

"Well, these look okay," said Baz. "Dwi8, come here and take a look at the powerhouse with me." The walky-talky followed Baz to the bulky structure of the powerhouse.

Leonardo walked towards the back, lights shining on the far wall. His light landed on large double doors at the far end. Myriad warnings and symbols of danger were plastered all over. Leonardo cranked open the doors. Stepping inside, his lights flashed into another cavernous space. He stood on a catwalk in the twenty-by-fifty-yard room. The catwalk ran the perimeter of the room twenty feet off the floor. A single set of stairs led down to the floor and engines. The huge, silent forms filled Leonardo with a mixture of awe, slight dread and unease when they were running; now they were like sleeping giants laid flat by an unseen illness. He remembered fondly looking at the *Wellstone's* drives hours before debarking, their thrumming forms the size of houses. These seemed pathetic by comparison, though they were no less powerful. The quiet filled him with a sadness that stretched back years.

He returned to Baz and Dwi8, who were looking over dormant displays and dark control panels, their helmet and dome lights the only activity in the space.

"Well?"

"Nothing. Can't even get backup systems to kick in. Everything's offline. I bet it's way deep in there. Could be damage somewhere below. Can't tell until we can get in there."

"All right." Leonardo paced the room while Baz and Dwi8 tried to bring *Resurgam* to life. Shortly, Baz gave up. "It's gonna take more time. What next?"

"Dwi8, examine the hull, inside and out. Find all breaches. Fix what you can. That hole back in the corridor," Leonardo pointed behind him where they had come in, "is going to take some time. I want as much of *Resurgam* back in order as possible. Baz, finish up getting what you can out of Wal8. I want to see the flight records ASAP."

"Sir." The walky-talky left the engine room. They waited until it was out of range. Leonardo gestured to Baz and they switched to secure comms.

"Start talking, Baz."

"I have a bad feeling, Leo."

"Agreed," Leonardo said with a curt nod. He looked around overhead, helmet lights illuminating the darkness. "I didn't plan on spending my retirement this way."

"I bet."

"Maybe it's just a loose wire."

"Ha!"

Leonardo was always pleased when he made Baz laugh. "Sure. Maybe Hammond just forgot to set a timer."

"I'll go hunt down some supplies. We're going to need to eat, make sure the suit chargers are functional. Make sure we have some fresh air."

Leonardo left, stepping over the ledge of the corridor outside, pausing to notice the blown-out remnants of his ship. He looked overhead at the mangled struts and buckled supports that barely held together during the crash. He marveled at surviving a crash only to find they might not live another day or two. He and Baz might be able to rely on suits for a few weeks at most. Then what? No going back into sleep berths without power. So they would die, leaving Dwi8 behind. Dwi8's batteries would run down in five hundred years or so, perhaps long enough for a rescue team to find their suited, desiccated corpses waiting for help. Or be dug up by another bunch of archaeologists like the ones who lay dead in his ship.

Hoping the walk would clear his head, Leonardo made his way forward. At the cargo bay, he went to the hole punched through the airlock doors and stood looking out at the planet. The ship was as cold and lifeless as this world. Outside was the dim illumination from its weak star. Inside was overpowering darkness.

He made his way through the gloomy corridors, pausing briefly at the mausoleum that the crew quarters had become. The darkness and cold of the ship amplified the lifelessness around him. There was only the sound of his breath in his helmet, the shift of his suit against his skin, the faint thud of his boots as he walked, the smell of his own body. An almost empty, mile-long vessel devoid of power, light and atmosphere instilled anxiety in him. He shrugged this off and began to piece things together in his head as best he could.

There was so much to be done. They would need to get the hull repaired as soon as possible. This was challenging without the nannies. Under normal conditions, they were constantly at work, rushing through their tubes and capillaries to repair minor breaches and damages all over the ship at a moment's notice. What rendered *Resurgam* powerless felled the tiny machines as well. While they had supplies and tools to do some repairs themselves, the ship was built for the nannies to do most of them. Dwi8 was adequate for the job, but he was no replacement for a few billion nanomachines eating their nanoslurry and defecating hull materials.

It would be a tremendously difficult job. The three of them had to comb over every millimeter of a ship a mile long and three hundred and fifty yards in diameter, with the barest minimum of tools for the job. Leonardo knew to expect no pleasant surprises and expect many hidden unpleasant ones. They could very well find their oxygen supply leaked out and frozen in a puddle under the ship. Or that upon getting power systems back online, some wires had gotten crossed in the crash causing a fire or explosions. Multiple bad scenarios played out in his head. Few positive elements rose up from the sea of doom he foresaw.

"Oh, who the hell do you think you are kidding, old man?" he muttered, coming to a halt. Repairing a ship like this to try launching it off the planet was hopeless. *Resurgam* wasn't built for landing and here he was acting like he could lift the damn thing back into space. The only thing he hated more than busywork was assigning it. Yet he dropped right into habit without thinking. He hoped the effort at keeping morale up—he snickered at the thought of three people (one unconscious) manning a freighter this large as a "crew"—wasn't nearly as transparent as he feared. Baz wasn't stupid, nor was Drina. But the alternative of sitting and waiting passively for an unlikely rescue was enough to motivate Leonardo into saddling Baz with tasks that amounted to mousing checkers around a board with no end in sight. If they got power back but were never rescued, at least their final days would be lived out in reasonable comfort. And there was the possibility of getting off in *Sparky*.

Leonardo balled his fists, looking for targets. Would it have been better to die in the crash?

Shaking his head, Leonardo turned his thoughts back to the matters at hand. It might be possible to seal off sections of the ship, creating pockets of sustainable atmosphere while traveling between them in suit. Then they could focus on getting *Sparky* ready and loading everything they'd need to get off this planet.

Perhaps when the hull was repaired they might solve the mystery that got them here. It was tempting, but Leonardo knew worry and inaction were luxuries they could ill afford.

He came to Drina's quarters. No change in her condition. She was still unconscious, monitored closely by the berth's medical systems. Underneath all the mediblankets and her suit, the Astrogator's body was kept alive by machines. He pondered this for a moment. How peculiar that the berth's multiple redundant systems and independent power supplies had kept her from the deaths that met the rest of the crew.

For that matter, how exactly did he and Baz escape death as well?

"And for what?" Leonardo muttered.

He pondered another horror: should Drina awaken, she'd be nothing less than furious to find herself stranded in the ship on an unknown, lifeless planet. Given her unique position she would be unable to leave the ship. Like all Astrogators, she was hard wired into the very information structure of *Resurgam*. An Astrogator's disengagement was not something one could perform with any old tools on board. It was a lengthy, delicate process that still—over two centuries since the first ship was fitted with a living female astrogation computer—resulted in the occasional brain-damaged Astrogator.

He had to consider she wouldn't awaken for only a second before banishing the thought.

Leonardo let his headlamps shine on two small posters over Drina's desk. The first was a formal portrait of Astrogator General Hera Forrest. She sat ramrod straight, flanked on one side by her Zeus-class warship, the *Ainiaan*, and an antique astrolabe on the other. Standard adornment for every Astrogator's quarters, Drina's copy was free of the shrine-like accoutrements most Astrogators usually put around theirs.

The other poster depicted a general resemblance to the UFW's logo, with the thirty-one worlds represented by multicolored spheres spread around intertwining olive branches. In the center instead it repeated the motif in the portrait, depicting a winged woman in a work suit holding a Zeus-class destroyer and an astrolabe. Below this, in what Leonardo knew was Drina's "angry" handwriting, was scrawled, "BOOTSHOD, STERILE AND TIED TO THE FUCKING SHIP."

The honor of being an Astrogator had long soured on Drina by the time they journeyed out to Baaklum Cha'am. Not everyone who graduated from the UFW Academy of Astrogation was installed in the position of prominence that was every young cadet's dream. Many became part of Astrogation support teams. Luckily, Drina had graduated with high honors from the Academy and was installed in the *Wellstone*. In their first few years together Leonardo and Drina were both bright, shining examples of the UFW's military wing, defending and providing colonies with safety, security and freedom.

Yet for the last two years, Leonardo had been rather happy that his wife was restricted to her quarters by the thick cables that snaked into her skull and spinal column. The woman he married and loved had become two different people. There was the one who was completely professional when present with the crew. Privately, she was as cold and distant as the planet beneath the ship, bitter about her literally immobile position, with a husband she no longer seemed to care for as she counted the days until their divorce.

The incident at Newhope 15 worsened things. She'd already been talking eagerly about her disengagement, and even though it was two years away she was counting it down to the minutes. Each mission was marked off as one less thing that stood between her and retirement. She'd had schematics of old sailing vessels on her pedia and often talked about returning to the Yucatan on Earth where they'd trained for the *Wellstone* assignment.

Newhope 15 changed everything.

He left her quarters, fighting images that could no longer be held back. He stood at the wall, banging his fists, ignoring warnings from his suit.

... bodies strewn around the cargo bay, converted into emergency shelters for the miners and their families. Now it was pooling with blood as men, women and children tore themselves apart in their last agonies. The stench was horrible. First torn apart by the sudden and total decrease in pressure from the terrorist's bombs, when atmosphere was restored the flash-frozen bodies defrosted and began to cook in the heat. The fires at the bow kept the crew from getting down to the cargo bay for several hours. By then it was beyond too late. Leonardo stood at the open door with a fire axe in hand, mouth agape. He fell back as the crew streamed into the hold to begin their long and horrific clean-up...

Leonardo regained composure, stood to his full height and returned to the cargo area. There was little he could do for Drina until power was restored. Let her machines keep her alive until they could get the ship working again.

If they could get it working again.

CHAPTER FOUR
Walking & Talking

"Crashed on an uncharted, deserted planet in a ship full of corpses and your ex-wife—"

"Uh, you say something, Leo?"

"Huh? No, just talking to myself."

"Already, huh? A good sign."

Baz was in the cargo bay, clearing a path through the debris of exploded containers to get to the emergency lockers. It was nearing what passed for night on the planet outside. They'd been awake for about twelve hours without much stopping. Their emergency suits were supporting them but they'd need real food soon. The hi-space journey was cut short, only about two weeks out of the projected six. Not surprisingly, waking to the disarray of the crash and putting some order to it was making Leonardo very hungry.

But eating in the D-FAC was impossible until power was restored. He stood at the hatch, staring into the empty room. Everything was cleaned and stored away, ready for reactivation nearer their destination. Long steel tables reflected the light of his headlamps. Dead displays hung from the walls, unable to show the usual steady, blaring stream of media, stim-shows or motivational rah-rah videos from Jason's archives or UFW satellite intel. All the food in the D-FAC was made from nanoslurry. Without the food nannies to make it, there was no way they could get anything edible from the galley. Food-grade nanoslurry in its raw form was largely inedible and tasted horrible. Leonardo rummaged around through boxes and shelves but didn't find so much as a pack of old crackers. Thus the search in the cargo bay for emergency supplies, which normally were saved for rescue missions when refugees or disaster victims would be brought aboard.

A beep in his ear caught his attention.

"What's up, Baz?"

"I've done all I can. Just can't figure it out. As far as I can tell, everything's fine. Himanako kept the engine room inspection ready at all times," Baz said.

"Well, when we get power maybe we can get a ball cam to poke around inside there."

"Okay. What now?"

"I'll come to the bay. We'll get into those lockers and see what emergency supplies we have."

Leonardo arrived and they cleared a path to the emergency lockers where they found food, water and an emergency habitat shelter. They dragged the habitat to a clear space at the center of the cargo bay. Leonardo put it down, kicked the activator and left it to work. He didn't need to watch to know that soon a strong dome would form, capable of sustaining a breathable, temperate atmosphere inside for at least two months.

Back by the lockers he found Baz holding a green cylinder about three feet long. It was scarred and blackened along one end. Along the side it read "Emergency Blast Charge" in UFW block script. He looked up and Leonardo saw puzzlement on his face.

"Why do you think this was discharged?" Baz asked.

"Might have gone off during the crash." Leonardo waved a hand at the debris. "I bet we'll find a nice big hole somewhere in the floor or in one of these containers."

"Like over there," said Baz, indicating the hole in the airlock.

"Right."

"Huh," said Baz. Leonardo followed Baz's gaze over his shoulder at the survey team's container. One of the large doors was blown open, the contents spilling out. Baz shined lights on the container doors. The insides were disheveled and blast scarred.

"Well, look," he said, gesturing at some gouges at the hinge. "I guess that's it right there. Some kind of malfunction blew the interior bolts. Spilled all their crap out into the bay. Doesn't seem quite right, but ... Nice packing job, assholes." Baz hissed and dropped the cylinder. They silently continued to dig out the bay. Soon they'd cleared out another bank of lockers. Leonardo opened one, dug into the contents and held up four ration packs.

"Beans and rice or teriyaki steak and peas?" he asked Baz.

"Uh, I'll go with steak." Baz took the foil pack and held it against his faceplate. "Shit."

"What?"

"There's no tube in this suit. How're we gonna eat these?"

"Huh. Good point." Leonardo turned around. "Well, the habitat's done. Let's go eat in there."

During their excavation of the debris, the small box had turned into a bright red dome twelve feet high and forty feet in diameter with a large, brightly painted yellow UFW emergency marker on top. They stood in the airlock as the doors shut and the atmosphere was replaced. Their suits beeped when the cycle was complete and they stepped into the habitat.

All UFW Type-55B Emergency Shelters were designed to hold up to forty people in cramped but adequate conditions. It was spacious for the two men. The sloping ceilings were low, barely three meters at the center of the room. The interior was a dark red, with the emergency marker acting as a window that let in light, amplified it and converted it into heat or stored it in batteries. The walls were rimmed with a low bench. In the center of the floor was a small, circular pedestal just one yard high that housed comm systems, shelter controls and a small heating unit for cooking or warmth. On the far side of the shelter was a latrine.

Leonardo pressed a small button just under the chin of his helmet. His HUD flashed a warning about unsafe atmospheres at him. Leonardo pressed the button again and the graphic cleared. His helmet disconnected with a slight sucking noise and a quiet pop.

The air inside the shelter was a mixture of plastic and yeasty smells from the recently extinguished nannies. The temperature was a cool 60F, though he could tell from the glowing red coils of the brazier at the center it would rise higher soon. He could smell himself now that newer scents were arriving upon him. The smell, ammonia and a sweet and sour tang, told him the suit's scrubbers were failing. He and Baz would be beyond rank soon, as they simmered in emergency suits with failing cleaning capacity.

Baz took off his helmet, took an extra sniff of the collar and made a face. He dropped his ration packs onto the bullseye pattern of the brazier and let his helmet fall to the floor. Leonardo unclipped his gloves, dropped them in his helmet and threw both at the wall.

"Nice," said Baz. "Haven't been in one of these in a while. They've changed them a little bit since the Forties. I got stuck on Tiger Eye for a while back in '43 and we stayed in one of these until Search & Rescue came."

"Tiger Eye?" Leonardo made a face, remembering four-yard-high sulfur drifts and microfine sand everywhere. "Yuck."

"Wasn't so bad, especially if you're escorting a bunch of CIS Teen Crusaders from one of their desert hideaways after an FMR attack. Some of their leaders were especially *grateful.*"

"I don't want to know," Leonardo laughed, pulling a cushion out from the low bench. It slowly unfurled like a giant tongue from a sleeping animal's mouth.

When their food packets heated up, the men tore them open and devoured the contents. They said nothing as they dug into the rations heartily. Eventually Baz cleared his throat.

"So how long do you think we have?" Baz asked as he licked the interior of the foil bag clean.

"Depends," Leonardo answered. "We have plenty of supplies from emergency stores. A few months, I think. This shelter can recycle air from whatever we can scrounge off the planet's surface. The planet seems pretty stable. Not too much indication of meteor activity so we don't have to worry about the planet getting hammered by that or, the ship either."

"So ... three months without power, six with?"

"Yeah, just about."

"Okay."

"And that's without a Search & Rescue team coming in. But I won't wait for them. We could be in some desolate system's backyard or way out in uncharted space for all we know."

Baz nodded, licking the foil bag with a careful, lazy focus. "I was thinking," said Baz, eyeing the inside of the foil bag, "about the nannies that build these things."

"Yeah? What about them? They extinguish quickly. Something about keeping them alive in storage, I think."

"Yeah but we've got other shelters out there, right? What about rigging those nannies to get to work inside the hull?"

"Hunh," Leonardo said, nodding as he thought it over. "It's possible, I guess. Hull nannies and shelter nannies eat and shit two different things. But maybe we can get Dwi8 to talk to the activator and retune them until we get power."

"I'll go give it a shot," Baz said, rising up.

"Right behind you."

They got into their suits. Leonardo cursed at putting the stinking helmet back on. Once outside, they went to the lockers and removed another shelter unit.

"Dwi8, check in." Leonardo waited until the walky-talky pinged a response.

"I am in the starboard hull access. I've almost completed the survey of the hull damage."

"We need you down in the bay now."

"Coming, sir."

Baz removed an activator from within the shelter's container. The tiny nonsentient computer inside lay dormant, awaiting the activation of its processes. Baz tugged the wires gently from their sockets.

"Don't be too gentle, Baz. Those things're designed to drop from orbit to a hard landing." Baz snorted and tugged the final wire free. He hefted the shoebox-sized activator in his hand.

Leonardo saw Dwi8 come down the stairs from an upper catwalk. It stopped at some large debris in its way then leapt over the pile and landed quietly near the men.

"Sir."

"Dwi8, I need you to reprogram this nanny activator box. We want to see if we can get it to jumpstart the ship's nannies and repair the hull fractures."

"Yes, sir. I have completed my analysis of hull damages. Would you like that now?"

"Let's tend to this first." Dwi8 nodded and took the box from Baz. It took the wires extending from the box and held these near a small circular aperture in its chest panel. A corresponding socket formed from a clear plastic surface.

They walked to the nearest capillary access hatchery. Leonardo had his doubts about the outcome. Shelter nannies were built to adapt to any environment, as emergency shelters were deployed on many different worlds for different needs. One world might have a corrosive atmosphere of hydrochloric acid, another might not have any atmosphere at all.

But Leonardo had never heard of this being attempted with shelter nannies before. Hull nannies were built to certain specifications and ate a very specific diet of slurry, the top secret complex material that made up a hull's composition. Theoretically, someone could slip the wrong recipe to the nannies or even altered nannies into the capillaries and then the hull could be weakened or the nannies programmed to simply devour the hull. Thus hull nannies were programmed to be aggressively hostile to any foreign element in the capillaries, destroying anything that might accidentally enter the system.

Then Leonardo realized many of the safeguards were offline with the ship devoid of power. *Might work after all*, he thought to himself. Anything was possible in this situation.

Dwi8 unplugged the wires from its socket after a few minutes. "Sir, I did my best to configure the nannies to the hull's specifications."

"Then let's give it a try." Dwi8 led the way as the men followed.

"Dwi8, you have an analysis of the hull damages?" asked Leonardo.

"One hundred and thirty-two minor fractures in the hull, mostly microscopic, all repairable. There will likely be other damages that appear if the ship becomes operational again."

"Let's make that a 'when', Dwi8."

"Yes, sir. *When* the ship becomes operational again. There are nineteen large-scale damages to the hull. We have enough materials for repairs, though it will be easier with full power."

"I see."

"Sir, I've made some other observations. May I share these now?"

"Yes, Dwi8." Leonardo was glad for some conversation, even with a walky-talky. The bouts of silence were beginning to get to him.

"All lifeboats and escape pods are accounted for. No one attempted to launch them."

"That figures," said Baz. "Everyone was dead before we hit the atmosphere."

"Agreed," said Leonardo. "Dwi8, when exactly did the disabling of the ship occur?"

"Approximately four seconds after we left hi-space, sir."

"No time for us to do anything, then."

"No, sir. Also, none of our astrosats or distress beacons were launched."

"Shit," said Baz. He stopped dead in his tracks and turned to face Leonardo. Dwi8 walked a few more paces and stopped to turn around. "Are you fucking serious?"

"Easy, sailor."

"Quite serious, sir," said Dwi8.

"Leo? C'mon," Baz held up his gloved hands, casting strange shadows behind him with his wrist lights.

"I know, Baz. It would be helpful if they were deployed and transmitting. But they're not." Leonardo turned to the walky-talky. "Any idea why, Dwi8?"

"No, sir. I cannot tell without AI systems online."

"Add another thing on the 'Not Working' list," said Baz. He stopped behind Dwi8. "Okay, here we are."

They were in the port corridor at a nondescript point in the wall. They faced the way their HUDs showed the glowing outline of a door marked *"HULL REPAIR SYSTEMS AND MAINTENANCE. AUTHORIZED SYSTEMS AND PERSONNEL ONLY."* Baz banged against it with a fist a few times.

"Gonna have to bust it down, Dwi8." He waved the walky-talky towards the door. It turned to the captain as if waiting.

He and Baz stepped back. Baz tapped the captain's arm and indicated a closed comm channel.

"You know, sometimes I wish you'd picked a different persona for the walky-talkies. Something a little peppier. Wal8 was always a little holier than thou—"

"You're not going to hurt its feelings if Dwi8 hears you, Baz."

"I know, I just—"

"And remember, I got it off a Religious Services vessel for cheap. Capt. Delahunt owed me a favor. The imam there had configured it to discuss the Reformist Qu'ran—and a few bits from other religions—in the off hours."

"I remember," said Baz. He jerked a thumb at Dwi8 as it worked on the door. "This one is part butler, part little brother, and part soft-headed cousin who huffs sealant fumes." Leonardo laughed.

"Regina told me that *Resurgam's* previous captain liked that." Leonardo barely flinched when speaking her name. He pushed through it and spoke. "Remember that I tweaked Dwi8 a little, too. Got rid of the English accent. Couldn't get it all the way back to default settings without wiping its whole memory, but at least it didn't sound like some old fart."

"I guess," said Baz. "I think it got a little more messed up in the crash. Kel8 wouldn't have let all this shit go down. It'd secure itself with all eight limbs and then blast the hell out of whatever it found. I loved watching that son of a bitch aboard the *Wellstone*. What an ally it would have been now."

"I miss Kel8 too, Baz. At least I got Jason transferred from the *Wellstone*."

While they spoke Dwi8 was waving a hand slowly over the door outline looking for a certain point. Finally the walky-talky selected a spot and drew its fist back. The walky-talky punched into the wall with tremendous force, driving its arm almost up to the elbow into the wall. Leonardo winced, adding that damage to a mental list of repairs. The walky-talky braced against the wall with its right hand as it worked inside the wall with its left. Leonardo thought of how he or Baz would be swearing, sweating and struggling at this. The walky-talky worked at the problem with a calm and grace Leonardo had only seen in martial arts masters at bootcamp or long forgotten in himself.

The outline of a door appeared in the wall as Dwi8 found an internal release. Dwi8 removed its hand from the wall and aimed both hands over the thin slots on either side of the door. Its hands became very thin and flat as the digits slid further into the space around the portal. Dwi8 began imperceptible manipulations around the door. Suddenly it pulled the door free, oily hydraulic fluid and wires spraying out from inside the doorway.

"Good thing security's down," said Baz. "Otherwise Dwi8 would have shit his electric pants. I've seen guys get turned to hash trying to do that."

Dwi8 dropped the door next and walked in, followed by Baz and Leonardo. The long, narrow service room was just over two meters wide by five long. The walls bore stenciled schematics of the ship, as well as displays for diagrams of all ship's functions. Three large horizontal tubes bulged out from the far wall. The upper tube was bright red. The bottom was matte black. The light blue tube in the middle had a box on its front with a variety of small sockets and gauges. Dwi8 held the activator in place above it. A protruding pipe from the tube fit perfectly into the box. Dwi8 put a hand on a lever and flipped it down. It held the box while plugging another cable from its chest panel.

"What do you think he's doing?" asked Leonardo.

"Looking into the capillaries. Whatever killed the nannies might still be in there. Then again," said Baz, "he might be asleep."

"Dwi8," Leonardo said, raising his voice, "what do you see?"

"Sir, there is no activity at all. Everything in the capillaries is dead. "

"Speculate."

"It relates to the damage on the rest of the ship. But the nanobes have their own power. I suspect something may have happened before the crash, possibly a viral malfunction of the hull repair system."

"Does it relate to the hull breaches?" Leonardo asked, knowing the answer almost as he finished saying it.

"Doubtful, sir. The capillaries would have sealed off at the nearest subjuncture. Repairs would have immediately begun."

"All right," said Leonardo. He stood there unmoving, without a clear idea of what to do next.

"Dwi8, how long will it take the shelter nannies to propagate and repair the damages?" asked Baz.

"I believe roughly twelve hours, provided they can use the hull slurry."

Leonardo looked at Baz.

"Okay then. All we can do is wait. What're we gonna do?" asked Baz, hands held up.

Leonardo yawned then straightened up. "Come to the crew quarters and take a look at what happened to them."

"Great," said Baz, turning towards the door.

"Dwi8, stay here and observe. Let me know if there's any changes."

"Yes, sir."

They left for the crew quarters, silently making their way up the dark corridors. As they entered, Leonardo paused and looked around longer than before. Things looked different now, which he attributed to the lifting of the sleep berth chemicals in him. Usually crew quarters were spotless during a hi-space trip. Before entering hi-space, lockers were secured and belongings stowed before the crew was tucked into their berths. Leonardo personally inspected them before and after every journey. He made sure it was always a model of order at all times.

Now it was a gray, metal mausoleum, tidy like a well-kept crypt.

Leonardo let Baz enter first to examine the bodies. The lieutenant paused by each berth, shining wrist and finger lights inside each then moving on. When he was finished, he sat on the steel table in the center of the room and shook his head.

"These people should be alive and walking around with us. Instead of ..." Baz waved his hands. "Dead."

"Exactly. Why them and not us?" asked Leonardo.

"No idea." Baz got up and looked at the berths again. At the far wall, he opened a hatch to expose a small blank display screen next to a panel of buttons and switches. "This berth systems control isn't going to tell us anything until we get power back."

"Heard that one before," Leonardo said.

"I suppose the isolation of the officers' quarters may have helped us." Baz leaned into a berth. The sign above indicated it held the remains of Sgt. Karsh Somogyi, Cargo Specialist. "But this cranial trauma is really bizarre. They're exploded like something attacked them from inside. Maybe something they ate. Something viral."

"I doubt it. That would have affected us, right?"

"Yes. We had full contact with them at all times during this mission. Couldn't be poison. Our food wasn't separated. So what's different?"

"No idea. It's just more stuff that doesn't add up. Dwi8 has no medical functions, only limited first aid. I can't do an autopsy, can you?"

"No. And no, thanks, no" said Baz, wiping his gloves and waving the idea away.

"Let's go back to clearing the bay. We can find some hull repair plates and get working on that. Also, take what's left of Wal8 and hook it up to the comm setup in the shelter. Then we can look at the flight records. If they're intact."

They went back to the main bay. All loose debris was thrown into far corners until the space was finally restored to order. After eight hours of cleaning they returned to the shelter, with Baz dragging the intact parts of Wal8 behind him. Inside, Baz set about connecting Wal8 to the comm unit in the center pedestal. Leonardo wondered what might come of it. Little remained of the walky-talky that was functional. Baz held its severed head in one hand, peering into the neck for a connection. He swore and hissed before rubbing his eyes with a free hand.

"It'd be easier with a HUD, right?" asked Leonardo. "Guess they'll regret stripping them from us."

"Yeah. Wish I even had my lenses in. I'd be able to focus some more. Maybe there's a magnifier somewhere in here," said Baz, poking around in a small compartment in the base of the pedestal.

"The pedestal doesn't do a smart connect?" Leonardo said, peering underneath.

"No. These things are bare bones. Only the essentials. Meant to get people out of the elements and alive, not living large while waiting for S&R. We'll have to let the designers know about the barbaric lack of automatic connection and robotic forensic tools when we get back." Leonardo smirked.

Baz tugged out a handful of wires from the pedestal's base. He pried open Wal8's chest panel and poked around, stripping some wires with his teeth then roughly splicing them together for a connection. He looked for corresponding wires and sockets on the walky-talky's head. A few bright flickers and images began to appear over the pedestal. Leonardo leaned in.

"It's not the best connection. Hell, not even a good connection." A blue square suddenly flickered between them. "Surprised I even got this," said Baz.

"What about your dermals? That little jobbie you got on Hallowed Ground?"

"Uh, yeah, might work," said Baz. He took another wire from Wal8's chest panel and rolled up his sleeve, exposing three small sockets on his wrist. He stuck the wire into one with a slight wince and slapped his forearm a few times. A skinboard appeared, revealing a simple QWERTY layout in raised bumps on his flesh.

"This always itches like a bastard after I use it," Baz said.

"I'll get you some aloe," said Leonardo. Baz laughed then typed at his arm. The screen flickered again, showing a star map. Leonardo leaned in.

"Okay," said Baz. "Wal8 says we left the Baaklum Cha'am survey site at the Dark Rims near K'axob. The walky-talkies put us to bed, securing the deep sleep berths as we approached a drop-in point. Drina jumped to hi-space outside the gravity well on the far side of Xibun. On our way back to Earth, Jason picked up an Astrogator's distress call. Since we're a UFW Emergency Rescue Vessel, the AIs automatically answered the SOS. Once they finished recharting to the new coordinates, the Twins dropped us out of hi-pace right into some weird debris. Nothing like that should exist out here. It was thick like a planetary ring. Anyway, not an E-class planet in sight and we took a direct hit from that debris before we could jump back in."

"Yeah, that matches what I got from Dwi8," said Leonardo. "So where are we?"

"Gimme a sec." Baz tapped away again. "Looks like the ID from the SOS was ... Frontis? Yeah, look's like Frontis."

"Frontis? Frontis?" Leonardo thought for a second, staring at the floor. "No. Doesn't make sense. The Frontis system is well populated. There are no ice planets or anything like this in it. And its star is a red dwarf, a K class. That sun out there is a weak white G or maybe an F."

"Good point." Baz tapped at his arm a bit more, shrugged and looked back at Leonardo. "Wal8 says Frontis."

"Well, Wal8's fucking wrong then," Leonardo barked. Baz pursed his lips and shrugged. Both men stared silently at the flickering holoscreen. After a moment Leonardo said, "All right, get Dwi8 in here. Connect it to Wal8 to confirm. We're missing something."

"Dwi8's not as advanced as Wal8. He's low-level servile."

"Right, but it can at least filter through the data better than we can at this point and maybe see some things we're missing."

"Okay." Baz grabbed his helmet and called the walky-talky then keyed at his arm some more, drawing up garbled data. Both waited silently for Dwi8, Baz tapping away at his arm pad and Leonardo brooding. He knew he'd raised his voice unnecessarily at the XO, but wouldn't admit it. The situation was frustrating, hopeless and it was harder to mask his fears from his only conscious crew member. A side effect of the deepsleep was irritability, but apologizing to an underling would be seen as weak, even to his old friend.

"Huh," said Baz. "Now this is interesting."

"What's that?" Leonardo looked up from the floor at the screen.

"Something weird in the black box transcript. It's a log of Jason's upper functions during the crash. I'm looking at it in second-by-second breakdown. Come here."

Baz moved over so Leonardo could read it as well.

Y: 2468/M: 5/D: 23/T: 3:58GZCT: DISTRESS CALL RECEIVED. APPROX.
DISTANCE 1.43 LIGHT YEARS. EST. DEVIATION -
Y: 2468/M: 5/D: 23/T: 4:00GZCT: ROUTINE MAGENTA 3536 ENGAGED.

Y: 2468/M: 5/D: 23/T: 4:01GZCT: EMERGENCY AI-PILOT OVERRIDE.
Y: 2468/M: 5/D: 23/T: 4:01GZCT: ¬˙ˆfπœ¨¬˜©¨†∂f©∂.
Y: 2468/M: 5/D: 23/T: 4:01GZCT: POWER SURGE.
Y: 2468/M: 5/D: 23/T: 4:01GZCT: ERROR! ERROR! ERROR! ERROR! ERROR!
Y: 2468/M: 5/D: 23/T: 4:01GZCT: FORCE HI-SPACE DECELERATION.
Y: 2468/M: 5/D: 23/T: 4:01GZCT: µ∫˜ç∫√f©˙ß∂©˙øπ©˙∆˙fß
Y: 2468/M: 5/D: 23/T: 4:01GZCT: EMERGENCY NAV UNITS ENGAGE.
Y: 2468/M: 5/D: 23/T: 4:01GZCT: HI-SPACE DECELERATION ENGAGED.
Y: 2468/M: 5/D: 23/T: 4:01GZCT: FHDSHGFGE^@&A7265616
Y: 2468/M: 5/D: 23/T: 4:02GZCT: COLLISION/ COLLISION/ COLLISION/
Y: 2468/M: 5/D: 23/T: 4:02GZCT: EMERGENCY PROCEDURES.
Y: 2468/M: 5/D: 23/T: 4:02GZCT: HULL INTEGRITY 92%.
Y: 2468/M: 5/D: 23/T: 4:02GZCT: EMERGENCY NAV AI ENGAGED / SEARCH E-CLASS PLANET, MINIMUM DISTANCE
Y: 2468/M: 5/D: 23/T: 4:02GZCT: HULL INTEGRITY 90%.
Y: 2468/M: 5/D: 23/T: 4:02GZCT: SUITABLE E-CLASS PLANET FOUND.
Y: 2468/M: 5/D: 23/T: 4:02GZCT: HULL INTEGRITY 82%.
Y: 2468/M: 5/D: 23/T: 4:02GZCT: ENGAGE CRASH PROCEDURES.
Y: 2468/M: 5/D: 23/T: 4:03GZCT: DGIEYUFGE17861876
Y: 2468/M: 5/D: 23/T: 4:03GZCT: PLANET ATMOSPHERE BREACHED.
kY: 2468/M: 5/D: 23/T: 4:03GZCT: HULL INTEGRITY 78%.
Y: 2468/M: 5/D: 23/T: 4:03GZCT: SURFACE CONTACT IN -
Ωfßf≈ß∂√∫©∆f∂∆©f≈¥∂©∂R490`-`-1-; 1'1'; 1L10`-01-1.,/,/.,/.`.,`

"Huh. Very peculiar," said Leonardo.

"You're telling me," said Baz, pointing to the display. "Jason pretty much just shit the bed when we came out of hi-space."

"Obviously. Something went horribly wrong."

"It looks normal except for these breaks here." Leonardo pointed to the gibberish in the fourth line down. "What is this?"

"'MAGENTA 3536?'" Baz said aloud. "No idea. Doesn't sound like something in the protocols. I don't remember them all offhand but it sounds out of place."

"After that," Leonardo said, pointing further down the screen, "it all just goes to pieces."

"But Jason thought everything was fine, or at least going normally enough to engage in orbit procedures," said Baz. "I mean, I'm sure if I got deeper into the logs, I'll find him running some queries, but ..."

"It's safe to say that it fell apart and Jason tried to keep it together—" Both were startled and turned as they heard the muffled clunk as Dwi8 emerged from the airlock.

"Sirs?" Dwi8 said, taking in the sight of its fellow walky-talky in pieces on the floor before looking at them.

"Dwi8, come here and plug into Wal8. I want to see if you can access any more than we can."

"Yes, sir." Dwi8 walked towards them and lowered down to the pedestal. Baz took the wires from his arm and handed them to Dwi8. The walky-talky plugged it into its chest panel. With the connection made, the holoscreen flickered as text, images and information blurred across the screen dozens of times faster than Baz's attempts. Dwi8 turned towards Leonardo. "Sir, what shall I look for?"

"What is this 'Routine Magenta 3536'? Some sort of emergency protocol?" Leonardo asked. The walky-talky nodded and looked at the flickering on the screen. After a minute it stopped and looked at Leonardo.

"It is an unknown protocol launched at the time of the ship's exit from hi-space. Author, origin and time of insertion are unknown as well. But it is not among normal emergency procedures." The walky-talky looked at Leonardo, almost expectantly. "It is also encrypted."

"Encrypted?" Baz and Leonardo said simultaneously.

"Yes, sir. It appears to have been launched from a foreign package three seconds after the exit from hi-space."

"Why?" Leonardo asked aloud, to no one in particular. "How did it get introduced?" Leonardo said to Baz. The walky-talky made no attempt to answer. Leonardo shifted his gaze to his XO.

"You got me." Baz held his hands up. "Maybe Wal8's damages made it misread these logs or something."

"I doubt it. There's no further degradation of the files there like you'd get with that. The corruption occurs after the foreign subroutine shows up. Doesn't add up," Leonardo said, running a hand across his short black hair. "Dwi8, what's happening with the hull?"

"Sir, no activity to report. The nannies remain inactive. This may be due to a period of communication between the hull and shelter nanobes. Or they may be neutralized."

"Nothing?" Leonardo asked.

"No, sir."

"*Any* communication with them?"

"No, sir. Nothing from the activator nor with the nannies themselves." Leonardo looked at Baz, who cocked an eyebrow.

"There's always some low-level communication between them and the AIs. No communication at all? Means they're dead," said Leonardo.

"Hmm," said Baz, nodding. "Bad sign."

"Dwi8, if there is no activity in a few hours, tell me. Then you can return to normal duty."

"Sir, there is video in Wal8's memory. It is time stamped to correspond to the crash. Should I reclaim it?"

"Yes. I think we've done enough to the ship for now." Leonardo rose and slid his suit on. The inside was cool, clammy and reeked of overuse. "I'm going to check on Drina. Keep working with Dwi8, Baz."

"You got it," said Baz, nodding. Leonardo donned his helmet and left the shelter. The airlock hissed open, air misting as he departed and stalked off towards the bow. Angrily he kicked aside debris and barged his way through the forward hatch. He tongued the secondary recorder active from the roof of his mouth and began sublingually updating the logs.

His lights spread illumination drunkenly across the walls and down the empty corridors. He wasn't sure if he was lurching from fatigue or mounting pressure but he made little effort to correct it. The stumbling felt good in a way. Leonardo chuckled, finding it hard to ignore the colossal ridiculousness of the situation. In thirty years of command, he'd been up against grave danger and remarkable odds only to emerge unscathed. Thirty-two combat missions with minimal losses. Eighteen Search & Rescue missions with one hundred percent recovery. He'd been among the most highly decorated captains in the fleet and admired by all. His entire career as a captain was held up as something for any officer in the UFW to aspire to.

"My boy scout," Drina would say, pulling at the short, dark curls of his hair as she kissed him. They always laughed about it, as if it were a harmless joke.

Then...

Newhope 15.

Either it wiped the slate clean or permanently blackened his record; Leonardo was sometimes unsure of how to look at it. He was lucky to be given the *Resurgam* afterwards. Friends pulled many strings and called in favors to get him assigned to the middle-aged freighter. Two years on board *Resurgam* without incident and he began to feel almost okay again. Almost. Like the nightmares might stop. Like he wouldn't spend so much time locked up in his quarters bitching to his holographic oracle Horacio. Like he might not need any more treatments, rehab stints or chats with the doctors over a secure LDT line so the crew couldn't hear his shouting and excessive swearing (a weird, displaced sense of honor kept him from openly cursing the UFW Admiralty out in front of the crew). Like maybe he could get by without drinking too much. Like he might be the man he once was.

Now this.

Captain Leonardo Reyes De la Valencia: boy scout no more.

As he banged through the corridors, Leonardo remembered his mother, Augusta, sitting at the worn table on the bow of their houseboat with women from the anchorage at Hollow Point, drinking into the night. When they gathered to play cards and drink their toxic homemade liquor, Augusta spoke a language he didn't recognize as he lay in bed and listened to her in the dark. It wasn't Chinese, Amerese, Espanol verdad, twen-cen English or even Portuguese. It was a strange language that rose from the back of her drunken throat like slow animals. They'd go on all night until conversation reached a fever pitch. Then Augusta would lurch from her seat—he could still hear the scrape of the aluminum chair legs against the corrugated metal floor—and shout in Soceam "Just when I think I'm out—they pull me back in!" The women would laugh raucously, usually waking up Leonardo's little sister, Adina. He'd get her back to sleep as the women's drunken laughter went on into the night.

In Drina's quarters, Leonardo checked her vitals. Nothing had changed. Her machines were desperately trying to heal their queen. She lay as unconscious as at her arrival on the planet. Leonardo leaned against the wall and slid down, resting his elbows on his knees as he came to sit on the floor.

"It's gonna be a while before this is over, Dree," he said. "You'll be angry when you wake up. No surprise. Thought you'd be free of this old man. Can't do anything about it. Better get used to it. This situation's pretty unbalanced. Fubared to be exact." Leonardo knew she couldn't hear him. Even if she were conscious, her berth would keep her drugged. Still, it felt good to talk to her.

"Let's see. Where would we have been? We'd have gotten back to Titan orbit. *Resurgam* would be decommissioned and you'd be going through your disengagement. Then where would you have gone? I know what we'd planned to do *together*. But now that that's been scrapped ... Where would Drina go?" Leonardo looked at her desk, various pictures and drawings taped to the board above: mostly pictures of tropical beaches and fish from Earth.

"Of course. Where would any Astrogator go after being wired into a ship for twenty years? Especially you? You'd stay with the plan. You always wanted to go there. Back to your fish and your turtles on a quiet stretch of beach. You'd pick a little hut, something small and clean, good open shelter with a view of the ocean. You wouldn't need much there: just a bicycle to get to the village for groceries maybe. A sailboat. Maybe a radio. You'd have some books and perhaps a pedia for when you got super bored. You'd get a nice tan and walk the beach all day. Swim any time you wanted. Cut your hair short, grow it out, and cut it again. No cables in it. No regulation length."

Leonardo stopped and listened to the silence around him. He could hear the almost inaudible hiss of the open comm line in his ears and a rustle as he breathed. He closed his eyes and imagined Drina's voice.

"Me? Shit, I have no idea. We had a plan, but ... I was going to get myself fixed up nice for you so I'd look less like your father, maybe with a few scars left for conversation. Don't see the need for that now ... So I have no idea. Definitely not going home. You knew that; the Golden Coast is nothing to return to, not even these days. There's not much else I want to see on Earth. I'd planned on hanging around with you and letting you figure it out." He paused for a moment, looking at his gloves.

"I guess I've grown used to you telling me where to go and how to get there."

He hadn't planned for a solo retirement. He'd be content almost anywhere and hadn't really given a post-military life much thought. It was all he'd known for over thirty years. He'd seen most of the UFW's reach and very little appealed to him. Their plan was simple: Drina wanted to build a boat. They'd sail around, he'd get to read as much as he wanted while they piloted around the recovered coasts of South and Central America.

But the plan had changed when some big problems ripped their marriage apart right down the middle.

Leonardo looked at Drina's desk, spying an old book. She always had some antique books with her, sometimes preferring them to the much more versatile pedias everyone else in the galaxy carried around. Leonardo made fun of her love of these smelly, old, fabric-bound things, even though she'd grown up without them. He'd see them washed up on the shores all the time, bloated like the corpses tangled in the concertina wire with the other flotsam, and thought of them as dead and useless next to a nearly indestructible pedia.

He picked up the book, a reproduction of a recent title. He looked at the spine: "Hail the New Anchorites: Evolution of The Astrogator During the Second Great Space Age." One of Drina's favorites. She liked it so much, she had it fabricated antique-style by the ship's maker. He grunted, glanced at her sleeping form, then opened it and began to read.

CHAPTER FIVE

The Astrogator As Modern Anchoress

By 2099, human exploration of space was coming to a standstill. With the delay in expansion caused by a fourth World War (March 28, 2030 - October 11, 2067), humanity had lost precious time for both exploration and the scientific study needed to get humans safely out into space. The establishment of the United Federation of Worlds in 2104 helped create a cohesive framework for a united human effort to reach beyond the borders of its own moon and home system and begin exploring its closer neighbors.

Establishing a permanent lunar presence was the first priority. The foundation for Lunar Base One, or "Hecate," was laid in 2118. An international team of construction workers, scientists, doctors and teachers left a war-torn Earth to lay the foundations of what would one day become a glorious subterranean city on the Moon. Abundant supplies of Helium 3 (h3), necessary to power the fusion drives of space-faring vehicles, were thought to exist in the lunar soil. But the great dream was not to be: extensive tests indicated the amounts of h3 were insufficient to establish a lunar fueling station. Eventually Hecate did grow into a powerful base from which to begin exploring the solar system, but scientists had bet a great deal upon the existence of h3 in abundance. Undaunted by this single setback—this was, after all, a generation that had recently seen the destruction of over a billion human lives in almost four decades of bloody war—the UFW looked to Mars in 2120 for sources of h3.

From Hecate, workers moved out to build the massive Apollonian Shipyards at Ocean of Storms, which became the birthplace of the early interplanetary missions. It was here the Mars von Neumann probes were built, as well as the Praxis Venus probes. To this day, using imported h3 from Mars and Jupiter, Hecate and the meters at Ocean of Storms remain vital to the presence of free humans and their advancement through space.

This investment of time, effort and sacrifice paid off. By 2150, humans had set foot on Mars and built permanent bases, stepped onto the surface of Venus with Mariner 8 *and* Venera 11 *in heavily armored suits and even touched upon Mercury with the* Messenger 15 *mission. By 2170, Mars was being slowly but successfully colonized. The fledgling UFW was setting its sights beyond the solar system to Proxima Centauri Alpha and Barnard's Star. By 2200, humans had spread out towards all ends of the solar system.*

   But there were still major obstacles to overcome before humans could venture further than Sol and its satellites. Interplanetary travel that didn't mean a one-way journey was a distant dream, hampered by the limitations of existing technologies. Though fusion engines had become widespread, they still did not develop the thrust necessary to get humans to other systems and back in a reasonable amount of time. With the technology available to them, UFW astronauts would have taken 20,000 years to get to Proxima. Hardly short enough to develop a return flight plan.

   Barring the difficulties in propelling humans through space, there were the issues of what to do with humans themselves during those journeys. How would they keep even the most minimal crew fed during six months of space flight? What about life-support needs, water and solid-waste recycling and disposal? Feeding a crew on a journey through space would require massive stores, even with crews in rotating hibernation or sleep shifts. Not to mention keeping their mental faculties intact during a trip through space. The sanity of any crew had to be maintained; confinement in small spaces for months or years at a time would result in the even most stable crew going mad. Nowadays, in this age of human expansion across the galaxy, these concerns seem trivial. We can travel light years in the time it took our ancestors two hundred years ago to travel across the Atlantic Ocean by boat. To the people of those times, these questions seemed insurmountable enough to keep humanity cramped in our own home system like gnats circling rotting fruit.

   But this changed. Beginning with the creation of higher-yield antimatter engines in 2189 by Misha Choudhury at UFW Sea of Rains Testing Grounds (Until recently all records of the engine's development were a closely guarded top secret. Though some records have been released, many details remain classified) humans saw a reasonable hope at reaching the stars and beyond. Choudhury's successes were noticed by the UFW and thus began the massive and secret project at the behest of the UFW High Council. But Choudhury's efforts wouldn't benefit only the UFW. Military, government and commercial entities were eager for higher-speed space travel and what it could bring them. After years of secret work in the difficult lunar conditions, Choudhury finally created a working engine, capable, as he claimed in a famously outlandish press conference, of sublight (SL) and faster-than-light travel (FTL). Choudhury's engines could potentially deliver humans to distant planets and solar systems in a fraction of the time it would take with conventional engines, at just under light speeds.

   After extensive computer models and tests using drone ships, test flight with humans began. But these test ships equipped with the Choudhury engines soon brought up new issues.

   On July 15, 2189, Test Pilot 06820 (in official documents pilots are only referred to by partial serial numbers) set a course for his ship KX-16 Delta Daddy *to go to Pluto and back. By Choudhury's calculations, the trip should have brought the pilot out and back in less than twelve hours. Radio contact with Pilot 06820 was maintained throughout the entire trip. All was going well as the pilot engaged the engines after safely passing Earth. Pilot 06820 could be heard giving speed counts and engine readings one second before stopping. Repeated attempts to get Pilot 06820 to respond failed. The pilot's final words were, "My God, it's ... all ... gone—" Contact with* KX-16 Delta Daddy *was finally lost when it passed beyond Pluto with engines going full bore. (Under the Interstellar Sacred Graves Act of 2190,* KX-16 Delta Daddy *became the first monument to the deep-space race. To this day, vehicles still report sightings of* KX-16 Delta Daddy *in deep space, with its mummified pilot still strapped in behind the controls).*

Telemetry readings from KX-16 Delta Daddy *showed troubling results in the pilot's brain during the flight. It was only after engaging the Choudhury drive that he became delusional. EEG readings showed Pilot 06820's brain registering excessive levels in the gamma band, the waves that represent consciousness. Despite the damning evidence of the telemetry, without a ship or pilot to examine, all the research teams could do was speculate on the causes. The only plausible explanation doctors could find was that some unknown energy or force was produced by the Choudhury drives and this contaminated the cockpit. Choudhury violently denied this, however.*

A second test vehicle, KX-17 Microstoria, *was fitted with an updated Choudhury drive shielded with antiradiation materials. On September 30, 2189, the second test proceeded with normal take off from lunar orbit and safe passage past Earth. Yet upon engagement of the Choudhury drives its sole occupant, Pilot 2113, became delusional, saying, "Oh, God! ... The light—" followed by silence. Vital signs showed the pilot to remain alive for a short time after losing consciousness, but he soon died.* KX-17 Microstoria *exploded an hour later. Telemetry results showed Pilot 2113's brain reacting in the same way as Pilot 06820's: overstimulation in the 40hz gamma band of brainwave activity. If the new drives would only kill human pilots as they neared their optimum speeds, humanity would never achieve its dreams of reaching the stars. The team at Sea of Rains knew there was no point in sending more humans out if they were going to die as well.*

Scientists pored over telemetry, flight logs and visual data. Numerous simulations were run to determine the causes of pilot dementia. Scientists were unable to reproduce the results in labs. Either the drives were generating a field of some kind that caused pilots to go mad or something else unknown. Pilots 2113 and 06820 seemed destined to go down as the only two men ever to travel beyond the solar system, though they had barely even left it. Choudhury vehemently championed his work and the safety in performance of his drives right up until his own death in May of 2190 in a hover-car accident while in South Africa.

Three more test flights were done, each with the same results. The UFW considered putting a stop to them; not from public outcry, as they were conducted in secret, nor from protest by pilots as they lined up by the score to fly the Choudhury drive-equipped test ships. Scientists continued to pore over the problems with the engagement of the drives. Finally, a team of neurologists at Lunar Sandia came up with a possible explanation. Neurologists noted that all pilots' EEG readings showed intense activity at the gamma band, the frequency at which consciousness occurs and can only be diminished by deep anesthesia. It slowly became apparent that something in the human brain simply couldn't tolerate near light-speed travel. Something in the perception of it became too much for the brain to handle.

"Literally, too much information appears to occur at those speeds," said Dr. Orvis Kwon. "The brain is not such a fat pipe after all."

So how could humans travel if they had to be asleep during the voyage? Man seemed to be bound to short hops and journeys only within the solar system, never to see worlds beyond the sun but through telescopes. A sixth and final test was conducted on January 5, 2190. The XR-21 Ancrene Wisse *set off with two AIs on board, one for navigation and one to monitor the Choudhury drives. The pilot was an unnamed female, known only to this day as Pilot 23. The suggested course was departure from the Moon while engaging Choudhury drives in between Earth and Mars. Then the pilot was to astrogate a course out to just beyond Sedna and back to Earth, braking around the Van Allen belt.*

Pilot 23 proceeded as planned. EEGs from the flight showed intense gamma activity immediately after the Choudhury drives were engaged. Flight recorders document this from Pilot 23's cockpit transmissions:

Pilot 23: "Choudhury drives engaged for 5.4 seconds. Hull holding together. Still feeling pretty lucid, fellas."

Hecate Mission Control (HMC): "Roger, 23. Maintain contact."

Pilot 23: "Speed approaching .85 light speed. Drives steady at 55%. Visibility—oh, wow. The light. The light. I see it."

HMC: "Pilot 23, please report visual. Do you have a visual to report?"

Pilot 23: "Seeing it ... Light."

HMC: "Pilot 23, please repeat. Repeat."

Pilot 23: "It's okay ... Guys, it's ..."

HMC: "Pilot 23? Do you copy? Disengage drives and engage autopilot, Pilot 23!"

T+1:13......................LOSS OF ALL DATA.

At this point all instruments pointed to the last known coordinates of Pilot 23 but showed nothing. Energy signatures in the area read a huge output from the Choudhury engines, like burn marks from an intense fire. But the ship had disappeared.

Another investigation was launched into the test mission. No single person was found at fault, and the investigating UFW committee concluded yet another pilot succumbed to the Choudhury drives. Telemetry readings from Pilot 23's brain differed from those of the previous pilots: a short period of intense gamma activity in the frontal cortex, followed by a sudden drop-off of consciousness. Then another wave pattern emerged just at this point, which researchers pored over but at first could not determine. It was eventually agreed to be a kind of alpha state, followed by an unknown mixed wave pattern, later named Mu Sigma Nu due to its curious form.

But where were Pilot 23 and XR-21 Ancrene Wisse? *After a week of searching beyond Sedna via long-range telescopes, it was concluded that Pilot 23 had either crashed, disintegrated or gone into deep space like the others. A secret memorial service took place at Hecate. Those in attendance would later say it was as much for saying goodbye to the hopes of ever traveling beyond the realm of the solar system as paying tribute to the life of a brave pilot.*

Then one month after Pilot 23 first left on her mission, a sudden burst of energy was spotted outside of Sedna. Long-range telescopes spotted a ship. Close observation revealed it was the XR-21 Ancrene Wisse. The vessel appeared in good shape as it returned to Hecate on autopilot. But attempts to hail it went unanswered. The XR-21 Ancrene Wisse was recovered in lunar orbit and towed into dock at Ocean of Storms. Upon entry into the ship, rescue crews were shocked to find Pilot 23 alive but barely conscious, suffering from malnutrition.

Once her condition improved and a full recovery was ensured, a debriefing team was sent in to find out what happened, while analysts looked over the data from flight recorders and ship's instruments. Pilot 23 was kept in seclusion at a treatment facility emptied out but for her.

Intense secrecy surrounded the circumstances of Pilot 23's miraculous return flight. Ocean of Storms was locked down. To this day, few know the exact details of her voyage. When reports finally emerged, the media could only say that Pilot 23's mission had yielded significant results that warranted further study. Further press conferences and interviews yielded little more information. Further UFW silence led to rumors that what happened to Pilot 23 indicated that the team at Ocean of Storms felt these results had to be kept secret at all costs for the safety of the human race.

After months of study, speculation and discussion, Pilot 23 was asked to fly another test craft with updated Choudhury drives installed. She eagerly accepted. This time the ship would carry a small crew of volunteer observers and the two AIs to control the ship's systems.

On April 2, 2191, KX-22—dubbed Ignus Lux Sanctum by Pilot 23—took off from Hecate. Pilot 23 engaged the drives between Earth and Mars. She had been given instructions prior to the mission to attempt to astrogate the ship towards Barnard's Star, 5.96 light years away. The Choudhury drives on-board Ignus Lux Sanctum were engaged for fourteen seconds before experiencing the blackout period. Upon regaining consciousness, Pilot 23 found she had achieved part of her mission. Astrogation instruments indicated she was just outside of the Barnard's Star system. After securing her own status ("I actually pinched myself," she recalled), she called down to the observation team, but received no response.

She left the cockpit and went to the observation deck and beheld a horrible scene. Images taken by the recovery team and leaked to the media at Hecate showed the observers all having suffered intense physical trauma: their faces inside their helmets showed they had endured a prolonged agony before dying. Telemetry showed this all occurred early in the journey. Medical sensors showed elevated brain activity of a type never seen before. "The subjects died from overexposure to an intense stimulus," read the final report.

After making her grisly discovery Pilot 23 secured the ship and returned to Earth. The entire mission lasted less than two months. Upon return to Hecate, Pilot 23 was placed on medical leave for several months. More details emerged later on, with reports saying she was distraught by the death of her passengers, unable to attend the full military burial of the observation crew. Analysis of the flight data and instrument *readings indicated no pilot error, however. The intensity of flight at sublight speed, coupled with the possible "Choudhury effect" was believed to have killed the observers aboard* KX-22 Ignus Lux Sanctum.

As of mid-2191, scientists were still puzzling over how Pilot 23 actually managed not only surviving but a return flight. Though the exact details may never be known, certain facts have emerged over the years. Neurologists could offer up only partial explanation, indicating Pilot 23 experienced heightened activity "of a manner never recorded" in certain sections of her brain, namely in the neocortical stem. Also, an acute difference in the way male and female brains processed information was mentioned, indicating that in the Choudhury-drive travel the astounding truth was that male brains simply were unable to take in the information the way female brains could. Researchers on the astronomical and flight branch of the investigation concluded that Pilot 23 somehow coupled her mind in a previously unknown method via the standard neural pilot interface with the astrogating AI, bringing the ship into a heretofore unknown and entirely different dimension of space or sent it into a speed mode heretofore unknown. By their estimates she achieved a rate of travel of over one light year a week.

One year, humanity was forever trapped in its own backyard, bound to thirteen planets and a small sun. The next, the galaxy seemed boundless. The UFW began to enlist pilots to test their brain patterns and chemical make-up in hopes of creating an army of pilots for a fleet of Choudhury drive-equipped engines.

By mid-2190, Pilot 23 had emerged from her medical leave and resumed active duty. By 2191, the UFW secret commission on Choudhury-drive travel had concluded that she was the only human capable of piloting Choudhury drive-equipped ships. Pilot 23 was brought before a delegation of the UFW high command in secret talks that lasted for months. The exact nature of these talks is shrouded in secrecy to this day. Pilot 23 met both with the council and President De Jesus himself in secret. Rumors emerged during the talks of cloning, alien technology (this was two hundred years before the discovery of the first Transparent Ones site) and other far-fetched theories.

This much is certain: the Astrogator program and humanity's expansion into the universe began at the conclusion of those talks in 2191. The Astrogator Academy was built on a far deserted corner of the Moon amidst unprecedented security. Almost immediately, ship builders began to plan for this technology and new engines were built for massive freighters at Ocean of Storms.

Within five years, the first women trained as Astrogators were deployed in select UFW vessels. Humanity's conquest of the stars was underway.

CHAPTER SIX
Low Resolution

Leonardo laid the book down.

That was his wife, one of the many women who sacrificed so much to ferry humanity through space. His *wife*. At least until she was disengaged; then she would be a civilian. He closed his eyes, letting the weight and exhaustion wash over him. Deepsleep fatigue was as real as it was oxymoronic. He whispered, "Wake me when—" to his suit as he slumped forward and sleep fell upon him in heavy curtains.

The dream unfolded in slow waves of light. It was his first EVA as a private back in '22. His tether was broken and he was free-floating away from the *Condado* as the rest of his dead platoon spilled from a hole in the hull out into the darkness and vacuum of space. He wasn't fearful, in fact there was a detached calm within him. It wasn't so bad, the lack of gravity was okay. He wasn't scared as much as sad he couldn't tell anyone else about it, the feelings of this strange freedom. All the stars, so far away yet right at his fingertips.

"Leo!" Baz's voice cut in to his dream. "I got something. Get down here now!"

"Baz?" Leonardo said, snapping awake. "Repeat that."

"I got something off of Wal8 you need to see now."

"On my way," said Leonardo. He stood and ran down the corridor. He got to the shelter and rushed the airlock shut, shucking his suit before the airlock fully cycled.

Leonardo looked at Baz, remembering Dr. Lowther on board the *Wellstone*, arms covered in blood, trying vainly to revive a miner's wife despite the massive amount of blood that pooled around her. Baz knelt at the pedestal, fiddling with wires extending from the guts of Wal8. Dwi8 lay down alongside him, motionless, innards laid open. Baz looked up at the disarray, then nodded as if to acknowledge what Leonardo was thinking. He returned to the work before him, speaking to Leonardo in a breathy, manic voice.

"Been working with Dwi8 to recover data and found a stretch of video ... I mean, what's here is mostly pretty boring stuff. Except for the last few minutes before Wal8 got terminated—"

"So show me," said Leonardo.

"Sure." Baz tweaked the small pad on Wal8's chest. The screen flickered before splitting in two over the brazier pedestal. "Left is video, right is the log." Leonardo saw a grainy, jumpy image of the cargo bay on the left with a counter rolling, and the steady scrolling of the automatic log of all ship's systems and operations on the right. "Mostly boring, right? Wal8's plugged into its charging berth. Here's the exit from hi-space—then the collision." Baz forwarded the recording and the screen changed. Objects began to float and fly about in the cargo bay. The log on the left sped up as emergency systems engaged. "So Wal8 gets up and tries to secure cargo against sudden gravity loss. He's going around, making sure everything's safe and there's as little damage as possible." Leonardo watched the hands and arms of the walky-talky adjusting and securing cargo containers.

"Obviously," said Leonardo, hiding nothing in his voice.

"Okay, now here's the impact." Baz sped up the recording again, stopping seconds before the crash. The image suddenly became nauseatingly unsteady, flying and tumbling around in the cargo hold. Wal8 stopped somewhere fifteen meters from his recharging berth. Suddenly, the screen filled with a container rushing toward it, pinning the walky-talky to the wall. Then a moment of stillness. The walky-talky turned to look towards the survey team's larger containers.

"See how nothing's moving? The ship stabilized here. Wal8 can't move, though. The thing's too heavy even for him." The screen showed no motion for almost two minutes on the timer at the bottom.

"All right." said Leonardo. "Then?"

"Wait." Leonardo glanced at Baz, who stared intently at the screen. They watched for several seconds. Then an explosion burst on the far right, ejecting debris into the hold. The damaged walky-talky attempted to turn its head resulting in a repetitious jerking. Smoke filled the cargo bay for a moment before being slowly sucked out.

"So that's the hull breach?" Leonardo asked, gnawing on his lower lip.

"Not quite. It's an *explosion*. But just keep watching," said Baz, pointing excitedly at the screens. Leonardo saw smoke disappear as the atmosphere vented. A pressure suited figure appeared on the right, carrying a long cylinder. Though the color was off due to the walky-talky's damage, Leonardo could see the pressure suit's tan hue.

"Who is that?" Leonardo asked. "Who in the hell is that?"

"No idea."

"What're they carrying? Is that the—"

"Emergency explosive charge I found out there? Yes. Watch." They walked to the survey team's container and attached the cylinder to the door's massive hinges. After a moment's fussing, the figure ran off camera. Another explosion filled the screen, blinding the walky-talky. When the light died down, the container door hung open, contents spilling out then coming to rest. The figure returned with one of *Resurgam's* antigrav sleds before climbing into the container. Shortly, a few objects of varying size were thrown out after it, reminding Leonardo of an animal rooting through a dumpster he'd seen on Pickney. After a few more minutes, they emerged carrying two larger objects in protective wrapping: one long and rectangular, about three meters by two, the other almost like a blunt pyramid with the top shorn off. These were placed on the sled and hastily secured. The figure stopped, turned to Wal8, then grabbed something off the sled and stalked towards the immobilized walky-talky. When it got within striking distance, they raised a thick metal bar and violently smashed Wal8 until it stopped recording and the screen went blue.

"Who was that?" asked Leonardo.

"No idea. I tried get a look at the name on the suit, but the resolution is too poor."

"Replay it," said Leonardo. Baz replayed it several times for Leonardo. Each time they watched it silently.

"Unbelievable," Leonardo finally said.

"Copy that," said Baz. The two men stared at the holoscreens in front of them. Leonardo dropped first to his haunches then sat hard on the floor. Running a hand through his hair he felt the cool fresh sweat break out across his forehead. A hundred thoughts flashed across his mind, dropping into an order and sequence that further scared him.

Finally Leonardo spoke.

"This whole thing was planned in advance," Leonardo said, his mouth dry. "Someone infiltrated the survey team, penetrated Jason's systems, forced the crash and ..." Leonardo's mind reeled with the breadth of the implications. "It's a massive operation."

"A setup," Baz answered quietly. "From way back."

"We need to know who that was and what they took," said Leonardo.

"And now," said Baz.

CHAPTER SEVEN
Obfuscate

For the next five hours Leonardo and Baz pored over more video from the dead walky-talky's archives. Without the right equipment, they learned little more than they had already figured out from the first viewing: someone on the survey team engaged in an extremely bold act of sabotage in order to steal artifacts from the site on Baaklum Cha'am. The answers were completely hidden from Leonardo and Baz beneath layers of confusion, disarray—and physical debris. Finally Baz disconnected Dwi8, allowed the walky-talky to patch itself up, and they left the shelter to re-examine the cargo hold.

"Be careful," said Leonardo. "We've inadvertently tampered with a crime scene. Some evidence may be completely gone."

"Yes, sir," said Dwi8.

"Roger that." Baz gave Leonardo a thumbs-up. "Had a cousin who was a cop on Lazuline," said Baz. "He said that most of the time crime scenes are ruined before people realize they're crime scenes. Still ..."

Their eyes and Dwi8's receptors were keenly trained upon everything, with a grim sensitivity to what they'd witnessed in Wal8's last recordings. The drab gray darkness of the bay was suddenly transformed into a shadowy minefield of hidden potential clues. Leonardo found the discovery of Wal8's demise darkened everything around them despite their piercing suit lights. Both men and the walky-talky stepped gingerly through the wreckage.

Baz shouted when he located the spent explosive charge before setting it aside. They pored over the cargo hold for another three hours, finding little else before their search drew them back to the survey team's quarters. They stood in the doorway with Dwi8 behind them.

"So in the video we saw one explosion then another. Which was first? The one that made this hole here," Leonardo said, pointing to the hole in the survey team's quarters, "or the one in the bay doors?"

Baz was silent, looking between the two holes gouging the hull.

"Sir," said Dwi8. Baz and Leonardo turned to face it. "I believe the smaller explosion was the first. Judging from the size of the blasts and the video this would seem to be the earlier of the two."

"Good. Now ..." Leonardo stepped into the quarters, papers and debris sliding under his feet. "What was the layout of this unit before?"

"There was another berth over there and some lockers, I think," said Baz, pointing to the blasted ruin of the far wall. He turned to the wall box at his left, its dead screen yielding nothing. "Guess we're shit out of luck for getting anything from the units on board."

"Maybe. Dwi8, get names from their suit IDs," said Leonardo, waving at the berths inside the container. "Be careful and note anything out of the ordinary."

"Yes, sir." The walky-talky stepped in and began with the furthest berth on the left side of the quarters.

"Now what?" asked Baz.

"Let's look in that container of theirs." The two men left the habitat module and returned to the bay floor. Near the container they slowed their pace, noting the door's blast marks.

"See that? The damage is centered around the right-hand side and hinges," said Baz.

"Indicating the charge was placed between them," said Leo. The immediate area of the blast was twisted, blackened metal, darkening the tan of the container's exterior.

"Look here, Baz," Leonardo said. Baz stepped closer to look over Leonardo's shoulder. He pointed to the locking mechanism on the container. The rectangular lock bore a small screen with a keypad, buttons below it and an intricate lock twisted apart from the blast.

"Why not use the keypad? Why blow the door off?" asked Baz.

"Possibly due to the power outage but most likely—"

"Because they didn't have a combination."

"Right. Containers are locked up during flight—especially delicate artifacts. Combinations are held only by survey team leaders and ship's captains, right?" Leonardo said.

"Right. So it wasn't the team leader who did this then. Or you."

Leonardo grunted.

"Funny. Let's go see what's inside."

Baz and Leonardo stepped in. With the lack of oxygen, they felt rather than heard the door groan and grind as the rig was further twisted and mangled by their entry. They stood in a vestibule running the width of the container and two meters deep, separated by a white-nubbed rim on the walls and floors from the rest of the container. Beyond this, the container was divided by wide metallic gray shelves running near the end where larger objects were stored. Shelves could be pulled out on runners embedded in the floor. Currently they were locked as they should have been during transit.

"I doubt the manifest is online," Leonardo said to Baz, pointing at an olive-drab box mounted on the right interior wall. Baz opened it and tapped at the blank screen inside with no result.

"Nah, offline like everything else. Which is weird. It's self-powered. That's in case they get lost. Makes it easier for recovery. Oh, wait. See why it's off?" Baz knelt down to examine a gouge in the wall, near the lower hinge that was torn from the door by the blast's force. Torn and twisted metal exposed the internal wiring of the containers on-board electronics.

"Blowing the door trashed the power source," said Leonardo.

Baz looked around the sides of the control box. "I bet I can haul the drive out and view it from the suit." Baz disconnected the box while Leonardo stepped further inside the container.

The front area near the door bore the brunt of the blast though only a few items bore scorch marks or broke free from their restraints. The middle and rear were more orderly. Everything was secured properly in accordance with UFW requirements. If only they'd been so thorough about checking the background of the team members, Leonardo thought. He looked at items in the various cubbies and shelves. All were secured and bore the seals placed by Somogyi, the cargo master, before departure. Very little was disturbed after the blast, in fact; the person in the video was after something very specific.

"A-ha," Leonardo said, standing over an empty bin.

"What have you got?" Baz asked, removing the box with a final grunt.

"Whatever was in here was forcibly removed—look at the straps." Leonardo held up frayed straps, the ends glinting in the light of his headlamps.

"Yeah, that's a B&E," Baz said, looking at the box in his hands.

"They had something big here," Leonardo said. In the bin, molded secure foam poured in before departure bore an indentation of the missing object. From the video they'd seen, both stolen objects were bound in thick security padding, secured with UFW warning tape. The slot in front of him had held the rectangular object.

"So what was it?" Leonardo said aloud. The tag had only a number and barcode, corresponding to the manifest that Baz held. According to procedure there would be a copy submitted to the ship when the box came aboard. But it would be inaccessible without power. Leonardo wiped his forefinger across the barcode. A red beam from the fingertip swiped over the code, storing it in the suit's memory.

"Got the manifest out," said Baz, holding a small flat square of black in his hand. "Could probably patch this into Dwi8 or maybe even my suit," he said, patting his belt and chest panel down for sockets and connectors.

"Later. We need to look around in here some more." Baz nodded and pocketed the drive. He joined Leonardo. They moved towards the back, checking each bin. They came to a stop in front of a large bin where something about a yard wide on each side had sat. All that remained were torn straps and an ID tag. Baz swiped this with his finger. They inspected the rest of the container, but found nothing else amiss.

"Okay. Let's go look at the sleds," said Leonardo, waving his XO to follow. They left the doors open and walked to the sled pens, four smaller doors, each four meters high. The doors read from left to right "AGS1 Michael," "AGS2 Jonah," "Exoforklift 1 Brawny" and "Exoforklift 2 Valbo." The middle door was open, the emergency manual control slot broken. Inside, the compartment was empty.

"Of course it's gone," Baz said. Leonardo turned to look out at the hole blown into the outer doors. "They took the shitty one, at least."

"Been out there for how many hours?" Leonardo asked Baz.

"Thirty-six," said Baz. "What the hell for?"

"Where the hell is more like it," answered Leonardo. Both fell silent as they stared out into the blank wilderness beyond.

He left Baz to review the manifest from the survey team's container and returned to his quarters. Despite knowing it would be silent outside his suit, he nonetheless imagined the sounds of his footsteps echoing through the emptiness of the ship. Protracted suit habitation was beginning to get to him. He'd settle for the ship's stale, recycled atmosphere over his suit or that of the shelter any day. Suit life had been the hardest part of his training, not counting being blown out of a transport over Miyazaki-Koch.

Leonardo found entering his quarters somewhat comforting, like returning to a summer home in the dead of winter. He knew stress was increasing when he longed to hole up in his quarters rather than deal with reality. Leonardo wondered if Cook in the Pacific, Shackleton on Antarctica or Sabatini on Isis-8 felt the same way during their ordeals. Certainly they did, but Leonardo was not one to linger over comparisons between himself and great captains of the past. His own ignominy in recent years overshadowed any earlier accomplishments in his career.

Leonardo laid a hand on his desk. He kept his sparse quarters tidy, as opposed to the disorder of Drina's. He preferred a few personal effects with very few adornments. A star map of UFW territories adorned one wall. Leonardo paused at a series of photos hung above his desk: he and Drina on the UFW base at Tulum with her measurement scars fresh and healing; Drina sitting on her throne bed for the first time with a bright smile and a thumbs-up; he and Baz standing next to the enormous carcass of a bull loeden-strider on Polaris Kc. Turning from these he saw his pedia lying on the desk and grabbed it. After a brief wistful look around the room, he turned to leave.

He paused by the door, fist quickly pulsing in and out of a clench, before turning back towards his closet. He paused with a hand over the knob then pulled it open. Uniforms and his few civilian clothes hung in precise order on the top rack. Below were his shoes and a few pairs of boots. Leonardo bent down to reach behind these until he felt a solid angular shape at the back. He removed a wooden case embossed with a smiling fat Buddha, one hand raised in a wave as jovial as his big smile and crinkly closed eyes. Chinese characters shimmered around the figure.

"Bun-Ho. Good to go," Leonardo said before leaving the room.

He did his best to resist a compulsive check on Drina before quickly ducking in. She lay as still as she had when they crashed.

Back in the shelter, Leonardo shed his suit and hung it to air out. Baz sat in the middle, his own pedia in hand. He barely nodded at Leonardo and returned to reading. Leonardo noticed wires coming from the pedia into the back of the small black box Baz had removed from the survey team's container.

"Anything turn up?" Leonardo asked, standing over the XO.

"Yes, but not that it makes things any clearer. The two barcodes we picked up obviously relate to objects in the manifest. Here's one." Baz tapped the pedia's surface and an image popped up on the holoscreen. At the top were the number and barcode they'd collected. Underneath that were the words "Great Chamber/The Key." Below that were two items unlike anything Leonardo had ever seen before.

One looked like a very tall, white doorframe with a rounded upper arch. Its outer surface was made of a whitish material, either metal or stone, carved into a long u-shape like a bathtub with the bottom end cut out. On its outer edge, glyphs could be seen, so delicate and superficially engraved as to be almost unnoticeable. Inside the pale stone arch, globs of whitish, leaden metal attached to one another filled the interior, like gray wax at a candle's base. At the flat end of the frame stood several long gray bars of the stuff, reminding Leonardo of worn stones on a beach. Towards the top, they began to vary in size and shape, becoming perfect spheres or elongated, bending shapes. Some wrapped around the outer white edge, and these bore holes in the end, like sockets. The top pieces bore numerous indentations, as if to fit into something else. Leonardo could make out a single swirling character made up of a subtle pattern worn in the top leaden pieces.

"And just what the hell kind of 'key' is that?" asked Leonardo.

"No idea. I'm not a diggy. It's a Transparent Ones thing." Leonardo shook his head and snorted. Dr. Ortiz, the leader of the expedition, had wanted to question Leonardo at length about what Transparent Ones ruins he'd visited. Leonardo cared little for archaeology, preferring contemporary human history.

"What's the other thing that's missing?" Leonardo asked.

"This!" Baz said, clicking through the pedia's pages until he came to a new object. "It's actually two things." The label at the top of the screen said, "Great Chamber Objects 1 & 2: The Tuning Fork and The Egg." In the picture, there were two three-yard-tall objects, each covered in iridescent Transparent Ones glyphs. A black and yellow ruler to the side gave dimensions. Baz zoomed in on the object to the left. It was shaped almost like a huge tuning fork, one tine being a yard and a half shorter than the other. This was made of the same whitish, leaden substance as the inner portions of the Key.

"Fork and Egg?" said Leonardo.

"Makes me hungry," said Baz.

"Obviously the Fork. Okay. What's the other thing? The Egg?" Leonardo asked. Baz scrolled to the right. The other object was a simple white three-yard cylinder of stone like the outer portion of the Key, covered with similar inscriptions. Its surface was broken by a perfectly square hole a yard from the top. They both rotated slowly in the picture, exposing all sides to view.

"Huh. You know, most of the time, when you get more information, things get clearer," Baz said. "Not here."

"No," said Leonardo, running a hand over his hair. "Did Dr. Ortiz say anything about these when they returned on board?"

"Not that I remember. I didn't deal with the return prep. The rest of the crew did."

"What about Dwi8?" asked Leonardo.

"Doubt it. He does more maintenance work. That was Wal8's territory and he's got zip. You and I were on the bridge most of the time. We'd gotten that call from CENTCOM about FMR activity near Mars," said Baz.

"Hmm?" Leonardo said, something murky rising up from the depths of memory. Things prior to the crash now seemed like ancient history. It was refreshing to let his mind wander from the present concern. "What? Something about a ship?"

"Yeah, 'a peaceful mission testing new communications systems' is the missive they'd sent out right before the thing blasted away from orbit." Baz shook his head. "D-SAT RECON said they launched a ship."

"Oh, yeah," said Leonardo. "The FMR. Peaceful, my ass."

Leonardo hefted the Bun-Ho box in his hand. Two years before on an ordinary night he held a glass just like it moments before alarms sounded and the Martian separatists ended his life.

"I don't believe it. Not for a second. They're up to something. I'm surprised they stayed quiet for two years. It's probably going out to strip down a wreck or mine out an asteroid. They must be desperate for resources after all this isolation."

Leonardo sat by the wall and opened the box. Inside were six slender bottles and two short glasses. The label on the bottles bore the same smiling Buddha figure in gold and red relief. Above the Buddha's head read, "Bun-Ho! Good To Go!" and below "Authentic Chinese Whiskey." Leonardo cracked the bottle's seal with a snap. This caught Baz's attention; a quick jerk of the head and his brow furrowed deeply.

"Oh," said Baz, quietly. "I wondered how long it would last."

"What?" said Leonardo. Baz shook his head and returned to his pedia.

"Ah. It's the last of the stuff from the trip to Rogelio." Leonardo poured himself three fingers' worth and the same for Baz. He stood without spilling a drop and brought Baz the glass. Baz took it and looked at Leonardo dubiously.

"What shall we drink to?" Leonardo asked.

"Leonardo, I'm not so sure. I mean ..." Baz looked to the glass and then Leonardo.

"Lt. Al-Mushtarii, is there a problem?" Leonardo asked. Baz's gaze was like that of someone reviewing a hole in their suit. "Here's the situation: our ship crashed, most of the crew is dead, and my wife is quite possibly brain-dead as well. You and I have little or no hope of returning home. Do you think the situation might allow for a little liquid wrench? Think we could cut ourselves just a little bit of slack?"

"I guess so, Leo," Baz said, standing. "It's just ..."

"What, lieutenant?"

"Bun-Ho used to be for celebrations: missions accomplished, successful deployment, milestones, stuff llke that. We'd rarely finish a bottle. Last couple of years the Bun-Ho's flowed a little too freely since—"

"Give me a fucking break," Leonardo shouted, spilling some whiskey. He steadied himself, cocking his head. "If the captain can't drink when the chips are down when the hell can he?"

"Sir." Baz said, raising his glass aloft, lips pursed.

"Don't call me, sir, Baz. Don't be an asshole," Leonardo shouted.

"All right, Leo," he said with a tightly drawn smile. "Here's to ..." Baz drew out the words.

"To getting our asses home by any means necessary," Leonardo said wearily.

"I'll drink to that," answered Baz and they clinked glasses. Leo downed his in one swallow, while Baz sipped. Leo coughed dramatically.

"Bun-Ho!" Leo shouted. "Good to Go!"

"Yeah, right," said Baz, shaking his head.

"Thank you, Colonel." Leo tipped his empty glass at Baz and went back to his corner. "I shall be reading in my chambers. Alert me of anything untoward." Baz snickered, and sat.

Seated at the wall, Leonardo held his pedia, flicked it on and thumbed the screen. A menu popped up, containing the several thousand mostly historical tomes that comprised Leonardo's personal library. One in particular caught his eye.

"Ha. Speak of the devil," he said aloud.

"What's that?" asked Baz.

"Came across Rockland's 'New Red West.'"

"No coincidences, huh?" said Baz, tapping at his screen. Leonardo shook his head with a slight grin and began to read.

CHAPTER EIGHT
The New Red West

The transition of the planet Mars from a distant, untouchable celestial body to a Terran colony began in the early 21st Century with the intent to mine it for Helium 3 (h3) by the former United States government. The idea—initially seen as political smokescreen to divert attention from international crises instigated by the administration in power at the time—gained real consideration and attention as significant developments were made in space travel, artificial intelligence and lightweight durable materials capable of handling the rigors of space in the latter half of the century.

The unmanned missions of the late 2000s, starting with the British Giant series of von Neumann (vN) landers in 2069, increased the possibility of a human colony on Mars. Following the demise of NASA and the ESA, the rise of viable and profitable private space exploration companies in the late 21st century made space travel safe, easy and affordable—as long as one had no intention of returning to Earth.

The first manned missions to Mars began in the early 2100s, with the Ray Bradbury 4 in 2109. The missions went surprisingly well, given the length of the journeys and the harsh circumstances that awaited the first dozen colonists. Later missions gave colonists hope in the form of nanotech-equipped landers that became dwellings and automated greenhouses built by the British Giant Holz-11, a vN AI "How wonderful to arrive after a long trip and have a salad waiting for us," quipped Capt. M. K. Noyes of the Bradbury. An exaggeration at best, the Holz-11 had created a large crop of algae, which in turn became a food paste for colonists (when tourism was viable on the now hostile red planet, Terrans could visit the monument to the Bradbury missions, commemorated when relations were better between the two worlds. This and the kilometer-high Bear Tribute Wall of Mars commemorating all twentieth- and twenty-first-century explorers in space were destroyed live before media viewers in 2232 when the FMR officially seceded from the UFW).

Though humans were able to develop a robust foothold and even prosper for a time on Mars, colonization was not without its considerable hazards. Many early colonists died due to exposure after failures in the dwellings caused sudden atmospheric breaches. Outbreaks of disease were common in the first few decades, with reappearances of ancient Terran diseases taking unprepared colonists' immune systems unawares in the *bleak Martian "Plague Years." Communities such as New Seville, Bangor Drop and Utopia Flats became synonymous with tragedy and death. "New Frontier" ghost towns were a common source of fear and fascination for the later generations of colonists. But humanity prevailed, though existence was by no means easy by the late 2100s. On Mars, a hard living could be eked out if one was willing to live simply and carefully.*

Terraforming efforts began around this time in the great domed cities of the south and north. The New Soviet settlements of Lomonosov and Kunowsky achieved moderate success in the face of open ridicule, laying out domiciles and even growing Terran vegetation in the augmented Martian soil under the protective covering of their domes. Great strides were made in radiation protection and engineering plants to grow in the hard regolith. A typical bit of propaganda dispatched from Lomonosov read "The Pioneers of the Red Planet have made greater leaps in technology than their capitalist colonizers and their feeble attempts at recreating the imperialism of old on the new world. Lomonosov gleams like Leningrad in summer and is the pride of the New Soviet Union." Bulletins and brochures from companies eager to lure new colonists boasted of equally lush settlements, with less rhetoric.

Another effect of the migration to Mars was the furthering of the melting pot effect seen in North America in the twentieth century. While tensions between citizens from different nations initially remained as they had been on Earth, over time these were seen to diminish as more groups began to intermingle due to the close proximity of Martian dome life. Whatever the conflict their ancestors had on Earth it was common to see Israelis and Palestinians coexist harmoniously in communities and even apartment blocks, as well as Muslims and Jews, Muslims and Buddhists, Muslims and Christians and Fundamentalist Christians and other faiths. The same phenomena was noted amongst groups that were classically at odds over racial issues. While racism, ethnocentrism and xenophobia never quite died, it did diminish over time among residents of Mars.

It was at this time the wealthy on Earth began to see Mars as a new and better way of life, not a hardship for the poor and desperate. Some old-timers complained that these carpetbaggers were stepping onto the land via paths laid with the blood bones and struggle of the poor but eventually they grew to accept the ease and advancement they brought. Venture capitalists began to pour funds into mass colonization efforts and infrastructure developments on Mars, outnumbering the initial groups of one or two dozen that left in the previous century's colonization. In 2197 the first resort communities for the wealthy began to appear on the Red Planet. The great shipyards at Ocean of Storms and Lunapark sprang up as thousands sought a new life far from the crowded twenty-second-century Earth.

As Mars began to grow more self-sufficient, it became more independent, developing and utilizing resources at home and relying less on those imported from Earth and the emerging extrasolar colonies of the UFW. The Free Mars Republic (FMR) established in 2213, built a capital near Noctis Labyrnthus, called Colmena—nicknamed Hivetown for its subterranean layout. The FMR initially operated as a colonial governing body autonomous from the UFW. Later, the FMR would grow into a powerful government, controlling imports and exports of Martian goods and resources to Earth, rivaling the UFW in its breadth and control.

Scientific exploration of Mars had continued as a mostly unmanned proposition throughout the early colonial period. Back then, it was common for early colonists to build homes amidst roving labs and AIs, and even host the occasional lander in their backyards and ranches. Satellites dotted the skies, mapping the surface and creating the first communications networks on the planet (later abandoned when the use of HF communications became established, and then destroyed by the FMR in the Secession). The Great Mirror, invisible to the naked eye, melted the polar icecap until it too was destroyed by the FMR. Few scientists could fund an entire life on Mars—a return trip was largely out of the question until the late 2200s—thus, a twenty-second century expedition to the planet was a permanent move to Mars. Nonetheless, around 2175, manned scientific teams trickled in along with a steady stream of colonists, examining the planet for, among other things, signs of life.

The question "Is there life on Mars?" had been asked by humans ever since they first spotted the planet in the night sky: green men from Mars (how eerily prophetic that would come to be), "War of the Worlds", the classic literature of Jules Verne, Edgar Rice Burroughs, Ray Bradbury, Greg Bear and Kim Stanley Robinson (to a degree) all sprang from this question. But it became especially poignant in the late 1990s, when the existence of the "Mars Rock ALH84001" and the microbial fossils it contained was made public. Scientists were eager to discover more of the history of life—bacteriological and otherwise—on Mars. The landers of the twenty-first century found evidence first of water then proof that there was enough water to sustain life. Yet the actual existence of life on Mars eluded scientists for the better part of the twenty-first and twenty-second centuries.

The first scientist to discover definitive proof of the existence of prehistoric microbial life on Mars was Erich Maierson in 2198. Maierson documented vast amounts of microbiological fossils dug from the dry riverbeds of Mars, namely in the Tharsis Tholus and Kasei Valles regions. Karl Martinez and Gilberto Matsui's investigations also hinted at larger single-celled organisms that once inhabited Mars' surface at a time when its atmosphere was more hospitable to life.

But all studies into the life forms that inhabited Mars would eventually come to an end under a developing cloud of mystery within the FMR's increasingly bizarre and eventually aggressive methods. Scientists, despite bearing no political affiliation, became early victims to the FMR's terror campaign. The FMR officially stated these acts were the work of "bandits and pirates" operating unlicensed hovercraft in the wastelands. However, numerous eyewitness reports stated these bandits often wore poorly disguised FMR uniforms and used FMR-issue weaponry.

In 2291, Dr. Elliott Krome's expedition to explore the deep canyons of Mars ended when his entire team disappeared. Krome had hope the expedition would put an end to the centuries-long argument about intelligent life on Mars. He and his team were exploring the deep cave systems of Ganges Chasma and Hebes Chasma when they disappeared. The bodies were never found, nor were Krome's extensive notes and data ever recovered. In transmissions before his death, Krome hinted at major findings "that would change the very way we see our place in the universe." A Search & Rescue expedition in 2297, led by Krome's fiancée Dr. Nakomo Rama, to try and recover Krome's findings, led to the now infamous "Let Mars Bury Its Own Dead" standoff at the site of Krome's last known location near Ganges Chasma. FMR state media broadcast video of FMR soldiers dynamiting the caves shut—"to prevent imminent collapse caused by the reckless excavation work of the Krome expedition"—obliterating the hopes of ever solving the mystery.

Martian colonists, by now in their fourth or fifth generation, were also growing increasingly agitated with scientific expeditions and offworlders documenting what they considered theirs and theirs alone. Anti-intellectualism was added to the anti-Earth fervor gripping the now angry red planet. Those suspected of pursuing scientific works in fields relating to Mars history were deported, or more often "disappeared in the wastes and storms."

In 2305, the FMR began to extract higher and higher tariffs from exporters, citing unnamed "increased operating costs." Railgun operations were frequently interrupted by sabotage at facilities whose Terran owners were unsympathetic to the FMR. More and more colonists became tired of the demands of an Earth so few of them knew or remembered. "Regolithians," as the Martian colonists dubbed themselves, became openly hostile to the arrival of wealthier late-era colonists in the 23rd and early 24th century— "tourists", as the locals began to call them. Some newer colonists even returned to Earth, claiming the prospect of Earth-bound poverty preferable to the contempt of the established, old-guard Martian colonists. By 2330, emigration to the Red Planet had dwindled to less than half a dozen ships a year, as opposed to the twenty-four a year Mars saw arriving on its dry, red shores in the heyday of 2290. FMR President Roberto Maggiacomo formally closed all spaceports in 2332, with the official Martian secession from the UFW. Dozens of ships were mothballed and left to sit in the junkyard known as the JAAR (Jovian Asteroid Anchorage Ring) Lagrangian point between Mars and Jupiter in the hopes of a thaw in relations and resumption of emigration.

As of publication of this book, those ships remain there, still and cold in the darkness between planets.

Around 2325 the depopulation of the domed cities came to light. Nouveaux Calais and Nouveaux Bruges were robust well into the late 2200s, but newer cities like Portland Park and Auslandia were barely erected before their populations declined until they were completely abandoned in 2313. The infamous Two Mile Tower, the two-hundred-and-twenty-five-story hotel that took the lives of over fifteen hundred workers during its decade-long construction, stood even more starkly during this period as an emblem of the lost hopes and dreams of mankind's ambition and greed on Mars.

By 2320, strange rumors began to swirl like the choking red winds. Old time colonists were reputed to bear a greenish tint of skin, with their eyes a luminous yellow-green. Late-period colonists reported running into clans of skittish and hostile Regolithians, their clear-domed pressure suits betraying these new traits. Rumor had it this was a sign of living off food produced by the red lands. Was life on Mars physically harmful to humans after all these years? Was it changing colonists' body chemistry? Had generations been building up genetic mutations as a reaction to eating food grown in Martian soil? With the disappearance of scientific study on the planet, the general distrust of anyone prying into the old guard's lives and the silence of Martian authorities, these questions would remain unanswered.

FMR President Roberto Maggiacomo, himself the son of the builders of Nuova Venezia, tried to assure the UFW in his last planetary address in 2310 that a mysterious plague was to blame for the reports of discolored skin, eyes and hair. He claimed colonists living in bunkers built into the enormous lava outflow tunnels under the surface helped combat an unforeseen skin reaction to the Martian atmosphere. Maggiacomo even later went so far as to blame the UFW for focusing so heavily on its more prosperous child than on the "sins of the third planet." But Maggiacomo's own appearance in the last of his FMR bulletins of 2310 showed his face heavier, obscured by goggles. Eventually these bulletins ceased as Mars slowly closed its doors to the galaxy.

The existence of newly built subterranean cities was substantiated in 2320 when satellite images showed construction around the Cydonia region (the location of the fabled "Face of Mars", a popular source of "Life-on-Mars" theories among twentieth-century conspiracy theorists) and even more massive undertakings around Ascraeus Mons. Experts analyzing these photos estimate construction had begun around 2305.

Finally, the UFW sent a peaceful diplomatic mission to Mars in December of 2331 despite efforts of the FMR to keep them away with stories of terrestrial plagues, dust storms and unspecified "poor landing conditions." Mueller's Brigade was the media name of the infamous UFW landing party, led by General Ashok Benes-Mueller. Benes-Mueller was a decorated veteran of campaigns at First Lunar Base, the Idaho Revolt, the Mercury rescue parties of 2310, and the famous standoff at Europa against members of People For A United Solar System (PFAUSS) in 2298.

Benes-Mueller's team at first encountered nothing. The surface seemed devoid of any signs of life—human or otherwise. Terrans tensely watched at home via AI camera crews as Benes-Mueller's team made its way through deserted settlements and red-tinged ghost towns of what Poet Laureate Piper Malinowsky called "The New Red West." Everyone remembers where they were when Mueller's team approached the main airlock of New Reykjavik. Families watched in horror as Mueller's team discovered too late that New Reykjavik had been turned into a giant fusion bomb. Eighteen and a half billion people watched as the dreams of a better life on Mars disappeared in a blast visible from orbit. What had once been a place where humans could go to forget their divisions and live a prosperous, harmonious life had forever been changed into a closed, dark and violent world.

Thus began the real War of the Worlds.

The FMR formally seceded from the UFW, declaring January 12, 2332 to be the first day of the "New Martian Race." It forbade the UFW entry under penalty of death or being shot out from the sky upon approach. Maggiacomo demanded all non-FMR satellites be removed from orbit, then shot them all down before the UFW could comply. The UFW responded with sanctions and boycotts only to discover that Mars had become quite self-sufficient and deadly. After seeing the pointlessness of such feeble efforts in the face of a rogue state, the UFW mounted a military campaign set to launch in late February 2332. This was halted when FMR state media showed the launch of giant orbital gun platforms capable of destroying targets well outside of Mars's orbit.

On March 23, 2332, the UFW formally relented on all claims to the former territory of Mars and ceased diplomatic relations, all attempts at contact or reconciliation.

For all intents and purposes, Mars was once again a dead, red planet.

CHAPTER NINE
Under The Stones

Leonardo laid the pedia down, his head swimming slightly from the Bun-Ho, which he'd been drinking while reading. One of the few times he saw his father, Ernesto, he'd told little Leonardo of the great deeds of Valencia's past; among the first to the Moon and Mars. As a boy, Leonardo dreamed of going to Mars and tracing his roots. Older and wiser, he realized it would never happen.

"Captain?" came Dwi8's voice from inside Leonardo's helmet. He stood unsteadily and walked over to the helmet, picking it up closer to his ear.

"Yeah, Dwi8?"

"I have the names and locations of the crew members in the survey team's quarters."

"Okay, let's hear it."

"Going from the berth nearest the door: Prof. Juan Pohaska, anthropologist, Prof. Nwarkim George Ortiz, team leader and head archeologist, Prof. Dominic Malhotra, ethno-linguist and epigraphic expert, Prof. Juanita Sadat-Stein, geologist, Prof. Roman Cobb, astrobotanist, Dr. Robert Morrison, astrobiologist. The damaged berth was occupied by Prof. George Mussina, technoarchaeologist and Transparent Ones specialist."

"Mussina," said Leonardo, pausing a moment. "Okay. Dwi8, scan inside that berth for anything left of the occupant; hopefully some DNA's in there. Then survey the area outside the ship near the debris field. Call me if you find any trace of human remains."

"Yes, sir." With a slight crackle, the walky-talky closed the channel.

"Mussina, huh?" said Baz. "He got blown up?"

"Yeah, I think so. Did you have any contact with him?"

"No, not really," Baz said, stretching out on the floor, brow furrowed. "I remember meeting him when they came aboard and once in the D-FAC."

"Well, we were busy with the ship. They hit the surface right after we arrived. Plus, who likes hanging around with a bunch of dusty diggies?" Leonardo said with a snort. "Of course, now I wish we had."

"Sure," said Baz. "What if Dwi8 doesn't find any remains?"

"Then Mussina's our suspect."

"And if Dwi8 finds any DNA evidence outside the ship or in the berth?"

"I have no idea what to do," said Leonardo, looking into his glass before knocking back the last of his whiskey.

CHAPTER TEN
Power

They stayed in the shelter, awaiting Dwi8's DNA scan of the berth. A nagging part of Leonardo wanted to be proactive, staying in motion and doing something. A different part enjoyed resting, the warmth of the Bun-Ho in him and the comfort of being suit-free, even in the austere shelter. Leonardo flipped idly through his pedia. Baz studied the manifest from the survey team's container. Leonardo's calm was tempered with an oscillating anxiety while trying to keep from downing the entire bottle of whiskey in one swig. Once he caught himself actually leaning towards the bottle.

The shelter's airlock beeped as Dwi8 returned an hour later.

"Sirs? My examination is complete."

"Let's hear it."

"There is no evidence of human DNA within the sleep berth. Also no evidence of DNA up to fifty meters from the ship. Infrared, spectrographic, and x-y radio scans yielded no results of anything foreign to the general make-up of the surrounding soil."

Leonardo glanced at his lieutenant. Baz stared back at Leonardo without expression. Leonardo eventually broke his gaze and examined his lined palms for a moment.

"Okay. Dwi8, scan a wider range for anything odd in the surrounding area. Not just DNA or organic material. Parts of *Resurgam*, humans, things that look unfamiliar to the planet. Just ... Anything unusual at all."

"Whole fucking planet's unusual," muttered Baz after the walky-talky clanked out of the room. Leonardo turned to face Baz.

"Mussina," Leonardo said.

"So where the hell is he?" Baz asked.

"Good question. Damn it." Leonardo called out, "Dwi8!"

"Sir?"

"What are the general climate conditions of this planet?"

"Sir, the minimal atmosphere does not provide much precipitation of any kind. Thermal winds are steady at approximately ten to fifteen kilometers per hour."

"Why is there ammonia snow then?" Baz muttered.

"Dwi8, can you see tracks from the stolen sled?" Leonardo asked.

"Sled tracks? No, sir. Any tracks would be erased by the winds."

"Damn. Keep scanning." Leonardo cut the connection and stared at the helmet in his lap. "Where the hell would someone go in this place?"

"There's nothing but mountains, right? With the aerial surveillance units we could track something, maybe?"

"The upper bay's sealed shut so we're not sending anything out. Not *Sparky*, not the Fli8s. Nothing."

They fell silent. Leonardo thought of their Fli8 drones, massive black and grey like bats hanging silent in their bay above them. Intraorbital drones with surveillance and tactical capabilities, once deployed the Fli8s would find the sled with little difficulty.

"Leo, I got it," Baz shouted, startling Leonardo.

"What?"

"I just remembered—the sleds!" Baz said, jumping up and slinging on his suit. "The a-grav sleds! The survey team used them on Baaklum Cha'am! When we got the recall message, we brought them all up in a hurry." His suit began to chirp and beep as if rudely awoken while sealing to his body. "I bet the crew never cleaned them off after we retrieved them."

"Doubt it," Leonardo said, getting up to put his own suit back on. "Somogyi is— damn—was thorough about decontamination. Everything goes in through the lock where the vacuums, blowers and hyperbrushes get rid of—"

"Well, I got an idea." Baz sealed his helmet to the rim. "See you at the sled pen?"

Leonardo let his suit power up and fit onto him. He pondered another swig from the bottle and gave in. With his helmet on, Leonardo stepped into the airlock. Baz was at the sled pens under their remaining antigrav sled. He could see Baz running his left forefinger and thumb over the sled's bottom, a light blue glow emanating from the glove.

"What's the big 'a-ha'?" Leonardo asked.

"Somogyi maintained decontaminating protocols for sure. Maybe if I can get under this damn thing—nah, it's too heavy without power. Don't wanna use the suit or else it might slip on me." Baz climbed into the payload of the sled. He held his fingers out again, the blue glow cold and bright in the darkness. Leonardo heard his intense breathing over the comm link.

"Yes. Got it," Baz hissed, standing up and holding out his palm. While wiping his right hand over his left, a rectangular screen appeared. "I copied soil samples from Baaklum Cha'am and keyed the glove sensors to them." Leonardo looked at Baz's palm screen showing a spectrograph of the soil samples and next to it another spectrograph showing a perfect match. "Some tiny particles were way up in the cracks in this thing."

"Wow. Good thinking," said Leonardo. "I guess I'll never totally trust decon procedures again. Get Dwi8 to scan for a trail like this and we might find something."

Baz hailed Dwi8 and sent him the new search parameters. Leonardo looked out the hole in the doors. He found it odd there was never any night here. It was always varying degrees of light neither bright nor dark. There had to be some rotation for the weak gravitational field, but not much. Leonardo shuddered from the clammy feeling against his skin, partly from apprehension. The person responsible for their predicament was somewhere out there with two strange artifacts and a twisting trail of questions behind him.

"Dwi8's on it," Baz said as the ship shook violently underneath them.

"—the hell?" Leonardo shouted as they struggled to stand.

"Is that an earthquake? Is the ship coming apart? Think we're under attack?" shouted Baz.

"Dwi8! Report!" Leonardo could barely speak with the tumult underneath them.

"Tectonic distress. The planet is experiencing massive seismic turmoil. I'm not sure if—"

"Dwi8!" Leonardo called out as he and Baz were flung across the floor. Leonardo saw everything they'd carefully stacked thrown around again. The shelter slid towards starboard. Leonardo felt deep, groaning vibrations underneath them and saw the enormous, unmoored containers begin sliding across the floor as if on ice. He looked to the holes blown in the bay doors.

"Baz! Out! Now!" he shouted.

Their emergency suits were designed with built-in safety measures: should an occupant find themselves accidentally on the outside of a ship, they had limited chance of return. Leonardo pressed the tip of his thumb and pinkie finger together as hard as possible to activate the suit's emergency measures. Small, powerful explosive charges burst from the heels and calves of the suit, hurling him towards the door. With so little time to right himself he said a millisecond-long prayer and made himself as narrow as possible. The slightest miscalculation would crush him into the hull at a hundred kilometers an hour leaving a smear of flesh, bone, blood and suit materials.

Leonardo sailed through the hole, barely clearing the edges. He looked before him, blinded by the sudden emergence from darkness into the relative brightness of the planet's surface. He felt the suit's frame stiffen as it prepared padding for the crash. In three seconds the suit had enough time to balloon around him then deflate upon impact. Leonardo rolled, momentarily entangled in the loose folds of suit as it retracted back to normal proportions.

"Baz!" he shouted. Leonardo thought the worst as the ground rumbled underneath him again. Then a light blue projectile shot forth from the same rupture in the ship, inflating, then it hit the ground with a single bounce. Baz lay still for a moment as the suit deflated, then tried to right himself despite the tremors. These continued for a few drawn-out seconds before tapering off.

"Dwi8?" Leonardo shouted.

"I am here, captain," said the walky-talky. An overlay appeared on Leonardo's HUD, with a red dot indicating Dwi8's location a hundred meters away. "Safe and undamaged."

"What the hell was that?" Baz asked, standing and brushing the snow from his suit.

"A massive burst of electromagnetic disturbance occurred milliseconds prior to the tectonic disturbance. I recorded enormous levels of energy during the rupture that have now dissipated. There appeared to be a two-degree elevation in the planet's temperature, though it is dropping rapidly."

"What the hell would cause that?" asked Baz. Leonardo shook his head. "Tectonic activity? Something striking the planet?" he asked.

"No, sir," said Dwi8. "There would have been massive damage and atmospheric disturbance. Anything large enough to affect the planet in such a way would have broken it apart."

"Look, there!" Baz shouted, pointing off into the distance. They turned to look at the mountains off on the horizon. A gray plume rose up on the horizon, bifurcating the yellow fringe of hills. Leonardo zoomed in closer on the plume.

"Dwi8, what's that plume's composition?" Leonardo said.

"It appears similar to the ground and snow: mostly ammonia with some sulfurous vapor and some hydrocarbons," said Dwi8. "There are other elements such as metals and isotopes consistent with solar activity."

"Solar activity? What?" asked Leonardo. "Do you mean volcanic activity? Are we in a volcanic plain, by any chance?"

"No, solar, sir. The planet does not appear to have any current nor past volcanic activity. It is flat all the way to the hills. In fact, the uniformity of the land is unusually mathematically precise."

"Nice. Dwi8 likes the math of the landscape." Leonardo turned to Baz as he heard him snicker. "Are you okay?"

"Sure, just fine," Baz said, slowly standing and brushing snow off his suit. "Never better. I was getting too relaxed back there."

Leonardo turned back to the ship. The disturbance didn't appear to disturb it too much. He thought how much worse it could have been, their corpses smeared on the inside of the cargo bay like paste. Drina would be left to die in the ship all alone, perhaps never knowing what happened. "Not much happened to the ship. You see anything?"

"Not really," said Baz. "Close-up doesn't show much difference."

"No further damage, sir," Dwi8 said in its ever-calm voice. "Some minor changes in positioning. The ship is listing more towards port, but stable."

"At least we don't have to repair anything we'd already fixed." Leonardo looked around them for a moment. "All right, back inside." They trudged through the snow and returned to the ship by climbing the line back up through the hole in the bay doors.

The tremors returned the bay to its former state of total disarray and chaos. While it didn't surprise Leonardo it took a great deal of effort to remember his CIS beliefs and not think that the universe had singled him out for a giant flick of its great finger in order to personally inflict pain and suffering upon him. Despite his weakest feelings he knew he was but an insignificant speck in the grand scheme of things, a particle in the great soup that was their universe.

Baz, Leonardo and Dwi8 set about restoring as much order as possible to the bay. The work was tedious and boring but kept them busy. They dragged the shelter back to where they'd originally placed it, anchoring it to the bay floor in case of future disturbances. After several hours, they returned to recuperate inside the shelter and ate silently as Dwi8 resumed hull repairs. Leonardo's head swirled with questions, answers and theories colliding like the debris in the bay.

Leonardo and Baz ramped up the chemsleep before joining Dwi8 in repairs. Most of these hull repairs were simple enough to do with just suit tools. They worked steadily from bow to stern following Dwi8's microscopic vision wherever it saw a tear, and repairing these. It was more tedious than cleaning the bay, and frustrating because of the numerous cracks they found. Leonardo and Baz stopped only long enough to check their progress and occasionally eat.

After two days, they'd repaired all major hull breaches, with Dwi8 handling the difficult external repairs. Finally they repaired the engineering causeway. The ship was fully sealed and capable of sustaining atmosphere again.

Yet still without power.

"Okay," Leonardo said with a sigh. "That should do it. When we get power, we'll restructure the interior."

"When ..." Baz mumbled, shaking his head.

"*When*," Leonardo said firmly, pointing a finger at his lieutenant. Leonardo glanced at the clock in his helmet display.

"Whew. Okay, we need a real rest. Enough of this chemsleep." Leonardo walked back to the bay. "Dwi8, keep watch."

"Yes, sir."

Back at the shelter, they dropped their suits into piles by the door. Leonardo lay down on one of the couches, draping an arm over his face. He swallowed a small capsule that instantly diminished the effects of the chemsleep. He smelled the MRE Baz was eating at the brazier and thought of eating one himself. Seconds later he was asleep.

He dreamt of his childhood again. Mother and he were out in her skiff with the wheezing, spitting outboard, puttering through the canals of the drowned coastal cities near his birthplace, Hollow Point on the Gold Coast of Connecticut. Mama sat in the bow, clad in the lower half of a wetsuit and a tank top. Her arms were powerful, tanned and taut in the bright Connecticut sun. Her black hair shone in the sun. Leonardo always knew how beautiful his mother was and yet forgot it until dreams like this. She held her power rifle in one hand, a gaff in the other. She kept an eye on the depth scanner next to her, its beeping audible over the engine, telling them of approaching obstructions. Leonardo knew they'd only need a couple of smart buoys or salvage junk to capture and sell and they could live well on the houseboat for a few weeks. Leonardo hated the dangers of Mother's job, but it kept them better fed than most of the kids he knew. Mama was one of the best, most ruthless of Hollow Point's limpiaristes—the scavengers that worked treasure free from the old homes buried under the water at the Gold Coast's edges. Leonardo had plenty of friends whose mothers were maimed—or dead—from scavenging.

Mama pointed to the right—starboard, as Leonardo was learning to say—at the spire of one of the old homes. Leonardo shuddered as he turned, bringing them closer. Its paint was faded, metal covered in decades of birdshit. Mama had spied a promising bit of flotsam near the spire. The scanner read all clear.

Then there was a splash and a hollow clang as a metallic claw shot from the water, gripping the boat's hull. Both of them turned with horror as they saw a second arm shoot from the water, land near Leonardo and cling next to the other.

A smart mine rose up, bubbling from the deep, rusty with seaweed streaming from its sensor arrays. A long-dead aperture irised open and a klaxon blared. The metallic arms began to retract, pulling the skiff towards the glistening detonators that bristled off the mine, bright with seawater in the summer sun.

"Gun it!" Mother shouted at Leonardo. He tried the moment he saw the first arm but the old engine wasn't responding. With the scope to her left eye, Mama squeezed off several rounds from the power rifle. Bullets plugged the water, missing the mine. Leonardo stared as the mine drew them closer to the detonator plug.

He almost thought he saw the mine smile through the rime of rust as it struck the hull.

Leonardo shot awake with a scream, cold sweat running down his face and body as he swung his legs off the couch. He could still hear the klaxon of the smart mine from his dream. Then he realized it was coming from his helmet.

"Baz?" Leonardo shouted as he saw his XO rush to his helmet. They balanced them on their heads without the support of the suit rings.

"Holy Shit!" shouted Baz.

"Good God," Leonardo answered. Multiple holographic alert signals blared and symbols blinked from the HUDs. They seemed to last for minutes. Leonardo would later realize it had been seconds at most.

Finally there was a moment of silence followed by a simple three-tone melody.

"Captain?" said a male voice from within Leonardo's helmet, distinctly synthetic but not Dwi8's.

"My God," Leonardo said, gasping as he tried to speak despite a throat gone dry with shock. "Jason?"

"Yes, sir." Leonardo dropped his helmet, staring at Baz. He nearly wept as he realized he was hearing the voice of Jason, *Resurgam's* AI.

The ship had come back to life.

CHAPTER ELEVEN
Luminescent

They scrambled into their suits, which bleated and whined at their hasty donning. Leonardo's HUD was filled with numerous, blaring alarms. Subpersonas of the ship's numerous systems screeched and bombarded his vision with error messages, damage alerts and warnings that had been dormant since the crash. He muted these and pushed warning symbols aside with a glance. The airlock took an eternity to cycle.

They ran to the bridge, ignoring lifts that might be functional again, being so used to walking everywhere that it only occurred to Leonardo as he ran past the fourth lift. While running, further warning symbols and status readings shot out as
they passed various sections of the ship; the alarm from the crew quarters' life-support steward alerting them to the dead crew members. They ignored these, running through brightened corridors.

The bridge doors opened slowly, gears frozen and sluggish with intense cold. They were greeted by all displays flashing "REINITIALIZING. PLEASE STAND BY." Holopanels were also sputtering and reconfiguring back to life.

"Jason. Sitrep?" Leonardo shouted, entering into the horseshoe of the central command unit. He dropped into his chair for a moment then stood again, too excited to remain still.

"Captain, all ship's systems are rebooting. I am creating subpersona now to address critical situations. I have questions when you are ready."

"Me, too. Repair status?'"

"Sir, atmosphere replenishment has begun on all decks. Main cargo bay has two large breaches in starboard side doors, bulkhead and outer hull. Also, the connecting corridor to Engineering has been breached and is therefore offline. I am still calculating damages and assessing stability."

"Jason, stop atmosphere replenishment in all areas except for the bridge and Asgr. Valencia's quarters."

"Yes, sir. Redirecting life-support replenishment to bridge and Asgr. Valencia's quarters."

"Jason, this ship is in bad shape. Continue scanning and reinitialization sequences. Call when ready."

Leonardo eyed the blank screens, displays and panels on the bridge. Normally in a situation like this all hands were at their stations and a holo of Drina shone next to him. Even with his helmet on and ship's systems keyed in to his HUD, the ship was eerily subdued to Leonardo. He heard the soft pinging of Jason's persona, letting him know the AI was attending to the ship's recovery. Normally only a few seconds would pass and Jason would return with a detailed report. Leonardo was unsurprised the AI took nearly a minute to detail the full status of the ship.

"Sir," Jason spoke as a detailed listing of ship's systems appeared on Leonardo's display, "we appear to be planet-bound. We have been here for quite some time."

"Jesus, Jason, where've you been?" snorted Baz, stabbing at a panel by the door with his gloved finger.

"Yes, Jason. The entire ship has been disabled without power." As the AI kept updating ship's status, Leonardo verbally informed Jason of the situation.

"I see," Jason said when he was finished. The AI's voice was coming clearly through Leonardo's left ear as opposed to the omnipresent voice when his helmet was off. "I am pleased you and Lt. Al-Mushtarii are alive."

"As are we, Jason," said Baz, closing the panel door. "Jason, how long to get the ship up to basic functions? Accounting for time to get most atmosphere restored and systems online for starters."

"During hi-space travel all nonessential systems were shut down. Major systems are still offline. Power was restored momentarily and surged, but I shut nonessential ship's systems off during damage assessment. We have battery power, and the main power stack in Engineering should be back online soon. There are several small hull breaches around the ship—"

"I thought Dwi8 caught them all," said Baz.

"These just occurred in the last few moments, sirs. Repressurization and the intense cold created explosive decompressions and tears in the bulkheads throughout the ship."

"Okay." Leonardo watched Baz shrug and turn toward the forward displays.

"Captain, hull systems are fully inoperative. Repair management systems are unresponsive."

"Yes, Dwi8 tried to jumpstart them with an activator from a shelter pack, but it was no use."

"Highly unusual."

"There's a lot of that happening around here lately, Jason," said Baz, tapping at a blank display panel. Leonardo saw Baz startle as it suddenly came to life underneath his hands. "Okay, now we're talking!" Baz began to tap away at the holokeypads underneath his gloved hands.

"Captain, you are aware the crew is—" said Jason.

"Yes, I am, Jason. Do you have control over sleep berth systems?"

"Yes, sir."

"Immediately freeze all berths. I want to examine them at some point soon. There will be a funeral at some point after we settle the rest of the ship."

"Yes, sir." Jason paused. "The berths are all frozen. Shall I do the same for the berths in the survey team's quarters?"

"Yes. I'll have Dwi8 seal up the hole in their container."

"Done, sir."

"Thank you, Jason."

"Sir, as for Asgr. Valencia—"

Leonardo leapt from his chair and out the starboard door of the bridge. He ran back to her quarters, barely remembering to disarm the reawakened security measures.

Emergency power had banished the darkness that clung over everything for the past few days. The machinery around Drina's throne had come to life, displays and activity monitors all going. Drina's medibots were active again, their spidery automatic arms moving over the still form cradled on the throne. The holodisplays showed her condition and the status of bodily functions.

"How is she?" Leonardo asked breathlessly.

"Still unconscious, sir," said a voice. Leonardo looked to his right and saw the apparition of a tall thin female with a white tunic materialize at the foot of the throne, looking down at Drina. "No real improvement in her condition. She is stable, nothing else." The woman's voice was softer, lacking the urgency of Jason's. Leonardo scowled at the woman and mudraed at her. Nothing happened.

"Lose the avatar," he said. The woman disappeared. "What do you mean *stable*?"

"Sir," said the disembodied voice, "She appears to be fighting a comatose state. Very dangerous. From what we can tell, she was in the Transit State bringing the ship home. Something during the crash affected her. It is unclear as to why she would not have revived. The astrogation AIs detected nothing though there was ..."

Leonardo looked up from Drina's face as he heard the hesitation.

"What? What is it?"

"Sir, the Astrogator has some odd internal injuries. The frontal and outer neocortex shows significant damage, as if from an attack of some kind." Leonardo felt his stomach drop and mouth go dry.

"Go on," he said.

"There's never been anything like this recorded before. Files show nothing like this anywhere. At a guess it looks like damage from feedback in the system. Interference in Astrogation interfaces, for example."

"We believe the ship was probably sabotaged by someone in the survey team," said Leonardo, wondering if he could go get another bottle of Bun-Ho.

"That might be the cause." It paused. "Something else is odd."

"What's that?"

"There are certain medications an Astrogator uses in the line of duty."

"Yes, I am aware of the use of lucidogens in her line of work," Leonardo said dryly. Most UFW pilot positions had specific medications or drugs (in addition to neural wetware implants) tailored to assist neural implants in the demands of service and a captain had to know who was taking what on his ship.

Officially, anyway.

"Asgr. Valencia had elevated levels of diaphanoxamine in her bloodstream and cerebrospinal fluid." The medibot paused. "Diaphanoxamine is commonly used in regulated doses to assist with smoother transitions in and out of the Astrogation state and communication with their AIs. It produces a time dilation effect and hyperawareness, while significantly enhancing certain cognitive functions."

"And?" Leonardo said, hoping the AI noticed his impatience.

"In the levels found in her blood, diaphanoxamine begins to have a deleterious effect on cognitive abilities. Time dilation increases, cognition decreases as does consciousness. Test subjects, when given high doses, reported perceiving reality like they were watching movies at incredibly slow frame rates yet didn't care. At that level the infinite detail of mundane things became fascinating. Subjects were found staring at a blank page for hours, examining the fibers with a heightened awareness, heightened vision, and hearing for instance. Some subjects tested a one hundred fifty percent increase in sensory awareness overall, to the point of—"

"Enough," said Leonardo, and the AI stopped abruptly. "What's your point?"

"Sir, the levels found in Asgr. Valencia's blood indicate addiction. Her blood levels look as if she's built up quite a tolerance for it. Diaphanoxamine and other lucidogen addictions have been cited as the cause of several accidents involving UFW ships in the last ten years. Some fatal."

"All right. When she regains consciousness, I will speak to her about it. For now take precautionary measures. Ration her usage ... Find a counseling persona for her to speak with." Leonardo held his breath and counted to ten to subside his rage.

Again? How had this happened?

"Yes, sir." The AI was silent for a few moments. "There is an upside."

"Oh?" Leonardo saw none in a situation where Drina very nearly killed them all. "What is that?"

"It probably saved her from further damage. Neural, that is. Incorrectly interfacing prevented her from being more seriously injured."

Ironic. Leonardo stared at the floor. "Keep me posted on her condition. Any changes, any at all, contact me."

"Yes, sir." Leonardo went to his quarters and grabbed his lens case from the bathroom. He caught a quick glimpse of himself in the mirror. Beneath the faceplate of his helmet was a mess of a man. Pale, coppery skin, dark eyes ringed from too little real sleep, an emerging black beard flecked with white; the same old scars, too, but a certain desperation in the eyes. People used to say he was handsome. The last two years had wrung that out of him, leaving him more haggard than anything else. In the right light he looked okay. Not now, though. Leonardo turned from the mirror. His skin felt clammy and his heart was pounding. The medibot's words spun around in his head, colliding with the implications.

Drina was abusing one of the main tools of her trade, putting everyone's life at risk. *Again.* On the other hand, it may have kept them from getting killed. Leonardo shook his head, putting a hand to his brow. Drina was addicted once more. He wasn't sure what was worse: his drinking or Drina's drug use. Neither had served them well. Neither would get them off the ship.

Leonardo entered the bridge, momentarily startled to see Baz standing at the front displays, helmet next to him. A quick glance at his HUD showed life support fully functional. Leonardo jammed his thumb under the chin of his helmet and took his helmet off. He was surprised at how relieved he was to breathe the air, as laden as it was with the tang of newly recycled components and little fresh oxygen.

"Sir," said Jason, the omnipresent voice resonating from the walls. "I've repressurized and stabilized the upper decks. Everything from the bridge to officers' quarters have full life support."

"Thank you, Jason." Leonardo took his seat and dropped his helmet down on the floor next to him. Raising a hand to his face he felt the rough material of his gloved fingers on his clammy skin. Angrily, he tore off the gloves and threw them at his helmet. Baz turned and cocked an eyebrow at him. Leonardo held his breath until Baz spoke.

"She okay?"

"Uh, not so good," Leonardo answered. He looked out past his XO to the flickering blank displays. "Medibot says she suffered neural damage during the crash. Not from getting jostled around, but from the attack on the ship's systems. Her frontal and neocortex is damaged. She's fine, just comatose."

"That sounds ..." Baz looked at Leo for a moment and then at his hands. "I'm sorry."

Leonardo nodded.

"Well, we do have most systems back online. I propose we find out which sensor arrays are functional and get a better sense of what the hell's out there to find that frigging guy."

Leonardo nodded wearily.

"Did the medibots give you any kind of prognosis? A timeframe for her recovery?"

"No. They didn't know, really. It's ... complicated."

"'Complicated,'" Baz said, repeating the word with a spin of sarcasm and incredulity. "How?"

"Baz ... They found high levels of diaphanoxamine in her blood."

"Why wouldn't they? This soon after the crash, she had to use the stuff during flight."

"Apparently, her levels are consistent with someone who was ... abusing it."

Baz's silence seemed to make the room temperature drop slightly.

"Oh. I get it." Baz strode across the width of the bridge a couple of times. When he spoke again his voice was high and angry. "So she's out of her mind on diaphanoxamine and you're drunk. How the fuck couldn't you two crash the ship?"

"Lt. Al-Mushtarii, I am still your commanding officer." Leonardo stood, his fists clenching so hard he could feel nails gouge into his palms. "Stand down."

"You're a drunk CO, sir. And now I find our Astrogator has been tweaking so hard she's nearly shriveled her brain away?"

"She is my wife and your superior, Lieutenant."

"Stop calling me that, Leo. What the fuck?" Baz came around into the horseshoe and stepped right up to Leo's face. "I've known you since I got posted on the *13 Colonies*. I've grown up under your command. I've known you longer than you've known her. We've put shit like Captain and Lieutenant aside at times when there was a bottle in front of us. Now the bottle I won't drink from is between us, and all of a sudden I am Lt. Al-Mushtarii? Fuck you! You bring up rank whenever things get too close—like the truth. So again, I say *fuck that shit, sir*. If you have a problem with me, sir, go ahead and fucking shoot me now. Because I have serious doubts that we will get the fuck off this rock alive with just one sober guy, an ODed Astrogator, a drunk captain and a low-level walky-talky."

Leonardo stepped toward Baz, cocking his arm back. As he leaned in to punch, Baz drew back, ready to block. Leonardo faked an undercut from the left, connecting with Baz's ribs. The force of the punch, amplified by Leonardo's exosuit, connected despite the impact pooling of Baz's suit. The lieutenant fell back on the panels then hit the floor. Leonard landed a boot on Baz's chest. Baz grabbed him and twisted, throwing Leonardo back. Leonardo rolled over and stood up, reaching for his piezoknife. Baz stood, his own knife ready, the high-pitched whine of their tuned blades loud over their hoarse breathing.

"You insubordinate little shit! I ought to chuck you outside naked. You're an insignificant little prick of an officer. I am Leonardo Reyes De la Valencia, decorated captain of the UFW Fleet. I'm a veteran of the Nine Campaigns of the Bug Wars, the Colorado System insurgency—"

"—and the UFW's worst basket case of a commander, in the last ten years responsible for the deaths of fifteen hundred and thirty-five colonists: men, women and children. All dead. A captain who hasn't run a major mission in two years—"

"Shut that fucking mouth before I carve it off your fucking face, you—"

"Instead you've been running freight, garbage, taxi runs for diggies and insignificant washout diplomats through the backwaters of the galaxy. You're only still a captain because you called in some favors. I'm only here because I took a hit for you." Baz stepped closer, pointing at Leonardo with his knife. "If I hadn't you'd have been jailed—or worse. Someone took pity on your drunken ass, got you this fucking bullshit command so you could still collect a pension and retire with some tiny shred of dignity. You and your *fucking. tweaker. wife.*"

Baz punctuated these last three words by stabbing at Leonardo with the point of his glowing white blade.

Leonardo threw his knife at Baz's head. Baz ducked as the knife sailed past where his left eye had been milliseconds earlier before it struck the rear display and tore a hole in the screen as it stuck fast to the wall.

"Lucky you're not dead," Leonardo growled.

"You'd be dead without me, Leo." Baz reached back and pulled the knife from the display. "I've kept your ass safe way too long for you to throw shit at me." Baz held both blades in his hands. "I'm not about to let you kill me before I can get the fuck out of the UFW."

"You wouldn't know what to do with yourself outside of uniform."

Baz laughed, short and hard like he'd been punched.

"You got that right. Anything else would beat batting clean-up for you all the time." Baz looked at the knives in his hands. The clean white blades were tunable to varying blade strengths, able to puncture through almost any material their user selected. Both men knew Baz could make the blades pierce Leonardo's suit like a hand through water. Baz hefted his blade as seconds ticked by on the quiet bridge of the ailing *Resurgam*.

Baz looked at Leo then the knife in his right hand. He shook his head.

"You're right. I'd have no clue what to do outside of uniform. Maybe there's a colony somewhere that needs an administrator for their rehab center."

"Doubt they'd hire someone who swings a knife at his superior," said Leonardo. "Nor someone without the balls to step up and command."

"I never wanted to command," Baz said, shaking his head. "I was always fine being XO. Why the fuck would I want to command? I saw all the bullshit it got you." Baz flicked his knife off, slid it back into the sheath on his belt and handed Leonardo his blade. As Leonardo reached for it, Baz withdrew it at the last second. "I assume this isn't going to end up hilt deep in my skull just yet, Leo. *Sir?*"

"No, no just yet, Baz." Leonardo glared at Baz and accepted the knife. Leonardo sheathed his blade and folded his arms over his chest. Neither of them moved.

"I'm not command material. We both know that," said Baz. He looked out over the bridge. "I never liked the view from up here. Too high up. Too far to fall."

He went back to the outer ring of displays and controls. "I'm a little too inclined towards rash decisions and outbursts. Oh, what's the other thing that comes up in reviews. 'Doesn't function well in ambiguous situations.' I know full well who to thank for being in the UFW all these years."

"You're an insubordinate fuck who should have been shoved into an airlock with his papers in his ass." Leonardo stared at Baz with smoldering disgust. "Fortunately you're a damn smart fuck who's useful in sticky situations. I've always known that the moment I cut you loose I'd regret it." Leonardo looked around the bridge. "This ship is a sorry excuse for a command."

"S'all right. Two years of this ashcan and then full pension beats rotting away in prison or being iced for a couple of decades." Baz sighed and looked at Leonardo. "Look, Leo, I just—"

"Forget it. I'm surprised we didn't try to stab each before."

A silence fell between them for a moment.

"How should we proceed?" asked Baz.

"I need some guidance," said Leonardo. Baz nodded and he left the bridge to his XO, grabbing his lens case as he left. He returned to his quarters, stripped down, showered, and put on a clean uniform then his lenses.

His eyes weren't quite used to them and he swore; they were colder than usual, having been frozen for so long. The lenses covered his entire eye. There was a slight tingle as their self-adhering surface made contact with the proximity sensors in his room. He blinked repeatedly as images, test patterns and short codes flickered across the lenses four times and then a connection was made. A status display appeared in his lower right field of vision, three dots blinking from left to right in succession. He looked down and hard to the right, and the display swung to center. Leonardo looked at the short list of commands and chose: *Guide Consultation*. "PLEASE WAIT" flashed in his vision as he made his way to an unmarked door near the bathroom. Leonardo placed a hand on a square in the door and waited. The square glowed green and the door slid open with a barely audible sigh.

The walls were white with tiny circular indentations evenly spaced over all surfaces. They reminded Leonardo of a cracker or some very fine upholstery he'd seen at a hotel once. Inside the small room was a reclining seat. Leonardo sat in the chair and let the door close behind him. A sudden silence, so deep and intense that he could hardly hear the rustle of his own clothes, engulfed him as he settled into the seat. He closed his eyes and saw darkness except for a small red triangle that blinked until it turned blue. He felt a gentle pressure at his temples and something warm and round gently snuggled over his outer ears. Leonardo took a breath, exhaled and opened his eyes.

He sat in a terraced garden overlooking a lush green valley.

Ornate stone villas dotted the opposite hillside. The sun was beginning to set over distant hills. Everything was alive, green and bathed in the golden light. An overhead arbor covered in grape vines filtered some of the yellow sun. Leonardo looked down at the ancient worn stones under his feet. His boots were replaced by simple leather and twine sandals. His feet bore smears of dirt as if he'd walked for some time. He wore a loose shirt and white linen pants that fluttered in a light breeze from off the valley. Before him was a wrought iron table upon which was arrayed a selection of cheese, sliced fruit, breads and meats. Next to this was a carafe of dark liquid, which he knew would be a sweet, full-bodied wine. Two large, clear glass goblets were placed next to the carafe.

"It is pleasant this time of day, no?" said a voice behind Leonardo. Leonardo startled though he was waiting to hear the voice. He felt a hand on his shoulder as the speaker came around to stand before him.

"As always," said Leonardo, turning his head slightly.

Before him was a man well under six feet tall; if Leonardo stood he would have towered over him. He was older, perhaps in his eighties or even nineties, with a vitality evident in his carriage and the graceful strength as he moved. His skin was olive and tanned, likely from working in the vineyards below. The man's hands were strong and veined from regular work. His face was handsome and kind, with cragged, weathered skin, and ringed by the soft, short-cropped halo of hair. He wore a clean white shirt, unbuttoned to midchest, exposing more tanned skin and sparse white hair. He wore simple khaki pants with clean black leather sandals. The man turned from the valley and looked at Leonardo with a faint smile.

"And how are we this afternoon, Leonardo?" the man asked.

"Fine, Horacio. You?"

"Well, as always." Horacio sat down in the chair opposite Leonardo, drawing it close to the table. He grabbed the carafe in one hand and a goblet with the other. In Leonardo's hands this would have meant spilled wine and stained clothes but not a single drop that left the carafe missed the goblet. He poured himself a generous amount of wine and placed the goblet on the table. He took the other in his hand, and tipped the carafe towards it. "Some for you?"

"No, thank you," Leonardo said, holding a hand over the goblet's mouth. He noticed his was less veined and darker than Horacio's, though not as old or strong. These were the hands of his youth. He was always younger in this place.

"Very well, then. Let me know if you change your mind. I'm very pleased with this vintage." Horacio placed the carafe on the table and brought the goblet to his nose. He sniffed then sipped, closed his eyes and broke out in a smile. A trickle of wine seeped from his mouth and he wiped at it. "Forgive me. I am careless sometimes."

"I find that hard to believe," said Leonardo. Horacio was always immaculately dressed, never wore anything fancy; his clothing never appeared disheveled or even dirty though not in the antiseptic depictions of a fantasy construct. Horacio carried himself with poise and stature, knowing exactly where he was in his world.

Leonardo knew exactly where Horacio was in *his* world: tucked away in a series of redundant servers deep in the ship. Horacio was a top-level, Alpha-grade Turing-compliant AIAI unit. Artificial Intelligence Advisory Instructors were standard equipment on ships for many years. At some point during human spacefaring, captains needed more guidance when communication with UFW Central was impossible or when other crew members might not be trusted with high security matters. The AIAIs ("shamans," "guides" and "guidance counselors" in jest) were programmed with exabytes of instructions, scenarios and methods never discussed in officer training. They were designed to give a commander insights others might not see. Guides were always a last resort. Each was programmed by the ship's captain with an appearance that made them comfortable and relaxed so they might open up more. Especially if near destruction waited outside while they lay on a couch in their quarters.

A captain created their Guide's avatars themselves. Some chose from a stock of common characters from literature or media; Leonardo knew of more than one captain whose Guide was chosen from porn omnivids. Another's Guide was a stuffed animal he'd had as a child.

Leonardo created Horacio, his mother's last lover. Leonardo fondly remembered the visits to the real Horacio's estate when he was a little boy. In the earliest visits, Horacio would show them the fields and vineyards of reclaimed land not far from the Golden Coast of Connecticut where Leonardo grew up. Leonardo was too young to care but as an adult he often wondered how Horacio had acquired his wealth and the ability to build the estate in a part of Earth only recently taken off the list of demilitarized hazardous zones. He'd dammed rivers and moved tons of earth to recreate a place he said his ancestors had owned centuries before in Italy. After horseback tours around the land, they'd eat lunch and Leonardo and his sister would nap under an arbor like the one he sat beneath now. In later years, Leonardo came to realize his mother's true relationship with Horacio. Where and how did a woman who lived off of coastal salvage meet a man of such wealth? No doubt, the paths he traveled often crossed into the low places Leonardo's mother inhabited. Leonardo often wished Mother had agreed to marry him before she died. Perhaps it would have forestalled her own mysterious death.

"I find that hard to believe, Horacio," said Leonardo. "Everything about you is a study in conservation of movement and energy."

"Ah, Leonardo," said Horacio, with a gentle laugh. He set his goblet on the table and interlaced his hands behind his head, leaned back and stared up into the arbor. "I've had many years to hide my clumsiness."

Leonardo looked hard at the man before him. "You do it well then, Horacio."

"You look troubled, boy. And a problem not shared only grows worse. So ... Tell Zio Horacio what is on your mind." Leonardo sighed, shook his head and began to tell the tale of leaving Baaklum Cha'am and crashing. Doing his best to leave out no detail too small—Guides needed to know everything—Leonardo noted Horacio's calm, pleasant expression, as he listened to music, or sounds of birds in the distance. He smiled and laughed at the appropriate places, though these were few. When Leonardo finished, Horacio raised his goblet to his lips, taking a long draw and swirling wine in his mouth as he looked out at the valley below.

"Anything else?" he finally asked after a long silence.

"No, that's it."

"Quite a pickle," said Horacio, rising from his chair.

"To say the least," Leonardo snorted. "We could die here."

"Yes, true," said Horacio, nodding and surveying his virtual valley. "We will all die eventually." Leonardo usually played along with the Guide, suspending his disbelief as if he wasn't wired up and lying on a couch in his crippled ship. Not this time.

"Horacio, you will never die. You do not exist in this place. You—the real you— you're *long* dead."

"Be that as it may, you, the *very* real captain of *Resurgam*, have come to me for consultation in a desperate hour." Horacio turned and picked up the plate of fruit from the table, offering it to Leonardo. "How do you like these apples?" he said with a wry smile, nodding at the fruit.

"I get it. Very clever," said Leonardo as he waved the plate away. Horacio laid it on the table then crossed his arms over his chest again. "I suppose I am feeling ... overwhelmed."

"It is understandable, Little Leo." Leonardo winced at the diminutive name. "Your situation is the worst you've ever come to me with. Not the worst ever, but not pleasant by far."

Leonardo gave in and reached for the carafe, pouring and spilling wine. He felt everything, the weight of the glass filling, wine splashing onto his hand, even the smell of it. He wondered about staying with Horacio for a few days of real time in the comfort of the arbor, with the view of a verdant valley untouched by strife. The taste of the wine was exactly as he expected: fuller than any wine he'd ever tasted with his flesh and blood tongue, enhanced by the power of desire.

"So what can you tell me?" asked Leonardo.

"What can I tell you?" Horacio said, striding slowly about the arbor, arms aloft. "Many things! Do you want *stories*? I have those in abundance. Triumphs of old, or of recent battles and their decisive outcomes. Do you want *facts*? I have those as well. I can give you the details and show helmet-camera footage from every soldier in every battle on every planet from every star the UFW has visited and encountered the FMR. So many strategies and scenarios. We could sit here for months discussing the tactics of all history's battles."

"I think I'd like that right about now."

"If it's what you *truly* want I can give that to you." Horacio tapped a finger to his lips. "But I don't think it will help you." He leaned against a railing. "You can compare battle statistics, research various strategies, etc., on your own in the comfort of your quarters." Horacio gestured as if Leonardo's quarters lay beyond the doors behind them. "That will not serve you now. You need to shed some things before you move on, Little Leo."

"What I need right now, Horacio, is some goddamn help. I have a severely damaged ship, a missing passenger who is the mysterious man who may have caused it, and no clear way of getting our asses off this crusty rock."

"Yes, I know you do, Leonardo." Horacio sat back down, sliced off a hunk of cheese and popped a grape in his mouth along with it. "I will say that right now, the solution is not in some ..." Horacio waved his hand around and looked skyward for the words. "... attack plan."

Leonardo groaned and rose from his chair. "You know, I think I'm executing Command Imperative One here. Capt. Leonardo Valencia, Op. Code 44-4-1. Horacio, I order you to give me a solution and a plan of attack."

"Very well," Horacio sighed. "Your situation as you present it to me seems to have a ninety-eight percent chance of failure. There is no precedent for total failure of a ship's systems." He sat up and leaned forward, putting elbows to knees, laying his palms out to the sky. "This is why I propose you shed your thoughts about this situation and find another way. You are, historically and statistically speaking, the captain most likely to succeed against odds like these."

"So it's hopeless?"

"Not exactly—"

"Fuck." Leonardo looked out over the valley, greenery spread out before him as far the eye could see. A cool breeze rose up from the valley, bringing scents of plants, a hint of manure and moisture. He was again tempted to drop it and sit down to engage Horacio in idle chatter until the sunset, whiling away the hours with imaginary food and drink. Despite the fact that events in virtual took place at a rate of one thousand virtual seconds to every one in real time, Leonardo had little time to waste here.

"So what are you telling me, Horacio?"

"Leo," Horacio said softly, coming to stand next to him at the railing. "What it is you wish to accomplish?"

"I wish to get off this damn rock."

"Nothing else?"

"What else is there?"

Horacio turned to face him. Leonardo fought the urge to push him over the railing, despite knowing in virtual he would just reappear seconds later behind him. "Little Leo, you need to ask why this man went to all this trouble of getting a ship to crash and run off into the snow with stolen artifacts."

"He's most likely dead now."

"You don't know that. Someone so eager to risk so much probably had a plan to succeed and survive." Leonardo looked at Horacio, seeing a small smile play across his lips. "And a very good reason to survive at that."

"Which might be?"

"I have no idea," Horacio said, throwing his palms skyward again. He left the railing and grabbed his goblet. "I'm just a humble vintner."

"Fine. Where should I start?"

"Have you debriefed Jason yet?"

"No."

"I suggest you start there."

"Obviously," snarled Leonardo. The real Horacio would have slapped him for that kind of insolence.

"Also," Horacio said, ignoring Leonardo's tone, "you've not checked the effects of the survey team to see if there were any diaries or records of some kind. How did their survey go?"

"Fine, I guess. One member got injured. We had to bug out after getting the call from CENTCOM."

"Then I'd suggest looking there."

"Okay, I will. I'll check back with you later."

"Do that. I shall be here."

"Goodbye, Horacio." Leonard turned to go.

"Oh, Leonardo!" Horacio called out. Leonardo turned back towards him.

"Yes?"

"I do hope Drina recovers. I understand there are certain stresses to your relationship, but she is a good woman. You both carry many burdens on your shoulders. Don't judge each other too harshly."

"Thank you, Horacio."

He turned to leave through the French doors. As usual, he never made it. Darkness enfolded him and he felt his brain shift slightly as it left the virtual world. He waited a moment and slowly opened his eyes.

He was back in the small white room again, far from the world where the old vineyard glowed in the afternoon sun.

CHAPTER TWELVE
Above & Below

Leonardo rose from the chair and checked the time in his lens display. Only a few minutes had passed while he was in with Horacio. He wished he could make real world time go so fast. He left the oracle room and then his quarters with a sigh. A quick glance in on Drina showed her in the same monotonous, unchanging condition.

He found Baz on the bridge poring over readouts on a forward display. He turned around at the sound of Leonardo's footsteps.

"I got the nannies back online. Had to jumpstart them with a fresh batch from an unaffected pod. Little cannibals are eating their ancestors now."

"Good. That'll get the ship patched up better faster than we will."

"Copy that." Baz looked Leonardo up and down and smiled. "Uniform, huh? Wondered why you took so long."

"It feels good. I suggest you do the same. Clean up and then head down to the main bay. I want you to find me any diaries among the personal effects of the survey team. Specifically the lead diggy."

"You mean Ortiz?"

"Yeah, him. Also, anything else that catches your eye. Then go to the upper hangar. Make sure the FLi8s are ready for a little sightseeing mission." Baz nodded and left.

Leonardo sat in his chair, settling in as his lenses acknowledged the chair and assumed a passive role before the displays.

"Jason, avatar, please."

There was a blip of light in front of Leonardo's seat for a moment and then a young Asiatic man stood before him dressed in UFW fatigues. The simple insignia on his chest identified him as Bridge Officer Jason. "Yes, sir?"

"Can you tell me how and why we crashed, Jason?"

"Yes, sir." The avatar's eyes closed for a second and reopened. "We proceeded normally until I picked up a distress signal. As a UFW Rescue and Research vessel, we are bound to answer an SOS. Upon charting the new coordinates, I dropped us out of hyperspace into an uncharted debris field." Jason stopped and frowned slightly. It looked down towards its feet for a moment as if in shame, though Leonardo knew this was impossible, then returned its gaze to Leonardo. "Now here is a discrepancy. When we received the distress call, I believed we were near Frontis as the Astrogation AIs told me. However, upon exiting hi-space, we were in reality nowhere near Frontis. It appears that during the voyage, an illegal routine presented to the system earlier caused Astrogation systems to go offline. Asgr. Valencia was injured in an attempt to get us back into hi-space." Leonardo swallowed hard. So Drina had tried to bring the ship out of a hi-space nosedive; the resulting stress on her and the ship must have been enormous. No wonder she was so badly injured. He nodded.

"Proceed."

"We were not in empty space, but an anomalous debris field which is where we sustained damage to the drives. At this time the illegal subroutine Magenta 3635 began to propagate in the network and *Resurgam* began experiencing catastrophic failures. I set about finding a suitable planet for emergency landing procedures. Records indicated that this planet we are now resting on," here Jason pointed to the floor, "was in fact E class and temperate ... But—" Jason held up a finger, then placed a hand to its cheek as if in contemplation. "I did not see this before. The astrogation records were tampered with. The planet we are now on was shown as Kelso-Gardiner 2 in the Frontis system. Yes. Temperate and E class."

"How did this happen, Jason?" Leonardo asked. The avatar stood penitent with its hands folded in front of.

"Numerous illegal routines and trojan packages were introduced by an unknown party and method through different avenues. The first was via standard blood screening by the medibots upon arrival on the ship. Subsequent elements were introduced in volumes traded over the ship's data networks between members of the survey team and Mr. Somogyi and Mr. Hammond. A final element was introduced in the return blood screening during retrieval of the survey team from Baaklum Cha'am."

"The source of the introductions?" asked Leonardo.

"All of these appear to have been done by George Mussina."

Leonardo clenched his jaw.

"Sir, a security breach like this requires high level AI processing to break deep encryption or collusion of some kind. It is quite shocking. These subroutines and packages gained an unprecedented level of access to all my systems and information." Leonardo could almost hear indignation in the AI's voice. "They supplanted existing records and falsified documents. I was led to believe a nonexistent ship was in distress, and a planet was where it was not. Furthermore—"

"Yes, Jason. I understand. We were all deceived."

"Sir, please," the avatar held out a hand. "These routines shut down the hull nanotube repair systems. They are also responsible for killing off the crew in their berths."

"How?" Leonardo asked, his attention piqued.

"One of the packages contained a routine designed to directly attack neural implants. A pornographic dream plug-in of some kind, traded between Mussina and the crew. Specifically Mr. Somogyi and Mr. Hammond."

"Damn." Leonardo breathed deep and slow. Neither he nor Baz had implants of any kind, having been stripped of them as punishment for Newhope 15. It was deemed a fitting punishment and also the belief of the UFW that the captain of a vessel as simple as *Resurgam* did not need them. Leonardo and anyone else who piloted a ship knew a captain needed implants to run any spacefaring vessel. What really salted the wound was that the entire crew were outfitted with the latest neural implants while he and Baz struggled with the outdated technology of lenses and proximity sensors.

And yet it was this lack of implants that saved him.

"Is this also why Asgr. Valencia is in a coma?"

"Partly. There were other medical issues as well."

"Yes, there were." Leonardo thought for a moment. "So, where are we?"

"Given that all ships systems were compromised by the illegal Magenta 3635 routine, I was unable to accurately pinpoint our location at the time of the crash. I am still unsure where we are due to the difficulty of astrogating from within hi-space."

Leonardo groaned.

"Care to make a guess?"

"I do not guess, sir. With all due respect that is for magicians and gamblers." Leonardo resisted an urge to kick the avatar in its nonexistent groin.

"Where do you believe we are, Jason?"

"We are on the planet where the distress call originated. Somewhere between Baaklum Cha'am and Earth, sir."

Leonardo laughed.

"Never thought I'd hear or see an AI covering its virtual ass. When will I know where we are, Jason?"

"Soon, sir. I've created a subpersona that is retracing our steps from the hi-space exit to our present location. We can then recover correct astrogation records and find out our exact location via pulsar astrogation. If you wish I will devote more resources to the sensor arrays, but it will limit efforts to repair the ship."

"Later. Right now I want you to help Colonel Al-Mushtarii get the Fli8 units ready."

"Yes, sir." Jason nodded. Leonardo rose and walked through the avatar.

"Baz?"

"Yeah. I'm still down in the diggies' box. Found Ortiz's journals in a locker under his berth. I think you should come down here, too."

"Why?"

"Show you when you get here."

Leonardo arrived at the main bay, walking all the way due to a deep mistrust of the lifts' stability. The walk cleared his head somewhat. As he got closer he could feel the air thinning slightly. His HUD told him the atmospheric levels were just short of fully restored. He found the auxiliary entrance to the right of the main doors open, with a pink, gooey material spread around the edges. He stepped into an elongated, rigid metallic tunnel leading to the entrance of the survey team's quarters, where it terminated. Inside he found Baz showered, shaved and in a clean uniform, kneeling by one of the berths.

Leonardo paused and held a hand under his nose as the smell of decaying bodies permeated the room.

"Nice causeway. Messy sealant, though."

"Sorry," said Baz. "Didn't know I was being graded."

"It'll do. What have you got?" Leonardo asked.

"I was looking for Dr. Ortiz's diaries underneath his berth. As I got up, something caught my eye." He pointed to the berth and Leonardo knelt down next to him. Baz pointed at a seam a few millimeters wide and of similar depth, where the berth's door met with the frame. "When these berths close up for travel, they seal up perfectly, locking the occupant into the atmosphere inside, right? Now follow the seam from here to here," Baz said, pointing from the bottom to the top of the berth.

Leonardo let his eyes roam along the seam. His optics saw nothing until midway up he found a tiny hole surrounded by the smallest of burn marks. Leonardo leaned slightly to the right of the seam, peering into the berth through the thick clear glass. On the temple of the corpse's head was a wider burn mark, centimeters in diameter.

"*Murdered*," said Leonardo.

"Yes," said Baz. "Clean shot to the head."

"Looks like a narrow beam from a piezocutter. Standard equipment for anyone doing a lot of digging."

"Yeah." Baz stood. "Now look at all the other berths and you'll see the same thing."

Leonardo walked to the next berth and peered closely at the seam and an identical burn mark. All the berths' seams and their occupants revealed the same thing: a nearly invisible burn outside, with a larger one on the head of the body inside the berth. Leonardo looked at Baz.

"My guess is he murdered them all right before he blew that hole over there," Baz said, gesturing to the blast hole, now filled with foam sealant. "That's a nice touch for a guy who knew they were dead already."

"Like he had scores to settle." Leonardo walked over to the table, where a few scorched pedias lay. The one on top was a luxury model made from ebony, with gold inlays on the buttons lining the bottom. At the top it read *"Dr. Nwarkim Ortiz"* in gold letters.

"The good doctor's own personal pedia?"

"Yup."

"I'll take a look through it." Leonardo gathered up the other pedias "And these, too. Let's go to the upper hangar. I want to inspect the Fli8s."

"Yeah, I was getting to that. Then I found out someone killed all our passengers."

They made their roundabout way to the upper deck, avoiding damaged areas. In a functioning ship that was properly pressurized with atmosphere fully restored, the journey was more straightforward: up the starboard side stairwell, left at the door and up the wide central stairs and through doors there. But they made their circuitous journey around through corridors and levels until they arrived at the port entrance.

Baz and Leo arrived at the doors to find a red light flashing over the door, in addition to an alert flashing in their HUDs.

"Atmosphere's still low in there," said Baz.

"We can get everything done from Secondary."

They walked further down to another door marked "Secondary Control." Leo passed a hand over the seal and they stepped inside a small drab room with dead displays and reinforced diamond-pane windows looking into the darkness of the bay. Faint blue light shone down from small windows high above. They looked at the displays only to see a blinking triangle surrounding an exclamation point: "Please Wait" it read. Baz flipped a switch in the room and lights shone out into the hangar, illuminating little more than a few meters past the windows. Then Baz flipped more switches and the main bay lights came on. The upper hangar was smaller than the main cargo bay at seventy-five meters long and forty meters wide. Gray walls sloped in towards the heavy doors.

"Displays are up," said Leonardo, pointing to the holocontrol panel illuminated before them. "Run a check."

Baz set to work on diagnostics as Leo looked for the Fli8 units hanging near the ceiling: two dark, elongated and curving shapes clinging to the recharge bars. Two small lights over each only shrouded them in more mystery. Leonardo tapped out commands on the holoboard in front of him.

They began to unfold simultaneously like monstrous gargoyle dancers. What began as long, slim black pods unfolded into huge black wings. As these opened they revealed the body underneath; thick, ovular bulks with strong legs tucked up into the belly. Near the claws, flares of powerful engines roared to life. Pointing towards the floor was the "head", all smooth with slight protrusions near the front containing sensory equipment. When their wings fully unfolded, their claws released from the bar and the machines dropped in free fall. It still thrilled Leonardo to watch this, always wondering if today was the day they dropped like stones to lie motionless on the floor. But flipping over at the last second, their legs sprang out from underneath and each landed on the hangar floor with a soft thump. The wings folded up and they marched to the window, looking less avian and more like fearsome metal dogs, thirteen feet tall in their restrained metal glory. They stopped before the control room window and squatted.

"Hello, boys," said Leonardo.

"They look good," said Baz, smiling. He glanced at the display under Leonardo's fingertips. "Ready to party."

"Oh, yes they are," said Leonardo, chuckling as he typed at the keyboard.

"Too bad we don't have anything heavy-duty   "

Leonardo coughed loudly and Baz looked at him.

"Do you ..."

"Oh, I do." Leonardo laughed and tapped a final series of commands, nodding towards the window. Baz saw two rails emerge from slots in the floor. From a wall to the left, lockers opened to reveal emergency oxygen scrubbers on racks. These slid aside to reveal a deeper hidden container. This rolled forward and stopped in front of the Fli8 units.

"Captain, *Resurgam* isn't authorized for heavy weaponry," said Baz.

"True," said Leo.

"Then what the hell is ..." Baz said, pointing out the window.

"I didn't call in all my favors in at once, you know," Leonardo said, turning to Baz. "Forty years of service and you tend to build up a surplus of 'em." Leonardo typed something else, ending with a mudra over the panel. "Some of my fellow captains thought it unfair for me to go light into the depths of space."

The racks rose three meters high with several rows of armaments on each, containing identical amounts of weaponry. Each rack looked more fearsome than the next; weapons bristling spines and protrusions from sleek shells. Leonardo found them glorious, beautiful and terrifying. The Fli8 units stepped forward as mechanical arms of stevedrones sprung from the floor and began to install the weaponry onto their undersides.

"That's a lot of firepower there."

"General Baptiste owed me big. A case of Bun-Ho got me all of this. I can't imagine how he got it off his ship." Leonardo laughed. Once the stevedrones finished loading up the FLi8s, the arms and racks of weaponry disappeared into the floor. The drones stepped back and stood at attention.

"Give them the soil sample you picked up off the sled," said Leonardo.

"Sir." A moment later, they heard a second ping. "Orders received. They're ready."

"Launch on my mark," said Leonardo. "Now."

The drones stepped back, squatted deep, and widened their stance. From their undersides came a white glow. They rose slowly from the floor, legs drawing up inside them. The steel wings unfurled and their bodies changed shape, becoming long and angular. Red lights flashed as the ceiling opened into a large square portal. As the drones went through they grew translucent before disappearing altogether. The last trace of their presence was a subtle, wavy distortion of the air around them that dissipated as they became completely invisible.

Baz and Leonardo looked at the display. On a red landscape, two yellow triangles marked "ALPHA" and "BRAVO" showed up on the screen. Telemetry created a detailed picture of the planet's surface; topography, elevations and land formations gave greater character to this planet.

"Let's go to the bridge and watch everything from there."

On the bridge, Baz took his seat just inside the horseshoe at the foot of the Leonardo's chair. Leonardo sat and held Dr. Ortiz's pedia in his hand. He activated it and began to read the journal entries from the dig.

CHAPTER THIRTEEN
Baaklum Cha'am

August 2, 2468
We have arrived at Baaklum Cha'am! The others must think I'm mad to be so excited to arrive in this backwater of the galaxy. Behold this inconsequential, dull gray orb looming outside my porthole. I am terribly excited about the amazing discoveries about the Transparent Ones and their civilization this planet could yield.

Assembling the team was arduous, with pleas and bargains, many scheduling complications and last minute changes. Once I finally got everyone together, I realized that the archaeological talent I have assembled will be the envy of academia: Prof. Juan Prohaska, anthropologist, Prof. Dominic Malhotra ethno-linguist and epigraphic expert, Prof. Juanita Sadat-Stein, geologist, Prof. Roman Cobb, astrobotanist, Dr. Robert Morrison, astrobiologist and—from out of his long retirement—Prof. George Mussina, techno-archaeologist and Transparent Ones specialist.

Securing the presence of Dr. Mussina is a major achievement in my career as he is one of the people most familiar with the work of Dr. Krome, leader of the last (and fatal) expedition to Mars before its Secession. Dr. Mussina is notoriously reclusive, having been working privately for the last twenty-odd years. It's Dr. Mussina's hard work that's brought us to Baaklum Cha'am in the first place.

I must rest now, for tomorrow we go planetside!

Tuesday, August 3, 2468
During our postrevivification briefing, Prof. Cobb shared his theories that Baaklum Cha'am was once a thriving planet covered with lush vegetation. The Desmond probes sent ahead mapped it and revealed dry riverbeds, ocean plains and water-carved canyons. Craters mar the surface from a long period of meteoric bombardment. This was so severe it wore down many natural features, like a potter smoothing out clay.

Soil samples taken by the landers indicate this was once indeed a fertile world— roughly three billion years ago. Another past catastrophe turned Baaklum Cha'am's atmosphere toxic to all but extremophilic life; for now it is a cold, inhospitable world. Sulfur gives the planet a slight yellowish tint as it blows around in unpredictable and massive storms. The scale of the surface temperature runs from the coldest, about -170 *degrees F (-113C), and the warmest is about 17 degrees F (-8C). Dr. Mussina says it is not unlike Mars in some ways. From his offhand remarks about that forbidden world, one would almost think he'd been there!*

Dr. Mussina's research dovetails quite nicely with my own. We have both been studying the Transparent Ones, the graveyard civilization that settled many worlds of this galaxy. I have been developing a theory of their migration patterns across the galaxy, while Dr. Mussina says he has been working on deciphering their scientific achievements. Dr. Mussina believes Baaklum Cha'am contains the solution to many of the mysteries of this ancient race. For one thing, he hopes to finally crack the mystery of the Transparent Ones' baffling technology. It is his knowledge, hope and optimism in this, among other things, that led me to accommodate him so much.

I can hardly contain my enthusiasm and hopes for this dig. If all goes as I hope and have planned these last four years, the work we do here will lay the blueprint for future generations of archaeologists as we discover further evidence of the Transparent Ones' existence beyond our own galaxy. The true extent of their civilization may never be known, given the size of the galaxy and the billions of years that separate us.

August 9, 2468
We have found the remains of a vast Transparent Ones settlement! It is a large group of buildings covering an area of 15 square kilometers. Sadly, as with all Transparent Ones sites, it's in ruins and my hopes of finding an unmolested Transparent Ones settlement are dashed once again. Age alone would not account for the ruination we see. Most of the sites appear to have been intentionally destroyed. The damage is from more than age.

So little is known about the Transparent Ones: what they looked like, how they lived, their language and their culture. They were named The Transparent Ones as they built on so many worlds yet left so little evidence of themselves. The shadows of their civilization are everywhere yet these mysterious inhabitants of such vast and complex settlements are long, long, gone. Great blocks of stark white stone and minute fragments of strange metals are all that remain. Despite our science we are as puzzled about their technologies as a monkey looking at a pedia.

Baaklum Cha'am is more of the same yet nonetheless wondrous. I am amazed at Dr. Mussina's certainty a settlement was here. Probes showed nothing but kilometers of empty, dead wasteland. Yet as we reviewed maps he circled a rocky region dotted with white stones. Satellite photos revealed no Transparent Ones ruins. We were all stunned by Mussina's accuracy. He claimed it was a lucky guess based on habitation patterns gleaned from his studies of previous worlds the Transparent Ones visited. He has promised to show these to me when we return to Earth. It's almost unbelievable but his theory and hunch proved to be correct, so who am I to judge?

Looking at all the information at hand there is an apparent pattern to the Transparent Ones settlements. They obviously needed a certain atmosphere to sustain themselves yet their choice of planets always met with dire ends. Every one of these worlds was once rich with vegetation but over time became cold, arid, and inhospitable.

There is no indication of what caused changes in their atmospheres. Did they poison the atmospheres of every world through their own negligence? It seems unlikely for a race with such a broad reach.

Furthermore, every planet is almost the exact same distance from the stars they orbit; a distance that should yield a stable, fertile growing world. Yet at every Transparent Ones settlement, geology and atmosphere are exactly the same: great white stones, an abundance of sand and a world with a thin, ravaged atmosphere.

It seems highly unlikely that a culture so incredibly advanced, with such a spread across the galaxy could exercise such poor judgment—or had such bad luck—in selecting worlds to settle. I doubt we will ever know the truth in my lifetime, despite the best efforts of Dr. Mussina and myself.

While the others are just beginning to map out potential work sites, Dr. Mussina went straight away to digging in a far-flung corner of the settlement, using his own tools while politely but firmly declining any assistance. Though I have my own work to attend to I am very curious about what he will turn up.

Tuesday, August 10, 2468
Another great discovery!

The settlement has a subterranean component! In the ten Transparent Ones settlements discovered, there has never been an underground dwelling. It's amazing that this went undetected by the probes. Prof. Stein was taking soil samples in the northwest corner of our dig when she fell into a hole that suddenly opened beneath her. Myself, Cobb and Morrison ran to her aid. As we gathered around to pull her free, the sand around us continued to open, revealing a vast trench. We were certain we were about to die as it proceeded unabated, with a dull grinding sound, until it finally ceased, revealing a slanted entranceway. Once Stein was safe we scanned the space for stability. The walky-talkies installed an elevator and we carefully lowered ourselves into the abyss.

We stood in a chamber ninety meters high, two hundred fifty meters long and one hundred thirty-eight wide. Illumination beamed down from the formerly dark vault of the ceiling. Both ceiling and walls are built from the same white stone found aboveground and at all Transparent Ones settlements—despite the fact that it is not a type of stone indigenous to any of the worlds they settled upon (did they import it all from somewhere?). The point at which Stein fell through is a ramp into the chamber. Despite retracing her footsteps, Dr. Stein is unsure what she did to trigger its opening. Unlike stairs, which may give a hint as to how tall the builders were, a ramp tells us nothing. Its gentle decline is comfortable to human height and pace but yields no clues as to the Transparent Ones method of ambulation. Dr. Morrison can only say they were either given to huge spaces or were so massive themselves this was simply a root cellar.

Upon adding to the lighting of the space with our own equipment, we discovered an even greater surprise. The walls of the room are covered with writing! It is raised in gold characters gleaming across every wall. No Transparent Ones site has ever been found with writings intact. It seems to shift in color as one walks along looking at it. The writing appears both logographic and hieroglyphic, making deciphering it challenging. I have set Prof. Malhotra to this formidable task.

The floor is made of a single smooth and unbroken surface, as if poured or polished. Indentations and markings create patterns suggesting there were once objects or furniture attached to it. Instrument readings taken on the walls of the chamber yield nothing. The dense stone is impenetrable to our equipment, which would indicate why it went undetected by our probes.

Dr. Mussina shared my excitement upon entering the chamber. "Indescribably glorious!" were his first words upon seeing it. "I suspected it would be here." Rather amazed by this, I asked him how he knew about it. "You don't think they built only aboveground, do you?" he said with a smile. "It's only reasonable to think they had some subterranean buildings." He declined to make any further explanation. Despite his confidence he said he has never seen anything like it. This from a man who has visited all ten Transparent Ones sites!

We do have our work cut out for us, though. High winds have picked up, blowing the gray and yellow sand of the surface down into the chamber. I have requested that the captain of Resurgam *send down an enclosure for the entrance into the chamber.*

August 12, 2468
I admire Mussina's dedication. Not only has he been in the chamber every day before anyone else, he has worked the past two nights in there. I suspect he's even been sleeping in his suit!

He is now focused on one particular section of the chamber, a recessed area one hundred thirty feet high with a thirty-foot raised platform the others have dubbed The Hearth. Mussina says it is central to the chamber and that in fact all the writing points back to it literally and conceptually.

Prof. Malhotra privately told me he thought the claim was audacious, considering no one has cracked the Transparent Ones' language. "It's kinda like a baby lookin' at an ol' STOP sign and telling you it were the lost works of Shakespeare," he said to me rather petulantly in his Mississippi accent. I reminded Malhotra that despite all his own achievements, Prof. Mussina's made it highly likely that if anyone else were to crack the Transparent Ones' language it would be him. I may have stepped on Malhotra's professional toes, which is not hard. Malhotra's insecurity and scholarly battles are as legendary as his epigraphic skills.

I must admit I harbor a growing degree of skepticism about Dr. Mussina. His claims are outlandish, but then he is Dr. George Mussina. For the last twenty years he has worked so consistently outside the sphere of respected academia and published so little that one wonders how he manages to make a living at all. Any mention of him is largely suspicious—and highly skeptical—due to this. He's held no university positions beyond graduate work and has no corporate sponsors. It makes for a curious sort of scientist. His "private funding and research," as he calls it, must be quite lavish indeed.

His emergence from retirement does revive the old questions, though. And his behavior so far doesn't douse the flames under them either.

Wednesday, August 25, 2468

Work continues apace on the Great Chamber, as we have dubbed the room discovered under the surface here on Baaklum Cha'am. The Hearth yields none of its secrets so far, yet Mussina is studiously copying its symbols and has gone so far as to have commandeered one of the high-powered research computational AIs I brought with us. Despite my better judgment I have allowed this, as I believe it will propel all of our work forward greatly. After all, Dr. Mussina is funding a good portion of this mission himself, a fact I declined to share with the others lest it give them the wrong impression. And even though the others do not know this, it will be challenging not to show deferential treatment to this mission's biggest backer. I may have to begin rationing time on the other unit so we all get equal use.

During our lunch break in the main shelter on Monday, I asked Mussina—during a rare time when he chose to eat with the group—about his theories of the Hearth and the Great Chamber. Mussina began to lecture on the Transparent Ones at large.

"The tendency is for archaeologists to ascribe a religious nature to all ancient inscriptions despite any evidence supporting it. 'Man is the measure of all things' as Pythagoras said. But the Transparent Ones," Mussina went on," were an ancient technological race. When they built this settlement here on Baaklum Cha'am, their culture was at its zenith." He paused for a moment to take a bite from his sandwich. He continued, speaking around a mouthful. "It's a technology so advanced as to be absolutely transparent—hence the name!" he said. "This technology allowed them to do things most civilizations could only dream of. Thus, their reach began far away and extended well beyond our galaxy. On a Kardashev scale, one being the level of our present technology and three being highly advanced, the Transparent Ones were a six." This drew gasps and not a few derogatory snorts from the others. Mussina brushed this off, continuing.

"There is this idea that the Transparent Ones had bad luck or poor judgment in picking planets to settle on, or perhaps that they polluted these planets with their own waste then vanished to another pristine world to start all over again and repeat the process. In light of their advanced technology, this insults the Transparent Ones while simultaneously illuminating the average human's stupidity. Present company excepted, of course," he said with a dismissive wave of the sandwich and a smile. "The Transparent Ones didn't search for planets to live on. They didn't need to after a certain point."

Here Dr. Mussina paused so long I almost bade him to continue. But just as I opened my mouth he opened his and completed his thought.

"They built planets to live on."

The rest of the team erupted in furious shouts, half of them demanding Mussina clarify what he said and the other half condemning him at the same time. I considered calling the captain of Resurgam *and begging him to bring a security force down to calm them. But Mussina rose with a particularly comfortable smile and strode out of the dining hall, sandwich in hand. The furor dimmed down into a silence as deafening as the preceding eruption. As a group the team turned to me and I simply had no reply. The silence hung over the room for the remainder of the meal.*

Afterwards, I sought out Dr. Mussina in the Great Chamber and asked if we could speak privately. He agreed but postponed until he was finished.

And later that evening when he entered my quarters, I noted a certain air of agitation about him. He was looking haggard, though upbeat—almost manic. I asked how his work was proceeding, and he said, "Splendidly." I asked when he might share his findings with the group as everyone's work could benefit from it. Mussina gave a queer smile and said, "All will be revealed in good time, Dr. Ortiz."

I asked what he meant by his last words in the mess hall.

"Well, it's quite obvious, I should think," replied Mussina. "If one looks at the characteristics of planets where the Transparent Ones left settlements, the similarities are quite striking: same atmosphere, same geology, same stonework, same botany— what's left of it—and same temperature. Even the planets' locations in relationship to their stars is identical. Mathematically identical, I should add. Look it up."

I told him I had noticed the similarities already. I asked him about the ruined condition we always found their settlements in and his thoughts as to how they arrived in that state of decay.

"A lot can happen in two or three billion years, Dr. Ortiz," he said with that smile I'd grown to become wary of. "I am sure the Transparent Ones made a few enemies along the way. Some closer to home than one might think."

Ignoring the offhand comment, I asked him about the depth of his knowledge and whether he had built upon his published work during his twenty-year absence from academia.

"One could say that, yes," he answered. "Let us just say that at some point in researching the Transparent Ones I came across evidence of their encounters with others in the galaxy."

I was stunned as there has been no indication of other cultures that anyone knows of. I begged him to elaborate.

"Really, Dr. Ortiz? I am somewhat shocked that you think it was only our own civilization and the Transparent Ones who existed in this galaxy. Such thinking would be acceptable to someone in the twenty-first century perhaps, but in our hyperenlightened and gilded twenty-fifth? Really. So many inhabitable planets and so many viable stars and only two races? No. Statistically impossible! The Transparent Ones made their way across the galaxy and made friends and enemies along the way."

"Who?" I found myself whispering.

"Really? And tell you the punchline before I tell the joke? I think not." He smiled and shook his head. "No, the truth has remained buried for billions of years; it can stay unknown for a little while longer." He paused and looked up at me. "Though I might be willing to share some of my knowledge sooner should this dig prove fruitful. For now, I must say goodnight."

I told him I eagerly awaited this opportunity to look at his work and advised him to rest, as there was more to be done on Baaklum Cha'am. He agreed, though he admitted being so excited about his discoveries sleep was often difficult.

Later in my own room, I researched his claims about the Transparent Ones. Calling up all the research on the various Transparent Ones settlements, I saw things with a different eye than before. Just as he said, there was indeed a remarkable similarity to every planet they'd inhabited. Not surprisingly, a Dr. George Mussina stated all this in a paper in an obscure archaeological journal on the very same subject filed shortly before we left Earth. I must have forgotten about it when I was preparing for the journey.

So with this new knowledge do I discount the information Mussina cited since it was he who wrote it? Or do I accept that he may know very well of what he speaks?

I'll sleep on it.

September 4, 2468

We have begun to branch out in our digging. Prof. Cobb has located some fossilized plant life. Malhotra has composed a theory about Transparent Ones linguistic formations. Our combined efforts will put together quite an impressive body of work!

Mussina's efforts have kept him to his far corner of the settlement. Just as well. He's become increasingly taciturn and elusive in his dealings with others. The team has been sharing one AI, as Mussina has commandeered the other entirely for himself. Sharing and cooperation is of no interest to him. When he was last working in the Great Chamber, he would ignore requests for assistance from those nearby or simply walk away. He has taken to muttering a great deal to himself. When engaged in conversation, he waves it off, making no effort to be polite.

Mussina spends his nights working in his corner, light gantries illuminating the area. He shoos off any who approach, saying we will disrupt his work. Dr. Mussina—I remind myself he is a professor, despite this behaviour—seems to forget we are all trained to handle artifacts with the greatest care.

At this point I would decline to recommend Mussina for any future digs, even if he pays for them entirely. Until he addresses these attitude problems, he is a weak link in any research group.

September 28, 2468

Sadly, I am looking forward to the end of this dig more than continuing our work here. Prof. Mussina's behavior has outstripped his value. I would rather have a dozen inexperienced, drunken, fornicating undergraduate students than one George Mussina.

Group work proceeds slowly, though it's not just group dynamics that challenge us. The very alien nature of the Transparent Ones civilization makes our work incredibly slow. We have come to believe the floor may have held seating or fixtures, though their purpose remains a mystery. Where these items went is anyone's guess. Looters? Did the Transparent Ones themselves take them? The Hearth seems to contain great possibilities but refuses to yield but a handful of secrets. What does the Chamber have to hide?

Mussina works in his corner continuing his alienation of the group. The others now openly complain about his unprofessionalism. Some have even broached the topic of academic censure when we return to Earth. An expedition is hard enough to manage without having to soothe the bruised egos of several scientists used to having their own damn way!

Malhotra is the most bothered of all. He's concerned Mussina will decipher the Transparent Ones writing before he does. I don't see how, given that Mussina's work is more recovery and restoration in nature than translation. This is the first site where so many artifacts have been found. Mussina prefers rooting around in his corner to deciphering the writing in the Great Chamber. But Malhotra insists Mussina is going to steal his work, going so far as to make outlandish claims about Mussina.

"You ever noticed his color, Ortiz? Don't he seem a little green to ya? His skin's got an unnatural clarity and tint to it, don't you think?" I told Malhotra I hadn't given it much thought, as I was working on a planet holding a vast settlement of the greatest civilization the galaxy—perhaps even the universe—has ever known. I suggested Malhotra do the same.

A few more weeks and we're heading home. Sadly, I'm looking forward to this.

October 11, 2468
Tensions have reached an all time high. No one will go near Mussina, especially after what Malhotra told them. He returned from surveying rock formations above the Great Chamber and demanded we speak privately.

In my quarters, Malhotra told me his story.

"I left the Great chamber and climbed to the top of that rock pile near base camp. I thought I'd seen some inscriptions. I was surveying the surrounding area, thought maybe we'd missed others. I look over towards Mussina's hole. You can hardly see anything with those black tarps over it. Well, I seen him step out from behind one of those things and look around. Then what does he do? He takes his helmet off!"

I asked Malhotra to repeat himself, hoping I'd heard wrong.

"Yeah, I said he took his helmet off. Hell, I know how crazy it sounds, man! I wouldn't believe it if anyone else had told me but I saw it with my own goddamn eyes, Ortiz. The man ain't human! Ain't even a man! Maybe he's an AI! Maybe he's a Martian! Hell, maybe he's a clone! Oh boy, if he's a clone then your ass is on the line. You know the rules, Ortiz. Biological Security Division will bury you so deep someone'll be digging your discredited ass up someday."

I told Malhotra to retire to his quarters and rest. He snorted and stood up.

"Don't treat me like a baby, Ortiz! I got more credentials than you got clean shirts. It was a major gamble for me to come here, what with my standing. You know I thought Mussina was just a washout, a digger with money and no history? Hell, now I know he's something much more dangerous."

With that, Malhotra left. Obviously the stress has become too much for him. Despite all his achievements, I doubt Mussina has mastered the ability to breathe thin nitrogen and sulfurous air at a temperature of 191K.

I am confident Mussina is as human as I, though more difficult to get along with. I almost prefer him to Malhotra. At least Mussina keeps to himself.

October 15, 2468
Today we had a major discovery!
I was cataloguing the impressions in the floors of the Great Chamber. The others were working on their own, when Mussina descended in the elevator and strode down the Great Chamber's ramp, pushing something on an antigrav sled, shouting like he was entering a bar and calling us over to the Hearth.

"I know you've all been wondering what I've been up to. Especially you, Malhotra." Mussina said, smiling as Malhotra's face went slack. "I am sorry to be so extreme about maintaining the sanctity of my work site, but I have worked on digs with many so-called 'professionals' whose clumsiness left artifacts irrevocably damaged. You will forgive me for being so harsh, but what I am about to show you may explain my extreme actions."

He stepped to the Hearth and laid a hand on the tarp covering the payload of the sled. "As you may know, I have worked on all ten of the Transparent Ones sites. At Cit-Bolon-Tum, I came across something I would rather hesitantly call a 'book.' It was created on sheets of a highly flexible metal, thinner than paper yet wholly indestructible. A map in the book clearly showed a star system, a planet in that system and a Transparent Ones settlement there. Another page in this book showed a map of that settlement and some things that would be found there—provided they had not been looted nor any degradation had occurred. Which is highly unlikely given the Transparent Ones' mastery of complex metallurgy—oh, please forgive my digression! As I was saying, the book told of a certain planet in a star system. Lady and gentlemen, we are in that star system. We are on that planet. We are at that settlement."

"Prof. Mussina," I said. "Forgive me but am I to believe you took this 'book' you found on Cit-Bolon-Tum, a UFW protected archaeological site? I've never heard of any 'book.' Furthermore, there are restrictions to removing artifacts from sites—"

"More importantly, what kinda shit is this?!" shouted Malhotra. "A map? A book? Mussina, you crackhead, I think you've been exposed to the atmosphere here. Ortiz, get the medibots ready to treat a very sick man!"

Mussina smiled and reached under the tarp. Malhotra stepped back, no doubt expecting a weapon, and relaxed as Mussina removed a thick, silvery-blue scroll and threw it at Malhotra's feet. It landed not with a metallic clang but softly like paper. We gathered around Malhotra as he picked it up. I noticed with chagrin the seal of the UFW Exoarchaeology division was placed on a corner, thus allowing the item to be transported from the site. Dr. Mussina must know people in high places. Something as valuable as this usually stayed in vaults for handling under the most protected of circumstances. I am frankly jealous that I had never seen it.

It was like a large, square book about half a yard on each side, with several pages of the same thin metallic material. The front was covered with a single Transparent Ones character, while each of the pages was covered with more of the writing. It was not unlike one of our own flexible pedias one carries in the field, yet it was still an *astounding artifact. Some pages contained pictures that moved as we looked at them, and spoke in a strange language of clicks and scratches. Suns rose and fell on planets, and stars moved across skies. Celestial objects leapt from it and hovered over it, leaving trails and lines with markings in Transparent Ones script. Malhotra flipped through it quickly while Mussina continued. So little time for an artifact of such immense importance, yet I had to listen to him!*

"The book—for lack of a better word as it is more like the highly advanced ancestor of one of our pedias than anything else—appears to be a cross between a brochure or an operator's manual of some kind. I took a big chance with my interpretation of what's on those pages, which led me to that southwest corner of the settlement. There, I dug out a large portion of the ruins to uncover something I found 'mentioned' in the book." Mussina pulled back the tarp to reveal an object over a yard in length. Its outer section was made of a whitish stone carved or molded into a long u-shape, like an ancient bathtub with the bottom cut out. On its outer edge were delicately carven Transparent Ones characters. Inside the white stone, globs of a leaden metal filled the interior. Some wrapped around the outer white edge, and these bore holes in the end, almost like sockets. At the top there were numerous indentations, as if to connect to something else, another piece. I could make out a single Transparent Ones character made up of a subtle pattern worn into the top of the leaden pieces.

"Another rock, Mussina?" said Malhotra, fighting to maintain his dignity. "This looks like some melted hunk of plastic. It could be from a gypsy ship that crashed here." I noticed Malhotra's jerky movements. His agitation was beginning to worry me.

"To a mere epigraphist like yourself, yes, Prof. Malhotra. Yes, it's just a rock. To someone like Dr. Ortiz, or myself, who has studied the Transparent Ones our entire professional lives, it is something else. It's more like ... Well, it is a multipurpose instrument. For now, we'll call it 'The Key.'"

Mussina lifted The Key, which appeared quite light in his hands.

"As I said, one of the few things I have learned about the Transparent Ones is that their technology was at its height when they built here and at Cit-Bolon-Tum. At the time these settlements were built, things were so complex as to be deceptively simple, hidden in plain sight. Thus, this Key is so random that it looks like molten metal. Remember, we are primitive sea creatures taking tentative steps onto land in comparison to the Transparent Ones."

"Mussina, y-y-you're talking gibberish," said Morrison, folding his arms across his pressure suit. His stammer always worsened when he was excited or nervous. "I'd like you to s-s-start making sense now. I have some samples I'd like to get b-back to."

"Morrison, you won't have any interest in your precious samples in about one minute. But very well, I'll make it simple for you impatient clods." The smile was wiped from his face. "The Transparent Ones had the technology to build planets, as I said before. Watch closely. This Key is an element in that process."

Mussina turned to the Hearth, shone a light from his glove at the upper right corner of the Hearth and read aloud, waving the light in a seemingly random fashion over the ancient script: "It reads something like this:

'When the elements have been aligned and the system is correctly ... fulfilled,
the Egg is at hand.
All parts as one, the Key opens the Immortal Doors
and the Womb shall build a containing Shell as desired.
May this home be a safe dwelling and harbor great work, thoughts, deeds and
actions,

'blah blah blah' and words to that effect. You get the idea."
"What the hell are you saying, Mussina?" said Malhotra, his face red behind his faceplate.

"Dear Prof. Malhotra, this object here," Mussina hefted the thing in his hands, "is part of how the Transparent Ones made the planets they built their settlements upon."

"There you go again! Prof. Ortiz, I demand that Capt. Valencia be notified that—"

Mussina cut off Malhotra, stepping past him. He walked back towards the center of the Hearth. He stepped onto our elevating platform and raised it six meters higher. There above his head I could see a faint indentation I hadn't noticed before. Mussina raised the Key over his head and pressed it to the wall. There was a sound of rushing air and a muffled metallic bang deep in the wall behind it. A deep groaning emerged from below. The walls trembled as the Hearth, which appeared to be one solid piece of stone, split in two. Light poured out from inside. We instinctively raised our hands, though our visors instantly accommodated for the increasing brightness. The object now hung in midair, above where Mussina had let it go. He drew the hovering platform back as the doors opened to their fullest.

We were now looking upon a smaller chamber with thirty-meter ceilings and five meters in depth. The indentation sloped down gently from the top to the floor. The walls were smooth and glowed a dull red like burning coals. Inside were a pair of two-meter-tall objects, each covered in Transparent Ones writing. One was shaped like a huge tuning fork with one tine about a half meter shorter than the other. This was made of the same leaden material as the inner portion of the Key. The other object was a simple column of unblemished white stone like the outer portion of the Key, with more inscriptions on it. They both hung in midair, rotating slowly as they had for billions of years. The Key slid into place between them without touching and began pulsing with a yellow light, the writing on its outer white ring shining brightly, their iridescence giving them a swirling appearance as if they were written in oil on water.

There was stunned silence from the group, the only sound being a faint hissing coming from our life-support systems.

"How did you ..." asked Morrison.

"Unimportant," said Mussina. "Prof. Ortiz, I recommend we return to Resurgam immediately. A discovery like this needs to be examined closely under the right scientific conditions," said Mussina. "The elements of the Egg can be safely removed from one another, I assure you. This alignment is merely a storage mode. They are safe unless *someone initiates the action sequence. Which is quite impossible without the right knowledge."*

I told Mussina I would consider it, though inwardly I agreed immediately upon seeing it. The UFW needs to see something like this right away. Here on Baaklum, Cha'am we are incapable of properly examining this astounding collection. We need the top facilities of the UFW research labs.

After examining the Egg with the others, I returned to my room to note this new finding. Then I saw the communication from Resurgam. Their captain has gotten orders to return home immediately. I returned to the group and informed them of our departure tomorrow at 0700.

October 16, 2468
We've had an accident.
After Mussina's 'demonstration,' the group slowly and carefully studied the chamber he had uncovered. Obviously, everyone was fascinated with the discovery. But we had to pack up, so there was little time for all but a cursory examination. Mussina left the chamber as Malhotra followed him up the ramp. I returned to my quarters to pack my things. I was engrossed in filing away my notes when Prof. Posada appeared at my door. "Malhotra!" was all he said in a breathless whisper, and I followed him out, donning my suit at the airlock.

We ran to the ridge above the dig site where we found the rest of the team—minus Dr. Mussina—assembled around Malhotra. He'd taken a fall from the top of the ridge. He was unconscious, helmet visor cracked, but Stein had sealed it with emergency sealant. From the angle of his limbs, it was obvious he had suffered numerous broken bones. Fortunately, he was still alive. Morrison and Stein got the antigravity sled and we brought Malhotra down to base camp. The medibots stabilized his condition, and judged him fit for transport. We will bring him back to the ship tomorrow, as a sudden storm has picked up, preventing Resurgam's lander from retrieving.

It's unclear what the professor was doing out there. Malhotra had been spending a great deal of time on the rock pile near our base camp. He told me he was looking for more artifacts but I suspect he'd been spying on Mussina. I wouldn't put it past him. That he claimed Mussina could breathe the atmosphere here on Baaklum Cha'am, I put off to stress.

But I had my doubts about another aspect of the accidents. I went to Prof. Mussina's quarters where I found him sitting on his bunk, dictating into a pedia that he hastily put away as I entered. I asked Dr. Mussina if he knew what might've happened to Malhotra.

"Birth, I imagine," was his response.

Since he was last seen with him, I clarified. Mussina smiled and said he'd left the Great Chamber, Malhotra pelting him with questions, begging to share credit for the discovery since Malhotra had so much knowledge that could be helpful to Mussina.

"As if I need his help," said Mussina. "All he wants is to preserve his delicate place in academia. I've nothing to fear from that Hindu hillbilly. He was probably so busy trying to dig up some last-minute artifact that he tripped over his own clumsy feet. But I

do hope Malhotra recovers. He's done some useful things and he is ... entertaining at least."

I asked Dr. Mussina what he wanted.

"What do you think? I want to see what this technology does! I want to find out what led to their downfall, and I have some clues and evidence as to what it was. I could care less about notoriety. You know how they view my theories. The constant struggle that I faced in my earlier career to have my theories heard and work validated is why I abandoned working within the scientific community in the first place. I spent twenty years toiling in the fields at various digs, surrounded by fools. Then I spent another twenty working privately while my ideas were considered outlandish and largely forgotten. And those that didn't fade from memory soon became accepted. Why should I struggle to keep small-minded, petty individuals happy when I could work on my own? So there's your reason why I work privately and preferably alone, Dr. Ortiz," he said, waving a hand at me.

I was about to bid Dr. Mussina goodnight when he stopped me.

"You know, Dr. Ortiz, I am extremely grateful for your efforts on this dig. Please don't misunderstand me. You are the reason I came out of my retirement to this planet."He smoothed out his hair. "There is the matter of the things we recovered from the Great Chamber. These artifacts we are bringing up are highly technological pieces. The UFW would be very eager to get their hands on them for their own research labs. Their quarantine procedures are so draconian that we'd never see the pieces again. They could end up languishing in a warehouse somewhere while we grow old filling out forms, writing appeals and waiting to examine them in order to bring their meaning to light. I know it is unorthodox—ha ha, what about me isn't?—but is there any way that you could perhaps spirit the pieces aboard? Perhaps by adjusting their labeling slightly?"

I told him I wasn't comfortable doing that.

"I understand that. In exchange for your efforts in the name of science, why of course when we get back to civilization I would gladly credit this discovery to you. I'm no fan of being in the spotlight, as you may well understand. I will simply return to my private work. Truly. My career is nearly at an end, but this would be quite a feather in your cap. It would be an honor to turn the responsibility of bringing these artifacts to the public over to you, sir."

I told him I would strongly consider it and left Dr. Mussina to pack.

Back in my quarters, I weighed the various circumstances. While I don't trust Prof. Mussina completely, I doubt he would have tried to kill or injure Malhotra. It's clear Mussina holds Malhotra in rather low regard. Even more obvious is that Malhotra was deeply bothered by Prof. Mussina's abilities. I see little reason not to agree with Mussina's theory of how Malhotra fell. He was no doubt trying to salvage his reputation, though he need not worry. I will see to it he is well taken care of on his journey home.

At Mussina's suggestion, I must be circumspect in speaking with the captain about the exact nature of the artifacts. I wouldn't want to cause him any undue alarm nor would I want to leave the objects (what do I call them? The Egg? The Globe? The Stones?) here on Baaklum Cha'am. I will inform him of their delicacy. Separate storage of the items found in the Great Chamber should reduce the risk of accident. Though I am not even sure what they do. Mussina seems to think they hold the potential for great power. I trust him to show me their true nature when we get them into a laboratory for study.

Oh, the time! I must finish packing. So much to do before they come to retrieve us. I do so look forward to returning to Earth.

CHAPTER FOURTEEN
Absolution

"That asshole Ortiz!" Leonardo shouted and threw the pedia at the wall.

"What?" said Baz in alarm, spinning to look at him.

"He brought unauthorized, potentially lethal alien technology onto my ship without telling me." Leonardo fumed quietly for a moment. "If he wasn't already dead, I'd kill him myself."

"Those things Mussina stole?"

"Yes. They're some kind of heavy-duty alien tech." Leonardo picked up the pedia, tossed it to Baz and told him the short version of Ortiz's diaries. In the silence afterward, Leonardo rubbed his chin, noting the stubbly growth. He'd failed to take his inhibitors but didn't much care. "Get me the manifest from their storage unit."

Baz put the information up on the display between them. He held up a finger and scrolled down. Pictures of artifacts and flora retrieved from the planet appeared in midair, names and numbers underneath them. Baz stopped at items marked in red letters. "After I uploaded this, I reconnected the manifest to the concierge box in the storage unit. And ... Yep, those're the things he took. But look here," said Baz, noting four red lines. "We thought he only took artifacts. Seems he took some other stuff, too."

"Their research AIs?" said Leonardo.

"What do you think he needed them for?"

"The information within?" said Leonardo. Baz shrugged. He leaned forward in his chair, looking at the main display. "What're Alpha and Bravo telling us?"

"Not much, unfortunately. We're learning more about this planet's topography than anything else right now." Baz switched to the feed from the Fli8 units, false color images, noting temperature, gravitational and atmospheric variations. A blue star indicated *Resurgam*, with the Fli8 units yellow triangles some distance away. "They're fifty klicks out. We're inside a flat-bottomed crater, a hundred klicks across. Walls are about five klicks high all around. Very uniform and very even."

"Just like Dwi8 said." Leonardo remembered Ortiz's conversation with this Mussina from the journals. "Mathematically precise."

"Exactly." Baz pointed. "You see the geological stuff it's turning up? Spectrogram is weird; things clumped together in bizarre combinations. Mixtures that shouldn't hold together are spread over the surface in strange ways; again in very uniform patterns. Some of this should be producing adverse reactions bad enough to eat through the hull or—shit, they should have exploded the moment this planet formed." Leonardo watched the readout as it reproduced the unnatural uniformity, a latticework of minerals overlaid by another layer and then another. Something came to mind, something else Mussina said to Dr. Ortiz about the uniformity in Baaklum Cha'am's make-up tugged at him.

"This is the surface. Anything about the crust?"

"Nope," said Baz with a shake of his head. "Alpha and Bravo are using their best and biggest scopes to no good."

"As if the planet doesn't want to be seen," said Leonardo. "Just like the scans of Baaklum Cha'am."

"Now that you mention it, yeah, I remember that bugging me. Hey, Jason?"

"Yes, sir."

"Are you able to penetrate the surface at all?"

"No, sir. I attempted to do so but interference yielded nothing below a shallow depth. Instead I have been training the arrays on constellations in order to determine our location."

"Okay but how shallow was it?"

"One meter, sir."

"Shit," said Baz, with a tone of amazement. Leonardo noticed something on the manifest.

"Jason," said Leonardo. "Send Dwi8 out with one of the core samplers from the survey team. I want at least five samples from a diverse group. Every five kilometers or so."

"Yes, sir."

"One more thing."

"Sir?"

"Where the hell are we?"

"Unclear, sir." A screen appeared before them and split into a series of four star maps. "These are the Dark Rims at K'axob." The upper left screen grew a yellow ring around a slowly blinking star. "Sol is here." The lower right screen drew a ring around a small yellow star. "Somewhere in between them," said Jason, as the upper right and lower left screens' frames glowed yellow, "is this planet."

"You've shown me this before, just in a different way," Leonardo noted dourly.

"Yes, sir. Now, here is the current atmosphere." Four images merged into one. At the bottom was a rounded metal surface of some kind with low domes and antenna and protuberances poking out. For a moment he couldn't tell what it was. Then Leonardo recognized it as the port surface of the ship, near the bow. "Something is preventing our sensors from probing outside the atmosphere."

"So nothing new?"

"No."

"Keep me posted." Leonardo looked at Baz, who threw his hands up in the air.

"Guess we won't get any transmissions, huh?"

"No. None at all."

"This is impossible. Jason's got stuff in this ship that can practically look through a planet. Now we can't even see underneath the surface nor beyond the sky."

"It's like looking into the ocean when I was a kid," said Leonardo, staring at the atmospheric readout on the display. "It got cleaner as I got older. Most of the time, containment shields on the wrecks kept the waste in. Eventually they got these weird fish they'd bred that drank the oil. *Gutbunnies*, they called 'em. Ugliest things ever, like a fish turned inside out. Anyway ... My mom'd sometimes rent a jenny and get it to suck out the oil from those things. Sell it off to the other *limpiaristes* or keep it for herself if there wasn't much to share. But when the shields'd fail, you'd be out on the water and all of a sudden there'd be this darkness pooling underneath the surface. Then you had to get back to shore or your engine would catch fire or worse."

"Jesus. I thought growing up on the Ring communes sucked. Planetside sucks much worse."

"It was an especially shitty part of Earth. You were either born into it or got used to it."

Baz nodded and returned to the display in front of him.

Leonardo stared at the screen, brooding over the situation. Then a blinking red dot appeared in the lower left-hand corner of the screen. He opened it and read the message.

Leonardo jumped out of his chair and over the horseshoe faster than the hairs on his neck and arms could rise up in alarm. Baz turned at the disturbance.

"What the—"

"She's awake! *Drina's awake!*"

CHAPTER FIFTEEN
Marooned

In Drina's quarters alarms shrieked before Leonardo barely remembered to disarm them. The medical avatar stood over Drina, ghostly hand at her wrist. It looked up at him.

"I didn't want to alarm you, sir, but—"

"Never mind that," Leonardo said, approaching Drina's throne. He knelt and took her hand. Drina's eyes fluttered.

"She still needs rest, but should be responsive."

Leonardo gazed at Drina's face. Her skin was a metallic white, cheeks propping up dark circles smeared beneath sunken eyes. The cables in her hair fluttered in response to any minute movement in their mistress's body.

Drina opened her eyes with labored, fluttering blinks. She looked first at the avatar then Leonardo. Her eyes showed mild confusion. A light furrow appeared across her brow as her lips parted.

"Are we still married?" she asked Leonardo in a rasp.

"Uh, yes," he said, unable to suppress a small smile.

"Shit," she said, closing her eyes. Leonardo looked at the medibot. The avatar glanced at the monitor above her bed.

"She's unconscious, sir." Leonardo stood, releasing her hand. He didn't expect a romantic reunion but couldn't stop the cold feeling as his heart sank down into his belly.

"The best thing for her right now, I guess." He slid down next to her bed and put his head in his hands. "Avatar off." He sat immobile, relieved and trying not to think. He listened to his breath and the occasional rustle of Drina's cables as they moved in her sleep.

He heard soft coughing and looked up at Drina. She was awake, eyes open. He sat up, knelt by the bed and she looked at him, expressionless, as if reading the instructions for an appliance.

"Hey," Leonardo said.

"Hey."

"How do you feel?" Leonardo asked.

"I feel ... like shit, honestly. This is the worst re-entry ever. The medibot's being frigging coy, too. Won't tell me what the hell's going on. Said there were some problems with the ship. Where's Ramon—I mean Dr. Afrika? Still asleep?"

"He, uh ...." Leonardo faltered at the mention of the doctor.

"You know, it's just ..." She closed her eyes and swallowed, which caused her obvious pain. "I want to be done. Uck. My throat hurts." A nearby tube drifted to her mouth and she drank.

"I feel the same way."

"Are we still holding near Titan? Medibot says there's a problem." Leonardo stifled the urge to snort at the understatement.

"Not exactly." Leonardo got a chair and sat. "Drina, we've crashed." She opened her eyes wide at him.

"What?" she asked. "How?" She looked around then stopped, staring at him without quite seeing. Leonardo knew she was consulting her implants, struggling to get information from the astrogation systems she used like another sense.

"Don't bother. You're disconnected from the network until you get better."

"What?" Drina spat, then sank deeper into her pillow. Leonardo saw, with relief, how the small burst of aggression wore her out.

"Easy. You're lucky to be alive." He leaned back. "Don't push it by getting upset."

"Okay. Fine." She swallowed with effort and a wince. Leonardo watched her grow calm. "What happened?"

Leonardo told his wife everything while she lay on her throne, eyelids fluttering, cables reshuffling and jaw clenching at the particularly hard parts. As Leonardo outlined the strikes against them, he could tell Drina was beginning to lay blame at his feet. He left out what the medibots told him. When he was finished, she lay quiet for a few minutes, soaking it in. Finally, she opened her eyes.

"When can I access to the network? I can work out some routings so when we get into *Sparky* then—"

"Not so fast. You're in no condition to resume duty. The medibots need to do tests to see if you're okay. If you survive that, then maybe I will."

"Leo, I'm not a baby. I've seen duty in much worse shape than this."

"Doubt it. We've got time to get you back in shape."

"Please don't give me your 'fit for duty' crap, Leo."

"Drina, look—"

"Half the time you're better oiled than the engines on this ship," she said, eyes closed. Leonardo stood and kicked his chair back to the wall.

"Jesus wept! For a moment I was actually happy that our *Astrogatrix* was alive and conscious." He let the slur sink in. "Astrogatrix" was an epithet cooked up in the early days of the UFW by backwards thinking men fearful of a woman in charge of their ships. Though not something he personally felt, he knew its effect on Drina was the same as for all other astrogators. He drew himself up to full height and adjusted his sleeves. She fumed as much as her fatigue would allow.

"Listen to me, Asgr. Alexandrina Valencia Reyes: *Rest*. That's an order. You need it. Especially since you're coming back to active duty cold fucking turkey off of diaphanoxamine."

Drina's lip twitched slightly. Leonardo left her for the bridge then did a sudden about-face. The last thing he needed was Baz and his questions. How stupid to get excited about Drina reawakening as if she'd be happy to see him. He knew full well she'd be no different: coldly civil in public, acidic in private. That he expected she'd wake content to find herself still marooned in their marriage on a dead planet made him angrier. Even the sounds of his footsteps through the empty halls mocked his infantile emotional expectations.

He went to the D-FAC. The lights came on instantly as he stepped in. He approached the food fabricators and poked buttons absently, seeing the same "UNAVAILABLE" appear on-screen every time. More lousy MREs, he thought, though he wasn't even hungry.

He turned and looked out over the chilled, empty sterility of the room. He needed something to occupy himself or he knew he'd hit the Bun-Ho and hard. He dropped onto a seat and allowed himself a few moments of uncharacteristic self-pity. The cold recycled air made the ship feel even more like a mausoleum, a museum to the hopeless effort of the last few years of his career. How tired he was, always checking up on the ship and waiting for the next problem to crop up and set them back. His uniform was dialed up to keep him calm and relaxed, but the cracks were beginning to show and deepen.

"No self-pity," he muttered to himself, remembering his mother saying this when he was little and whined about not having a toy he wanted due to their poverty.

Their situation had to change soon. He wasn't sure how much he could take.

"No self-pity." Louder this time. His drill sergeant, Markus Kloos, shouting at him after a day-long hike along a ridge in Bolivia.

They could just pile into *Sparky*. Scuttle *Resurgam* remotely and Drina—when she was healed—could get them to charted space without having to actually astrogate. There would invariably be questions, but Leonardo was considered such a lost cause that any lie he told would be passed off as the words of a drunk. It wasn't like his career could get any worse.

"No. Self. *Pity*." He shouted this time. His voice echoed off the tables and cold dead display screens. He could no more desert this situation with all the unanswered questions than he could banish his fear with shouting.

A ping sounded in his ear just as a small red triangle appeared and blinked in his left eye.

"Leo?" said Baz.

"Yeah?" Leonardo answered.

"The Fli8s turned up something very—"

"On my way."

On the bridge, Baz had the real-time video from the Fli8s on the central main screen. Both showed the ice-covered planet, two different regions hardly different from the other.

"What?" asked Leonardo, slightly out of breath.

"I was just watching the one on the left. Nothing too surprising; a lot of snow and ice. Then this one on the right began to pique my interest." Baz wound the video back. It showed the lip of the crater, wide and long, in a bright green arc across the screen. Suddenly from out of the white and shades of gray in the snow a red dot appeared. Followed by another. Then another.

"And those are?" Leonardo asked.

"Tracking points. Fli8 caught the scent of material from Baaklum Cha'am on the sled. Like bread crumbs, right?" Leonardo nodded. "Like the old fairy story."

"A trail to grandma's house?" he asked.

Baz turned with an eyebrow cocked. "Wrong fairy tale." He pointed to the screen. "You get the idea, though. Voila ..."

A red line snaked from the hulk of *Resurgam* to where it stopped and blinked at the crater's edge.

"Now check this out," Baz said with a rolling mudra. The feed zoomed in close to the planet's surface. The rocky edge of the crater blended with snow into rough walls rising from the endless waste—except for a well-concealed cave.

"Trail stops cold right there." Leonardo nodded. "He didn't go over the wall. Those sleds don't climb that well, but—"

"Nope. I had Fli8 zoom in there to look for any indication of that. Nothing." Baz tapped at the display, pointing to a small square with a multicolored readout of the crater wall. "Check out the thermographic image in the inset. There's about +3K difference. He went down that fucking *hole*."

"How big is it?"

"About four meters across and three high."

"Where're the Fli8s now?"

"Alpha's holding steady over the cave. Bravo's cruising somewhere else on the planet. And look what it turned up." Baz waved a finger at the left screen. The image flickered back to a view of the planet's largely flat and desolate surface. A red circle appeared and blinked over an indistinct feature of the landscape. Baz flipped his wrist and the image zoomed in. There, on a rocky outcropping sat a gray, hulking, man-made object. An overlay measured it out at seven meters from each of the four stabilizing feet and six meters high from the ground up to the end of the wide barrel pointed at the sky. Strewn near it lay a mass of deflated landing bubbles and a parachute.

"It's a—"

"KALI-728 EMP Cannon," said Baz. "Looks like it was dropped off recently. Just before our arrival perhaps?"

"Fuck."

"It probably helped disable the ship. You never know what those things'll do in certain atmospheres."

"So Mussina was rendezvousing with someone or a group."

"Yep. And they're down in that hole, I bet."

"Have Bravo maintain position there. If it finds nothing else man-made on the surface, then we'll let it blow that cannon up."

"Got it." Baz began typing into the holokeyboard in front of him.

"We have to get into that hole," Leonardo said. "Someone's got to follow him."

"I'll go down there once we make sure the surface is clear," said Baz without looking up from his keyboard.

"No." Leonardo shook his head vigorously.

"Well you sure as shit aren't going, Leo. *Captain*."

"But—"

"Can't send Drina, either," Baz said without looking up from the keyboard.

"Obviously, smart-ass."

"We can leave Dwi8 here and do the recon ourselves," said Leonardo.

Baz turned around, mouth open to speak.

"Hear me out. We'll set him up and have him on repairs. It should be reasonably safe."

"Famous last words," said Baz.

"Perhaps, but we can go out and be back in a few hours. Jason will protect Drina. We've got an antigrav sled. God forbid, anything happens, Jason'll put her in *Sparky* and butt the hell out offworld."

"What if we encounter 'them' out there?" said Baz.

"Then we deal with *them*. We're gonna meet *them* either way, might as well try and see what we're up against, right?"

"I guess. Okay, I'll get ready as soon as I finish this," Baz said, typing. "Fuck! Everything'd be a hell of a lot easier with implants."

"Implants. That reminds me. I forgot to tell you why we're alive and the crew is dead." Baz looked at Leo. Leonardo tapped his right temple.

"Implants?" Baz said.

"Yes," said Leonardo. "Something in Mussina's illegal trojan routines killed them all. They traded media plug-ins with him. Possibly the same thing that tried to get at Drina."

"The Sublime Christ At Rest," Baz said, rubbing his forehead. "I guess the demotion was good in one way. Well, except for Drina."

"How is she?" asked Baz.

"Alive. Cranky, but she's okay. The 'bots say she's fine. But she needs more help."

"I'm sorry, Leo."

"Thanks. I'm not her favorite person these days."

"I noticed."

"You'd be blind if you didn't. She blames *me* for the crash, for one thing." Leonardo sat down. "Frankly, the blame rests on everyone's shoulders. A bunch of things we should have seen coming got past us. I hate when it comes down to rookie moves. We're gonna catch hell for the lax measures that allowed this."

"Don't be too sure. This has never happened before, Leo."

"But they—whoever Mussina and his cohorts are—found a big hole in our defenses; infiltrating an archeological team, getting aboard a ship that gets overlooked and then pulling this off took some work. As if our return weren't going to be hard enough."

Both men stared silently at the screens before them, revealing an ever-widening array of information that never seemed to coalesce into a clear idea of what they were dealing with.

Further and further, darker and darker, as Leonardo's mother always used to say.

CHAPTER SIXTEEN
Revelations

A ping sounded in Leonardo's ear, startling him from his troubling thoughts.

"Sir," came the voice of Dwi8. "I've completed the survey of the planet's soil. It was quite difficult to get acceptable samples. The coring device could barely—"

"Thank you, Dwi8. Upload what you found and then meet Col. Al-Mushtarii and I in the main bay. We have another job for you."

"Yes, sir." Leonardo beckoned Baz and they left the bridge.

They met Dwi8 in the main bay. The atmosphere had been fully restored, though it remained cool. Leonardo smelled a sharp tang of unfamiliar odors. He traced the source to where Dwi8 stood in a puddle near the airlock doors, precipitate from outside melting around its feet. Its shiny black exterior was wet with melting ice and sulfurous smears. Five core samples lay near it in clear sample tubes, next to the coring device. Leonardo thought Dwi8 looked like a child come in out of the mud to clean up before dinner. Baz and Leonardo went to a display panel by the bay door and beckoned Dwi8 over.

"Baz, hold on a second. What are the chances someone's out there watching us?"

Baz regarded the display of his pedia for a few minutes, scrolling through the images from the Fli8 drones.

"Doubtful," said Baz. "If they did, they would have shot both Fli8s out of the sky or come to finish us off. Or that EMP cannon would've shot them down. I think that it was just armed for only one or two big shots. No, I'm sure they think we're all dead. Otherwise there would be some kind of sentry at that hole."

Leonardo thought it over while pacing back and forth. Baz was probably right; they were safe from reprisals—for now—but they were unable to repel an attack by an unknown enemy with unknown firepower. Then again, not sending Dwi8 could make them sitting ducks.

***

He left the bay and checked in on Drina. Leonardo found her resting as before, with little change in her condition. He drew a chair up near her throne and sat, waiting. Eventually she let out a sigh and turned to look at him.

"Leo ..." she said, drawing his name out with a weary tone.

"How do you feel?"

"All right."

"Good. Eaten anything?"

"Not really. The 'bots are feeding me some nasty paste but it makes me feel better."

"You're down a few quarts, so ..." He let his words trail off, not knowing where to take the conversation. Small talk was never his strong suit, especially when larger issues loomed.

"Leo, I—"

"Look, Drina. No one's perfect. I know things are terrible right now. Worse than ever. But we have to work together."

"I know," she said, as if swallowing bitter medicine. "I just—"

"I don't know how you got the extra di-hex, I just need to know you're gonna be clean enough to function on this crew."

Drina looked at him with slowly building incredulity.

"With all due respect, *sir*," she said, without any respect. "I am not the only one with a substance abuse problem. Sir."

Leonardo counted to ten slowly, patiently drawing out the numbers in his head like hauling nets up from the ocean depths.

"Drina, I know what you're thinking. But what happened was everyone's responsibility: the whole crew, you, Baz and me. Now—"

"Leo, you were drunk at Newhope. You were drunk! The FMR snuck in with the miners and set those bombs off because you were fucking drunk! Don't give me some bullshit about spreading the blame around. It's all your—"

"As if you weren't out of your mind on the di-hex when that rescue got fubared."

Leonardo stood up.

"You were so fucked up I had to cover for you that day. Damn it!" he shouted, kicking the chair so it flew and banged into the doorway. "Everyone was slacking at that! We got caught off guard. 'Just a quick rescue,' I said. Didn't think it'd be a sneak attack by the FMR. So what if Baz and I were playing cards? You were too messed up for watch duty anyway."

Leonardo stabbed his finger in her direction with the last sentence. He dropped his arm to his side and saw the collection of printed photos stuck on the wall near her door. One was of them together at a table, a cake covered in candles between them, celebrating the eighteenth anniversary of Drina's Integration Day aboard the *Wellstone*.

***

A week after that picture was taken, they were docked at Pellas Station.

A distress call came in. A mining operation on one of the gas giant Newhope's moons was experiencing geological instability after the explosion of a major pocket of methane they'd opened while drilling. The UFW wanted the miners out before everything collapsed, despite the pleas of the DN Powers Mining Company to keep them there. The

FMR had been sighted in the area and they didn't want to take any chances despite the wealth of minerals at stake.

Leonardo volunteered the crew, taking the *Wellstone* out of orbit and into hi-space two hours later.

Leonardo remembered being woken by Jason when they entered the Newhope system. The mission was a routine retrieval of the miners and their families, with a crew of repair walky-talkyies dropped planetside to shore up damage for a safe return. The main bay was reconfigured as temporary shelter for the miners. Food stores were stocked with nanny-made supplies and there were several thousand tons of MREs. The *Wellstone* was ready. Leonardo loved a mission like this: smooth, fast, everything going as planned. Even with minor hiccups, he liked the effortless flow as everything fell into place.

He felt a serene confidence as they slid into orbit above the massive orange planet. The evacuation was orderly. Seismic readings from the *Wellstone* indicated the planet was more unstable than originally believed. Over fifteen hundred men, women and children were evacuated in less than twelve hours using the *Wellstone's* biggest troop transports, the *S. L. Dunbar* and the *Arjuna*. Families were housed in shelters on the floor of the bay, checked by medics on arrival and given a warm meal the moment they were cleared. Leonardo felt a sense of pride as he stood watching these families, tired and exhausted but grateful as they stood in line waiting for food. He marveled at the ship's ability to turn itself into a refuge for people fleeing mortal danger as easily as it turned into a stronghold for battle. The long rows of cots separated by canvas walls stretched off to the other end of the enormous bay. It wasn't comfortable but it was safer than where they'd been hours before. Their belongings and the mining equipment stood in long containers stacked by the doors of the bay.

"Everything has a place and everything in its place," said Baz as they reviewed the manifest before signing off. They'd live here for a week before being placed in a mining community on Snowdown.

Leonardo arranged for movies to be shown in the bay; something harmless like a Frontier Family Tale or old Earth stories he had on file. "I love these old cartoons," Baz said, watching an ancient battle between cat and mouse waged large on the wall. The evacuees sat and watched the movies, eating real popcorn Leonardo scored in a poker game from the grain carrier *Newton's Fourth Law*. He watched for a while before he and Baz went to the officers' mess to play cards.

Drina was scheduled to be on watch. He went to her quarters to brief her, stopping short just inside the doorway. She sat on her throne, eyelids fluttering and a weak smile across her face. Leonardo shook his head, switching off the overhead light. She was deep in the di-hex and wouldn't be any good for at least twelve hours. So they could slowly cruise the Newhope system until she was sober.

Leonardo produced a bottle of Bun-Ho Premium Blend and opened it while Baz dealt cards. They drank, played, and ate popcorn. During their third round, Baz was winning when Jason summoned Leonardo.

"There appears to be a problem with some of the colonists, sir."

"Deal with it," said Leonardo.

"They asked me to speak directly to you, sir. It seems they do not like dealing with me."

"Something their administrators can't handle?" Leonardo said, tipping his glass back into his throat. He looked at his cards and wondered if Baz wasn't cheating again.

"It appears someone believes their children's toys were accidentally stowed away in a container. The children are scared and can't sleep without them, sir." Baz snickered and Leo shot him a look, then smiled.

"Remind them the containers are sealed while we are under way and will not be opened until we reach Snowdown." Leonardo laid a card on the table and Baz made a face.

"Sir, I have. They are very adamant , saying we are not providing adequately for the welfare of their children. Also some are complaining that there are religious items that they cannot be without in the containers."

"Religious items?" said Baz. "What kind of—"

"Tell them we'll get the children some warm milk," said Leonardo. "As for the religious—"

Leonardo heard a distant boom. The ship rocked. Alert symbols flashed in his HUD and began to flood with urgent status reports.

"Jason? Sitrep."

Leonardo and Baz leapt from the table, scattering cards, popcorn and glasses. They ran to the bridge.

"Explosion in the cargo bay originating from one of the containers the colonists wished to open. There's catastrophic atmospheric decompression. I've sealed off all areas and—"

Two more muted explosions came from far away and brought another jolt to the ship.

"Jesus, Jason! What the hell is happening?" yelled Baz as they entered the bridge. It was alive with activity, twenty crew members scrambling to control the situation. Screens flickered and dozens of voices chattered over comm lines as the entire ship jumped into action. Leonardo ran into the center and took over from the duty officer.

"The second explosion occurred at the other end of the bay near the forward doors. Emergency teams have been sent in."

"Seal that hole up now," Leonardo stepped into the horseshoe and scanned the six screens before him. Two showed the fore and aft sections of the main bay. Leonardo saw the enormous hole blown into the hull. The camera shook as the vacuum tore away anything that wasn't secured; bodies and debris flew out. Corpses collided midair or with the jagged edges of the hole, torn in half as they were finally sucked out into open space. Repair walky-talkies and stevedrones crawled out from their nests like giant metal spiders, immediately going to work at the hole with sealant foam and reinforcing plates. Inside the hull, nannies worked to seal the hole with their larger counterparts. Jason's voice rang out into the bridge.

"Fire control in the port and starboard corridors is disabled. Analysis indicates use of heavy incendiaries."

Leonardo looked to the left screen showing the corridor leading down to the main bay. What wasn't obscured by smoke showed the corridor engulfed in flames, fat flaming droplets of the incendiary substance dripping from walls and ceiling. The corridor was sealed off from all human contact until fire teams suppressed the fire.

"Jason," yelled Leonardo.

"The second and third explosions came from IEDs left in the corridor by two of the colonists. No, sir, it appears to have *been* two of the colonists."

"What?"

"This is from camera 19, port corridor, thirty seconds prior to the explosion," said Jason. The central monitor switched to the same corridor, now free of smoke and flame. From the left came a group of colonists behind six soldiers. Suddenly one of them broke through the column of soldiers, running towards the doors. The soldiers spun round and raised their rifles. The runner, a heavyset man, turned and flung open his vest revealing some kind of mechanism hidden underneath. He slapped a hand to his chest while shouting something before the camera went white from a blast that emerged from the man's chest. When the flash receded, bodies were aflame.

"A suicide bomber?" said Baz.

"Looks like it," said Leonardo. "Starboard cameras?"

"The same, sir," said Jason. "Though different methods were used." The screen flickered to a view of the opposite corridor. A trio of soldiers led a group of colonists slowly down the corridor, one of them pointing and speaking. The colonists were a group of a dozen or so children with three adults, two females and one male. They moved along slowly, the children looking around while the soldier spoke.

"That's Cpl. Leung. Told him to give small group tours of the—"

Baz stopped speaking as a woman in the group rushed forward as in the other video. She lunged at the soldiers, made a movement inside her vest and said something, her face wild and ecstatic. Then came the explosion. After the flash the small bodies encircled in smoke writhed before succumbing to the flames.

"Children. My God ..." said Leonardo. "Used as human shields ..."

"Bastards," said Baz, rising from his seat. He looked at the real-time view where fire roared unabated and the doors remained closed. "Goddamn it, Jason, where's the fucking fire control? Now!"

"Sir, fire control is inoperable. The atmosphere was flushed after the explosion but these incendiaries can burn without oxygen. It will take approximately three to ten minutes to get into the corridor. Repair teams are still resealing the main bay." Leonardo watched helplessly as they worked furiously.

"Baz, you have the bridge. Jason, I want a medical team ready at those bulkhead doors!"

"Already in place, sir."

Leonardo leapt from the horseshoe and ran down the corridor to the lift. He punched the button and the doors opened. Stepping inside, he placed a palm on the panel and shouted, "Valencia. Emergency override. Speed restraints off!" Leonardo barely had time to brace against the back wall before the doors slammed shut and the lift shot down the length of the massive ship. The g-force was not so strong that he couldn't move inside, slinking along the walls until he got near the front. As he did, the lift shuddered to a halt, the green light above the doors glowing as they slid open.

He stepped into a corridor filled with several dozen emergency-suited crew members eager to rush in and save whom they could. Leonardo searched around and found the ranking officer.

"Sgt. Tamro!" he shouted.

"Sir!" the sergeant said, turning and saluting. "We're unable to get into the corridor, sir. The explosion was so intense that the mechanisms are temporarily jammed. Nannies are working to get the doors open."

"At ease." The sergeant relaxed. Leonardo made his way to the bulkhead besides the doors. He put a hand near the door, feeling heat emanate from it. He turned to a wall panel nearby and opened a video feed from the main bay.

Stevedrones had nearly sealed the hole as others crawled over the walls near the containers, closely examining them. This time they were opened and searched carefully, looking for hidden traps and explosives.

The shelters, which had minutes before stood like so much laundry hung out to dry, were gone. A few supports stood from moorings in the floor while stray cords fluttered in the tug of vacuum. There was almost no trace of human life on the floor of the bay. Leonardo switched between cameras, even switching into the views of drones on the floor. No sign of thirty-five hundred people. Were they all sucked out into space?

They waited in the corridor for nearly an hour. The door mechanisms were heavily damaged, only opening with effort from the nannies and requiring a final effort by the soldiers to pry them open. As they did this, Leonardo suited up in protective gear and grabbed a fire tool from a rack, eyeing the blade and hoping for a chance to bury it in an FMR insurgent's head.

Finally they opened the shield doors into the corridor.

Smoke poured from within, oily, black and cloying. The fire control crews dove in first, dousing the flaming walls with foaming flame suppressant. The emergency crews went in through the tunnel of safety and went to work on the inner doors. Leonardo followed them, fire tool in hand. He worked with the men to get the door open, cursing and grunting alongside as they forced the heavy slabs apart.

A narrow crack opened in the four-yard-high door, and a child's hand slid through, covered in blood. Something blocking the mechanisms cleared and suddenly the doors flew open. Human bodies tumbled down onto the crews, knocking them back in a wave of corpses, disembodied limbs and gore. The whole mess dropped and slid through the door and slid to the ground in a wet, slippery avalanche. The crewmen scrambled out from underneath it and recoiled, caught between the last throes of the fire and a wall of dead bodies. Leonardo stood slack jawed in the midst of his horrified men. The fire tool slid from his hand and clanged against the floor.

The bodies spread out before them in a thick, gory tangle for almost a hundred feet into the main bay. Piled high near the portal, they thinned out further away; those were the ones who died before they could even get close to the doors. It was all too easy to see what had happened: first, the explosion came and those nearest suffered least. Those not immediately sucked into space held on for dear life only to succumb to the tug and deprivation of vacuum. Those farthest from the hole panicked and ran for the exits, which were blocked by the suicide bombers. These people died in the ensuing panic. Those trampled underfoot were almost lucky; the rest endured slow death by asphyxiation and the boiling away of their internal liquids for an excruciating minute or more. The bodies at the top of the piles bore evidence of being torn apart by others in desperation.

Once the hole was resealed and atmosphere restored in the enormous bay, the bodies lay waiting identification and eventual disposal or preparation for returning to their home worlds.

From faraway, Leonardo heard voices. He was practically blind to the signals and status reports flashing in his HUD. All he could see was the ghastly, improvised killing floor in the middle of his ship.

"Sir!" shouted Tamro, piercing his horror and breaking him out of his grim reverie. "Sir, how do we proceed?"

How to proceed through and move into action amidst such atrocity? he wondered. How could you proceed when your entire being screamed at you to run and bleach out the mind with whatever was handy. Leonardo's training and years of experience evaded him, leaving him feeling of small, afraid and alone.

"Tell the men to move forward carefully," Leonardo said after a pause. He shook his head and blinked a few times to snap himself back into reality. "Move through and look for survivors. Secure the space. Uh ... Follow me."

"Yes, sir!" shouted Tamro. "All right, people! Listen up! Captain wants us to move out and stay sharp! Eyes out for survivors."

The whole damn thing is wrong, thought Leonardo. He felt something inside him shut off. The buzz from the Bun-Ho was long gone. He wouldn't need to adjust his chems now to keep himself alert and aware. Later, he'd wonder if AIs felt this way, seeing and acting yet not feeling anything. A twinge of realization would work through him and burn something awake briefly when he saw a dead child or a small arm or leg torn from the body that had owned it. Then the numbness would slam down again and he'd move along.

When they finally secured the space—Leonardo wasn't sure how long it took, whether it was minutes, hours or days—he went to the epicenter of the blast. Walky-dogs flitted about on multiple limbs, the flash of detection equipment from their headpieces and snouts blinking as they took hundreds of pictures a second for Jason to analyze. Leonardo tore his fire mask off and spoke.

"Jason, what was it?" The walky-dog nearest looked up and sat on its haunches, limbs folding up as a display screen materialized before him.

"Sir, it was an IED of unique design using highly common elements mixed to deliver a maximum yield. I believe in the hurry to get them aboard before another quake, this container was overlooked." Leonardo looked at the display and saw the forensic recreation of a complex contraption loaded inside the container. It would always bother Leonardo that later forensic examinations could not determine the exact make-up of the explosive.

"And the suicide bombers?"

"A similar compound was used, tuned to the chemistry of the wearer's DNA. The devices they wore were injectors that turned their blood explosive." Jason showed him the video of the two bombers, side by side. The explosions replayed and zoomed in on their abdomens.

"Who were they?" asked Leonardo.

"We've found evidence they were from somewhere near Sol."

"Sol? Who would be out here committing terrorism? The miners were loyal to the UFW."

"Yes, sir, but—"

"Play the feed on repeat. Focus on their faces." Leonardo watched the feed again. They looked unfamiliar and normal at first, growing disturbed and agitated in the moments before detonating themselves. The male said something, mouth moving over and over again.

"What is he saying?"

"It appears to be, 'The Harvestman will emerge again.'"

"What does that mean? 'The Harvestman?' Define and analyze 'Harvestman.'" Jason acknowledged, the walky-dog nodding in assent. After a few seconds it spoke.

"Harvestman. Arachnid species from Earth. Phalangids or Opiliones are eight-legged invertebrate animals belonging to the order Opiliones in the class Arachnida, in the subphylum Chelicerata of the phylum Arthropoda. Over 6,300 species of Phalangids have been discovered worldwide on Earth. Harmless arachnids known for exceptionally long walking legs, compared to body size. The difference between harvestmen and spiders is that in harvestmen the two main body sections—the abdomen with ten segments and cephalothorax, or prosoma and opisthosoma—are nearly joined, so that they appear to be one oval structure; they—"

"Enough," said Leonardo. "How does it relate?"

"Unclear. It seems to bear no relevance to anything we have found. I will continue to check records for any information."

"You said they were from Sol, Jason."

"Yes, sir. From *near* Sol, but not Earth. The group in the port corridor was being led back to the brig. I've just gotten the reports from the rescue teams. These colonists carried talismans of a peculiar nature and documents. I have determined the talismans to be of rock found only on Mars." Leonardo shuddered. No mention of Mars was ever good. "The documents carry specific instructions to carry out acts on Newhope 15."

"The FMR?"

"Yes, sir. The Free Mars Republic was most certainly behind this attack."

***

"I took the hit for you, Drina."

Leonardo paced slowly around the room, hissing out his words.

"Didn't check the colonists in like I should have. Protocols are there for a reason. If I'd followed them, I would have noticed the rigged container. I turned off the biometric scanners since I figured everyone would be agitated anyway, so that's all they would read. I got cocky. And you were so out of it, I let you off the hook. My poor wife"— Leonardo shook his head in mock pity—"Ha! My poor, dear Astrogatrix. I let them think I had completely dropped the ball, when it was you tweaked out of your mind! Came out of the bay with blood all over me while you were still cross-eyed and painless on your fucking throne." He waved dismissively at Drina, rolling his eyes. Leonardo righted the chair and sat, running his hands through his hair.

"I was so angry. Something so stupid and simple fucked us up for life. A routine check—something a rookie captain would have seen—nearly got us all killed! Yet I couldn't stand to think of what they'd do to you. Me? They'd chuck me in a brig for a few years or maybe just run some therapies on me. You? If you were lucky, they'd force you into an early disconnection and completely ruin your life. You'd be stuck somewhere for dereliction of duty and then what?" Leonardo looked at Drina and then away. "I guess ... I figured I'd deal with it when we got back to Titan. But no one expected the FMR would be there at Newhope. I ignored warnings about some chatter. Wrong! They pinned the whole goddamn thing on me"—he stabbed his finger at his chest, words and spittle hurling from his mouth—"Renewed hostilities. Thank God for good friends or God knows where we'd be! It was all I could do to get us this heap." Leonardo looked at the ceiling then back to his hands.

They were silent, Leonardo's angry breathing calming and quieting as the minutes passed. He stared at the floor while Drina looked at her hands, cables fluttering around her head. They looked less like angelic attendants to him than snakes. She smiled wanly and let out a weak chuckle.

"Look at us now a few years later. Another guy sneaks on board and tries to blow it up."

Leonardo nodded.

"I didn't see that before. Huh. Funny. Not really, but ..."

Leonardo listened to the low hiss of the air vents and the whine of a small fan somewhere on Drina's throne. Finally she cleared her throat, which sounded like a shot in the room.

"You didn't have to save me, Leo. I know you meant well, but—"

"A good captain always—"

"Please," she said, so loud and direct he stopped short. "I'm sorry you protected me on Newhope. I should've told the truth. I was afraid. I knew everything would be lost. I knew what they'd do to me. I'd be imprisoned at Fuller's Beach in permanent sunset. I've heard stories; girls go crazy out there."

"Yeah, and staying on the throne's kept you *so* sane."

"Leo ..." Drina said, her voice tired. "C'mon. Please ..."

"I'm not saying it's any better in the captain's seat. Obviously it didn't keep us from our respective vices, did it? I just think we both might've been better off telling the truth."

Leonardo stood and brushed at his uniform. "We sure as hell wouldn't have ended up out here."

"No, I guess not." Drina shook her head. "Shit, at least you get to walk around the ship."

"Well, why don't you take something for the anxiety?"

"Uh, I think we both know where that led me."

"Yeah, right. But something else. You've got therapies you can use! Come on, you've only got another couple years and then you never have to sit down again if you don't want to."

"There's only so much virtual time and scenarios a girl can take. So many therapies, or going virtual all the time, you can feel the difference. Start to see the pixels, even."

"Drina, look," Leonardo said, sighing, "I don't know what to tell you. We're doing the best we can. Just hang tight, okay?"

Leonardo saw the cloud pass over her face. "I guess I can't take a lover in the meantime, huh? I mean, Baz *is* gay and—"

"Goddamn it, Drina!" Leonardo shouted, rising off his seat with the words. "She's dead! Are you happy? It's done and she's dead. Her skull exploded inside the damn *berth*. I lost my whole goddamn crew, including her. I'm sorry I ever had anything to do with her—but enough! It's over. Forever."

A heavy, leaden silence hung between them, emotional smog cloying the air. Leonardo clutched his hands tightly together. He saw the crescents his nails dug into the skin on the back of his hands.

"I wouldn't have taken up with her if I felt you were interested in this marriage. You got into the di-hex and gave up way before Newhope. Now you're making me pay for it? No, not anymore." Leonardo stood up, putting the chair back near the table. "When you're feeling a bit better—no—when I *say* you're better, we'll put you back on active duty. Until then, rest. Go virt, maybe. Or get di-hexed up, for all I care."

"Yeah, go have a drink while you're at it, old man!" she yelled at his back. "Go and—"

Leonardo crossed the room in two strides and leapt onto Drina's throne.

Proximity alarms screeched and he felt the dampening field crowding him, protecting Drina in a field that felt like steel wool on his skin. He grimaced, moving in closer, feeling the electric drill effect work into his brain, telling him to back off. He grasped the front of her uniform in his hands anyway, crushing the fabric in his fingers. Security systems shrieked in vain against their captain. Drina's machinery began to whine and squeal, lights flashing at the elevated levels of activity in her condition. Out of the corner of his eye he saw the avatar appear, shimmer then disappear as if embarrassed. Leonardo looked her in the eyes, sweat on his brow. Drina held her breath, eyes fearful and half-furious as she held his gaze. The cables in her hair jumped around nervously, like small, anxious dogs at the end of their mistress's leash. Leonardo hissed through teeth clenched like a containing wall stressed to its limits.

"The problem with you, *Astrogatrix* Valencia, is that you think it's all about you: that you have the worst of it, some kind of divine right to the blues. Must be the fact that everything on this ship is centered around you and your needs. Poor Drina, poor little sorry-ass centerpiece of the ship. Poor little goddess. Stuck with a man old enough to be her father. All wired up and no place to go." He flicked at her cables with one hand and they recoiled. He grabbed her tighter before she had time to move. "No one's ever had it easy, little space princess. Especially now. Don't think just because you're wired into this room you get the shittier end of the stick. I'd gladly take your place if it meant never having to see my hangar bay turned into a slaughterhouse. Or if it meant never seeing the woman I love destroy herself."

Leonardo let go and dropped her back into the berth. He stood, panting, the alarms quieting as he stepped back from her berth. Her machines began to calm down around her, interface cables clustering close to her skull as if in sympathy.

"I'm sorry for what I did, Drina. I'm sorry for protecting you." Leonardo stepped back and walked out. Stumbling on his way out, he said, "Maybe you should think about what you've done to us."

He thought he might have heard her crying as he walked down the hall and turned into his quarters. His jaw was jammed shut so tight he felt pain in his ears. "Fuck it," he said to his walls. At that moment Leonardo wanted to hear nothing and feel nothing.

He went to his closet and rooted around. Digging around his boots and parade shoes, he came across another varnished wooden box with gold lettering on the face. "BUN-HO PREMIUM" it read in the bright gold lettering.

"The good stuff," Leonardo muttered. Normally he would have waited for a special occasion to open the box, but with none on the horizon he tore it open, breaking the clasp off. Inside were six bottles of beloved Bun-Ho. He took one out and ripped the cap off. Leonardo tipped the neck back and welcomed the burnt, stinging pierce of the raw whiskey as it went down his throat. He wiped his mouth with his sleeve and looked around his quarters.

"Sunset," he said aloud, walking to a chair and dragging it in front of the large blank wall across from his desk. "Earth. Late twenty-first century. Eastern Yucatan coastline. Extend time." The wall began to burst with color and coalesce into the image of a horizon, scant clouds framing a burning sun. Oranges and yellows striped across the wall as the sun burned in the sky.

He was a quarter into the bottle when Baz pinged him.

"Leo?"

"*What?*"

Silence for a second.

"We're going on a little sightseeing mission, you and I. Remember?"

"Yes," said Leo. "I'll be right down."

"Okay, hurry it up."

Leonardo took four more pulls from the bottle, slammed it down on the table and swore. He canceled the sunset and left his quarters, throat burning like his mind.

CHAPTER SEVENTEEN

Occulate

UFW TOP SECRET CONFIDENTIAL BRIEFING MEMO
August 28, 2466
OVERVIEW
Lt. Col. F. V. Riccardi, Lead Investigator, Intelligence Harvesting Specialist
Following the incident at Newhope 15 and the attack on the UFWSS *Wellstone* (under the command of Capt. Leonardo Valencia) the incident fell under the jurisdiction of the UFW Intelligence Service. I was placed in charge of this investigation once the *Wellstone* was towed to dry dock at Port Nautilus on Bakuba.

All intelligence gathered to date indicates that the FMR is preparing a large-scale event against the UFW. What that operation is I cannot determine. Due to their insularity, excessive secrecy, formidable capabilities and incredible ability to elude detection, this commission has found it difficult to ascertain the exact nature of these operations.

Since the beginning of hostilities between the FMR and the UFW, several attempts have been made to insert undercover agents within the FMR's ranks. Over one hundred and twenty attempts have been made at a rate of almost one per year. All have been unsuccessful. In addition to attempts at direct infiltration of the FMR, other avenues have been explored. These began with several simultaneous attempts to infiltrate the inner circle of individuals known to work the less populated edges of the Jovian ring communes as well as private enterprises operating wildcat mining and unauthorized archaeological operations outside the purview of the UFW Xenoarcheologic Authority (see attached report of the case "UFW vs. Coralone Corporation" UFWJS985a.ii3.12sda.44a).

The last attempt made was in October of 2467 with the deployment of an operative installed aboard a single-occupant orbital vehicle disguised as space junk. Despite the risk of destruction by the massive orbital platforms surrounding the planet, this was felt to be an excellent means of infiltrating the FMR. The vehicle drifted into Mars orbit in a manner consistent with inanimate objects and debris adrift in deep space. As was hoped the craft entered orbit unmolested. Using long-range telescopes it was observed descending into Mars's atmosphere. Following the landing a massive sandstorm welled over the landing site and it was never heard from again.

It is my belief that any further attempts to gain entry into the FMR are futile and will result only in further loss of vital personnel. Efforts should be made and all emphasis place on heightened security, surveillance and prevention of what will undoubtedly be a catastrophic attack of devastating proportions.

Information gleaned thus far via soft interrogation has been disappointing and of little use, revealing little more than proof of the continuing personality cult that is the governing method of the FMR since its inception. Despite my continued requests for the necessity of enhanced techniques, UFW High Command has not granted permission due to human rights concerns voiced by the office of Pres. Liang. It is my opinion and that of this reporting body that the threat of another terrorist incident of greater scale than the Newhope incident necessitates the use of higher-yield interrogation methods.

Thus the reporting body and I wish to go on record as being in opposition to the executive orders against using these techniques.

Nonetheless, it is my duty to report my findings thus far.

Of the few surviving FMR agents from the Newhope incident none were forthcoming with any details other than name, serial number and date of birth (information which is useless as we have no records of births on Mars and within the FMR since the 2332 secession). Few spoke in anything but heavily accented, terse sentences comprised of little more than gibberish with a nearly religious fervor. All praised the FMR and the eventual demise of the UFW at its hands.

All mentioned the name "Harvestman" (see video) with a reverence usually seen in fanatical religious groups. Mention of Harvestman appears sporadically in surveillance footage from various raids and covert operations, first appearing during the July 2457 action on the Antigone communes orbiting Venus and the thanahexagene rings broken up by UFW tariff agents on Lazuline during the same year. Those heard saying it offer little in the way of explanation, merely that their actions and those of the FMR are done "in the name of Harvestman and his struggle for freedom."

With so little information to go on, I can only make vague assumptions and giant leaps as to the identity of Harvestman. These are:

1. FMR Founding Pres. Roberto Maggiacomo. Given the fervor with which the FMR carried out its sweeping campaigns of reform and terror as it rose to full power, it is be reasonable to assume Harvestman is a code name for the last known President of the Free Mars Republic. The problem with this theory is that even with the cryostasis technology of 2332, Maggiacomo would be 176 years old. Even with infrequent and selective decanting and excellent health measures, it is highly unlikely the man would live sixty years longer than the average human lifespan under top medical care.

2. Ex-Black Bag Commander Roger "Bishop" Wasielewski. Rumors of Bishop surviving the final assault on Hora are as plentiful as the subsequent sightings of him. It must be noted that official confirmation was never made of his death. However, it is unlikely a man dependent on regular injections of synthetic pituitary extract could live for long on the run without arousing suspicion. The enduring stories of Bishop give criminal elements a symbol of hope. Rallying around the Bishop (a personality cult in and of itself) provides them a source of joy and spiritual sustenance, considering his former role

as a ranking member of the Church of The Infinite Sublime (and the source of his nickname). Some credible sightings have been made of a man similar in build and appearance to Wasielewski on Golden Pine (see Appendix VII). But it is unlikely that this is anything more than a coincidence. Nonetheless, Bishop's background is being scoured for any possible pro-FMR leanings or statements.

3. An as yet unidentified individual or individuals. The possibility that Harvestman is actually Salvatore "Rocco" Casto has been considered but is unlikely (Despite Casto's avowed fondness for the FMR, it is perceived as a relationship of convenience to further his criminal enterprises). That Harvestman is actually a group of individuals has been postulated but again seems far-fetched at best.

If frustration at a clear understanding of who or what Harvestman is perceived in this report then so be it. My previously stated opposition to the limited interrogation and intelligence-harvesting methods granted me by my superiors is understood. I have taken great strides to work within those parameters. But I must go on record here and reiterate that I have warned of the possibility of a negative outcome unless greater steps are taken to gain information about the identity of Harvestman and its methods and intentions as they relate to the FMR.

Please review the enclosed materials in the form of surveillance, interrogation and reconnaissance videos. I await the review of this report by the UFW High Council and will abide by its ruling.

Sincerely,
Lt. Col. Fiorvante V. Riccardi, UFW Intelligence Service

CHAPTER EIGHTEEN
Discovery

"I think it's time we bury the crew."

They were silently putting on armored pressure suits in the prep room outside the main bay when Baz spoke. Though he was unhappy about donning a suit again, Leonardo was glad it wasn't the stale emergency suits. Their armored recon suits were far more comfortable and equipped to allow them longer use times.

"Now?" said Leonardo.

"Worst-case scenario of this is we don't come back and Drina has to scuttle *Resurgam,* then the crew doesn't get a proper burial. Seeing how they died, it's the least we can do."

"You're right," said Leonardo.

Once in their suits they got the antigrav sled from the bay and returned to the crew quarters. There, Baz and Leonardo initiated the sarcophagizing process of the berths. Witnessing the burial of his crew (and not the least Regina), Leonardo watched each berth envelop its occupant in opaque, airtight sealant. Then the berths opened one by one, slowly lifting their inhabitants out for easy removal and stacking on the antigrav sled.

"Did these guys have any burial instructions? Religious preferences?" asked Baz, leaning against the control stick of the sled. Leonardo checked his HUD then shook his head.

"They were all CIS," said Leonardo. Church of The Infinite Sublime, the dominant religion among UFW crews, seemed less a religion to Leonardo than a deification of science as a religion in and of itself. *Whatever gets you through the day*, as his mother would say, *as long as it doesn't get in the way of mine.* "No specific burial instructions. Burial in space acceptable."

"Remind me of that when we're back out there," muttered Baz.

Leonardo stepped out of the way as Baz piloted the sled out into the corridor and down the hall. In the bay, Baz stepped off the sled and looked at Leonardo. Leonardo was looking over at the survey team's quarters. Without a word, Baz joined him. Together they went in and removed every body from its berth. This was a much harder process as Mussina's sabotage had rendered their sarcophagization systems useless. So Leonardo and Baz wrapped each one in their berth clothes and bedding before stacking them on the sled on top of the crew members.

"What are we going to do with the bodies?" asked Baz.

"Exactly what I was thinking." Leonardo looked at the broken core sampler Dwi8 had used. "We can't bury them. The ground is impenetrable."

"Leave them in the snow?"

"Undignified."

"Cremate them?" Leonardo looked up at Baz.

"Sure." Leonardo thought about burials he'd presided over in the past. Normally a dead crew member would be sarcophagized and laid out in one of the smaller bays for twenty-four hours; after a formal ceremony the body was jettisoned into space.

They moved the sled into the Engineering Section's machine shop. Baz moved the bodies into the compact disposal unit. Once stacked, he closed the door and set the controls for a short intense burst. Baz stood back as the timer counted down.

"'Mercy upon them and accept them into the infinite grace,'" murmured Leo, reading from a text Jason supplied and beamed to his HUD.

"'Born from atoms, reduced to ashes, for they are nothing in the face of the infinite sublime,'" answered Baz. The timer pinged loudly. A muffled *woof* and a flash from inside the chamber and it was done. The men waited as the safety systems turned off and opened the door.

What had been bodies was now rendered into a single compacted rectangle of dark gray ash sealed in clear film at the bottom of the chamber. Leonardo took this and Baz followed as they walked to the smaller airlock. There Leonardo paused a moment then flung the cake of ash away from the ship. It arced high over the surface and began a slow descent towards the ground. The delicate film opened, releasing the cremains from within. Gray dust drifted out over the surface and streaming tendrils began a graceful drop to rest on the ground forever.

Baz backed the remaining antigrav sled out of the pen and glided over to the larger airlock where Leonardo hopped on. The doors closed behind them and alarms went off in their HUDs as the airlock cycled. The outer doors finally opened and Baz edged the sled forward to the edge.

They peered down at the twenty-meter drop to the planet's surface.

"Hold on," said Baz. Leonardo grabbed the railing as Baz backed the sled up then slammed it forward. They sailed out the airlock and over the planet's surface for several hundred feet before coming to a soft landing. The sled kicked up a small amount of ice and dirt before cruising again.

"You do something to this sled?" asked Leonardo.

"Himanako hot-rodded it." Leonardo laughed as they sped across the ice.

"Did you tell Drina where we were headed?"

"No. She'll be fine."

"It's not her I'm worried about."

"Jason's got orders to bug her out in *Sparky* should anything happen to us."

Leonardo checked his HUD. One of the FLi8s hovered five klicks above them giving him a slight feeling of security.

The journey overland was smooth and uneventful. Baz slowed as they approached the crater walls.

Ahead Leonardo saw the cave about a hundred meters up the wall. The slant of the crater rim was steep, almost eighty degrees. Rocks of varying sizes and shape littered the mouth of the tunnel.

"We gonna make it up there?" asked Leonardo.

"Yep. Just hold on tight." Baz gunned the sled hard and Leonardo held fast to the railing as the sled moved quickly towards the crater wall. They sped up the incline with barely a bump. Leonardo heard the late Himanako's illegal thrusters kick in at the sled's back end. They ascended the side easily.

"Duck!" shouted Baz. Leonardo crouched just as the mouth of the cave swallowed them. He felt a light scrape at his back as they brushed the ceiling. The sled bounced once as it neared the floor then steadied. Baz came to a stop a few meters in.

"You okay?"

"Yeah, fine. Nice driving." Leonardo looked around the tunnel. It was almost perfectly circular. He shone his lights on the walls.

"These walls," he said. "Incredibly smooth."

"Volcanic? Lava tube, maybe?" asked Baz.

"Doubt it. This is machine tunneling from the *inside*. You saw the rocks spilling out as we came in?"

"Yep," said Baz. "Means Mussina didn't do that, for sure."

Leonardo looked into the darkness of the tunnel. His HUD showed a subtle increase of temperature and faintly elevated radiation.

"Okay, proceed quietly. Be prepared to back out fast."

"Sounds like my first—"

"That's enough, sailor."

Baz gunned the sled forward at a slightly slower pace. The sled's lights lit the way. Ahead was clear, smooth tunnel for several hundred meters. Leonardo noted the slow increase in temperature as they descended further and further. By the time they were two kilometers in it had risen by twenty Kelvin.

Ahead, a pinprick of light began to expand into a widening sphere.

"Baz," said Leonardo, tapping his XO on the shoulder and pointing. Baz slowed and let the sled hover in place.

"You zoom in and it's only more bright light. Seems like it might be the source of the temperature rise, too."

"Steady on," said Leonardo. They moved deeper into the tunnel. Leonardo wondered if they encountered anyone, if they would even be able to turn around. His HUD was having trouble displaying due to intense EMF interference. The images shuddered and froze then clicked off and on before stabilizing only for the erraticism to repeat again. The temperature kept rising but every other indicator was blinded by the interference.

"Baz, wait," said Leonardo, as the temperature suddenly kicked up thirty degrees in as many meters. The light at the other end was beginning to shine brighter on the walls, looming in the distance. "We're nearly blind now. You see anything up ahead?"

"A lot of light."

"Steady on. This is making me nervous."

They slowly edged forward until finally their faceplates darkened, compensating for the brightness. "All right, turn the sled around and let's proceed on foot."

"Jesus, you see the radiation levels?" asked Baz as they stepped off the sled. "They're insanely high. Never seen anything like this before."

"What the hell is producing them? A power plant?" Leonardo said. They walked cautiously another two hundred meters to the end of the tunnel. A few meters from the end they clung to the walls and crept to the edge. Without their faceplates the light would have blinded them permanently. Leonardo's motion detector showed nothing for the next forty meters. A few seconds later, they carefully peered around the corner.

They looked upon something astounding enough to reduce both Leonardo and Baz to total silence for minutes. Leonardo would never have imagined what he saw a scant distance from where they crashed. As with everything else since the crash, the more they saw, the greater the mysteries became.

The tunnel ended in a rough lip, really a mound of huge stone chunks. The cave before them was massive, perhaps thousands of kilometers across. The brilliantly lit interior was exposed, showing him almost nothing but featureless rock going up around him in all directions. Everything glowed from the yellow light that generated the intense heat they noticed descending into the cave.

The entire planet's hollow, he thought.

The interior was a dull yellow color, bleached by the heat, and spherical, with the ground curving away into the distance. It was impossible to judge the size due to its vastness. Leonardo guessed the cavern took up the planet's interior.

A fiery scene spread out before them. The source of all the light, heat and perhaps even the planet itself was a massive object glowing in the center: a fiery display of solar energy enclosed in a space that shouldn't have contained it. *A small star inside a planet*, Leonardo thought, as if admiring an insect on a leaf. His HUD overlay told him it was over four kilometers across. It was a yellow like Sol, its surface roiling and burning as solar furies churned in an open nuclear reaction. Angry flares belched and blasted away from its surface, lashing out only to be stopped at an invisible barrier of blue flashes. At several equidistant points large polygonal structures each a half kilometer in size hung at its equator, linked by pulsing blue beams of light. These must have created the flare barrier that contained the orb, like the invisible electric cages used in the ten-dollar traveling zoos of Leonardo's childhood. A tighter latticework of triangular shapes connected by bright points of blue light ten meters across was visible around the star. These glowed in reaction to flares across the star's surface, their purpose as yet unknown but ostensibly keeping them in check. The ground shook every time one of the flares lashed out at its cage.

This miniature and secret sun hung in the subterranean sky, illuminating and pounding everything with its baleful, heavy glare. Leonardo's Geiger counter pegged itself long ago into an "n/a" reading. That much radiation should have killed anything near it. Including them.

"I think we're in way the fuck over our heads," Baz whispered. "God, I wish we could call for backup ..."

"Mussina did all this in three weeks?" Leonardo asked in a hoarse whisper.

"No way. Not even with all the brand new UFW R&D tech he could get his hands on. I mean, nothing we have ... Nothing they have could do something like this. It's impossible. Unless ..."

"He could have done it with what was recovered on Baaklum Cha'am, I bet," said Leonardo.

"This kind of thing—I've never seen anything like it, but—it'd take a lot—I mean, years and years—of planning. I mean ... how the hell do you do something like this?" Baz shook his head.

"Certainly Mussina could tell us," answered Leonardo.

He ducked as motion to the left caught his eye. A dark polygonal shape came into view through the distorting heat shimmer.

"What the?" Leonardo said. "You see that?" He zoomed in with his helmet optics.

"Son of a ..." Baz said.

It was a spacecraft, smaller than *Resurgam* by half, all black with landing gear. Its engines were older Choudhury drives. Yet it bore no markings. Leonardo glanced at his HUD in vain.

"No ID codes," Leonardo muttered. "No surprise there."

"What the hell is that thing doing in there?" Baz asked.

"Where the hell did it come from?"

"Don't know. Can't ID that ship."

They zoomed in on the suited figures underneath the ship. Leonardo looked closely at their upper shoulders and helmets.

"You see that?" he whispered, though he knew they couldn't hear him.

"Those insignia!"

The figures moving about underneath the ships wore FMR uniforms: black pressure suits with an orange circle outlined in green, with an obscure character in yellow over the left arm's triceps.

"What the hell is going on?" Baz asked. Leonardo couldn't answer.

The suited figures were moving objects from their ship to the stolen antigrav sled. Leonardo and Baz could see a desktop AI, a research unit—no doubt the one taken from *Resurgam*—and a figure behind it viewing a pedia. The figure wore a UFW suit.

"There's Mussina," Leonardo said to Baz.

"Asshole." Baz turned to Leonardo. "What're they doing? Are they leaving? I mean, what the possible fuck is the FMR doing here?" Leonardo held up a hand to silence Baz, thinking all the same things.

"Look there!" said Leonardo. He pointed to something fifty meters away. At first it looked like a human scaling the rock wall. When the head turned it wore the featureless face of a walky-talky. They watched as it climbed towards a pyramidal structure topped by a large dish antenna emitting a thin white beam towards the star.

"If we caught that walky-talky, we could learn what the hell these creeps were up to," Baz said.

"Too risky to go out there. If they don't kill us the radiation from that globe of fire will. Wait a second. Do you have a data wasp on you?"

"Yeah, I think so." Baz rummaged in his suit pouch and drew out a small silver sphere. He smiled. "The good old SLLT5."

"What kind of walky-talky is that?" asked Leonardo.

"Uh, less than human features make it a Zeitlin 7. Or maybe a 6. Yeah, a 6. See its I/O port at the back of the neck?" Leonardo zoomed into a small aperture on the AI's back.

"So can we get the SLLT5 to download the memory drives?" he asked Baz.

"I'll get right on it," Baz replied with a smile.

Using his HUD, Baz uploaded instructions to the SLLT5. A light on its surface blinked twice and it flew back from Baz's palm.

Leonardo prayed it wouldn't be spotted as it flew towards its target.

"Watch," said Baz. The SLLT5 latched onto the walky-talky's neck like a hawk to prey. The data wasp held tight for a few seconds before it disengaged and flew back to Baz's waiting palm.

"Nice work," said Baz.

"Damn. Look," said Leonardo. Baz turned to look. The ancient Martian walky-talky held still for a second, hands on the ladder and a foot on the ground as if in thought about which foot to raise next. Then it slowly tumbled back, rolling down the incline towards the ship. The planet's light gravity made the descent comically slow, dust and rocks flinging up and around lazily as the AI tumbled down.

"Let's get out of here," said Baz.

They scrambled back to the sled and barreled out the tunnel back to *Resurgam*.

CHAPTER NINETEEN
Inside

Once safely back at the ship they stripped off their suits and raced to the bridge. Leonardo was relieved that no followed them out from the tunnel. He spent the whole voyage back turned to face the tunnel, a bolt thrower in his hand. Both Fli8s reported no activity at all.

They sat at a console on the bridge and Baz connected the data wasp to Jason.

"Here it is," said Baz. He pointed to the display on his right, showing the downloaded data from the Martian AI. After Jason's scans for virii or more of Mussina's trojans yielded nothing, numbers and text flickered on-screen as Jason collated the data. The main display showed a menu with options, the Zeitlin Robotics logo in the upper right corner.

"Jesus Christ! How old is that thing?" said Baz. "Text menus in a browser? No neural link? No audio command? A holo, maybe?" Baz sighed and tapped the holokeyboard. "Okay, what's first?"

Leonardo looked at the screen. In large white letters on a blue background was a list of specs:

UNIT TYPE: ZEITLIN 6
FORMAT DATE: 11/26/2389
UNIT NAME: QuaD6

Then there were a number of menu options: "Video playback, Data Storage, Data transmitted, I/O logs, Processes, Setup, Toolbox, Special Ops," Leonardo aloud. "How about we check into Data Storage?" Baz punched some keys on the holoboard in front of him and a listing appeared.

"Heh, just as I hoped! This must be their primary AI," said Baz. He ran a finger down the list. "It's got every last shred of data they have on it. Their ship's AI is probably damaged, and they only *just* stole the survey team's. Why else would they keep this hunk of crap at ninety-eight percent capacity? I'm amazed the damn thing can walk! It's packed to the gills."

"I wonder if they're doing backups," Leonardo said. "Having one AI do heavy-duty work and all data storage is foolhardy, but I suspect they don't much care. These Martians are obviously up to something big with resources stretched thin, cutting corners. Like they don't expect to be caught or answer to any superiors if they make mistakes."

They took a cursory look at the massive amount of data. There was a great deal of information about energy output, solar formations and a huge amount of gravity-control theory that evaded Leonardo. He wasn't sure what it meant but knew it had everything to do with the sun burning below them.

"All right, Baz, let's see some video."

The first, dated six months before the crash, showed the Martian walky-talky loading heavy-duty, military-spec crates into the dark hold of a ship. These were standard containers for a journey: water, food, and medical supplies. This went on for several minutes. Baz was just about to select another file when Leonardo spotted something in the background.

"Go back a few seconds," he told him. Baz jogged the recording back. They watched as the walky-talky piled containers then turned to grab something.

"Freeze it," Leonardo shouted, pointing at the display. "Look there."

Beyond the ship a fairly typical spaceport scene unfolded: the long expanse of landing area, buildings in the distance, stumpy landing lights, chain-link fences and numbered signs. Beyond the tarmac, the rocky ochre landscape gave way to red hills behind an illegible sign.

"What's that sign say?" Baz asked, squinting at the display. "Jason? Center focus and enhance." The image zoomed in and pixels formed legible words. The sign was dirty and weather-beaten. Through the dust, they read "ATTENTION! Accès Interdit: zone de cargo seulement! Passagers à l'arrivée: rapportez-vous à l'Autorité Astroportuaire de Nouveaux Paris. Informations supplémentaires disponibles auprès de l'Autorité Astroportuaire, bureau 55A."

"New Paris?" Baz said. "*Mars*. That's New Paris on Mars."

"Remember the alert from CENTCOM? About the cruisers leaving Mars? New Paris was where those ships originated." Leonardo scratched at his chin then tapped his teeth with a finger. "Very interesting. Let's see another."

The next recording was a few months later. It opened on a grimy flight deck. Warning signs glowed and lights flashed; a launch sequence was in progress. Now a different walky-talky assisted a human in a black pressure suit into the cockpit of a medium-sized spacecraft. A figure from the side came forward, took the hand of the pilot and pressed it to its own faceplate. Others clad in pressure suits stood nearby as the pilot clambered into the ship. Leonardo saw an FMR flag plus a yellow pyramid on the arms of their pressure suits.

"Bet that's their commander," Leonardo said.

"Is it a farewell ceremony?" Baz asked. "Because that's a permanent goodbye if I ever saw one."

The pilot slid in and the hatch closed behind him, vapor blowing out from the gaskets as they sealed. The walky-talky stepped off the gantry as the ship slid into the launch chamber. A door with a thick window closed and a series of lights to the right went from green to red. "God, look at the gunk around those indicators" Baz muttered.

"That thing's an ancient piece of crap! My grandma drove those things into the Jovian asteroid belt for fun."

"You're right," Leonardo said, leaning back into the chair. "At least a hundred and fifty years old. Late colonial period, easily."

The small ship disengaged and slowly drifted away. For a few minutes it hung in black space until the engines flared and it sped off. Those standing on the flight deck grouped around the window. For several minutes there were only the figures at the window jostling for a better view of the darkness of empty space.

"Jesus, God. Martians are boring," Baz muttered. He sped playback until there was a sudden flash.

"Holy shit!" He quickly rewound it. They viewed the massive explosion again as the vehicle sped into the depths, quickly becoming indistinguishable from the darkness. Then the flash came again in real time.

"Suicide mission," Baz said, leaning back in his chair. "Thus the teary goodbye."

"But why are they still standing there?" Leonardo asked Baz. "Why a suicide mission if they're in no apparent immediate danger of—"

The next flash was blinding, flooding the displays white for several seconds until the walky-talky's filters compensated and the image restored. The figures stood still as though afraid to move. The screen jostled as a shockwave sent them reeling before they regained their balance. A smaller flash occurred seconds later and they rejoiced, clapping each other on the back and congratulating each other for a full minute. Matter roiled and boiled on the screen, turning into a dark mass with orange streaks glowing through it. The commander clapped his hands over head then jerked a thumb behind him. The group followed him out. The walky-talky remained on the flight deck continuing to record. The indicator lights changed back to green as atmosphere was restored.

"Jason, focus enhance center twenty-eight percent."

"What the hell happened?" said Baz.

The action was occurring a hundred million kilometers away from the ship. The craft was gone. Where it had been was a smoldering sphere, a red-hot coal hanging in space with tendrils of smoke slithering away from the planet. The surface was an angry spitting mass of churning red and black. Hot tongues flared out from the surface. A cloud of smoke, debris and gases began to form around it.

"What happened? Did it hit an asteroid or something?" Baz asked. "It must have been carrying some heavy ordnance to stir up the surface like that."

Leonardo sat and thought for a minute.

"No. That's not what happened, Baz. It's like ... what we're seeing is ... like birth in action or something," Leonardo answered. Baz cocked an eyebrow.

"Leo, that's a little purple even for you. What the hell do you mean?"

"Remember what Mussina said? About the Transparent Ones having the capability of building planets? He didn't know it from that map he found at Cit-Bolon-Tum. *He'd seen it happen before his own eyes*." Leonardo pointed to the screen.

"That's a stretch," Baz said. "But I'll bite in light of what's down below us. So *when* did he see it?" Baz asked, scratching his face. Leonardo only now noticed the trimmed beard on his XO's face.

"Here," Leonardo pointed to the screen. "He was on this flight. He's probably the one with the command insignia. The timing was perfect. We picked Mussina up at an outer-rim service station, Zungu 21. He probably arrived from the location we're viewing right now."

"Look. It's getting bigger."

The globe expanded, its churning surface growing darker. They watched as it grew to the size of a small moon. Its growth seemed to pause for a few minutes, with the surface coagulating into an ugly mass of planetary scar tissue. Occasional bursts of hot gas and matter spewed forth. Eventually the surface quieted and grew dark.

Suddenly two massive explosions came from opposite poles, blowing two giant holes in the planet. Magma, dust and ash were thrown from the interior. Just as quickly it slowed. Finally, the debris ceased stirring and gracefully formed into rings outside the holes in the planet.

"Accretion?" said Baz.

These rings collapsed and warped, eventually flattening and widening into a disc shape. The discs drifted and covered the holes they burst from. They watched the fiery discs burning before becoming sealed inside the planet. Then slowly the holes closed from inside.

Baz and Leonardo sat slack jawed and silent, watching as the planet on-screen cooled and formed ice on the surface. By the time they could speak, a thin, hazy atmosphere was beginning to form, obscuring the lessening tumult on the surface.

"Planet building," said Leonardo. "Never thought I'd live to see that."

"Almost didn't," said Baz, rubbing his face.

"Not sure how I feel about it."

"Funny," Baz said. A faint smile played across his face.

"What?" Leonardo asked.

"It's like a ... Symmes hole," Baz said, pointing where the disc seamlessly joined the planet's surface.

"A what?"

"A Symmes hole. When my father was dying, he got kind of demented. Very demented. He swore off his meds and thought the Earth was hollow and people inside were out to get him. Kept begging me to go back to Earth—as if—and destroy the Symmes hole at the North Pole. I did a little research on it, because I was curious as to what the hell he was talking about. Turns out that six hundred years ago there used to be a whole cult that thought Earth was hollow and these two holes at the poles were entrances into the interior. Now I wonder how crazy Papa really was."

"You think UFW Astrophysics has any record of an anomaly like this occurring?" Leonardo asked Baz.

"Let's see. I got date, time, source and—oh, here we go. Got some coordinates for you, Jason." Baz dragged a finger over the display, highlighting a string of numbers on-screen.

"Sir," Jason said. After a moment he replied, "This occurred in the Stokes system. Planetoid location is Stokes 6. I have a question, Captain."

"Yes, Jason?"

"Records indicate that the Stokes system has only five satellite planets. Recheck?"

"Proceed." There was a second's pause before Jason signaled completion.

"Recheck complete. The Stokes system does have only five satellite planets. The sixth planet is new."

"Dear God," Baz said.

"Please hold, Captain. I am making some calculations." Leonardo wondered what Jason was up to. "I have analyzed constellations in the video. I can say with ninety-nine percent accuracy that we have crashed in the Stokes system. We are on the sixth planet."

Baz and Leonardo looked at each other.

"So what the hell did he make this hollow planet for?" Baz replied. "And how did they get a sun inside it?"

Leonardo was silent for a moment. Eventually he turned and looked Baz in the eye.

"If they can build this," he said, "what else can they do?"

CHAPTER TWENTY
Enveloped

They continued scouring data from all sources for clues about the situation.

Leonardo watched over real-time telemetry from the FLi8 units while Baz closely reviewed the footage purloined from the Martian walky-talky. Leonardo found the surface of the planet remorselessly mundane while wondering who knew what was happening down below.

Baz grunted and tapped Leonardo's shoulder. Leonardo looked at the haggard XO, who smiled optimistically. "Check this out." He mudraed the playback. "From a few days ago."

It showed a darkened place, a cave or a perhaps a planet at night. The lumbering Martian walky-talky was preparing a staging area of some kind. Eventually several space-suited figures emerged, descending from a ramp in the underbelly of a ship. The walky-talky finished and stood behind the group. The whole scene was dark and obscured, strangely murky, with the only illumination from the ship's weak utility lights. These illuminated numerous cables snaking all over the ground. The Martians gathered in a semicircle underneath the ship, each standing at a mobile workstation. Leonardo and Baz could hear the staccato chatter of radio communications now between them.

"Look," said Baz, pointing. "It's Mussina. See the suit?" Leonardo nodded.

Mussina, in his stolen UFW suit, stood at the center near the stolen research AI and another mysterious object.

"That's the AI they got from us—I mean 'stole,'" said Leonardo. He could almost make out Mussina's face under the helmet, the heavy goatee and dark, bushy eyebrows. Leonardo peered at the unfamiliar object for a moment until he realized it was a stolen item from Baaklum Cha'am, the larger half-bathtub object. They stood in shadow, their suit lights shining on the consoles in front of them.

"Turn up their chatter," said Leonardo.

With a crackle as introduction, voices garbed in static and digital interference filled the bridge.

"All right, launch the Sower." This was the voice of Mussina. Off in the distance, a small, bright blast of light shone against the surface and a black cone rose into the dark sky. It provided faint illumination like a single candle in a cathedral.

"Ready the power couplings." Mussina took a stylus from the object in front of him and touched the outer rim of the artifact in a very specific manner. Wherever he touched lit up colors and shapes, holographic and iridescent images rising over the rim. Leonardo remembered similar ones from the pictures he'd seen. Mussina was tapping in a deliberate order as if it were an incantation or equation.

"Ready, commander." A figure behind Mussina raised a hand to signal the others.

"Where's the Sower?" asked Mussina. "Give me a placement confirmation."

"Coordinates match, sir. Sower in place, Commander."

"Ready the particle attractors."

"Particle attractors ready."

"On my mark. Five. Four. Three. Two. One!" Mussina made a quick movement, then yelled, "Fire all beams!"

Simultaneous beams of light from units spaced along the cavern floor shot into the sky and filled the screen, shaking with energy. For a moment the screen washed out in white so blazing the audio buzzed from it. Then everything in the formerly dark cavern was suddenly lit in harsh, glaring light. Intense heat radiated out in shimmering waves, distorting the feed further.

"I'm amazed such an old walky-talky could withstand that," said Leonardo, "let alone the humans."

Mussina now hunched low over his arcane objects and devices, hands waving in abstruse gestures. The other Martians held fast to their workstations, bracing against successive shockwaves from the blast. Their voices had gained a strained tone, struggling against the unseen yet powerful force.

"Planetary surface and crust integrity holding, Commander."

"Containment systems?"

"Containment is holding and matching the growth of the Seed, Commander."

"Keep the pericarp field at one hundred percent. I want no leakage."

"Emitter levels stable, sir!"

"Gentlemen," said Mussina, holding tightly to the table in front of him as he pointed overhead, "What you see here is our future. Salvation lies not in reconciliation but in the final vanquishing of our master's enemies. Billions of years of debt is about to be paid in full!"

"'*Billions of years of debt*?'" said Baz. Leonardo shushed him.

"Growth accelerating, sir. It seems rapid. Too much so."

"This is to be expected, Mr. De Paula. It will accelerate at a steady, healthy pace for a time before it finds stasis and holds. The Seed is eager to make the Sower proud. The Son will be a strong and steady thing."

"Exchangers kicking in now. Reflexive relays firing at maximum."

"Good, good. There's some energy coming right back to it now, I see."

"Containment shield at full, sir."

"Good! Quad6! Come!" The AI lumbered towards Mussina. "Go to the containment field's main generator housing. Make sure those beam armatures in the gantry are stable." Leonardo watched as the AI walked out from underneath the ship. When it had left the shaded protection of the ship's underside, the fireball's intensity raged a hundredfold stronger. Radiation waves spread from it, ripples cascading down from each pulse and throb of the growing infernal sphere. Leonardo and Baz could now see it clearly in the sky, flares lashing out like tongues of snakes. Leonardo saw the floating containment units spread out evenly across its surface, closing off the last gaps where the flares blasted the interior of the planet: one at the bottom, another at the equator, and the others spread evenly across the equatorial rim. The AI continued to move up the incline towards the now familiar pyramid housing the containment beams.

"Stop it right there," said Leonardo. Baz mudraed and the image froze. "So now we know how they made it."

"Do we?" Baz was scratching at his beard. "There was a whole lot of mumbo jumbo in that snippet. These words like 'Sower', 'Son' and 'Seed.' Did he really mean 'Sun' as in a star or 'Son' as in male child? From what we saw, 'Sower' is some sort of payload rocket carrying 'Seed' which looks a lot like the device they sent out on their corsair that originally made the planet."

"Not sure," Leonardo said, crossing his arms over his chest, frowning. "Either way, it's a bad pun, though it does seem to relate to components in the operation. 'Sower' being the capsule and 'Seed,' 'Sun' or 'Son' being the product of some kind of fusion reaction. Even without actual telemetry we can see that the energy output of that thing is immense. They need huge amounts of power just to contain it let alone make the damn thing."

"Mussina said something about exchangers. Maybe they have something capping the output from it and recycling it to contain it."

"Perhaps," Leonardo said, nodding. "It's amazing they've survived this long. Does little to clarify anything. All right ... What else do you have for us to look at?"

"About nine hundred petabytes of data, video and audio." Baz called up another file. "This is from about one week ago."

Baz flicked his fingers and playback resumed.

They watched Quad6 walking up the gangway and inside the Martian ship. After the airlock, it moved through the decrepit ship. The painted walls were peeling and almost rotten looking, covered with peculiar writing. Rusted struts were visible amidst evident fire damage. Shadows clung to the edges of the dimly lit hallways of the ship.

"That ship's been through hell ... surprised it's still flying," Baz muttered.

Quad6 entered what passed for the bridge, a cramped cumbersome design. It was semicircular with meter-high viewing ports along the far end. The command chair loomed high over everything else. Consoles spread across the outer wall with crew members seated at the hopelessly outdated equipment.

"Manual control faces!" Baz shouted. "Jesus drove this to carpentry gigs." Leonardo laughed even as he felt the hairs on his neck stand up. For some reason he was dreading what might come next.

"'Quad6, halt.'" It was Mussina's voice. Quad6 turned to face Mussina seated in the captain's chair wearing the bottoms of his UFW pressure suit and a soiled undershirt.

"His skin," Leonardo said to Baz. "Look at his skin." Baz nodded. Barely a week of being on the Martian ship had done strange things to Mussina. Leonardo remembered how members of the survey team found Mussina's skin tone odd, even fake. Whatever he'd been disguising his skin with was wearing off; it had a gleaming, greenish tint to it now. His eyes were nearly luminescent, yellow with irises faded and barely visible. His thinning hair was no longer black, but had begun turning a bright, lurid blue, as if afire. His green skin seemed diseased where lesions had broken out on his arms. Small white medipatches with tiny red crosses were plastered on his skin but obviously doing little to heal the patient.

"Lesions," Leonardo said.

"Radiation is bad in there," Baz said. "They took a major unhealthy dose when they ignited that sun. Their suits are clearly not armored. Whatever they're using for containment isn't strong enough. Even without the clown make-up, Mussina'd be glowing in the dark. I wouldn't want to be his liver right now. It's working overtime to process the antirad meds in addition to the radiation. If they have a functioning medibot on that ship it's probably about ready to break down from overuse."

Mussina stepped down from the captain's chair. Leonardo hadn't realized he was so powerfully built. When he met him at the pickup from the Outer Rims Depot at Zungu 21, he seemed smaller. But then he was most likely playing down his strength and size. His weakness from life on a lower gravity planet would have been a dead giveaway to the team that he was not terrestrially born.

"Gradman, De Paula, Marsonek, Heredia." He barked out the names with impatience. The crew members, similarly green skinned, with light blue hair and luminescent yellow eyes, rose to stand at attention in front of him.

"Their eyes are glowing in the dark," whispered Baz. Leonardo shushed him with a wave of his hand and listened.

"At ease," Mussina said. The men relaxed. "Gradman. Updates on the Sower?" A man stepped forward, tall and thin, with fewer lesions than Mussina.

"The amplifiers are in place, Captain. They will be fully charged in approximately seventy-two hours. Containment systems are working at ninety-five percent capacity. I'm slightly concerned about their stability, though we can maintain that throughout Phase Three."

Mussina nodded. "Fluctuations are to be expected. Were we in possession of a complete Seed and Son generation set it would be entirely stable. But I'd keep an eye on the regulators for now. I want clean signals at one hundred percent throughout the final transfer." Mussina turned to the second man, a shorter, stocky figure. "De Paula. Geology?"

"Planet's holding steady. No faults or fissures. Surface and crust integrity are fine. EMF output is normal for this system. Gravity dampers are working as expected. The Seed was perfect in germination. The Egg will be successful in gestation. No errors.'" De Paula spoke slowly, like he was drunk, droning in a monotone.

"Why are they all sweating?" Baz asked. Leonardo noticed the same sheen on their skin as Baz did. Profuse perspiration glistened on their skin and dampened their hair. They wore only the lower halves of their pressure suits, and some were shirtless.

"Environment controls must be on the fritz," said Leonardo. "Maybe they're running life support at low levels to conserve energy. I wonder what the hell happened to that ship."

"Of course, it's entirely possible that they're containing a small sun not a hundred meters from them." Baz snorted and they continued to watch.

"Good work," Mussina said on the screen. "Your calculations were impeccable, De Paula.'" Mussina faced the next man, Marsonek. "Dr. Marsonek. Medical status."

Marsonek broke rank, wiping his brow with a soiled rag. He was older than all the others save perhaps Mussina; an unaugmented late seventies, balding, wispy hair pasted to his sweaty scalp.

"We were wise to bring as many medical supplies as we did, captain. Despite our best efforts, life-support systems are still largely geared towards this ship's original, more human inhabitants."

"'More human,'" Leonardo whispered. "So this wasn't a fully reverse-engineered vehicle. It's most likely a commandeered ship. This man's most likely a doctor pressed into keeping them alive for the short term."

On-screen, Marsonek wiped his brow again and continued.

"Between the ship's life support and the intense conditions of the Seed out there," Marsonek pointed behind them, "'I'd say we have about forty-eight hours left before we die of either radiation poisoning or systems failure. But I trust we should be finished by then." He offered a weak smile. "With the work, I mean.'"

"'Thank you, Doctor,'" said Mussina. He laid a hand on Marsonek's shoulder and reached into his tool belt with the other. In a single fluid movement he drew a piezocutter out and slapped it onto Marsonek's forehead. It made contact with a small flash. Marsonek barely had time to draw in a single sharp breath before he dropped to the floor, the hole in his head neatly cauterized by the cutter's heat. The men standing at either side of him looked momentarily startled as they stepped aside to allow the corpse to fall between them.

"Dr. Marsonek was clearly ill. His protestations would have cost us precious resources." Mussina waved the cutter over his head, the blade whining in the air as if complaining about nothing to do. "What we do here is no laughing matter. We are here for the good of the whole, not anything else. What we do here is for the Martian people and our Greater Cause. Is there anyone who shares Dr. Marsonek's attitude? If so, I promise you that death by this instrument is far preferable to what we have ahead of us if we fail." Mussina looked around at the crew before replacing the cutter on his belt. He put a hand on the shoulder of the last man in line. "Mr. Heredia, you are now Chief Medic and Life-Support Systems specialist. Check to see that Dr. Marsonek left everything in full running order. Though Gestation and the Transit Mechanism will be completed in two days, I want life-support systems functional for two weeks as a precautionary measure. As eager as he is, a few more weeks will not matter to the Harvestman." Heredia nodded and stood taller under his captain's glare. Leonardo threw out a pause mudra.

"*Harvestman?*" asked Leo, leaning forward. "Did he say Harvestman?"

Baz kept his eyes on the screen for a moment then looked at Leonardo.

"I thought I misheard it myself. But yeah. He said it, all right," said Baz.

"Damn it," whispered Leonardo, dropping his head in his hands. The same name that came from the lips of the terrorists two years earlier was now uttered by Mussina. He waved and playback resumed.

Mussina snapped his fingers at the walky-talky. Quad 6 stepped forward. "Take this body to the Recycling center then check outside that all the equatorial anchors are holding steady. Report back at once." The walky-talky bent to pick up the corpse and turned to leave. It was at the door when Mussina called out, "Wait!"

Mussina stepped into view again on the right and approached the command chair. Just behind the raised chair was a large display. It looked as if it were hastily added to the bridge, with its rough exposed wiring and heavy glued corners. Mussina rapped on a control panel with the back of his hand. "You! Wake up! Wake up in there! I want to show you something." He waved the AI closer.

As the AI stepped closer, Leonardo and Baz could see into the display; a female from the collarbones up, lit from consoles glowing dimly around her. She appeared to be floating in a dark pool of blue, viscous liquid. Leonardo thought at first it was a corpse. Then the dim yellow eyes blinked as they peered out from a pale green face. Lank, pale blue hair framed a sallow mouth and nose that floated in the liquid like rotting aquatic plant life. Crude neural connections were made to her skull, invading the brain of the floating figure. The skin around the interface points was raw, bloody and cracked like a compound fracture. As the AI adjusted to the light around it, the interior of the display became more visible. The gaunt, floating woman seemed to be in tremendous pain.

"Oh, God,'" Leonardo said.

"Listen to me!" Mussina shouted at the woman. She writhed as she came to, squirming despite being trapped in the pool. "Listen to me! This man here has been granted the freedom of death you so desire. I promise you, if you take us where I want to go, I will let you die." The woman began to cry, shaking her head and moaning incomprehensibly. Mussina banged a fist against the chair. "Shut up! Shut up! Don't tire yourself out by whinging! Save your strength." Mussina waved off the AI, and it plodded away.

Baz stopped playback.

"What the hell has this monster created?" Leonardo whispered. "Who puts a torture chamber on the bridge of a ship?" He shook his head in disbelief. "What the hell is it?" Leonardo asked, pressing his hands to his temples. His stomach was a cold knot deep inside him.

Baz kept his eyes on the screen, face screwed up like he was enduring some small but nagging pain.

"It's a very crude support chamber, though by now it's a cesspool."

"Support chamber?" Leonardo shouted.

Baz glanced at him then back at the screen, nodding.

"But that's—Do you mean he's trying to ..." He couldn't finish his sentence. Baz looked at the floor and nodded.

"It makes sense but it's horrific. They've hacked the ship to put an Astrogator in. Mussina's made a crude support chamber for permanent long-term neural linking. But they did it badly." Leonardo silently absorbed Baz's words. "It's totally, horribly clear now. Mussina couldn't get them all the way out here in the time he had in a ship that old without an Astrogator. It's barely capable of interplanetary hops. It's the only way they could get out here in time. Piloting into the planet's interior? That's a million-in-one chance of survival."

"Oh, my God ..." Leonardo said. "He didn't—"

"He's not going to release her until they've completed their mission. Which I'm pretty sure is a suicide run."

"I can't even imagine what it could be ..." Leonardo said.

"Whatever it is, they plan to do it in less than three days," said Baz.

CHAPTER TWENTY-ONE
Narcosis

Leonardo paused outside Drina's quarters. Viewing the footage from the Martian walky-talky deeply disturbed him. That Mussina was planning some sort of strange and terrible experiment was in itself troubling. The existence of a small sun only a few kilometers under his feet added to his unease.

But the existence and abusive treatment of an Astrogator was worse.

Leonardo, a UFW captain of twenty years, with over three dozen combat and exomissions to his name had seen the worst the galaxy had to offer.

What horrified him was that humans were often the cause.

Astrogators were goddesses of the modern age. Entire AIs were devoted to them on-board ships. The UFW served them and their every need. Families of Astrogators—women who had achieved disengagement to live a normal life paired with a partner (usually their former captain)—got preferential treatment in everything from housing, emigration, even medical care. Leonardo knew, Drina's bitterness aside, that it was no small feat to spend twenty-plus years of your life physically attached to a spacecraft. The risks were great and the sacrifices enormous. Through these women, humanity stretched its collective wings beyond a small wet, blue rock out into the cosmos. Without women like Drina, captains like himself would rest in suspended animation for months, years or decades, never to see Earth again. Crude misogynist slurs like "Astrogatrix" aside, Astrogators were more important than even the Choudhury drives that propelled their ships through space.

Captains knew this best of all. Leonardo never questioned the rules making arranged marriage between an Astrogator and her captain mandatory; he fell in love with Drina shortly after meeting her. He didn't need to be reminded of the countless studies and data citing the benefits and supporting marriage between the two most important positions on a ship; the loneliness of an ensign's life, even with female crew members aboard, made a partner on-board all the more appealing. Astrogator Romanticism flourished even without the myth of Pilot 23 herself demanding the inclusion of the "paired unit" clause before she turned herself over to the UFW and became the first Astrogator General. Leonardo needed none of that to know how essential his wife and all the women like her were to humanity's very survival.

Their strained and wrecked marriage did nothing to dispel him of his beliefs. And seeing the harsh, barbaric treatment of a woman blessed with such a gift was horrific to Leonardo's very core. Even though neurochemically hardwired with UFW conditioning to protect any Astrogator—especially his own—at all costs, as a human he felt horrified by what he saw. *If I am so lucky as to leave this rock*, Leonardo thought, briefly fingering the UFW insignia on his uniform, *I will drag George Mussina with me back to justice on Earth.*

He stepped into Drina's quarters where she lay, eyes open and staring off into the distance. He was unsure if she was watching something on her HUD or zoning out.

"Hey," he said.

"Hey," she answered, devoid of emotion. "Back for more?"

Leonardo shook his head. All the posturing and devotion moments before could have been lost to her defensiveness. He ignored the bait.

"How do you feel?" he asked instead.

"Physically or mentally?"

"Whichever way you want to answer." Leonardo pulled the chair over and sat. "I believe I'm done arguing with you, Drina."

She nodded. Eventually she turned to face him, her gaze as free of emotion as her voice.

"If that's the case, what brings you here?"

"The situation's gotten more complex—"

"Than before? Like crashing isn't bad enough?"

Leonardo had to laugh.

"Let me show you." He drew a holoscreen in midair at the foot of her bed and began with the location of the cave and went through everything he and Baz had viewed. Leonardo hesitated at the footage inside the bridge.

"What?" Drina asked. "Keep it going!"

"Dree, it's just that ... They've got an Astrogator and—" Drina's eyes widened— "She's not well. I think they've got her there—shit, I know they have her there under duress, and—"

"*Show me,*" Drina said, the set of her jaw hardening. Leonardo let playback resume. Drina watched the scene on the Martian bridge with a stony expression while tears formed in her eyes, sliding down her cheeks onto her uniform. Leonardo stopped playback when it cut away from the Martian Astrogator and closed the screen.

Drina didn't speak, simply sitting with her mouth working silently for a minute.

"Sorry," said Leonardo.

"S'okay," she said, nodding, wiping a single tear from her eye. She kept her gaze on her hands and slowly cracked her knuckles. "Just goes to show you when you think you got it bad, someone else has a shittier stick in their hand than you."

"Where have I heard that before?" asked Leonardo.

"I knew it," she said after a silence. "I felt her."

"You did?" Leonardo asked.

"Yes. Momentarily. When we exited hi-space and were just about to crash. A presence. A presence in the ... *Narthex*."

"Really?" Leonardo cocked his head to one side. "What did you say?"

"The *Narthex*." She opened her eyes and looked ahead.

"All right, so she was here before the crash?" he asked. Drina closed her eyes and a tear worked its way down her cheek again.

"Yeah," she replied, wiping the tear from her face. "It felt so odd to be so alone in there. Time stands still and a second feels like days dragging along. This is *without* the di-hex, you understand? I'm so used to at minimum five or ten others calling out to me. But there was nothing for ages. Then a presence developed, but not a normal one. At first I thought it was sort of my reflection, like my own injured mind's thoughts echoing and coming back at me like through a fog. Then I perceived it as a distinctly different entity. It was kind of a ... half presence, like someone who'd been drugged. But the odd thing is you can't access the *Mapparium* or even the *Narthex* unless you're fully aware. That's what diaphanoxamine helps with—in the right dosage, of course. It felt like I was back in the barracks listening to someone nearby talking in their sleep."

"Did she speak of anything in particular?"

"No," she answered, rubbing her eyes. "Well, I could tell there was a great deal of pain. When she could speak, it was as if I wasn't there. I mean, we can all tell when there are others in the *Narthex*. But she, this one, didn't seem to register when I was trying to contact her. She just kept babbling on about the pain, trying to break free, sending a message or something. And a word ... " Drina held her hand up for a moment as she searched for it. "Harvestman."

Leonardo nodded.

"Just like the terrorists used in the Newhope bombing. And we just heard Mussina say it in a conversation." Leonardo paused. "Drina, did she say anything else?"

"No. Nothing at all." Drina laid her head in her hands.

"I know how this must make you feel." Leonardo reached out and held her hand. Drina flinched before letting him hold her hand stiffly.

"I've never had to deal with one of us as an ... enemy before." Another tear formed and worked its way slowly down her cheek. "I don't think anyone has. I don't care if she's FMR. She's still an Astrogator."

"This is no collaborator we're talking about. She's there under duress, Drina," said Leonardo. "I can assure you of that. There's no way she's willingly helping them."

"I know. It's a strange situation to be in. It's like I have a window into the enemy ship."

Leonardo looked at her as a shiver worked its way down his spine.

"What?" she asked.

"Do you think you can contact her?" Drina looked at him for a second, her tongue working the inside of her left cheek. "If you're well enough, of course." Before she could answer, Leonardo flicked a mudra in the air.

"Medic? Medical status of Asgr. Valencia?"

The avatar appeared at the foot of the throne, and turned to Leonardo.

"Asgr. Valencia is in stable condition. Her cortex has been repaired and her metabolic levels are acceptable. She may resume normal duties in twenty-four hours, though I would like to check on her condition at least every four hours."

Leonardo nodded and the avatar disappeared with a nod of its own.

"It's your lucky day." He stood and let go of her hand. "Do you think you can contact her without them knowing?"

"I don't know." She looked at Leonardo, slowly closing then opening her eyes. "You want me to?"

"Uh, obviously." Leonardo looked out the doorway to the bridge. "Look, find out what their mission is. But don't let on that you're here. You may have to do a bit of play-acting or something. If she finds out she may let it slip. Mussina would attack and we can't hold him off. Him thinking we're all dead has been our biggest advantage yet."

Drina nodded. "What do you want me to do when I find out their mission?"

"Report back to me and I'll let you know. But we may just be able to save her and derail their plans. And hopefully get our fucking asses off this rock."

"Captain!" She said, in a mocking tone. "Such language in front of a lady."

"Yeah, I've heard the lady say much worse lately."

"But I had a right to."

"Maybe." Leonardo looked Drina in the eyes. "Drina, are you on board with me on this? No fighting now, I need a soldier. I need a professional."

"If it will get us the fuck off this rock you got whatever you need. Within reason," she said, one eyebrow cocked.

"Yeah, I know. No sex. You're safe from me. I'm sick of doing it on the throne anyway." Leonardo swallowed his piqued interest. He walked towards the door, turning around just as he stepped out. "Get some rest. You're going to need it. It's gonna to be a tough one, I think."

She nodded.

Leonard left her and went to the bridge. Baz was reviewing video, the screen jumping as images fast-forwarded along.

"Hey." He stopped and stared at Leonardo. Leonardo noticed Baz's sunken eyes in their sockets, exhaustion making his skin sallow and pale.

"Yikes, man. You look like hell. Take six hours and sleep."

"Real sleep?" Baz said, his brow furrowing. "I don't know if I can anymore."

"I feel the same way. The idea of sleeping while we're in the midst this crap seems foolhardy at best. But despite all the advances of modern science, real sleep still beats all." Baz rose and went off to his cabin, leaving the video paused on the fiery scene inside the planet.

Leonardo returned to his cabin, dropped onto the bed and fell asleep almost before his eyes closed.

CHAPTER TWENTY-TWO
Dominion

Leonardo awoke from dreamless, heavy sleep in exactly the position he lay down in, an arm over his eyes, the other hanging down off the side. Mother always warned him to keep his arms in the bed, saying the *cucuy* would pull him into the sea to serve in her drowned mansions. Leonardo finally learned his lesson when a water scorpion climbed up through the trash grate one night and pinched his little hand. He fingered the scar, remembering the scare he got. Only the beating Mama gave him for waking her stopped his screaming.

He rose from the bed and groaned, lowering his arm off his face. He rubbed his head and face, slapped his cheeks. Checking his HUD showed him he'd been asleep for more than eight hours. He swore and stumbled to the bridge. Leonardo found Baz sitting at the front console, arms across his chest, watching video stream by at high speed across the monitor. He barely nodded as he heard Leonardo enter.

"Sorry, I crashed hard," said Leonardo, trying to hide the guilt in his voice. "Coffee. Enhanced," he mumbled to the dispenser which moments later drew him a fortified cup of dark, steaming brew.

"No worries. I did the same. Jason was on top of things while we were out." Baz reached out for a coffee mug in front of him, taking a sip. "I had him split off a subpersona to do a deeper forensic search through their walky-talky. Looks like he found some interesting stuff."

Leonardo sat. The video speeding by made him dizzy. He closed his eyes and rubbed them. "Okay, I want to see that in a second. First, let's just do some brainstorming here." Baz turned to face Leonardo, sipping from his mug.

"I've got a feeling time is running out. Mussina planned to do something big here. I just can't tell what."

"Their sun isn't quite clear enough?"

"No, it isn't. The data is difficult to decipher—"

"—and not just what's in an alien language," Baz said with a nod.

"Alien language?" Leonardo said. "Where? What?"

"Near as I can figure. There's all that stuff in Transparent Ones script and a whole bunch of stuff Jason can't decipher. He says it's similar but still 'wholly inhuman.'" Baz held up two fingers of his left hand, signifying quotes.

"Alien, huh?"

"Yup. I know what you're thinking," said Baz, spreading his arms wide, shrugging while keeping his coffee from spilling.

"'Baz, there's no evidence of alien life discovered other than that of the Transparent Ones."

"Well, Jason's pretty damn smart. And I agree with him. Whatever the origin, there's so much of it and it points in many directions. Seeing the sun inside this planet made some things clearer but not much." Baz paused to sip. "For all its brightness, finding it sheds no light on why they built it here."

"Here's what I think," said Leonardo, leaning in and encircling the mug in his hands. "Mussina's crew commandeered a vessel and built this planet out here."

"If I hadn't seen it myself, I wouldn't believe it. Ok, sure. And if we can get that tech back to Earth, we'll be rich."

"Anyway, Mussina came on board with us, went to Baaklum Cha'am to retrieve artifacts from a Transparent Ones site. Mussina needed to bring these artifacts here and build this Sower and Son inside the planet. But then what? He wasn't going to stay here. They have to leave somehow."

"That's what the Astrogator is for. What exactly is that down there?"

"A small sun." Leonardo said.

"Okay, sure looks like it," Baz said. "Still, why make it way out here? What's the point? Energy?"

"Why inside a planet even?"

"Keep it hidden?"

"Why, though? From whom? And why hidden out here?"

"No idea ..." Baz shook his head.

"Think about it. The UFW would have seen them doing this with Phobos or Deimos perhaps, and shot it down or blown it apart. Even with those orbital weapons platforms."

"And this planet's made from something so dense sensors can't penetrate. So they could build it without attracting attention. You heard Jason: its creation was passed off as a natural event, like two asteroids colliding." Leonardo nodded, not feeling much clearer for sleeping nor having woken up. He wondered if the endurance drugs were even working.

"Another thing. What did Mussina mean when he said 'for the greater good or the whole?'" Leonardo asked. Baz shrugged. "What a weird way to inspire the crew."

"Not sure. I need to see more," Baz said. "That's key to understanding this. There's new stuff that's pretty interesting."

"Why not show me?"

"Because I like to hear myself speak," Baz said with a smirk. He ran his hand over the holokeys. A schematic appeared with data and markers. In the lower right-hand corner was an FMR logo. Some characters were in UFW standard, others Leonardo had never seen before. It showed a cone-like vehicle with an object placed inside, identified only as a cylinder with a pair of strange characters over it. In the background was a small planet.

"Looks like the corsair from that video earlier. The one that—"

Leonardo stopped in midsentence as the graphic animated. First the ship sped off towards the planet. The view zoomed into the craft's interior, pilot in front, alien object at rear. The vessel crashed into the planet, with the payload detonating just before impact. Both craft and pilot were destroyed, with debris from the explosion spreading out several hundred million kilometers. Near the epicenter debris stopped and retreated towards the center, glowing red and roiling with activity. Then the viewpoint zoomed in again as debris formed into a series of accretion rings that merged and grew into a sphere that expanded, adding fragments from the destroyed planet to its growing bulk. An overlay showed the size as a few hundred kilometers in diameter, growing at a rate of kilometers a minute.

A staccato crackling came over the speakers.

"Guess there's some audio." Baz mudraed and a synthesized voice narrated what they saw.

"—will form in time, a highly efficient retention sphere. Research shows that proper programming will shape the shell in any way desired. The shell is designed to organically collect and redistribute energy with one hundred percent retention. The thickness, density and conductivity of the particles are programmed into the device. This is the beginning of the work done by the Sower for the Son. Once the Seed is in place, the enclosing sphere—"

"Holy crap!" said Baz, stopping the video. "That's what they did in that other video. This is a *demo*."

"Of a Dyson sphere?" said Leonardo, rubbing his scalp. "Saturn Lab was working on those a few years back. That lunatic Dr. Yee and his team. I saw demonstrations there of a Dyson sphere about a half klick across. Highly unstable. Couldn't contain it for long. The last I heard they were still a long way away from building one. That was a few years back obviously, but—"

"Then there's no way the FMR could do that with human technology. I doubt they've been doing R&D on Mars for the last hundred and thirty-some-odd years. Clearly they recovered alien tech somehow—"

"Look, it's very simple: *Mussina*. It was Mussina. That guy's been all over the UFW's reach as an 'archaeologist' gathering artifacts. I'm sure he's got of lots of alien tech. We can't be the only ship he's duped." Leonardo shook his head. "It's small consolation that another captain may have unwittingly been smuggling Transparent Ones technology thanks to Mussina," he said.

"So what else?" Baz looked at the list.

"Here. Jason thinks this is of interest."

Another animation. This showed the cross section of a planet. Its hollow core was clearly visible, the crust a consistent ten kilometers thick. At each pole the crust ran thinner at only two kilometers. The interior was filled with a glowing fireball.

"So what?" Leonardo asked Baz. "We already know this. Hell we've seen this. Why show me now?" Leonardo despised his own testiness.

"Leo, it's just a little—Just ... *watch*."

The animation continued. The hollow planet moved to the upper left-hand corner and another planet took center, with green continents and oceans in blue. At first it looked like a generic planet. Leonardo's HUD generated a suggestion as to which planet they were viewing.

"Christ it's ..." Leonardo said, the pit of his stomach turning cold and wet.

"*Earth*," whispered Baz.

A target appeared in the middle of the Pacific Ocean. A yellow line connected this to the surface of Stokes 6. Between Earth and Stokes 6, a jagged pair of red waves broke up the yellow line, abbreviating the long distance separating the two spheres. They watched as the animation progressed: Stokes 6 moved closer, piercing the hazy outer edge of the ionosphere before disintegrating in Earth's atmosphere; as the planetoid disintegrated, the concealed fireball tumbled like a nut from its shell into the ocean. Miniature flares and waves of distortion erupted from its surface in ever-growing ripples. Devastation spread out from it exponentially, more powerful than even the meteors that struck Earth in the age of the dinosaurs. They watched as it took its toll, remapping the surface of the planet. The resulting shockwave and displacement destroyed everything on the surface, boiling away two-thirds of the oceans. The desolation was coldly documented with on-screen data.

"Any audio?" Leonardo asked, his throat dry.

"No. No ... None." Baz's voice was as grave and parched as his own.

They watched the simulated destruction of Earth continue.

Data scrolled down along the right-hand side in a cool blue stream as the visual display showed the outcome of Stokes 6's encounter with humanity's birthplace. The reconstituted icecaps melted, drowning hundreds of thousands of square kilometers of reclaimed coastal land and partially refilling boiled oceans. Continental outlines shifted dramatically, erasing boundaries and even many countries off the map again and again. Soon the planet became fully flooded, mountaintops worn down to long, narrow sandbars and archipelagos. Leonardo noted the area he'd grown up in, the Golden Coast of Connecticut, lay submerged under several hundred meters of water.

The animation held for a moment, pausing to show the submerged world before it began to change again. A time-lapse indicator showed developments blossoming forth over days, weeks, months and then years. A small rectangular window in the lower right-hand corner showed a chromatographic image: levels of oxygen, nitrogen, hydrogen and other elements listed in fluctuating amounts. Leonardo watched as a slow, uneasy realization came upon him: over a period of almost a year, the Earth's atmosphere would be dramatically recalibrated to kill *everything* on the planet. Temperatures rose too high in some regions and dropped too low in others. A readout for "picomatic microbial growth" soared all over. By the end of the simulation the atmosphere had been rendered toxic to human life.

The simulation ended and a dialog box appeared stating simply, "Operation Recast Complete."

Baz threw up, vomit splashing through the holokeyboard and hitting the console below. Leonardo stood abruptly and unsteadily, icy sweat breaking out all over his skin. The simulation, an agonizing two minutes and fourteen seconds long, replayed until Leonardo finally waved it off.

"Baz?" he asked breathlessly.

"They're going to use this thing on Earth. *Earth.*"

Leonardo looked at the image frozen on the display before him. In his mind the object repeatedly collided with the planet—Earth and its twelve billion inhabitants. The damage would be much worse than the meteor collisions that wiped out the dinosaurs sixty-five million years ago. No hope for anything to re-emerge as the new dominant species.

No species left.

"My God ..." Leonardo could barely speak.

"Okay, let's get back on track," said Baz without conviction. "So ... So they destroy Earth by hurling this planet at it."

"Yes, but how do they transport it there?" Leonardo sat down, shuffling his feet so the cleaner rat that emerged from a slot in the floor could clean up after Baz. "The FMR can't move a planet to another location, can they? The UFW certainly can't."

"No, I don't think so. I ... I can't figure that out." Baz rubbed his jaw and stared at the floor. He looked at Leonardo. "It doesn't matter much after what we've seen. Look at what they've done already. They infiltrated our ship, landed it without killing Mussina, and smuggled artifacts into the interior of this planet. Doesn't much matter if we can't do it because they certainly fucking think they can."

"I suppose they'll use their ship to do it. Otherwise they would have scavenged from *Resurgam* or just hijacked it. They'll use their Astrogator to move the whole thing. Somehow," Leonardo said.

Baz shook his head.

"Nope. The UFW tried that. 2443, on the *Eldridge* out of Winfield Base on Pluto."

"I don't remember that," Leonardo said.

"*Eldridge* was parked in orbit. The theory was a ship could generate a wide Choudhury field around the asteroid. They paired two Astrogators up and doubled the AI power. Amped up the drives with some enormous field amplifiers in the hold. Nothing happened, except the ship broke apart before the crew managed to escape. The AIs were destroyed. The Astrogators were both disconnected and placed on full disability afterwards due to the strain."

"Mmm," said Leonardo.

"Sorry, Leo, but I doubt the Martians would attempt this with just one older, abused, and depleted Astrogator. And those desktop research AIs they stole couldn't handle the calculations for a jump on a ship that size, let alone something on this scale. They've been spying on us, watching experimental flights. They know what's up."

They were silent for a while, lost in thought.

Suddenly Baz looked up.

"*The planet,*" he said.

Leonardo frowned at him.

"Look here. Why do they need all that power? Not just to hold that fireball in. Why build a Dyson sphere? Way out in the middle of nowhere? They're certainly not going to live out here. Their plan is to get the whole planet to Earth and destroy it." Baz stood up, wobbling for a second then finding his balance. "To do that, you'd need an immense amount of energy and computing power. The energy of a small *sun*, right?"

"Sure," Leonardo said, nodding, dreading every word of it. "I suppose."

"This whole planet is an energy source," said Baz. "Perhaps a battery even. It's going to get them out there somehow and then destroy itself; a suicide mission."

"What if they recovered something else from Baaklum Cha'am? Those other artifacts," Leonardo said.

"What?" Baz asked.

"The artifacts Mussina stole. We know one made the sun," Leonardo pointed below them. "That was the Sower. What about the other thing? Maybe it's some kind of alien supercomputer."

"Something else that Mussina took from the planet? Besides what we saw him using on the video of the fireball creation?"

"Yes."

"Sure. I mean ..." Baz leaned back in his chair to consider it. "Anything's possible, right?"

"Absolutely," said Leonardo. "There's got to be something that links this all together. We'll need to have all the data ready when we get back to Earth."

"We can't just leave, Leo. We need to do something."

"Oh, we will, trust me. I just need to have all the evidence in hand to give to the UFW."

"Okay then," said Baz.

Leonardo got up and went back to Drina's quarters. Her color and mood were both improved. She almost seemed pleased to see him.

"Oh, yes, I seem to remember this man. A little sleep does you good." She distractedly offered a smile and returned to some charts before her. "I've been running some figures and have found some pretty good routes out of here. When we're free of the peculiar magnetic interference of this planet, we'll be able to hit hi-space in no time."

"Good." Leonardo barely registered what she said. He was glad she was keeping herself busy. "Speaking of hi-space, any luck with contacting the other Astrogator?" Drina laid her pedia on her lap. Cables settled around her head with a quiet, fussy flutter.

"Somewhat." She stared up at the ceiling. "She seemed to recognize my presence. I fit in with her hallucinatory state. I asked her name. She said it was Tanya Balanz. I asked the name of her ship. She said it was the originally the *Hector Smith*, but after its capture they renamed it *The Great Heart Of The Supreme Brain* in honor of the first FMR President. What's his name? Maggiacomo."

"Figures," Leonardo said. Information popped up in his HUD. "The *Hector Smith* was commandeered near Sainbara. Back in the late twenty-three hundreds."

Drina nodded.

"She's been kept alive this long. She was twenty-two when the ship was captured. She's eighty-three now, a few decades past mandatory retirement, and she's been kept under extreme duress. I tried to ask her what they've been doing with her all this time, but nothing really came out other than ..." Drina swallowed and closed her eyes. Tears seemed imminent before she reopened her eyes. "They've tortured her, Leo. *For years.* Now it's torture for her to jump. They didn't kill her when they first captured her because they wanted more Astrogators and the technology, but they couldn't get it."

"I wonder how long it took them before they realized her DNA's locked tight with suicide pathogens. The FMR seceded before Astrogators appeared, so they would have no idea—" He saw Drina was rolling her eyes and flapping her hand open and closed at him. "Sorry."

"You don't need to tell me about my DNA's little secret weapon, Leo. It kept this ship and the *Wellstone* free of dirty diapers."

Leonardo had to laugh.

"And all along I thought it was my self-control and timing. So she didn't give you any idea of their intentions?"

"No. I doubt she's aware of anything. They keep her as uninformed as possible and drugged unless—"

A klaxon blared. Leonardo ran to the bridge at full speed to find Baz in front of the monitors.

"Sirs," came the voice of Jason from over head. "In running through captured data from the Martian AI, there were some files that were heavily encrypted. I've finally decrypted these."

"Let's see it then," said Baz.

"Recorded Transmissions," said Leonardo, reading the folder heading. Baz scrolled through the thousands of files listed before them.

"Whatcha looking for? Letters from home?"

Leonardo hushed him with a backhand wave. Filenames and codes blended in with one another in his swirling, fatigued brain.

One file stood out with its peculiar routing signature.

"'Miranda 222 UFW sat. REROUTE/MOLITRO 180424-68.'" Leonardo pointed to select it. A small screen opened, laid over the window of filenames. "That's from right after we crashed. Miranda 222 is an old comsat, I think."

"How old you want, man? There're museum pieces floating out there. Anything not shot down during space junk clean-ups is still up there. Not just around Earth, either."

"Miranda 222 is part of the legacy Extrasolar Relay on the outskirts of the solar system," said Jason.

"Right. I remember it from when I had to do a training EVA repair during my tour on the *ESS Putnam*," said Leonardo. "It was put up in the twenty-second century for high-speed comms with generation ships."

"So?" Baz said.

"See this reroute to MOLITRO? MOLITRO's in deep space. It's a networked transmitter, the first in a series stretching way out into the depths. Think they've been communicating on disused frequencies through old satellites?"

"Sure, I don't see why not." Baz looked off into the air for a second. "Sons of bitches could be using telegraph for—"

"I doubt anyone checks all of the Miranda's bands at all times. The MOLITRO network handles enough volume that you could send bits through without attracting attention. There are millions of transmissions going through it, in and out, every second. The FMR could easily receive and transmit."

"Possibly," said Baz, "even with an AI monitoring they'd mask it to look like interference, chatter or benign data. Maybe bounce around channels or frequencies. Let's see it." Leonardo nodded. Baz mudraed and a screen of static appeared.

***

"'Are we connected?'" Mussina's voice boomed loudly over the speakers, startling them. A garbled hissing came after. "'Is he there? Is the Harvestman there?'"

"Pause," said Leonardo. "Harvestman. Guess we'll finally get to meet the guy." He squinted. "Where's the video?"

"My guess is it's lost. Or maybe they had audio only. Why one side is more garbled, I don't know. Lemme see if I can fix it." Baz adjusted some filters at the panel, and shook his head. "No deal. It's distorted pretty badly. Whatever numbnut sent this couldn't dial his way out of a paper bag."

"Keep going," said Leonardo. The static snow unfroze, with Mussina muttering something unintelligible. The muttering stopped as he said, "Yes? Good!" His voice changed suddenly, becoming less overbearing and more like that of an eager child.

"Harvestman? Are you there? Excellent! Yes, I know it is difficult for you to journey to the surface. We would never have asked if it wasn't important. I can assure you it is worth the risk." Mussina paused, an irritating buzzing noise rising in the background. "Yes, Harvestman. I imagine it is difficult to see the surface of your world after all this time. The land must have looked wonderful in your day. How I wish I could have seen it when you were younger—What's that? Well, I understand you've not aged a great deal, but you must admit it has been a great while since the Uprising." More buzzing in response to Mussina's silence.

Leonardo looked over to Baz.

"Is that interference?" he whispered. Baz shook his head and looked over at the waveform for clues to the noise source. He looked back at Leonardo and held his hands up.

"'I know, Harvestman. You need not be reminded of the horrors. I cannot imagine the loneliness and isolation you have endured only to find yourself the sole survivor of ... Yes, yes, I will proceed with the detail of our plans. I know you have only a short time available to you. We know well the dangers—but oh, the rewards! When our work here is finished it will make that horror a thing of the past. Yes, yes, it will take time, but I assure you this is a first step towards your freedom.'"

"Sole survivor?" whispered Baz.

"Pause," said Leonardo. "Who's he's talking to? And this 'Harvestman'? Nothing on him since Newhope?"

Baz shook his head. "A superior, maybe? He's speaking with a great deal of deference."

"Yes, he is." Leonardo looked out the viewport. Stokes 6's snowy, wasted surface stretched out. He wondered when the snow would start melting, the landscape changing. Then he remembered a cave that led underground to the madman they were listening to. "What does he mean by 'Uprising'? What's he referring to? The FMR revolt? The attack at Newhope?"

"Maybe it's someone from Mars? Maybe the uprising he's referring to is the original uprising of the Martian colonists?"

Leonardo shrugged then shook his head.

"That was largely bloodless. Perhaps ... Is it someone alive from then?" Leonardo thought for a moment. "They would be around two hundred years old. They had good cryogenics there, from what I've read. They needed them during the Plague Years."

"Yeah, okay. Maybe. That bit about coming to the surface? Like someone's been underground? In hiding? Political refugee, maybe?" asked Baz, rising to get more coffee.

"The Regolithian Resistance did go underground—literally—in the early 2300s. Perhaps it's someone from then cryogenically frozen and now revived?" Leonardo turned back to face Baz at the dispenser. "My God! What if it's Maggiacomo himself?"

"Could be." Baz sat down. "This is all just conjecture. Perhaps if we listen to it all first?"

"Sure." More video snow and the sound of Mussina's voice.

"'I am sure you have been debriefed about my activities thus far? Since I left the sacred regolith? Yes, sir. The plans unfolded beautifully and aroused no suspicion. They were unaware of me. My work left me above suspicion. They were so hungry for knowledge of the Transparent Ones, at least what they want to know—hmm? Oh, that is the name given to the Observers, yes, your oppressors. As I was saying, when they saw the knowledge that I possessed, they sped up the processing of my travel documentation. Ortiz did as I said and secured the vessel with the same captain involved in the attempt to get another Sower and Son from the other site ... Yes, that one. The fools saw nothing odd in any of my requests. They agreed to pick me up at some backwater service station. Excuse me? It's a type of depot for fuel—It's irrelevant, sir. The fact is they accepted me with little inquiry and let me go with them to Baaklum Cha'am. Excuse me? Yes, I am sorry about the language barrier, sir, but without certain procedures it's impossible to speak to you as you would wish."

"Hold it," hissed Leonardo. He could barely turn to look at Baz and clenched his fists. "It was a setup. Goddamn Mussina set us up."

"Son of a bitch," said Baz, shaking his head.

"Newhope and then this?" Leonardo rubbed his temples. "Unbelievable. Could it have been set up from way back then?"

"Apparently, yes."

"Bastard." Leonardo bit a knuckle and shook his head. "I fell for it hook, line and—"

"Leo, don't. How the hell would we have known?"

"Fool me once, Baz." Leo stood and paced the bridge. "I got played. Big time. They've kept the UFW on High Alert since then. What do you think they're gonna do to me after this?"

"Well, worst-case scenario is they might never find out. God forbid, we might not be able to stop this from—"

"Spare me. I got played. I'm Mussina's bitch, end of story. Fuck it. I'll cry about it later."

Leonardo sat back down.

"Okay, what about this other stuff? Procedures? 'Language barrier?' What the hell does that mean? Who is he speaking with?" Leonardo asked again. In frustration he waved playback on.

"I separated from them the moment we arrived. The instructions I found at Cit-Bolon-Tum were explicit and perfect. The location of the Hive Builder was exactly where it was supposed to be and left untouched. I am sorry your people met with an untimely end there. Hmm? No, it was sufficiently long ago that there was hardly anything older than you, sir. You will have to compute that into your own timescale to fully understand, but I did my best to find any remains. The scope of destruction left little in the way of surviving organic matter."

"Stop," Leonardo shouted. Baz jumped. Leonardo whirled Baz in his chair to face him. "Mussina's speaking to this Harvestman as if he's been to Baaklum Cha'am and Cit-Bolon-Tum. But there have only been three missions out there besides ours: the first military survey, a colonization drone survey and one other exoarchaeological team."

"You're right. Doesn't really make sense. Like whoever he's talking to knows the planet personally from before any of those missions," finished Baz. Leonardo nodded. "Weird. That comment about almost sounding 'Martian.' I don't understand it at all. I mean sure, there's a slight accent, but ..."

From within Leonardo something rose up knocking the loose ends in his mind around before arranging them. Disparate facts and elements clicked together, bringing a very uncomfortable realization. With a wet descent of Leonardo's twisting stomach gut, he swallowed hard and willed himself to speak.

"It can't be ..." Leonardo said.

Baz looked intently at him.

"We're listening to him talking about finding artifacts no older than this Harvestman? Which, if the Harvestman is Maggiacomo or some old-guard FMR founder that means we're talking about one hundred or so years ago, right? That makes no sense. There weren't any expeditions out there a hundred years ago. It was only catalogued about fifty-seven years ago." Leonardo rubbed his forehead with the thoughts swirling inside. "Do you really think he's talking to Maggiacomo?"

"Sounds like it. Yeah. I can't imagine who else."

"Why the 'language barrier' and those procedures he mentioned? This is insane. I can't believe I'm thinking this." Leonardo stood and shook his head, trying to clear the unwelcome idea from growing in his brain. Was Roberto Maggiacomo, mastermind of the FMR Revolt, boxed up and frozen for a hundred years until now? If so, why? There was the well-documented struggle for Martian independence and Maggiacomo's belligerent hatred for the UFW in the final futile days of cold war diplomatic relations. It made sense in a way Leonardo didn't like. Maggiacomo was certainly crazy enough to try something like this. To be revived in order to help plan the destruction of Earth, though?

"When were the first Transparent Ones settlements found?"

"Dunno. Hey, Jason?"

"The first Transparent Ones settlements were found in 2397. Azh Bolom Tzacab was on one of the infertile moons of Alpha Centauri's Mykonos. Discovered by—"

"Enough." Leonardo thought for a second. "They must have defrosted Maggiacomo, debriefed him about all this stuff and asked for guidance. There's no way he could have been conscious during all that time. He'd have been 107 when the first settlement was found and his health was always poor. He was revered as a messiah. It makes sense that he would choose to be frozen and revived occasionally. Let's say for argument's sake that he was frozen for posterity to live to see the FMR emerge victorious—and Mussina here is debriefing him."

"Okay." Baz nodded. "So what?"

"I don't know. What else we can pull out of our asses?"

Baz laughed and waved playback on. Mussina's voice filled the bridge.

"In the interest of time, I will be brief. Sower and Seed are united. Farmer and Fielder, as you know, were recovered and brought to this location a few months ago. All the family affairs are in order. With the Hive Builder in place, the family shall be complete. Within a short time, the Family shall unite and rebuild the Home World. It will be glorious! There will be no more Opposition. One day you will walk its surface and it will be like your original home. Yes, Harvestman? Ah, I understand. Thank you. I wish I could say I will see you, but we knew our previous meeting was the last I would see of Mars. I am honored to have been a part of the rebuilding. I hope that one day—" The screen flickered for a moment and Mussina's face appeared on the screen. "What? There's an encryption tracer on us? Has it been broken? Cut the link now!" As Mussina spoke, the snow-filled screen shuddered for a moment then brightened with a new image.

Its brief appearance burned into Leonardo's mind.

In the hundreds of times he and Baz replayed those few seconds they memorized every detail, horrid and banal: the furnishings, the arrangement of everything in it and the movements of everyone in the room. How a certain chair fell, the steps and direction a running soldier went in. Leonardo would note how wrong he was in his earlier assessment of who the Harvestman might be, for couched in the final few seconds of video was the first and only glimpse of the Harvestman.

At that moment Leonardo and Baz joined the ranks of the first humans to witness a sentient being from another planet. And they would most likely be the last.

After the initial shock wore off and he had time to think, Leonardo remembered that as long as humans looked upon their reddish neighbor in the sky, they wondered who or what populated this planet. Leonardo himself had read Wells, Verne, Heinlein, Bradbury, Burroughs, Robinson and Asimov's tales of Mars as a child; little green men, voluptuous space women and three-fingered cyclopean invaders swooping in from triangular or saucer-shaped spacecraft were some of the more popular candidates for Martian inhabitants. Late twentieth- and early twenty-first-century science ruled out the existence of these beings and claimed Mars's only living occupants had been tiny microbial elements living millions of years before during a brief wet period. This microbial life found its way to the planet from bits of rock flung into space via fierce meteor impacts on neighboring Earth. The presence and abundance of water on Mars and discoveries in the late twenty-first and early twenty-second centuries did nothing to shake the determined minds of Earth scientists. Up until that very moment when these two men gazed upon the screen, scientists believed the highest form of life on Mars had been microbial at best.

The reality was far different.

To Leonardo and Baz it was plainly obvious Mars had once been populated by something far more advanced, complex and stranger than anyone ever imagined. What they saw was unlike anything either Leonardo or Baz had seen on all the worlds they had visited. Combing through the UFW archives Jason could find nothing that came close to what flashed on the screen for that brief, hideous interval.

The creature may have been insectoid at one point long ago—it was now almost entirely cybernetic. Its overall appearance was of multiple, jointed limbs spread out radially from a spherical trunk. As they emerged from the central body the limbs grew into detailed extremities. Some were more blunt looking; one was like a hammer, another like a large axe, but others were very finely formed for specific tasks with a six-fingered hand; another a long, narrow probing tool.

Amidst the array of limbs were strange, wide, scythe-like metallic shapes like human scapula overgrown and malformed. Amongst these were bizarre black stalk-like protuberances like charred bones sticking out of a doused fire pit. The creature resembled a burned metal sculpture or scrap cobbled together from an atrocious factory fire. Wires and thin cables connected the scythes, limbs and stalks together in a complex arrangement. To Leonardo's rational human brain, the arrangement of blades, wires and jutting stalk-bones should have come apart without being welded or bonded together. But it held together and more fantastically it *moved* together in a hypnotically graceful dance despite the frantic setting. As it moved, the light hit the scythe shapes in different angles; some shined while others were dull or reflected back absolutely nothing. It was a wonder it didn't slice itself apart as it moved frantically in the small, cramped room.

The central trunk of the body held the most curious part. Once past the initial horror of seeing it for the first time, Leonardo and Baz repeatedly viewed the recording. The metallic structure of the being's body was merely ornate armor formed around a central sphere of bright magenta light. It seemed to have some mass or substance, though what it was remained unclear despite Jason's detailed analysis. All the AI could tell them was that there was energy creating the illumination in that bright sphere.

The entire scene lasted only a few seconds. The garbled snow instantly gave way to a standard prefab conference room. At the far end of the table stood the Harvestman. On the wall behind it was the FMR seal, Mars looming large inside the familiar pink ring. An armed FMR soldier stood to the right, his black spacesuit and green skin out of place in the drab room. As Mussina shouted "Cut the connection!" the Harvestman sprang to life, limbs and antennas flailing. From some boxy apparatus inside the sphere came the hissing, screeching sound. The soldier sprang into action, knocking the camera with his rifle butt. The camera fell, briefly showing the floor of the room while lying on its side. Men ran across the room for a second before the image turned to snow. Shouting, angry voices continued for another second before the audio ended with a loud pop.

"Freeze that!" Leonardo shouted.

Baz slammed the holoconsole and the image froze. Leonardo made a small sound in the back of his throat, something between choking and a sigh. Baz turned to his right and retched. When he recovered, they both stared at the image frozen on the screen.

"What the hell is that thing?" Baz said when he finally caught his breath.

"*The Harvestman,*" said Leo breathlessly.

"Yeah, but it's—"

"*A Martian.*"

"I know, but—"

"No, it's not what I expected either. But ... I have no idea what I expected." Leonardo put his head in his hands. The reversal of several hundred years of scientific fact was hard to comprehend. Humanity spent the better part of the last two hundred years convinced they were alone in the solar system, if not the galaxy. Now these two men crashed on an isolated world suddenly found the opposite was true.

"Shit. I was expecting that face from old media. You remember that? The fat guy with sunglasses and a mustache. Not this fucking shit!" Baz waved his arms around in imitation of the creature.

"Baz, get centered." They sat still, intoned a centering mantra, then opened their eyes.

"Well, that's as centered as I am gonna get," Baz said.

"What do you think we have here?" Leonardo asked Baz.

"Something completely insane. I don't know what this Father, Sower, Sun or Son bullshit is but something's going to happen soon. All these code names—We know what it was. We saw the footage of that demonstration and that fireball down there." Baz pointed down. "They're gonna to try to destroy everything on Earth, Leo." Leonardo noticed Baz no longer said the word "Earth" with the casual disregard from before.

"Then they're going to make it a place where that thing can live."

They both looked toward the direction of the cave.

CHAPTER TWENTY-THREE
Causality

Leonardo stalked the ship, walking down the corridors on one side then the other. He'd left the bridge to think. Despite the two kilometers he covered, his perambulations couldn't shake loose the grim certainty of what Baz said. In a strange moment of clarity, he saw the situation differently than that of a human terrified for the safety of Earth. The simulation they had witnessed, coupled with the briefest glimpse of an alien being all led to a simple terrible conclusion.

One life form was systematically preparing to dominate another's habitat. Martians were seeking to inhabit Earth.

The irony of the FMR once being children born of human mothers was not lost on him. The rumors of gruesomely transformed Martian colonists aside, things had gone wrong all too quickly. He could hardly clear his mind for all the confusion. Behind everything, the gaping maw of his terror begged him to drown it out with sweet Bun-Ho. The thought of drinking made Leonardo quicken his pace, stamp his feet harder into the deck as he walked along.

Finally, he turned about-face and headed back to his quarters. He knew of one objective voice he could stand to hear.

   ***

Leonardo found himself sitting on the patio again, the sun high and hot above his head. It was noon in the vineyard. In his hand he cradled a cool metal goblet of sweet wine. A platter was laid out on the table before him: olives, feta, meats and roasted vegetables.

It took everything in him to not shout at the simulation to stop wasting his time and bring Horacio in. Time dilation or not, Leonardo felt the last sands were tumbling rapidly from their hourglass. Finally the old man emerged from the stairway to his left. He wiped his hands on a handkerchief, smiling as he saw Leonardo.

"Well, Leo. Not shy of the grape now, are we?"

"Spare me, dead man." Leonardo looked out over the fields, the sun burning down upon them, making him think of the fire of a sun much closer to him.

"Well, then. Things haven't improved, I take it? What news have you?" Horacio strode over to his seat as Leonardo began recounting events since their last meeting. The old man's expression was always the same: listening patiently, with eyes focused on a point far ahead. Leonardo laid out the developments of their situation before him.

"Interesting," said Horacio when Leonardo finished. "Well, you will certainly be providing for your future when you return to Earth. The discovery of sentient alien life. Leonardo Reyes De La—"

"How the hell do we get back?" Leonardo shouted, hearing his voice echo off the hills around him. "I have a crippled ship, *Sparky* seats three very cramped without an Astrogator stuffed in, and there's a sun inside this planet ready to explode any second. 'Return to Earth', my black ass."

"Ha! You sound like your beautiful mother. Well, you may not succeed with that approach," said Horacio. Leonardo begrudgingly admired the constant calm of the man's expression, virtual or not. "So you've told me the situation. What do you see as a solution?"

"Little and nothing," said Leonardo. He looked at his feet, worn and dirtied. "Our weapons are minimal. The things I've smuggled aboard won't hold us for long against what's down there. I am concerned about mounting an attack and somehow destabilizing the sun's containment systems; it looks pretty damn rickety. If we could somehow keep it together after we strike them, I'd feel better. But we have no time to study it. Attacking them seems more and more like a suicide mission."

"Perhaps. Leo, let me ask you something."

"All right."

"What would it feel like if you succeeded? What would that be like?"

"I ... I honestly can't say ..." Leonardo shook his head.

"No, go ahead ... Your imagination seems to be in need of exercise." Horacio popped an olive in his mouth, stripped the meat off with his tongue and teeth then spat the pit out over the railing.

"I think it would be amazing. I'd be stunned if we got off this frigging rock."

"Go on," said Horacio, plucking out a few more olives, popping them in his mouth and working the pits away from the flesh. Each pit went over the edge with practiced virtual nonchalance. Leonardo chuckled darkly.

Horacio dispensed with the last pit and cocked his head with a half smile.

"What's so funny now?"

"It'd be a nice turn of events in light of the previous couple of years. I've been in the shit for a while now. Plenty of people wish I'd died at Newhope. Returning with a prize like Mussina instead of a tribunal and another six-month-long review? That would be very nice."

"Hmm." Horacio scratched at his head. "And a suicide mission bothers you?"

"What? Of course it does. What're you saying?" Leonardo placed the goblet on the table and stood, pacing the deck as Horacio spoke.

"I'm saying I see before me the great Captain Leonardo De la Valencia, famed captain known for his good looks and astonishing luck. A man who was plucked from the garbage-filled canals of the rusty Connecticut coast where he fought augments in the ring for food and was eventually put into officer training at the expense of some mysterious benefactor. Hand-picked to serve the best missions and selected to command the finest warship ever built."

"Yes, Horacio. I am very grateful to you." Leonardo mockingly bowed before Horacio. "I never questioned who provided for my education. Without you I would be piloting a scow, scavenging among those Golden Coast ruins for a living and punching out off-duty cops and convicts at night to earn a little more."

"Leonardo, don't believe for a second that skill alone carried you through your whole career. You are talented and intelligent, yes; a good pilot, a good fighter and even a leader. Your rags-to-riches story—uh, riches such as they are for a military man—did get you much farther than someone raised in the 'Tainer Town hilltops of Hollow Point and schooled at the UFW academies." Horacio took a long swig from his wine, wiping his mouth with his hand. Leonardo turned and looked out over the impossibly green fields of the simulated vineyard. "Now you find yourself very far out on a small, thin limb and eager to be done. Am I right?"

"What're you saying?" Leonardo said, staring into the valley.

"I think you want to die out here."

Leonardo whirled to face the old man, whose complacent expression held. Horacio continued to look off into the distance.

"Yes, I think you'd rather die than take on a significant role in human destiny. Better to be a minor tragic figure than a significant flawed one."

Leonardo spat at the old man. Horacio looked at the spittle on his shirt as if a butterfly landed on it.

Leonardo lunged towards Horacio. With his hands a mere foot away from the old man's throat, he suddenly slowed as if passing into some invisible gelatinous material. He struggled to get hold of Horacio but failed.

"Safeguards, Little Leo. You know as well as I that it takes surgery you never had to keep you from thrashing out in virtual. Wouldn't want you falling from your chair as you attacked me."

Leonardo seethed for a few seconds then relaxed.

"I suspected the thought had occurred to you somewhere deep in your subconscious. It's perfectly understandable, but please don't shoot the messenger. I am programmed to say what no one else will without fear of sanctioned reprisals. Neither Baz nor Drina would, I dare say." Horacio gathered a pita in one hand, dropped in some feta, olives and a small dollop of pesto. He downed the entire parcel in one bite, washing it down with wine. With a small belch he rested his hands on his belly. He regarded Leonardo with a cocked head, spitting out the olive pits. "I propose a solution to your first choice: a suicide mission to stop their suicide mission."

"Fine," Leonardo said, sitting back heavily into his seat and picking up his goblet again. "I'm all ears."

***

168

Leonardo walked back onto the bridge, slightly shaken yet more purposeful and clear. Baz glanced briefly back at him before turning to face the displays.

"Hey," said Baz.

"Anything?" said Leonardo.

"No," said Baz. "Same old countdown to destruction and we can't see the clock."

"About that." Baz gave an imperceptible tilt towards him. "I think there's a solution."

"Which is?"

"I'm still working on the details." Baz turned to look at Leonardo with raised eyebrows. "I'll let you know soon. For now have one of the Fli8s buzz the tunnel and launch a string of transmitters down there. We're going to need some radio contact."

"Okay," said Baz, entering commands into the holokeyboard. "All set."

"Jason, keep your eyes peeled."

"Sir," said the bridge persona.

"Baz, go to the cargo bay and get all the explosives we have. *Everything*. Stack 'em all on the slow sled."

"Then what?" said Baz.

"I'll tell you when we're down there. I have to brief Drina."

Leonardo went to Drina's quarters. She was asleep. As he neared her throne, the proximity sensor awoke her.

"Hey," she said, rubbing her eyes.

"Hello," said Leonardo, sitting at the edge of her throne. "Catnap?"

"Yeah." She sat up and shook out her hair. She swept it back in her hands and wrapped it into a ponytail.   "They train you how do that or did you teach yourself?" he said with a smirk. Leonardo always marveled at how she managed to get the hair in without entangling the embedded cables.

"For the thousandth time, no." She shook her head and actually smiled. "What's going on?"

"Way too much," he said, drawing up a display in front of her. "Check it out."

She watched the playback of the Harvestman. When it appeared, Drina's mouth dropped open; her medibots registered alarm in a few sharp squeals, green lights flashed red. When playback ended, she leaned back into her throne and covered her eyes.

"Holy shit," she muttered, rubbing at the sockets fiercely. She dropped her hands and looked at Leonardo as if for some kind of reassurance. He had none. Drina shook her head. "The goddamn FMR. And that thing? That ... A Martian?"

"The last Martian."

"The last Martian?"

"Near as we can tell," said Leonardo, leaning back and scratching his head. "From what Mussina said, there was a cataclysm. That 'uprising' he mentioned? Something killed them all and drove this one underground. Imagine: all the Martians killed by someone or something and the Harvestman—that last Martian you saw—has been in hiding for *billions* of years."

"Hate to see what he's hiding from. But a thing that big you gotta hide pretty deep," said Drina, shaking her head and making a face.

"Yeah, well, if memory serves, no diggies ever got that far under Mars's skin before the FMR killed them." Leonardo turned to face Drina more directly. "I have a plan. Here's your part." Drina nodded and sat up. "Contact their Astrogator. Can you do that?"

"They're probably getting the ship ready. I bet they're even keeping her permanently in flight mode, which is stupid as it'll wear her out. She's fried as it is."

"You'll be able to contact her there?"

"Yes."

"Okay, then tell her she'll need to make a diversion. It's most likely a suicide mission, though."

"At this point, she's eager to die."

"Okay, tell her that roughly—" Leonardo consulted his heads-up "—twelve hours from now she should create a diversion when Dwi8 goes in."

"Going in for what?"

"Blowing them all up with an antigrav sled full of explosives."

"Subtle."

"No time for that." Leonardo smiled at her and stood. "We have to hit them hard and fast."

He kissed her and left.

***

In the bay, Baz and Dwi8 stood near the antigrav sled. All the explosives Baz had found were piled neatly on the sled. A half-dozen small green boxes rested atop a larger container three meters high by four feet wide. They turned as Leonardo approached. Baz wiped his brow and leaned on the sled.

"Aside from what I stowed up in the FLi8s' bay I don't even remember what we had," said Leonardo. "For all I knew the hottest thing we had was cayenne powder in the D-FAC."

"Oh, no. We got some heavier stuff," said Baz. He pointed to the small boxes. "Fusion explosives. Nothing too fancy, but good to keep around in case of emergencies. This big boy right here," said Baz, patting the larger box gingerly, "is polandium. I was surprised we even had this. It's stable when separated in two separate containers. When you break the seal and mix them it becomes highly unstable. Just a trigger could set this thing off."

"Hence the dynamite."

"Right."

"It's secure?" asked Leonardo, walking around the sled.

"Yep. We tied it down and rigged an oxygen detonator. Dwi8'll be ready to go in a minute."

"Dwi8?" said Leonardo. The walky-talky turned to face him. Leonardo caught a whiff of the planet on its surface, a small wave of ammonia and some other indefinable smell. "Take the sled into the cave. We'll be able to stay in touch. Enter quietly; make sure you are not seen. Then put the sled into overdrive and ram their ship. Hard. Try not to hit any of the solar containment systems. We still need to escape in *Sparky*."

"Yes, sir."

"We're depending on you, Dwi8."

"I will do my best, sir." Leonardo found himself overly concerned that Dwi8 got back safely.

"Baz?" said Leonardo. The XO looked at him and saw his face.

"Okay, Dwi8, secure all these containers here," said Baz. He followed Leonardo to the shelter. Both men looked around.

"Jesus. Glad we got the hell out of this thing, huh?"

"I was beginning to like it," said Leonardo as he slapped the surface. "Baz, are you sure Dwi8 can handle this? It's not a Battlin' Andy, it's just a regular servile walky-talky. It's got about as much strategic sense as a cork."

"Not much choice, is there? Wal8 would have been ideal, but ..." They looked at the gutted walky-talky in the shelter. "Dwi8's all we got. I'm gonna miss it."

"Send it out then meet me at *Sparky*. We have about twelve to eighteen hours before departure." Leonardo clapped Baz on the shoulder and left.

Sparky sat ready and waiting in its bay. Leonardo looked around the dark interior. "Lights!" he called out and the bay slowly brightened. Leonardo stepped inside and placed a palm on the armrest of the pilot's chair. The cramped cockpit lit up as the ship came online. System messages showed on his HUD as the ship ran self-diagnostics. He began his own check alongside it.

Baz appeared and took the seat on the right.

"Dwi8's off and running."

Leonardo nodded and together they continued preflight checks.

Baz got out and visually checked the engines. In the cockpit, Leonardo turned around to look behind him. *Sparky* held just enough space for one passenger and cargo— or an Astrogator complete with throne.

"Baz?" he shouted.

"Yeah?" Baz said from under the port engine cowling.

"Clear out anything we don't need in here. Make *Sparky* light as possible."

"Gotcha." Together they cleared out the cabin, leaving a bare minimum of MREs and medical supplies, making it as spacious as they could.

Together they made a final visual check. "That's about it," said Leonardo. He noticed Baz staring into space.

"Dwi8's getting close," he said, checking his HUD.

"Let's get to the bridge then." Leonardo called Drina.

"Dree, You ready?"

"Ready on your order."

"Proceed."

"Sir."

On the bridge, Baz immediately drew up several displays around him, video feeds from various sources. Leonardo vaulted the horseshoe and sat in his chair. In addition to his HUD, he created more views, fingers flicking in space as windows opened before him.

"Action stations." The lights turned red and the displays all switched colors for maximum visibility. Leonardo's five displays showed different views: Dwi8 driving the antigrav sled through snow, Fli8 Alpha monitoring the cave entrance, Drina on her throne, and two showing ship's status. He ignored the steady white "OFFLINE" overlay on the engine status.

"Baz?"

"All systems are go. Dwi8 wants to know if he can bring back a string of ears for us." Leonardo grimaced and shook his head.

"Not if he wants to meet a war-crimes tribunal to discuss his new collection." He let the grimace broaden into a smile. "Maybe one or two would be okay." Baz snickered.

"T-minus twenty minutes from cave entrance."

The border of Drina's comm window suddenly glowed yellow, requesting Leonardo's attention. Status indicators framed her face. He acknowledged it and the frame went green.

"Astrogator Valencia?"

"Captain, I made contact with their Astrogator just in time. Mussina is planning their jump in eighteen hours. I told her to stall. She'll be coming back half an hour from now."

Leonardo breathed a silent thank you to whatever god heard prayers all the way out here. They were just in time for mobilizing and still so far from out of the woods. A few hours more could have meant their death and the destruction of Earth.

"T-minus fifteen minutes to the cave."

Leonardo switched to the sled's on-board camera, seeing endless snow, the sled's progress noted by green numbers rapidly counting down. Fli8's display showed the cave entrance and a countdown of Dwi8's imminent arrival. When Dwi8 came to the cave entrance it held position, awaiting the next orders.

"Okay, Baz, have Dwi8 go in slowly. Bring Fli8 down to an attack altitude and hold. Route Dwi8's output through the SLLT5s to Fli8's transmitters." There was a brief pause and static in Dwi8's output as it went underground, then visuals were restored and Fli8 picked up the connection. Dimly lit by the sled's light, the AI piloted the sled down into the cave.

"T-minus ten minutes to the interior, sir."

"Drina?" On-screen she turned towards him.

"Sir?"

"We need that diversion now. Make it good and long."

"Yes, sir." Drina nodded, closed her eyes and lay back. The display faded to half-tone, reading "Astrogation Session in Progress." He could see Drina's face going slack in the orange of the monitor as she dove into the inscrutable interior world where the Astrogators performed their duties.

"Dwi8's feed is on main screen."

The big display flickered then filled with the antigrav sled diving deeper into the cave, meters from its destination. Leonardo kept focus on these readouts; despite all the regular sleep, chemical sleep and wakefulness training, he was worn down. Even to maintain focus on this mortal struggle, where a second's distraction could be costly, was hard for him.

"He's in, sir." Baz broke the reverie and Leonardo looked up to the main monitor. The SLLT5s fed several views back to them as well as Dwi8's point of view. Dwi8 stood silhouetted at the inner cavern's entrance, the light far brighter than before. Dwi8 compensated with filtering that hardly diminished the infernal glow.

"Look at the readings. It's stronger, Leo."

In the bottom center of the screen was a tiny picture of Fli8's feed. Leonardo called this up, and saw Fli8 hovering approximately a hundred meters over the cave's outer entrance.

"Have Dwi8 proceed carefully. Baz, can we tap into their internal comms? I wonder if they're—"

A blast shook the screen just as Dwi8 entered the cavern. The transmission broke up with static. The walky-talky righted itself, looking for the source of the blast. A fresh set of windows popped up, detailing the extent of damages the unit had taken.

"What happened?"

"Dwi8's taking on fire. Tracking's harder."

"Dwi8, ram it with the goddamn sled!" shouted Leonardo.

Baz worked furiously to protect the damaged walky-talky while getting it to execute their final plan. Leonardo watched Dwi8's faltering, jagged steps. At least the blast had not detonated the sled's payload. The walky-talky worked to turn the sled towards the ship just in time to see another bolt of fire from somewhere along the cave walls.

"Dwi8! Evasive!" Leonardo wondered if the walky-talky still recognized his voice. A snapshot appeared on-screen. "Jason! Analysis!" A picture emerged of an anomalous shape just under the Martian ship.

"Baz!"

"Ruger-Hock 55A power cannon. An old one but still in good—"

Another blast from the cannon knocked out Dwi8's transmission. For a few seconds they saw electronic snow, then the image returned. A brief second of Dwi8's transmission showed it looking down at shattered legs before a final blast took it out permanently. Dwi8's feed disappeared, replaced by static and jagged lines. Leonardo hoped it was another temporary dropout. Still the screen showed zero signal strength, zero telemetry; a sure sign Dwi8 was gone. They sat silently, the only sound the whisper of life-support vents and the quiet beep of Fli8's telemetry stream.

"Damn." Baz shouted and jammed his fist over his mouth. "They were expecting us."

"When we took out their walky-talky," Leonardo said. "We could have looked over the data ... more ... before ..." His stomach dropped as he rose out of his chair. He felt his fingers go cool and blood left his extremities. There was a clarity in him that fell like a cloak, covering him in the silence of the bridge now that the mission had failed.

There was only one more option.

"Baz, keep Fli8 at the cave. Then go the bay and get your combat gear ready. Prepare the other sled. I'll be in the hold in one hour."

CHAPTER TWENTY-FOUR
Casualty

Leonardo moved his chair closer to the console in front of him and a holokeyboard appeared. Frantically he began to type. He was going at it so intently that he thought the life support had dropped out until he realized he'd forgotten to breathe. He took in a gulp of air and resumed.

"Sir," said Jason, "I see you're initiating backup procedures. May I help?"

"Yes, Jason. Back yourself and everything else into the data center on *Sparky*."

"Yes, sir. Shall I inform Astrogator Valencia that—"

"No!"

"Yes, sir. Backup procedures initiated." Leonardo dreaded telling Drina of this plan. Emotional distance wouldn't make it any easier for him, he knew for sure. Despite all her training and professionalism, Leonardo knew Dwi8's failure would hit her hard. Given her limited ability to contribute, she would feel personally responsible for this becoming a potential suicide mission.

After finalizing the backups, Leonardo went to Drina's quarters. Despite all the rest and medical care, she still looked spent. Leonardo wanted nothing more than to give her all the time she needed for a full recovery. But he knew that hope was useless though his plan might buy her some time. If they were lucky and all went right, she might get to an outpost. He knelt down, placed a hand on her shoulder and gently woke her. Even the flutter of her eyelids spoke of a body struggling to recover.

"Hello, my darling," he said. He kissed her cool skin, tasting the sour toxicity of neutralized biotech in her sweat. She smiled and stretched, the cables jumping back and away from her head like startled sleeping cats. They settled down as she rose up in her chair.

"A kiss, huh?" she asked. She rolled her eyes and struggled to bring some lucidity into her tired, overwrought brain. "To what do I owe a kiss?"

"Nothing good, I'm afraid." He told her about Dwi8's destruction. "I was thinking that if we got Dwi8 in there, we'd have a good chance of getting out of here."

"Obviously," said Drina.

"Well ..." He sat down near her throne. "Now there's Plan B. Not the best scenario, but it's all we have." Drina nodded, keeping her eyes fixed on Leonardo's. "Baz and I will go in ourselves and terminate the FMR." Leonardo paused to let his words sink in. Drina nodded. "I'm not going to lie. There's a good chance we won't come back. We're outmanned, outgunned and not entirely sure what we're facing. By all indications they're expecting us. If Baz and I have to go in, I'm putting you in *Sparky* with all the data we've collected. You'll take it to Earth and—"

"No, Leo. *No.*" She swallowed hard and shook her head, jaw set. He saw her internal struggle; the training riding a close second to her emotions. There was something left of her feelings for him after all. As common as it was for them to argue, with all the training they'd had it was still more difficult than he could bear. "Why can't you attack them from the air? What about using something to drill down into the crust? We could all get into *Sparky* and ..." She stopped as she saw his expression.

"Drina. There's no other way. Neither of the Fli8 units have anything strong enough to pierce the crust. Even if we used everything they had, it would take too long. We're almost out of supplies. We left Jupiter with enough resources for a chaperone and escort mission. That was my first mistake. No one, least of all me, expected a need for more than basic weapons and supplies. Anything else we had was destroyed in the crash." She looked into her lap at her fidgeting hands, folding and unfolding, rubbing against one another. Leonardo could tell she was calculating something.

"Yes, Captain."

Leonardo sighed.

"Ok. My Astrogator has accepted the situation. But what about my wife?"

Drina said nothing.

"Remember the oath, Drina?" She gave a nod, looking over his shoulder. "We swore to lay our lives down for the UFW so that billions of citizens could live freely. We put our lives to the side so that others might live in peace, free from harm and protected from fear. We agreed we might even die in that service, protecting people from the FMR. Understood?" She nodded. Leonardo moved in closer to her and put his hands over hers.

"Spare me the heroic bullshit, Leo." She shrugged his hand off and wiped a tear away. "Keep up with that shit, I'll puke on your suit."

He took her hand again and applied the slightest pressure.

"Drina, I know we're done. I don't see us suddenly making up at this late date and reconciling."

"So you want to kill yourself?" she shouted. Horacio's words restung Leo.

"No. No, I want to live through this. Regardless of what you think. But we both know that won't happen if we don't do everything in our power to destroy these people. If we don't do our utmost, there will be nothing to go back to: no beach, no sea, no boat, no Earth, no UFW." Another tear rolled down her cheek, like the ones welling in his own eyes.

"Your tears," she said. A faint smile flashed across her face. "A rare thing, indeed."

"Not particularly heroic, is it?" He reached towards his wife and embraced her, clumsily squeezing her tight as she sat on her reclining throne. He felt how thin and bony she'd become. Suddenly, a sharp beeping sounded in his left ear. They simultaneously laughed and parted.

"Been a while since we've triggered the intimate contact alarms during high alert." She smiled, more in remembrance of good times past. Drina lifted herself and brought Leo's face closer and they kissed briefly to the sound of more beeping.

"Look, Dree, it's not over. We're coming back. Baz and I have some fun guns hidden away. I doubt those puke-green sons of bitches have anything like what we got."

"Except a miniature sun."

"Yeah, well, we won't let them use that." Leonardo sat up and tugged down the front of his tunic. "You'll be safe here. We'll be broadcasting and Jason is in charge of the ship while we're out."

"Oh, Jason's a good chaperone. When we return, I'll have him decommissioned and he can oversee school dances."

Leonardo stood and smoothed out his uniform, lingering. "Ok, so ... Contact their Astrogator again. Tell her to watch for another signal. Baz and I are heading in. We'll all be in *Sparky* within eight to ten hours and headed home."

He left his wife to her duty in her cocoon.

CHAPTER TWENTY-FIVE
Grain

February 12, 2191

Dear Mr. President,

I am grateful to hear that you wished to receive my correspondence despite being on a much-needed vacation/retreat. As a lowly scientist who remains in the comforts of his lab, I cannot imagine the pressures and demands of overseeing the wealth of planets and concerns of the many billions of people that inhabit the UFW's reach. I am in charge of a mere twenty-five hundred and am overwhelmed by that more often than not.

I must admit I find it a bit challenging to put an ink pen to actual pulp-fiber paper in order to correspond with you. But I respect your exclusion from contemporary media, communications and the affairs of the world for a brief time and also the security concerns of your staff. It is barely a minor inconvenience.

You asked that I brief you on the ongoing investigation into the latest tests of the experimental Choudhury drives. Forgive the assumption but I believe as a politician you may not be fully versed in drive dynamics and astrophysics. Therefore, I will do my best to explain my findings in layman's terms.

Following the test flights of 2189 my lab reviewed all data collected rigorously. To this day I am struck by two conclusions. The first is that the test yielded far more than we ever imagined possible. The second is that I wish my late colleague Misha Choudhury had lived long enough to see his legacy vindicated by the performance of his drive systems.

I think we can agree that Pilot 23's survival and return from a voyage in a vessel with Choudhury drives fully engaged is monumental given the losses we've suffered throughout the program. This alone makes the sacrifice of so many pilots and technicians worth it.

While I cannot speak to all details of the peculiar tale the pilot has recounted repeatedly in her debriefings (with a consistency that can only indicate an absolute certainty this was what she saw), everything else in her experience has led me to some startling conclusions. These have given me many a sleepless night, I am not ashamed to admit, due to their implications.

As near as I can tell the test flight proved something Misha always said in private but never declared publicly: that his drives would provide us with FTL capabilities and thus open up this galaxy and perhaps others to human exploration and colonization.

What it also opened up was something far beyond both our wildest dreams.

Dr. Choudhury believed the drives would allow FTL travel through space by themselves. What they actually appear to do is something far more radical. After careful study of the flight data and telemetry I can safely say that what Choudhury drives achieve is not necessarily FTL travel but in fact entry into a previously existing artificial system of FTL transit.

I'm sure reading what I just wrote gives you as much pause as it did in my writing it. The numerous implications of this are perhaps beyond even my understanding.

One thing is certain. While we have not as yet encountered evidence of other civilizations in the galaxy, apparently we have stumbled upon a system of FTL transport built by an unencountered race or the remains of a deceased civilization's work.

This discovery led me to a three-day migraine and one of my assistants into an alcoholic binge from which he is still recovering at a facility near Taos, New Mexico.

Once recovered, I set about further examining all data at hand and postulating theories based on this. I believe the data backs up the conclusions I have come to as well as the actions I believe should be taken.

As I said, Pilot 23 stumbled across a kind of galactic mass transit system. As evidence for this I cite not only her voyage to and from Barnard's Star (a distance of six light years from Earth) but her testimony as well. From this I believe the transport system is so large in scope as to be perhaps unchartable, though attempts will be made. And yet, if her testimony continues to hold true then we are looking at a highway in space—which I have dubbed "hi-space" for simplicity—allowing for travel in a fraction of the time it would take using conventional means.

This hi-space network of corridors is so precise and perfect in its construction that whoever created it were masters of science and technology on a level that can, without hyperbole, only be described as godlike in its breadth and scope. So many ideas and questions spring forth from this that I find myself barely able to present them to you in a coherent manner, let alone contain them in my head.

The first of these is that we finally have a way in which to travel longer distances by using pilots whose minds are intrinsically linked to the very vessels they steer. My team has created a preliminary method of doing so (as used by Pilot 23 on the last test flight) which, while requiring a medically challenging and potentially dangerous process of installing these pilots into their ships, will allow for this travel to become a reality. The truth is that despite the current state of our technology we are simply chattering primates in the presence of the hi-space network.

Another is that of Pilot 23 herself. The woman presents a problem, though not through any fault of her own. The problem is this: after numerous analyses, examinations and autopsies of all pilots involved, we cannot come to a satisfying conclusion as to what made her test flight experience so successful while those of all her comrades ended in disaster and tragedy. All twenty-five test flights were essentially identical: same route, same drives, all commanded by experienced pilots. There is really no reason why her flights should have been any different.

And yet they dramatically were, which leads me to another troubling conclusion.

The flights were successful due to something unique about Pilot 23 herself.

I have run countless tests in several lab environments, both real and virtual, which yielded nothing unique about her. She is a startlingly average human in every way: height, weight, build, intelligence and strength. Nothing sets her apart from her colleagues except for the fact that she did something no one else has done before or been able to do since.

This presents one essential problem.

Pilot 23 is herself a young woman with, considering her general good health and medical history, a few decades of service piloting UFW vessels ahead of her at best. Beyond that she would be past mandatory retirement for a career that is already one of the most stressful for a human being.

The answer to this problem would be simple but for one thing: the Unilateral Cloning Ban of 2061. The horrors of the War of the Duplicates remain firmly embedded in the human psyche thanks to our ancestors' pervasive media culture and the many memorials that stand today in almost every country on Earth. No one would ever wish to see that unfold again anywhere.

However the cloning ban *has* hampered many scientific efforts, even when permitted under the strict guidelines that allow labs like my own to function. The case of traveling hi-space is yet another example. Were we simply allowed to do so, clones of Pilot 23 would already be growing in preparation for the first widespread tests of ships equipped with them.

I understand what I am proposing is as close to heresy as one can get in this day and age. I also stake my entire career on this statement: without considering a partial, or perhaps temporary, secret lift of the cloning ban, we may never travel at more than a crawl across the galaxy.

Were that ban not an issue, then we could proceed with speed and ease in developing a program for travel in the hi-space corridors.

These cloned pilots (whom certain members of my staff have dubbed "Astrogators," a slight misnomer that I am nonetheless fond of) would be installed within their vessels for a period of perhaps ten to twenty years, directly linked to paired astrogation AIs by a hard-line neural link. A period shorter than this would not be cost-effective; longer would be deadly. These women would then be in charge of astrogating their vessels at all times, but especially during the periods of hi-space travel when their special skills would be needed most. They could successfully move vessels in and out of the hi-space corridors while the rest of the crew and passengers would remain in a state of chemical or deepsleep during the portions of the voyage that have proven lethal to conscious humans.

Tests indicate that with quantum entangled systems in place, communication with these vessels will be possible (communication between astrogators within hi-space may be as simple as any normal communications within range of our current radio and masercast technology. Only further tests with more astrogators will tell us the truth).

These vessels would never be out of touch from each other or the rest of the fleet in the event of emergency or military action.

But this is all moot so long as the cloning ban is in place.

I ask that you consider what I've written here not just in speculation, but in light of what we've already achieved and what we *could* achieve. Humanity stands poised on the brink of greatness, but for a great fear of repeating past mistakes. Despite our predilection for war and misery have we not also learned to keep from repeating the most grievous of our errors?

I know Pilot 23 is very keen to speak with you about her experiences. I know the visit you made to her in hospital was only a formal one, allowing for little in the way of conversation. Mr. President, I cannot state more emphatically that this woman is the key to our future. I would ask that you speak with her at length and soon.

I've enclosed her video testimony as well as a more formal and technical presentation of my notes. I hope they pass on to you and your staff so you can see what's at stake here.

I remain your faithful servant in the name of humanity, the UFW and science above all.

Be well, sir.

Dr. Uel Yee, UFW Saturn Orbital Laboratory Center

CHAPTER TWENTY-SIX
Debasement

"How's it going in there?"

Leonardo entered the main bay, finding Baz cranking open a gray container in the far corner.

"Pretty good. I wish I had time to dig through this shit and get in here." He tugged with one hand while he wiped sweat from his forehead with the other arm.

"All right. Let me help you." Together they pulled open the bent door. As he strained with the bent hinges, Leonardo thought back to his first time entering *Resurgam*.

She's a bitchy little tug pretending to be a freighter, he'd said to himself, *and I can't wait to be rid of her*. This was not the way he planned to leave the ship.

They were poorly armed for an emergency situation as *Resurgam*'s commission left her with minimum defensive capabilities. As part of Leonardo's probation, her battle modules were removed, as if he was somehow less reliable with heavy weapons. Whether any of their remaining equipment survived the crash remained to be seen. They finally opened the door.

"So?" Leonardo asked him, kneeling to catch his breath. Baz stepped, whistling. He looked around and sighed. Leo looked into the container behind his XO.

"Good news and bad news."

"Bad news first."

"The crash destroyed the Makatinis and most of our weaponry." Leonardo barely suppressed a wince as Baz said this. Makatini armored cycles would have been perfect for the assault. Small, highly maneuverable land/air fighters were what they'd need in the planet's interior. With the weaponry gone, they were even more hampered.

He glanced into the container full of smashed machinery, specifically two vehicles mashed together as if by a giant, malicious child. Other bits and pieces were cannons and rocket launchers, bent and smashed to bits under the crushed vehicles.

"Shit. The good news?"

"The rest of the secret stash will definitely put a stop to Mussina." Baz nearly sparkled at the prospect. "Or help us bring him back alive if you really want."

"Let's get that." They exited the container. As they turned away he caught a glance at the doors leading to the Rear Bay where *Sparky* sat waiting.

"What's *Sparky*'s status?" Leonardo asked, pointing to the heavy door.

"Still fully functional, Leo. Totally fine."

"Are you sure?"

"Sure, I'm sure, man," said Baz, turning away towards a large container. "No worries." Leonardo grabbed Baz's arm, whirling him around. The XO leaned away, expecting a punch.

"It's the only thing that's going to get Drina out of here, Baz, so when I ask you, I mean is it going to get her out of here?" He held Baz's gaze with tired, burning eyes.

"I promise you, Leo, that it will get whoever's in it out of here: you, me, or Drina. Whoever. Off the planet. Alive." Leonardo held him for a second longer and then exhaled, releasing Baz's arm.

"Good." He stepped back and they continued walking in silence.

"This is what we have left," said Baz. They stood before another container, a UFW multimodule designed to be dropped from orbit, ready and waiting for landing teams. They could be outfitted as field hospitals, living quarters, mess halls, mobile refrigeration units or command centers. *"UFW RESURGAM D2219/CREW GEAR"* was stenciled across the front. Baz waved a hand over the control sensor to his left and a seam opened in the unbroken white surface.

"De la Valencia, Leonardo Reyes. Captain. Confirm."

"Confirmed," said the container in a female voice. "Confirm secondary."

"Al-Mushtarii, Baz Jabril. Executive Officer. Confirm."

"Confirmed." The seam turned into segmented doors that opened out and slid into the wall. Lights immediately lit the interior. Walls divided up the container. A central corridor ran down its length. The box contained four walk-in lockers on a side, two at the back. Crew member names were stenciled above each compartment. Inside each locker were complete armaments for all ten of the crew. Leonardo walked back to his section and waved a hand over the wall pedia. The display blinked to life, showing the UFW logo, then the contents of his locker.

1 UBQ98 automatic multipurpose weapon with 4 blocks of nanomunitions

1 case Keller/Yung adhesive/corrosive blasting tape

1 Ghorran shotgun / 500 shells

1 Biehl Yakuchi gyrojet rifle with five boxes of two hundred rounds each

1 Colt 44 with 4 boxes of one hundred rounds each

"Everything in there, Baz?" Leonardo picked up an ornamental dagger that hung on the wall; a gift from Regina. She said it was used by her great-grandfather to settle a duel on an old ore freighter out of Mars.

It always goes back to Mars, thought Leo.

"Got everything, sir. Got Ghorran shotguns, my UBQ, bolt gun, blast tapes and grenades." Leonardo heard Baz rummaging about in his locker. "Ready for some fire."

"Oh, I suspect we'll see plenty of that." Leonardo looked back into his compartment. In addition to the weapons listed inside, each crew member had a small table used for cleaning and repairs. These spaces developed a secondary unofficial use as well. In every ship he'd ever served on, these became unofficial altars and shrines to the owners' religious entities or mementos from life back home.

Leonardo's was no different. He had a CIS Bible at the center in front of a small golden statue of Jesus. Above the statue were three pictures: one of the Earth that he took from *ESS McMullen* during his first voyage offworld; the second of himself and Drina on the beach in Mexico during the summer of 2446, when they were on leave just before being given command of the *Wellstone*; the third of Drina alone just after her successful engagement into *Resurgam*. Her dour expression in the third picture was a far cry from that joyful young woman in the first.

"Captain?" Baz said, walking towards him. Leonardo turned. Baz had taken his own shotgun out from its case and cradled it in a polishing rag.

"Ah, the hunter boy is happy again," Leonardo said. Baz smiled and looked at the weapon.

"I just haven't seen it in a long time is all. I want to make sure Enkidu knows I missed him."

"Ring boy, is everyone from your district partial to calling shotguns by name?"

"You use them a fair amount and get so close to them it's only fair." Baz patted the gun.

"On a ring commune, no less? The hull breaches must've been insane," Leonardo answered. He sat down on a crate of shotgun rounds. "Let's think this one out, shall we?"

"Alright. Who's devil's advocate, then?" Baz asked, cracking open the barrels and staring down the length.

"You," said Leonardo.

"Okay."

"Enemy plans to teleport this planet to Earth's orbit, blow up Earth and annihilate all life there. " Leonardo stopped. "Sounds insane when you say it out loud. Imagine the six-month debriefing this is gonna cause? All right ... We have no Battlin' Andys on board, correct?" Baz nodded. The armored robot soldiers nicknamed Battlin' Andys had been used in military engagements for over three hundred and fifty years. Leonardo often relied on sending them in wherever possible. Simpler than AIs but far more specialized than walky-talkies, they could take complex battle instructions and act as focused infantry units in a skirmish.

"Yes, sir."

"Fine. We sent Dwi8 down and they destroyed it. We're out a walky-talky."

"They know we're coming." Baz pointed the barrels of his shotgun up towards the light, looking for any obstruction.

"So we go in quick, hit their engines to strand them then we take out the substations."

Baz nodded.

"Take out the engines, there's a possible antimatter leak, then an explosion will destroy us and them. Destroy the containment substations and we're dead, too. Those things keep the fireball under control. Knock those out, we're toast." Baz blew down the shotgun's barrel. Leonardo thought of Dwi8, laden with explosives only to be shredded seconds after stepping out into the open.

"Send a Fli8 into the cavern to strafe their ship and leave the substations. Terminate the entire Martian team. Take their ship back to Earth."

"Can't. FLi8s are too big. And you risk blowing us up as well in both these scenarios. They'll probably have guns to keep FLi8s away. And if you're thinking of flying that piece of junk they came in on back to Earth, I'd rather float home."

"Good point. Jason?"

"Sir."

"Have Fli8 terminate the EMP cannon on the surface immediately."

"Yes, sir." Leonardo looked back at Baz with a smile.

"But they haven't detected it or us yet. What makes you think they suddenly would?" he said. Baz mulled it over for a moment, worrying a spot on the stock with his rag. He gave one last look down the barrel and closed the rifle. "Suppose they do see Fli8 and neutralize it."

"They just might." Leonard pulled the knife from its sheath, the blade curved at a dangerous angle. If it were used in a duel, it definitely would leave one party on the floor with no chance of getting up. Leonardo thought for a moment then shook his head. "Let's stick with Plan B: retrieve Sled 3 and load it up." He waved a hand at their gear. Baz nodded. "Drive the sled down, get as close as possible before they catch on. One of us hits the substation, and the other the ship."

"*A suicide attack.*"

"An attack," Leonardo corrected.

"Great." Baz turned silent, staring at the weapon in his hands. "But we still need a Plan C."

"Plan C?" said Leonardo. "Not sure we even have time for Plan B."

"Yes. What if we fail? Consider it." Baz looked at Leonardo.

Leonardo weighed their extremely limited options. What if they *did* fail? He peered up into the ceiling but saw nothing.

"Okay," he said. "Plan C is if this fails, then you come back—"

"Shit. I knew it." Baz slapped the shotgun's stock.

"Baz, get clear for a second. We know that best case it's a one-way mission. We've prepped *Sparky* for take-off and put it in standby mode. Get Drina inside. You and I head for the cavern. Fli8's already neutralized the EMP cannon so they can't use it on us. We take our targets down. If one of us gets hit, the other heads back here. If both us get hit, whoever can gives FLi8 the order to blast the entrance shut—"

"What?" Baz said, looking up from his rifle. "Leo—"

Leonardo cut him off with a wave.

"Look, it's likely we won't escape. Neither them nor us. They will be on the lookout for us. So you and I attack the ship while we leave the substations alone. If we're lucky, we can get Mussina alive to stand trial on Earth. If we survive, we get off the planet. If not, Drina leaves the planet before it's teleported or explodes."

Baz stared silently at his boots for a moment.

"All right, but what about if we jack our engines and open the magnetic core shields. The antimatter reactors will—"

"No deal. Remember? The core was jettisoned during the crash." Baz stared at Leonardo, rubbing the butt of the gun with his thumb. A sign Leonardo knew well. "Say it!" he said. "We don't have time."

"With all due res—Leo! So you've just given up?" He leaned forward, eyes intent. "What about seeing home again? Don't you and Drina have some plans for her diseng—" Leonardo waved him quiet.

"There's no other way. I've thought it over since we crashed. Even before discovering Mussina's plan. I knew we'd most likely die out here—"

"So you're just accepting defeat?"

"No. There's no backup. They destroyed Dwi8. FLi8 can't get in there. There's no other way." Leonardo stood up. "It's the toughest decision of my career." He hung the dagger on its hook and turned back to face Baz.

"My plans with Drina or yours don't matter. Our first priority is the safety of the UFW. Period. We stand between the safety of the galaxy and these maniacs. They have no intention of letting anything interfere with their plans, do they? They will not stop. And neither can we even if it means our own lives. Do I make myself clear?"

"Yes, sir." Baz held his gaze. "Yes, Leo."

"Now, as my friend, I can offer you this. I don't see any way of us escaping except in *Sparky*. My intent is to put Drina inside along with the backup drives from Jason so someone can figure out what they're using. You can stay here with her and leave. I'm not going to force you on a suicide mission. You have a choice. So make it."

Baz sat staring at his palms before rising and going back to his locker. Leonardo heard him rummage around, slamming doors and dropping things. Leonardo busied himself with straightening out his bench. Finally, Baz stopped making a racket.

"I've never once backed down from a fight," he heard Baz say. Leonardo turned around. All Leonardo saw was Baz's head suspended in midair, a tired smile on the face he'd known for many years and many missions.

"Let's do it." Baz said. "Only thing is: should I go like this?" Baz nodded down to his nonexistent body. "Or like this ..." His face disappeared and suddenly the space before Leonardo became an infestation of writhing maggots, complete with the wet sounds of their larval movements.

"It's the return of Mad Maggot Al-Mushtarii!" Leonardo shouted.

"Not since Purva Nigalsa," came Baz's voice from within the mass of writhing insect larva. "Remember those FMR thinking it would be a breeze to raid the fuel depot? Ha! Scared the shit out of them with this."

"It's damn effective but a dead giveaway against the rocks." The maggots disappeared and Baz reappeared wearing a flat gray cloak down to the floor. Leonardo reached out his hand. Baz slid his out of the cloak and they shook.

Baz followed Leonardo from the container, each carrying their weapons. They suited up, their body armor activated to accommodate the extra weight.

At the sled pen they loaded the remaining sled and got on. The back end dipped slightly as Baz pulled the control stalk from the back and plugged it in at the front. Leonardo stood behind him.

"Ready?"

"Go."

Baz flipped a switch and the sled rose with a soft rush of air. Dust and bits of debris blew away from underneath. He angled it towards the makeshift ramp he'd built for Dwi8 and piloted it into the airlock. Leonardo turned back to see the doors close behind them.

"It's gonna be a little bumpy, Leo," said Baz.

"As long as we make it there in one piece I can handle a little turbulence."

The airlock depressurized with a loud hiss, lights flashing on the control stalk. The doors opened out to the planet's surface. Leo took a deep breath in, seeing the pale blue light.

"Hold on," said Baz, and the sled lurched out the doors. They dropped a few meters as Baz ramped up the field strength and they made a gentle gliding descent towards the surface. Leonardo took look a behind him at the doors closing automatically and then down the length of the ship. *Resurgam's* gray topside was a stark contrast to her blackened and scarred underside.

He almost looked forward to seeing the last of her.

CHAPTER TWENTY-SEVEN
Redemption

With a gentle bump they landed, the sled accelerating away from the ship. The ground rushed past them in an ever-increasing blur. Soon they were traveling at a speed sleds weren't supposed to achieve.

"You been hot-rodding this one, Baz?"

"Yeah, a little," said Baz, turning back to smile and nod at his captain. "I never let Himanako or Hammond near it. I knew it'd be handy to keep one a little on the amped up side." The sled raced over the surface as Leonardo watched the landscape slide by.

"Baz, I need to speak privately to Drina. Beep if you need me." Baz gave him a thumbs-up. Leonardo pinged Drina, who appeared on the HUD overlaid on the surface.

"Hey," he said.

"Hey," she answered. "So you're off without saying goodbye?"

"I'm calling now, aren't I?" Leonardo said with a smile.

"What's your ETA?"

"About an hour. Anything on your end?"

"I told their Astrogator to wait for a signal. She'll know what to do."

"What's that?"

"She's going to drop them inside their sun."

"Jeez, we should have had her do that sooner."

"Not without them getting suspicious. Their drives have to be engaged before she can do it."

"We'll knock those out so she won't need to do that."

"Jeez," said Drina. "Great options."

"Not optimal, I know. It's the only way." Leonardo took a deep breath. "Look, Drina. I need you safe so we can get right the hell out of here when this is over. Okay?"

"Sure thing, Leo. I'll just move to *Sparky* when you guys leave the cave."

"I know you will, Drina." Leonardo looked aside in his display for a moment. "Jason's taking you there now."

"What? Leo—" she looked around her for a second before focusing over his shoulder at something.

"Drina, it's for your own safety."

188

"Leo, wait—" He cut her off.

Leonardo pictured what was happening. After he gave the signal to Jason inside *Resurgam*, an emergency passage would open, a gently slanting tunnel, wide and tall enough for a man to stand in, running from Rear Bay 7, where *Sparky* sat ready and waiting, right into Drina's quarters. There, Drina would be desperately fighting with Jason for control. Leonardo listened to her berate the ship's persona.

"Jason! I want manual control now, godammit!"

"Asgr. Valencia, the captain has not authorized that for your own safety."

"Screw my safety!" shouted Drina. In Leonardo's mind's eye, she thrashed on her throne. Under normal circumstances, her interface cables would extend to allow her to leave the throne. Now they would refuse to move beyond the normal range of motion, an alarm screeching every time she did so. The safety dome emerged from the ceiling, enclosing her in the throne. As Drina continued to yell at the AI, she slid backwards into the wall.

In emergency mode, Drina's throne became a mobilized enclosure moving steadily through the ship. Leonardo knew Drina would try to shut Jason down and stop the eviction from her room.

"Dammit, Leo! I can take care of myself!" she shouted. He wondered what the short journey was like. From inspections of the passage, he knew it was completely dark, the only light coming from her throne. Since she was facing backwards, the last light of her room would have slipped away by now.

"Leo! You fucking asshole!" Drina shouted. Leonardo sighed.

In Rear Bay 7, an umbilical column opened from the wall, connecting itself to *Sparky*'s portal. Drina would come sliding down the umbilical column to finally rest inside the small ship. The column would disconnect and the hatch would close. Leonardo saw the sudden closing of the portal as the light faded around his wife. Drina sat cursing the darkness for a moment before the ship powered up and her throne made connection to its power.

"Asgr. Valencia," said Jason. "We are now running ship's functions from within *Sparky*."

"You mean *you* are!" she shouted. "Leo! Answer me!"

"Hello," he said. "You're safe."

"Safe?" she shouted. "I'm trapped!"

"If anything happened to us while we were down inside there, you might not have made it to *Sparky*. And *Resurgam* is structurally unsound. A good tremor and you might not make it there."

"What if I get trapped in here?"

"Unlikely," said Leonardo. He tapped at his wrist pad, and *Sparky* swiveled upwards into a launch position. She could watch the bay doors open, amber lights flashing and crystals forming on the outside of the window as the atmosphere bled out.

"Now you have a good clear shot at getting out. First sign of instability, Jason's going to fly you away."

"I could have done that myself," she fumed.

"You'd have hung on until the bitter end. Then we'd all be dead."

She grunted and sat silent, glaring at him. He looked past her at the path ahead of them.

"We're not far now, I think. A few more klicks."

"I won't be able to see you."

"No, you can access the feeds from the SLLTs running down the tunnel. We have any any popcorn left?"

"Ha. Ha." Leonardo knew his wife. Her dedication was what made her bearable despite everything else. He knew exactly the number of displays Drina would set up around her: *Resurgam*'s functions on one, *Sparky*'s on another and the tunnel feed on a third. "Can I coach you?" she asked.

"An armchair general? I think not." Her image hiccuped a bit.

"You're breaking up, Leo," said Drina with a hitch.

"Suit's range is short. We'll be there soon and we'll switch over to FLi8 so it can relay to you."

"Okay."

"Signing off now," said Leo.

"Be safe," said Drina.

"We'll see you back at *Sparky*."

"You better," she said.

He laughed and the image blacked out. Leonardo looked at the path ahead. The tunnel entrance was close. Excitement and fear rose together in his stomach as if trying to jump out and grab something. Leonardo hefted the rifle in his left hand and steadied himself against the back of the sled. He thought of Horacio for a moment, remembering their last conversation.

"Baz?"

"Yeah?"

"What're you gonna do when we catch Mussina?"

"Kick his ass all the way back to *Sparky*."

"Sure," said Leonardo with a laugh. "I know that much. But after?"

"Oh, you mean after after, like if—I mean—*when* we get back. Well," said Baz, pausing. "It'd be nice after all these years not to fight my way around a port. I'm sick of all the bullshit we get wherever we dock. It'll be nice to be able to look people in the eye again. Mussina's head on a stick would buy us both a little respect."

"Agreed."

They were both quiet for a moment.

"One and a half klicks."

"Anything out of the ordinary?"

"Nope. Fli8 shows all clear up ahead."

"They're getting ready to jump, I bet."

"Maybe. I'm staying puckered just to be safe."

Leonardo laughed. They approached the cave entrance a few meters above the foot of the steep wall.

"Hold on tight!"

Baz pulled the stalk back and they leapt into the tunnel entrance. At the last second they lifted enough to skid in and come to a shuddering halt.

"Subtle," said Leonardo. Baz pulled the stick and the sled begrudgingly moved forward, lights illuminating the tunnel. SLLT5 ball cameras hovered every five hundred meters, transmitting information to the surface. They pushed ahead in silence, the sled bumping slightly over the rough-hewn floor of the tunnel. After twenty minutes, Baz slowed down. Leonardo saw the tunnel opening ahead. They were close. The jumping in his stomach increased.

"I'm gonna stop here. It'll be safer on foot."

"Agreed." Leonardo switched off his overlay and let ambient light lead the way. The sled glided to rest and they stepped off. Baz turned it around towards the surface. He opened a locker at the back and pulled out cargo webbing and a length of carbon rope.

"What the hell is that for?" Leonardo asked him.

"We're gonna need something to tie that bastard up with," Baz said.

"Good thinking." Leonardo slung his heavier rifle over his shoulder, holding the gyro-automatic in his right hand. They walked the final length of the tunnel, silently trudging towards the light. Leonardo knew Baz was keeping an eye on his HUD for the first sign of trouble. Things were deceptively serene. As they closed in a few dozen meters from the entrance, Leonardo noticed the temperature rising rapidly.

"I'd expect some automatic fire. They'll most likely have that on after Dwi8 showed up."

"Probably what took him down. I'll spy ahead," said Baz, pulling an SLLT out of his pocket. He gave it a twist and threw it. The spherical bot flew forwards a few meters before slowing under its own power. It held still for a second before speeding away. Leonardo opened a small window in his HUD, keeping his field of vision open. The bot saw nothing, sped away and stopped just at the mouth.

"If I were them, I'd have trained the gun to fire at the smallest thing that comes out of the tunnel. Easy to defend for them, but means a little more work for us—"

They stopped short at a pinging sound in their helmets.

"SLLT's getting scanned. Radiation differs from the output of the sun."

"Something's pointed over—"

A series of staccato blasts suddenly rained down around the mouth of the tunnel. The men slammed against the wall, raising their weapons. Leonardo held his breath for a few seconds until he realized the SLLT was still functioning.

"A KLE," he said.

"Friggin' Kellys," whispered Baz. "Always unreliable except for this one. Shit!"

"A missile ought to take it out," said Leonardo. He held up his rifle and talked to it through his glove, programming a firing solution. Leonardo pointed his rifle at the mouth of the tunnel and pulled the trigger. The missile shot out just before another volley pummeled the opposite wall. EM interference made tracking difficult, but Leonardo saw the missile take out the big gun on his HUD.

"Cloak up and move slowly," he said. Baz gave him a thumbs-up, shimmered then disappeared in front of Leo, represented as a dot on his HUD. They edged along the tunnel, weapons aloft, sensors feeling out ahead of them. At the tunnel's mouth, Leonardo enlarged the ball camera's window.

"Can't see much, Baz."

"The big gun's out for sure." Leonardo zoomed in and saw the Martian ship, the stern still smoking from the missile.

"They have smaller guns, too. Another by the stern. Must be dumber ones. They aren't tracking the SLLT. But they'll spot us no problem," said Baz. Leonardo scanned the nearby area, spying a pile of rubble to the right.

"We need a decoy. I'll take cover behind those rocks. When the guns are on me, you take them out," said Leonardo.

"Let me do the decoying. You go for the guns—"

"Baz, that's an order."

"Leo, you—"

He leapt out of the tunnel.

"Fucking jerk!" shouted Baz. "Sir!"

A hail of fire followed Leonardo as he ran across the rocky ground. Baz fired at the guns. Leonardo rolled behind the rubble just as a heavy volley pulverized the rock where he stood.

"Baz? You up?"

"Yeah, I'm fine. I think I got it, ya damn boy scout!"

"You'll thank me later. Still cloaked up?"

"Yeah, I'm not going maggot until I'm close."

"Good." Leonardo checked his HUD. "No movement. They're getting ready to take off. I'll target the ship. You go for the substations. We can destabilize that thing with enough time to get back."

"Roger that." Leonardo grabbed a roll of blast tape from his pack, loaded it into the rifle's launch tube and programmed another firing solution. He edged the weapon just over the top of the rubble pile and fired.

Shots rained down on his cover too late. The tape hit the tail of the Martian ship foreward of the engines. With a small explosion it unraveled, adhering to the hull.

"Captain, you're a bit late," said a voice. "Only by a few hundred years, but ..."

Leonardo froze.

***

Mussina.

Leonardo tensed up, peering at the engines, then ducking as he took fire. The engines were a clear target once the small guns were taken out. Leonardo fired at them. On his HUD, the missile weaved past slower projectiles and obliterated the guns.

"Nice shooting, Tex!" said Baz.

"It ain't over yet, Baz."

Leonardo's radiation indicator was firmly pegged into the red. He'd need weeks of antirad treatments if they survived. He peered over the top of the pile again; nothing shot back. Leonardo leapt over, landing low as he skulked towards the ship. The tape had begun to work around the hull. He had to be clear before it made it all the way around.

"These heroic efforts are foolish and ... ineffective," said Mussina. "Especially in the face of what is to come."

A tremor made him glance to his left as the substation collapsed with a blast from Baz's rifle. Leonardo looked overhead at the fusion maelstrom above him. The roiling surface of the fiery ball above them seemed unchanged. He dropped his gaze.

A door on the underbelly of the ship opened.

"Baz! We got co—" His words were cut off by particle beams shearing the darkness under the ship and hitting several points around him.

"Damn. I'm hit!" he heard Baz say. Leonardo dropped and looked behind him. He saw a flicker as Baz's cloak cycled through several different surfaces, maggots, skulls, and rocks until it flickered off. Baz lay on the hill in the opaque cloak, exposed, a gash near the bottom.

"Baz, stay low!" Baz rolled to his side.

"Suit took a hit. Got a leak. Think my leg is broke—" Multiple beams fired at Baz again, hitting his midsection.

"Baz!" shouted Leonardo to no response. Leonardo fired at the ship. With autotargeting he managed to hit someone lurking in the shadows under the ship.

"Got one for you, Mussina," Baz said, as a rocket slammed into the engines, blowing them apart.

"And I have something in return, fool."

Leonardo shouted as he watched Baz being body ripped apart by shots from a flechette weapon. Leonardo spied three figures standing underneath the ship, one left illuminated by the dying fires of the engines. Leonardo shot them, knocking the body over. The other two dropped low and fanned out, firing at him.

"You lieutenant is gone. Just like all the other impediments in my master's way. Like bits of dust they are blown from the golden form of his mighty—"

"Mussina, you're a dead man."

Leonardo took cover behind some boulders in the way. He saw the blast tape winding back to the top and working its magic, tightening until it would explode.

"No, sir, I am more alive than ever. Striking his enemies down brings me great satisfaction. I truly enjoyed that, captain. Now for you."

A shot to his right arm threw Leonardo back and flung his rifle to the ground. More shots knocked his right leg out from underneath him. Right arm mangled, pain seared through his body. Leonardo's suit automatically sealed, curling his arm into his side to keep him alive. Leonardo drew out his gyrojet pistol with his left hand and fired shots into the dusky shadows under the ship. A spark lit the darkness and someone lurched out, clutching their chest panel. Leonardo fired again and again, shots piercing the faceplate before the figure dropped to the ground.

"You're done, captain. Why not live your last few seconds of life without struggle. Let go and take your place as destiny strides past you on fiery limbs and sets the balance right?"

Leonardo lay back against the rock. The flaring sphere sun above him grew larger. His rad monitor showed the levels were ten times above lethal and rising beyond the range of his gauges. At least Baz's work was done: the orb was destabilizing.

In that moment Leonardo realized he would never see a real sun again. Gorwing up, he loved the warmth of summer days underneath Sol, riding in his mother's skiff, the water splashing in their wake. He glanced at the remote feed showing him the FMR ship. The blast tape had tightened its acidic grip, cutting deeper into the decrepit hull. Soon the Martians would be stranded.

"No. It's over for you, Mussina. This brief little war is done."

Leonardo grabbed his rifle, programming one last firing solution. At the last command entered the entire nanomunitions of his rifle converted into a series of missiles. Leonardo fired up at one of the orbiting containment generators looming overhead. Through the pain he watched them drive in and burst apart the rhomboid box. Debris rained down, angry flares burst forth like an animal lashing from a hole in its cage.

"Captain, do you think this will—"

On his HUD, Leonardo watched the magnetic blast tape shear off the rear of the ship. The interior caught fire for a second before succumbing to the poor atmosphere of the cavern. The ship sank onto its rear, the landing gear toppling over like empty boots. Mussina's voice slung curses out over crackling bandwidth.

"Bastard! All the work and effort of centuries and you think with your heroics you can climb down here and derail his greater destiny? I'll enjoy cracking your helmet open and watching as your brains boil out of your eyes. Your ridiculous efforts do not make this battle yours. Despite everything the Harvestman remains victorious."

A lone suited figure, trapped outside when the gangway was crushed underneath the ship, turned and ran towards Leonardo, weapon aloft.

Leonardo saw the stolen UFW suit and laughed. His own suit alarms trilled away, urging him to run from further exposure to the hellish subterranean environment. From his left pocket, he pulled a high-mass sticky grenade, flicking the safety off with his thumb. On his HUD, Mussina approached, weapon pointed low towards Leonardo's rocky hiding place.

Capt. Leonardo Reyes De la Valencia, once commander of the mightiest vessel humanity ever built, lay broken on the cavern floor under a small, dying sun. His body was wrecked but his mind remained clear. He pressed the button underneath his gloved thumb.

"No, he doesn't, you green bastard. *Earth* wins, Mussina."

Leonardo saw only a moment of light, feeling warmth and painless bliss.

Then nothing.

CHAPTER TWENTY-EIGHT
EPILOGUE

Drina's throat was sore and dry from screaming Leo's name as *Sparky* shot away form the crumbling surface of the planet. The skin of her face was cracked and drying. Tears pooled at her neck from the planet's weak gravitational tug. Exploding out of *Resurgam*'s hangar bay, they'd left seconds before the blast that killed Leo and Baz ripped the planet apart.

Now she felt the uncomfortable dampness seep into her collar, mixing with sweat. She ignored the chafing and jabbed hopelessly at the controls in front of her.

"Ma'am," said Jason. "I will retain control of the vessel until we exit the Stokes system."

"The hell you will," she said, hearing a voice dry and rough come from her parched throat. "Hand it over."

"We are not yet out of harm's way, ma'am."

The ship buckled as shockwaves raced past and Jason kept *Sparky* ahead of the debris field, the last efforts of Stokes 6 trying to claim them just as it had Leo and Baz. Drina could barely admit that her emotions had the best of her and piloting in this state would get them killed.

Soon they were flying out past the weak sun. Stokes' small yellow illumination grew slightly brighter as they flew by. They passed it, escaping the last of the debris that had almost trapped them.

"I am surprised the sun didn't collapse in on itself and form a black hole," said Jason. "Such a fascinating arrangement of—"

"They died back there, Jason." Tears again, oily from dehydration. "They're dead and you're talking about black holes forming in their grave."

"Forgive me, ma'am." Drina watched the sticks in the cockpit move as if ghost operators occupied the pilot's seat. "I thought it might ease your mind."

"Just shut up and get us out of here."

Jason stayed silent as they cruised further out of the system, leaving behind the tepid sun, insignificant planets and irradiated debris. Drina, already exhausted, lay shivering and spent on her throne. The displays around her showed the preparations for the longer journey ahead of them. She couldn't focus on the data, couldn't see the graphs in front of her. All she saw was the fiery blast and the last image from her husband's suit camera as it stuttered before cutting out. Exhaustion, grief and confusion blended together and her eyes lost focus as tears began again.

"Ma'am?"

Jason's voice pierced her fog and she wiped her eyes. She blinked at something in her HUD and Jason's avatar appeared, reclining in the pilot's seat.

"Ma'am, it's time we prepared for hi-space jump." Drina sat in silence for a while. Jason turned around and looked at her. "Ma'am?"

"No," she finally said.

"I'm sorry?" asked Jason.

"We're not leaving them," she said, voice clearer, regaining some authority. "We're not leaving *him*."

"Asgr. Valencia, we cannot—"

"No," she said again. "Turn us around. We're—we're going back ..."

"Ma'am," said Jason, releasing itself from the seat and walking towards her in a way no human could during flight. "With all due respect—"

"Fuck your respect, pick up the sticks and turn us around." She hammered at the holodisplays before her. They remained unresponsive.

"Lieutenant, I understand you are under an emotional strain now but —"

"You understand nothing," she shouted at the avatar before her. Jason showed no reaction, simply waiting. "You're incapable of understanding what ... what just—"

"Ma'am, I understand that if we were to go back, this is what we would find," said Jason. He gestured and an image superimposed itself over her other displays. "A wide field of debris, cooler now in the vacuum and substantially down from the unstable high temperatures directly after the blast. The high radiation levels would be challenging for this ship but if we were to sift around we might find an irregular arrangement of particles but no organic matter of any kind. Capt. Valencia and Lt. Al-Mushtarii were very effective in their destruction of the FMR and their miniature sun."

Jason closed the window with a flick of its wrist and folded its hands across its waist.

"I know that in the last few days of this ordeal, Capt. Valencia's voice showed considerably fewer stress frequencies in it when he spoke to you or of you. I know that his devotion to duty was such that were he and Lt. Al-Mushtarii still alive, he would consider this direct opposition to his orders willful insubordination."

Drina looked at Jason with tired, sore eyes. Jason's eyes were trained on her without any expression. It was, after all, just an avatar combining the parameters of the shuttle cabin in relation to the coordinates of her face so that it would appear to meet her gaze and provide comfort on a small, ancient human level.

"I also understand that we cannot make a hi-space jump without your abilities. If we do not, we will travel slowly for some time and run out of fuel well before we arrive anywhere near a populated area, shipping lane or well-traveled part of this sector."

Drina closed her eyes and tried to think of anything but exploding planets, fire bursting through ammonia ice and vaporizing everything inside and out.

"Capt. Valencia would want you to return to tell the UFW what has happened here."

Drina opened her eyes to find Jason turning away and sitting down at the controls again. She felt the vessel power down slightly, Jason conserving fuel as they drifted. All she had wanted to do was forget everything and be away from this place. But to leave Leo behind?

"So tired ..." she said, letting a hand flop on the blanket over her. Could she survive this pain?

She looked into the darkness before them for some time.

"Jason," she said.

"Ma'am?"

"Prepare the Choudhury drives for hi-space jump. Secure *Sparky*'s exterior sensors and tell the astrogation units to find us a course back to Earth."

"Yes, ma'am." Jason went to work, calculating and preparing the ship to leave the system. "Once the jump is complete you will be able to rest. When we arrive at Titan you can begin your detachment process."

"Damn right I will," said Drina, raising an arm to her holodisplay to begin the voyage home.

ACKNOWLEDGMENTS

This books is less about one man getting the time to write it than about the people who supported this writer in what he needed to do to complete it. I owe a huge debt of thanks to so many.

First and foremost is my wife, Alice, who is the most spectacular thing ever put on this planet (second to her is our daughter Sophia); Alice my beloved, your love, support, patience, insight and reading helped this go from a "What if?" to a book. Mere words do not express my love and admiration for you. I am married to an extraordinary woman. I am forever grateful to you for it (by the way, Astrogator Drina Valencia has lived in my head and heart for many years. While she is a composite character made up of many strong and human women, she is mostly based upon my own Astrogator, my wife, the being who gets us through the hard and soft places in life).

My daughter, Sophia. Pup, you've brought me so much joy in your person ever since the day you were born. I am so glad you chose me and your mother. You're in this book, too, in so many ways. Thank you for being awesome, my wise one!

My parents Richard & Gretchen Terhune, for bring me life and supporting me in all ways, not the least of which is reading a book in a genre you neither understood nor particularly enjoyed and for being honest about what you liked and didn't. And look—I finally did something with my BFA in English!

My brothers and sisters-in-law and their kids for all their love and support.

My advance readers, for they are legion and mighty: Kate Baker, Tommy Taylor of the Taylor Men's Clinic, Chris Bowe of Longfellow Books in Portland, ME, Joslyn Hamilton, Steve Landry of the Landry Pug & Crochet Ranch, JUNGLE JMC of the Scarborough Marsh Incident and last but not least all the homies of Rocketship Unicorn.

My friend Mary Bowe who has read just about every single goddamn iteration of this friggin' book and given me amazing advice along the way. Thanks must also go to Dorene for letting me borrow Mary from time to time to bend her ear. And then of course Emma and Olivia for being best buds to Sophia and cool young ladies in their own right.

Mary Robinette Kowal had a listen to a podcast Kate Baker recorded of the first chapter and then dropped some science on me, which I am eternally grateful for.

John Scalzi for his knowledge, patience, humor and mentorship to me and all the other members of The Speculative Literature Foundation's Mentorship program in October of 2006 as well as on Viable Paradise XII. Krissy has taught you well.

Elizabeth Bear at VPXII. The endurance and tolerance of the most inane of my questions is greatly appreciated. I've got your back and I'll crack it any day!

All my homies from VPXII. DORTY DOZEN ROOLZ!!! And a special shout out to Marko Kloos without whom I wouldn't have taken some great leaps in faith and publishing. Here's hoping this is one step closer to that Hugo sword fight!

My friend Katrina Archer at Ganache Media for her quick and powerful editing of this. Merci beacoup!

Cat Valente and Dimitri Zagudin for moving to Maine and being just totally frigging rad, especially Cat for shepherding me around Readercon and the publishing world, too. And Dima for brewing badass coffee.

All writers along the way who replied to my cold-emailing them and thus supported, inspired and encouraged me: Sandra McDonald, Peter "Megasquid" Watts, Paolo Bacigalupi, Philip Palmer, Alastair Reynolds, Karl Schroeder and Richard K. Morgan.

Mary Noyes and Chuck "Turbo" Utter for helping me bring my giant desk into my life so I could finish this work and do more great things with words.

To all my readers, known and unknown. I hope you find my books worth your while. I appreciate it.

And last but not least to the Universe, in its infinite and indifferent wonder.

Namaste!

Chang Terhune is the co-owner of Portland Power Yoga in Portland, Maine, with his wife Alice Riccardi. In addition to teaching yoga, he is an avid gamer, playing on both Xbox and PS3 (not simultaneously), a writer of science fiction and other stories, and a musician. A writer since he was twelve years old, "Harvestman" is his first published novel. Chang is currently at work on several books, including "Astrogatrix" the sequel to "Harvestman" as well as a book about yoga entitled "The Accidental Yogi." He lives in Portland, Maine with his wife, wonderful daughter, dog Sparky and George Foreman-Terhune, a cat.

Find Chang on the web at http://www.changterhune.com.